Melencolia I
Albrecht Dürer
1514

A crumpled copy of this classic engraving was employed as a
bookmark in the original manuscript, charting the unknown author's
progress. If you own this book, please feel free to use it likewise.

ROCK STAR'S RAINBOW

ROCK STAR'S RAINBOW

ROCK STAR'S RAINBOW

A NOVEL

KEVIN GLAVIN

KEVIN GLAVIN PUBLISHING
IRVINE, CALIFORNIA

Inquiries should be addressed to:
admin@kevinglavinpublishing.com

For additional information:
rockstarsrainbow.com

This is a work of fiction. Names, groups, businesses, events, and locales are used fictitiously. Any resemblance to reality or the people and places involved with it is purely coincidental.

Edited and Designed by Kevin Glavin
Frontispiece: *Melencolia I*, Albrecht Dürer, 1514, Public Domain
Author as *The Laughing Cavalier* / Hals, Adapted by Mark Peters

Publisher's Cataloging-In-Publication Data
(Prepared by The Donohue Group, Inc.)

Glavin, Kevin (Kevin Patrick)
  Rock star's rainbow : a novel / Kevin Glavin. -- 1st U.S. ed.

    p. ; cm.

    ISBN-13: 978-0-9825466-0-4
    ISBN-10: 0-9825466-0-2

1. Rock musicians--Fiction. 2. Celebrities--Fiction. I. Title.

PS3607.L38 R63 2009
813/.6   2009909640

Printed in the United States of America

For
my family.
It's been a long road, but we're almost there.

PREFACE

This engaging yet egregious work was discovered in the seat pocket of a plane flying from Los Angeles to Las Vegas. Tired of looking at watches and cologne in the gift catalogue, I searched for more intriguing reading material. With some effort, I pulled out a bulky package that someone had evidently left behind. At first, I hesitated to open it. I inquired of all in my vicinity, but no one ventured the slightest claim. As the image of Hemingway's lost Parisian manuscript trained by, I decided to investigate further. I gathered its ruffled and coffee-stained pages, which were falling out of a rather flimsy and tattered legal folder, and perused them later that evening as I sat losing with incredible style at the roulette table, betting on 00.

There is a popular saying: "What happens in Vegas, stays in Vegas." Well, not in this case. After consulting with counsel, I have determined that it is worth the gamble to publish this manuscript for the public's enjoyment, edification (if only through *reductio ad absurdum*), and potential horrification. The shocking nature of this reverse *Bildungsroman*, or more specifically, reverse *Künstlerroman*, of the rock star Rook Heisenberg (from the infamous band The Little Bang) searching for his lost innocence is of such explosive revelation that the general audience should be forewarned. (Younger, or more sensitive readers may wish to skip over certain sections that, however realistic, may be deemed offensive.) Nevertheless, this innocent traveler felt, torpedoes be damned, that its benefits might outweigh its harms and that people might get a kick out of it. This is my only hope, as I cannot attest to the work's truth, credibility, or literary merit. I leave that task of exegesis to the critics, of which I'm sure this book will have its share.

It is worth noting that along with the dog-eared vellum, some antiquated and experimental recordings of Rook and his ensemble were also found—in DAT format. Much like many a super-group's early archives, the sound quality is abysmal and bare, although the potential of the music itself is stunning, offering a glimpse into the first phases of this supernova of a band. The curious reader will soon be able to find some of these early experiments on the web as MP3s, under the now over-worn double entendre—The Little Bang.

As you scroll through these ramblings, please forgive any errors or mistranslations made during redaction. Consider the entire document [sic]. The original copy was an imbroglio—hard to decipher and written in a paroxysmal hand on eleven ill-marshaled yellow pads; there were many abbreviations which did not follow standard stenography and evidently were privy to only the author himself. Certain chapters consisted of several blank pages with obscure acronyms, as if the author were planning to amend the text at a more opportune time. There are occasional usages of Dutch, Russian, Cantonese, and Hindi apparently overheard during the rock star's travels that beg better colloquial transliteration by more adept linguists. There also exist gaps: this editor has done his best to "connect the dots" so as to present a more coherent narrative. The reader should also note that I made every effort to ascertain the original composer of these follies through the usual channels of media conglomerates, publishers, the local police, FBI, CIA, foreign embassies, lawyers, the airlines, agents, psychics, and even the rock star Rook himself. I was consistently rebuffed and met with the old chestnut "no comment." I would be remiss, however, if I did not hazard a guess. My suspicions lead me to believe that this is a draft of an unauthorized exposé of the reclusive Rook penned by Aitchkiss Killawathy, the recently deceased entertainment reporter. However, as I have already indicated, no affirmations or denials could be obtained from this unfortunate man's connections.

Lastly, it would be dishonest if I failed to mention that I have been aspiring to write a novel for years. Aspiring, and expiring, that is. My first attempt, *The Thermostat Is Out of Control*, was a sophomoric effort at satire, and consigned to the flames of youth. My second attempt, *That's All*, was written as an epistolary, and went the way of many Dear Juan letters—to the laughing stocks. This work, as the above suggests, was more "found" than written, more inspired by the Muse than born of any real labor; I am content with the title "editor."[*]

---

[*] The title, *Rock Star's Rainbow*, was this editor's contribution, as the work was unnamed. This signifier was inspired in part by a copy of the famous Dürer print, which was folded and apparently being used as a bookmark, marking the unknown author's progress. It rested on the last page, which seems to end in mid-sentence. Technically, the German master engraved a moonbow, but I trust the kind audience will understand the liberties taken.

So let us embark. I think you will enjoy this adventure. However, it is perfectly understandable if you are put off by such celebrity scandal. Keep it or toss it, it really doesn't matter, as perhaps is evidenced by its original author's apparent abandonment. The reader will be the judge of whether I should have left the crumpled pages discarded on the plane or not. Happy travels!

KG, Editor
Los Angeles, California
September 4, 2009

ROAD MAP

Don Quixote now felt it right to quit a life of such idleness as he was leading in the castle; for he imagined that he was making himself sorely missed by suffering himself to remain shut up and inactive amid the countless luxuries and enjoyments his hosts lavished upon him as a knight, and he felt too that he would have to render a strict account to heaven of that indolence and seclusion . . . .

—Cervantes[*]

---

[*] This quote from the quintessential picaresque novel was blazoned across the outside of the nameless folder upon a "My Name Is" sticker.

1

A HOLLYWOOD HOMECOMING

"What are you waiting for?" Ted Southhampton asked Rook Heisenberg.

Rook, staring at nothing in particular, took a towel from an eager female fan and wiped the sweat from his ruddy face, half-expecting to see his image transferred there.

"The perfect moment . . . ." said Rook, and as if he were performing a magic trick, handed the damp cloth back to the young lady.

"Yoicks!" she gasped, clutching the calico to her chest and jumping up and down. "I can't believe it!" Rook, with the detachment of a plastic surgeon, observed her bosom bouncing within her skimpy *I'm a Rock Star!* T-shirt.

"Well believe this, young lady—we're very busy here!" barked Southhampton. "We don't need your help." Then turning to Rook, he lowered his periwinkle glasses and said in earnest: "You've gotta go out again. Don't keep 'em waiting much longer."

"*Avrakehdabra,*" replied Rook, chuckling at his manager's tornado of a personality and corresponding hairstyle. Rook listened to the chants from the crowd at the Hollywood Bowl. *What am I doing here? What on earth am I doing here?* He continued to peer numbly into some vague memory, some blunted purpose.

Southhampton slapped his precious client across the face. "What's your problem? Will you stop your mumbling and wake up! You can't leave 'em without playing that last encore."

"Yeah!" echoed rock star girl, clenching her fists—holding her excitement tight lest she explode. Rook winked at her.

"I know," said Rook, turning his attention to the black velvet curtain that hung in front of him.

The band's first hit, "Los Angeles," had also become somewhat of an albatross for Rook; he had been playing it as their finale for some twelve years now. *Is not my life more than the same old song?* But he shrugged, kissed the surprised devotee on her lips, and hopped on his motorsickle, nicknamed Roxy.

"I can't believe it!" screamed the girl as Rook roared the engine to life.

"Neither can I," said Southhampton. And he placed his callused hand on the girl's bare knee.

The sound of the crowd rose as a roadie held a mike to the bike. Its purr flowed through the Bowl. The fog machine was going; Rook put on his aviator glasses, reared the throttle, and nodded at another roadie; the curtains parted, the mechanical universe (an elaborate stage set) exploded with fireworks, and he cruised onto the stage with reckless abandon, almost crashing. *Goddamn glasses!* Hazily looking out at the thousands, he procured a smile. A flash mob began, swaying to the backbeat. Rook jumped off the bike and grabbed the microphone and guitar.

He didn't say anything for a while. He teased them. He let their anticipation reach the breaking point, then: "Some of you older people might remember this one." He took a deep breath (which was left on the CD when many women said that that was their favorite part of the song) and sang: "Los Angeles, city of the an—gels. Give me a kiss—you pretty little an—gel . . . ."

He pushed his voice as far as he could; when he couldn't sustain it any longer, he ran his fingers nimbly up and down the scalloped fret board of his white Stratocaster, shaking out every last shade of tremolo. The band picked up speed, and the audience started to mosh. They bounced off each other with tremendous ferocity, like particles in the primordial soup. A red brassiere and ultra-ribbed condom landed on stage. The clean-cut security crew, in their smashing blue and yellow uniforms, attempted to maintain order, but the chaos overwhelmed them. A few people made it up onto the stage and ran around like they were on fire. One young man actually was (due to a mishap from the fireworks); he was extinguished and escorted backstage for some pampering by the band's private doctor.

Rook, meanwhile, oblivious to everything except his own enjoyment, ripped off his *Anarchy!* T-shirt and threw it haphazardly into the air. He jumped up and down—frolicking. Then he took off his spectacles, and just sat and stared out at the mass of humanity. He panned from face to face, catching his breath. He let the moment sink in. *I could do anything. Anything* . . . thoughts of sex, nudity, money, drugs, and death trailed through his mind like the adverts for some failed blockbuster. *How tedious.*

The Little Bang kept playing. Rook kept looking at the crowd. *All these people—looking for something. What? To relieve boredom. To escape the monotony.* Suddenly, Rook got up and dove into the pit—something he only did rarely. The fans caught him—he surfed about, and began to sing again. He held the mike out; people swore in several languages. They seemed to get more manic—punching, flashing, tossing turf out on the lawn—reaching a fever pitch. Finally, Rook rode a wave back to the stage. The band wound down then finished the song with a leaping crescendo and the obligatory smashing of drums, guitars, and amps.

"Hey all," Rook said, lighting up a smoke. "It's been quite the party. I love a party! And you're all invited to our next one! Good night!"

They bounded offstage, in the throes of celebration and sadness. It was the last night of their yearlong world tour, and they were back in their hometown of Los Angeles. Everyone had come to see them: other rockers, movie stars, industry people, politicians, sports greats, and of course the media. As they made their way through the sea of VIPs, Southhampton held out his arms and shook his head, smiling.

"Boys," he said, "great show, great show. But let's get out of this and into the meet and greet." He draped his arms around them as if they were valuable luggage, and herded them towards the private room where they could mingle with some semblance of order.

"I'm gonna stay out here a little while," said Billy Razor, the bassist (who got his stage name when the band was in its early stages—he would always be late to practice because of stopping at 7-11 to buy razor blades for his cocaine habit). He took a chug of a Heineken. "You always want to keep us moving . . . the tour's over now—there's nowhere to go except there," he said, eyeing a porn-star in tight, bright orange leather with matching lipstick.

Southhampton raised a wandering eyebrow towards the young lady. And as the memory of one of her scenes involving ice cubes went through his mind, he said: "Lovely, but we have some interviews to do."

"Interviews, splinterviews," said Chop Shop, the drummer (and a car freak), gazing at a tall drink of water in a bebe mesh tube top inadequate to restrain her top. "Will you look at her—I'm gonna interview her!" And Chop slithered towards her.

Southhampton pulled his windswept hair and grabbed the two remaining band members—Shitfaced, the keyboard player (almost always plastered), and Rook (the only band member to keep his original name—though he dropped the surname of Heisenberg—"It's too uncertain for a rock star," he would joke, although there was no relation to the famous physicist). Rook meanwhile was being pulled in three directions—by Southhampton towards the TV cameras—by rock star girl towards perhaps another towel, and by Anatoli Anti, the Russian-born, now famous Hollywood director who was trying to convince Rook to write the soundtrack and also star in his next U.S. film tentatively titled *Jail-Order Bride* (American marries girl from the Ukraine that he met on the internet and falls victim to extortion by the Russian Mafiya). Rook coughed and coughed and grabbed onto his manager for support; the rocker really just wanted to go home and sleep in his own bed for a change. Despite his love of parties, and although he couldn't articulate it, he felt overwhelmed with something, and if he could find the word, perhaps that word would be melancholy, or better yet—*Weltschmerz*. With a twist, he extricated himself and ducked into a private bathroom, putting his hands to his head. He splashed some cold water on his dolled up face and stared into the mirror at his beautiful brown eyes, professionally whitened smile, and high-maintenance hair.

"Who am I?" he asked. "Who am I really?"

For a second, he thought he saw a Spaniard dressed in Renaissance clothing upon a draft horse—*glimpses of a past life?*

"Come on!" shouted Southhampton, pounding on the door. "You're gonna start having acid flashbacks."

When is he ever gonna let me have some time to myself? When is everyone just gonna leave and let me have some peace? It's like a party where the guests never go home. Goddamn marketing machine. I need to slow down—I'm goin' too damn fast! I don't even know where, or who I am anymore. All I know is that I'm movin' a million miles an hour . . . .

Rook had wanted to give tonight's performance his all; he didn't know when the Little Bang would ever play again. He needed some time to recharge, refocus, and remake himself. He had also wanted to give Los Angeles an extra-special homecoming show. And he had, but they still wanted more.

He tousled his bleached blonde locks, popped a pill, and threw open the door. "Double-H," (Double-H was Southhampton's sobriquet for always clarifying the orthography of his name) "I love you, but I need some room to breathe," said Rook. Everyone suddenly became quiet and tried not to gawk.

"No problem!" said Southhampton, overly animated. "Just a word to the cameras, and perhaps to the wise, then I'll get you out of here!" He ushered the non-church goer over to the crew from Channel 11 as the flock resumed its chattering.

"Rook!" shouted Mindy Mountain, a pretty blonde reporter in a black business suit with no trace of dandruff. "How's it feel to be back home?"

Rook rubbed his ears. "Pardon me, my hearing's not what it used to be."

She leaned closer and Rook caught a whiff of her perfume—Shalimar Baccarat. "How's it feel to be back home?" she repeated, shyly smiling.

"Great, Mindy, great," said Rook, looking at her name on her press pass. "It's always nice to be back in L.A. We really appreciate the welcoming we've received. But if you don't mind, I'd like to go home now. I haven't been home in a year—I'm sure you understand. I'd like to see if it's still there." She laughed. Rook then whispered into her ear, to avoid the mike picking it up (it did anyway): "The hint of vanilla and musk in your perfume is driving me crazy. Come home with me."

Mindy stepped back a little and looked as if she were about to throw up. "I don't think my husband would like that," she said, fidgeting, but maintaining her smile for the cameras.

"I admire your commitment," said Rook, putting out his hand. She didn't take it—just looked at it and the absence of any sort of commitment. Rook smoothly slid it tight into his jeans pocket, and staring at her sparkly ring said: "Keep wearing that perfume—it'll drive Buster wild. A real bucking bronco I bet he is."

She turned and confronted him head-on, and with a look of direness, slapped him hard across his chiseled face.

"Why does everyone keep hitting me?" asked Rook, massaging the sting.

"Cuz you're an asshole," she said. "Let me ask you: how many women have you slept with this past month?"

"Don't answer that," said Southhampton, suddenly stepping in and trying to block the camera, which was still rolling.

Rook turned his eyes towards the ceiling, recollecting. "So far, seven, I think." For years, Rook had methodically kept to a rigorous schedule of spending quality time with a different woman every other day. Although there were occasional anomalies, primarily due to overindulgence in medicinals prescribed by the band's private physician—Doctor Vilhelm.

Southhampton put his hands to his hurricane hair. "I'm gonna have to call legal," he mumbled to himself.

"I rest my case," said Mindy. "Grow up. How long do you think you can keep doing this for?"

"As long as horny broads like you are around."

At this point one of her camera crew, a 350-pound bouncer holding a Panasonic and a place in his heart for Mindy, set his gear down and started towards Rook. Rook's bodyguards, who weren't quite as large but deadlier, started towards 350 with 357s. Southhampton stormed in between everybody, holding up both hands feverishly.

"Okay, this interview is over. Enough. Elvis has left the building. Let's go, let's go! God, why do I bother with you?" Southhampton asked Rook, pulling his investment away.

"For the money."

"Why'd you do that? What were you thinking?"

"Just having some fun. You should try it sometime."

"Fun at your own expense. Can you imagine the story she's going to run?"

"Well, it'll probably help me sell more."

Southhampton, now that they were far enough away from trouble, stopped Rook. "You may be right. But she had a point. She had a definite point. You can't keep doing this forever—this bad boy rock star act. You'll become a parody of yourself."

I already am, thought Rook.

"Just shape up," continued his manager. "Listen, take some time off, then we'll have a pow-wow session about what's next. Okay? Now let me get your limo," he said, with an air of self-importance that could inflate a mattress. Southhampton and the 357s pushed people aside, and the caravanserai made for the exit door, as the well-groomed, blue and yellow jacketed security hovered over the madness, trying to keep a lid on all the celebs, making sure they didn't destroy the place.

Maybe she's right, thought Rook, watching his feet move and feeling like they were someone else's—like he was in a movie. *Maybe I'm gettin' too old for this; Christ—it's my birthday tomorrow!* This sudden remembrance sobered him up and he looked around, adrenaline-charged, seeing all the faces in high resolution. Tomorrow, June 16, 2009, would be his thirty-third birthday. Normally, Southhampton or some spectacular hottie would jog his memory. This year, no one had. *I want a party! I want a huge ass party!*

Southhampton and one of the bodyguards, an Irish bloke named Gary, pushed Rook into the car, protecting him from the surging throng.

"Remember," said Southhampton, "relax. You deserve it. But think about things. Really! And I'll see you in a couple weeks." He tapped the top of the limo goodbye and it attempted to speed off. Before it did, rock star girl held out her hand desperately, getting it caught as the window rolled up. Rook grabbed it, and let her in.

"What's your name again?" he asked her as she sat on his lap.

She was about to speak, when Rook put his hand over her pouty mouth.

"Hey, Rich," Rook said to the back of the driver's balding head. "Whattya got back here? You got that stuff that I always like that I can't remember?"

Rich laughed. "You'll find it stocked as usual, sir. Don't worry," he said, although navigating a limo through the mob was indeed a challenge. "Home, sir?"

"Home," said Rook, gazing out at the people pounding on the bulletproof glass. They reminded him of the monkeys at a safari park his family had driven through when he was a child. He wondered if it would be safe to feed them. He took a drink and then another, then lit up a smoke and then another smoke. He exhaled into his date's lungs.

Rich maneuvered the long white leviathan slowly through the swarm, onto Highland, and towards the

Sunset Strip, as Rook made out with Girl #8 and looked out periodically at the scenery. *All those lights. All those palm trees. The perfect weather. It's good to be back in California.* As Rich pulled up Doheny, and neared Greystone Park, Rook wondered about all the rich people sequestered in these strange Beverly Hills hideaways. He wondered if they were all as strange as he was. He wondered what the people thought when they drove by with their Star Maps. One of these days, Rook was going to drive by "normal people's" homes and stare in their windows.

"What are ya thinkin' 'bout?" asked Girl #8, trying to catch her breath. Her real name was Monique, and she had traveled all the way from the heart of Texas to become a star. Unfortunately, it wasn't working out in the acting business, so she decided to do the next best thing—meet real stars. She knew a friend of a friend, and somehow got backstage, and now she was wondering how she could get this Rook to marry her.

"I'm thinking about marrying you," said Rook, smiling. He said this to all the girls, because this is what most of them wanted to hear. Monique became even more starry-eyed, her face all sparkly, and imagined she was indeed Rook's wife and kissed him accordingly with her collagen lips. Before they could come up for air, Rich had pulled into the drive of the gothic estate and entered the secret code, which was a Fibonacci sequence.

"Which rich bastard lives here?" asked Rook, pushing himself away from Monique. "Oh, I do." And he laughed and laughed and then began coughing again. He pictured himself as a knight returning to his castle after a successful battle. This battle, however, was fought with a guitar, and songs he had penned on whatever paper he had handy—business cards, magazines, napkins. *But what victory did I win?*

Before he could formulate a thought, and it is doubtful that he would have considering the increasing inebriation, Girl #8 was pulling him hurriedly out of the car.

"Good night, Rich," laughed Rook, tossing him a $1000. "A higher conquest calls!" And Girl #8 continued doing all she could to become Wife #1.

"Thank you, sir," said Rich, tucking the bill in his crisp, starched and ironed shirt pocket. *That will go to Becca's tuition,* thought Rich, of his daughter in her first year at Brown.

Rook and Monique and Gary scrambled to enter the house and Gary turned off the alarm system, which had been upgraded to account for the celebrity's ever-increasing popularity and concomitant risk. Bags were stacked and labeled in the foyer. *Tomorrow,* thought Rook.

"Anything else, Rook?" asked Gary, as the rock star and the groupie fell into a kind of childlike pyramid near the stairs.

"Yeah, bring up a few bottles and make us some green fairies." And suddenly the couple dropped their glasses and their smokes and a small fire started as the Everclear went up in flames.

"I'll take care of that," said Gary, quickly moving to douse the wildfire with (literally) the shirt off his back. As he cleaned up, his muscles naturally flexing (he was a former bodybuilder), Gary paused, looking at a bamboo plant that had been growing on the kitchen windowsill for some seven years. He had actually given it to Rook—

although he was sure that the party-tripping rocker had forgotten. "I'm moving tomorrow," said Gary, emptying the broken glass into the designer garbage can.

"What?" asked Rook, nibbling on Monique's ear; it tasted like clams.

"I hate to tell you, but now's a good a time as any. I'm moving."

"Why?" Gary had been Rook's closest and most-trusted bodyguard for seven years now. His favorite before—Salmon—was sent up the river for embezzling funds from the band. As Rook got richer and richer, he found it hard to trust anyone. Now he was going to have to open up his house and life to yet another stranger.

"Well, we're about to have another kid," said Gary. "And Megan, well, she wants to raise them somewhere safer—her hometown of Omaha."

"Omaha? Won't you be bored out of your mind there? Come on! Buddy!" But Rook was too tipsy to plea.

"I don't know. It might be nice to have a slower pace."

Gary stared at the bamboo plant. *Seven years—just like that,* he thought.

"But it's going to be so hard to find someone to replace you. Someone I trust," said Rook, belching.

"What can I do? My family needs me around."

"I need you around! When are you leaving?"

"Early morning." And Gary thought of his parents who were now both in a nursing home in Pacific Palisades and how difficult it would be to move them to Nebraska.

"Sounds like a song," said Rook, and he got up and gave Gary a bear hug. "I'm really gonna miss you, buddy.

Thanks for all your help." And he noticed for the first time Gary's freckles.

"No problem," said Gary, pausing. "I'll leave the stuff at your door." Gary then started heading towards his room. *Rich, stinking bastard,* thought Gary. *Do I really need to put out my hand? Hell, these people just don't live in the real world! I should ask him for the money. I really should.*

But instead he kept walking towards his room—at the back of the house, next to the maid's quarters with whom he had had an affair with for two months. He set down his gun and wondered if his wife would ever find out about his extracurriculars, as he put on an ill-colored tie-dye.

"Well, well," said Rook, talking to the plant in the kitchen as he splashed more cold water on his dimpled cheeks. "Where did this come from?" He threw the foliage in the limited edition gold leaf trash can on top of the broken liquor and smelly cigarettes.

Rook then bounded upstairs—towards the master suite—pulling Monique along with him as she hung on his leg. They made their way to the largest of the 8.5 bedrooms on the second floor. He ran his hand along the cool, gray marble railing, pausing at the smooth little obelisk at the end. Black Dog, his black lab, ran from down the hallway to greet him.

"Oh, hello baby . . . ." he managed, as Black licked him. "I've missed you!" Black ran around and around—she just couldn't believe her master was home. "Oh, you're a good girl. You don't care if I'm famous, you don't care about the next record, or the money—you just love me for me, don't you?" Black jumped up on him and practically knocked him over. "Oh, you sillywilly! Now tomorrow I need you to go out and make some money. Don't come home till you have $1000 in your pockets. What? You don't have any pockets? Oh, we'll have to do something about that!"

"You talk to your dog nicer than you do to me," said Monique.

"Well, dogs are loyal."

Rook brushed his hand along the cold walls as they shuffled down the long corridor of furnished yet empty bedrooms (occasionally they would be very full—whenever there were out of town guests or big parties). Black Dog followed them, sniffing their jeans, picking up the recent scent of Shalimar and a potpourri of fragrances and wagging her tail. Rook and Monique kerplopped on the edge of the Edwardian sleigh bed in the 2500 s.f. master and proceeded to trip the light fantastic. At some point, they both fell asleep, limbs entangled and akimbo. Rook awoke with a start; as if suddenly remembering something, he got up and grabbed the absinthe that Gary left outside the door with the silver antique fountain and everything. He downed his and Monique's lickety-split, lit up another cigarette, and then stretched out in an exquisite mahogany veneer coffin he had placed by the window under doctor's orders for "rehab" purposes. He left the lid open, but neither Monique nor his dog cared to join him. He listened to the two of them snoring from different parts of the room.

Birthday. Deathday. It's all the same. You come into the world alone, and you leave it alone. He thought of buying himself a nice birthday present, but what do you buy for someone who has everything? Rook stared at the patterns in the ceiling. He followed the traces of the stucco along until he remembered swimming in a pool as a child doing the backstroke—floating with his ears underwater so he couldn't hear; it was subdued and he floated effortlessly as if the universes were supporting him and the bright lights overhead were heaven calling. The bubbling of the fountain from the master bathroom enhanced this effect. In this manner, he allowed further recapitulations to come. How had he ended up here in Hollywood in the first place? Faces swam by, and fast-forwarded right up to the girl in the rock star T-shirt who was now dreaming away. *I really am a rock star!* He laughed loudly; it echoed strangely in the lonely mansion. He thought of pinching himself to see if it were all real, but then laughed at this as well. At some point, he hauled his weight to his king-sized bed and fell into the little sleep next to a girl whose name he did not know. Outside, the stars shone brightly, but could not be seen clearly through the smog.

2

WHAT DO ROCK STARS DREAM ABOUT?

In his dreams, Rook was not a rock star. He was sometimes the high school-loser, who sat daydreaming in study
hall, writing lyrics and creating beats. He was sometimes
the tough guy. He recalled seeing his counselor—wanting
to create a guitar class. The paunchy man smirked causti-
cally, twirling his pen. Rook twirled his shoelace and threw
the first of many professional tantrums, heaving a chair at
the frosted glass door, shattering the poor man's name.
Instead of doing the work assigned during his suspension,
Rook practiced guitar. He figured it was no secret—the
only way to become a true proficient was to practice non-
stop. And so he provided himself with his own education,
calling himself in sick once a week to play acoustic twelve-
string in the woods. *But why am I doing all this?* he
dreamed, forgetting. *Oh, yeah! Her!* Not just a girl—*the
girl*—the reason for everything. Of course, this story is not
new. Every artist has his Dulcinea. *But what was her name?*
He tried to remember the first time they met.

It was at a bowling alley in Iowa City. Actually, it was
in the video game area adjacent to the bowling alley—
where you could hear the sound of the strikes and the
Donkey Kong jumps simultaneously. Lightning! Suddenly

Rook's movie became silent, and all he could hear was the thumping of his chest—whoever she was, she was out of this world. He remembered catching a glimpse of her in school, but they had never really crossed paths. Her hair was short and droopy, dyed red with a streak of hot pink. Her jeans hung down just slightly, though she seemed completely unaware of anything too suggestive—an innocent goddess. She had a rosebud tattoo just below her waistline and another one on her shoulder blade—peeping out now and then from beneath her white tank top. Through the holes in her Levi's, her knees appeared rug burned. Thinking of her, Rook lit up like a pinball wizard beside the machine he was leaning against. Her hair reminded him of a racecar he wanted. Where would he ever get the money?

Now, he was rich, rich enough for a stable of racecars, but still this girl was irretrievable. He couldn't go back and change things—and even with money would it have made a difference?

Maybe. What ever happened to her? Suddenly, in his mind, he saw her boarding the London Underground at Piccadilly. But where was she going? *I want to go to London.* He saw her through frosted glass and willed himself there. Zooming as fast as he could, he jumped, but the train doors closed and the tube sped off, leaving him minding the gap with fragments at his feet. *You want what you can't have.*

Rook awoke and panicked for a second—thinking there was some mix-up and he had never completed high school. But gradually his reality reassembled itself. He recalled graduation day from high school in Iowa City and the last day he had ever seen Hula. Slowly, the pictures came, and he remembered everything about her with crystal clarity. He had asked her out that first night they had met at the bowling alley (if you can call drinking beer in the parking lot a date), but she was seeing someone else. That was near the end of freshman year. Then he saw her at the beach (really the Coralville Lake) that summer. Her boyfriend wasn't there—she was with a girl friend named Joanna, but her previous rejection still stung, so he kept to the safety of his buddies. They thought they were tough kids; they picked fights and tried to act real cool. Top of the social hierarchy, in a rebellious sort of way, they evoked fear and admiration. And this is how they were acting that day—horsing around, splashing each other, when Daniel, their fearless leader, began to speak.

"Shit! Is that Hula Kentucky? She's gotten hotter than hell!"

"No kidding!" the others echoed.

Rook, looking at them looking at her, but keeping his back to her, froze.

He made the mistake of glancing at Daniel.

"What's this, Heisenberg?" Daniel asked. "Freeze tag?"

They all laughed and Rook tried to laugh too, then he ducked beneath the water, swimming away silently, trying to keep track of where Hula had been standing. He thought he had made a full circle, but when he came up, gasping for air, he practically bumped into her. If someone had a camera handy, and had taken a picture of the future rock star at that moment, it would have swum its way through all the magazines and tabloids and biographies. Rook, wet hair thrown back, mouth forlornly hoping, eyes wide with fear, buried his love there, unsure. And so of course when he saw Hula's condescending smile, he dove right back to where he came from and swam away like a frightened fish. When he lost the breathing capacity of his primordial ancestors, he finally surfaced next to his buddies, and they formed a circle around him—laughing and pointing and spitting water. Aghast and all wet and about to go under again, Rook suddenly felt a force rise from within, and he went with its directives. Holding up his index finger, he smiled confidently, turned around, and waded up to Hula with his trunks pointing in her general direction (though off to the right). She was still standing where he left her, and deigned to turn her stunning profile towards him. Up to her waist in water, Rook watched her punk-red hair drip in slow motion and her body glow through her royal purple bikini. Rook's entire body and face, meanwhile, had an odd, twisty look like that of an over-salted pretzel.

"Hi," he said. "Remember me?"

Hula laughed outright. What else could she do at such a ridiculous come-on? But then, even at the age of fifteen, she was wise enough to know that girls matured faster than boys, and that Rook's awkwardness could not be helped.

"Of course I remember you," said Hula, wiping her hair back from her aquamarine eyes and glancing at his gangly physique. "You have quite a passion for Bud Light, from what I recall. And gymnastics?" She elbowed her friend and they giggled.

Rook winced. "What? Hey, it was all I could get. My gang and I got it garage-hopping."

Hula raised one eyebrow at Rook and his so-called gang. "Impressive," she said. "What other sort of hopping can you do?" And she turned and waded away as a gust of wind blew, looking like Botticelli's Venus, leaving Rook to think about what the hell he had done wrong.

***

Rook laughed to himself as he reflected on his youthful naiveté. *I did a hell of a lot of things wrong.*

***

Come September sophomore year, Rook looked for her in each one of his classes, but no luck. Then, as he was heading for the bus, he was surprised to see her standing next to a garbage can in the outdoor western quad. He wanted to approach her, but the sun blinded him, or did she? He couldn't really remember. He had never hung out in this particular area, wasn't part of this clique. He hesitated, pretending to read graffiti on the wall. There really was graffiti on the wall—a drawing of a dog with big bazookas. He shook his head and looked back at Hula. *What the hell.* He felt the same mysterious force carry him, almost against his will and better judgment, towards what he felt was pure.

He pushed open the door and a hard breeze blew. Stumbling outside, Rook was about to make his move, when a guy in a jeans jacket and spiky hair suddenly put his arm around Hula. Rook froze, waiting to see what she would do.

She laughed at something jeans jacket said, turned, and kissed him on the lips. Rook sunk away and stared at a book lying on the ground—*Dibs: In Search of Self.*

"Hey Heisenberg," said Jim Jam, a neighbor and former friend—before they joined different cliques. "What are you doing out here?"

"Uh, just looking for my book—that's it!" said Rook, picking up *Dibs.*

"We don't read that till next trimester," said Jim, who was also in Rook's English class.

"Just getting ahead," said Rook, sneaking one more glance at Hula before he left. She was now aware of him, and staring at him suspiciously. Rook held up the book and waved. She turned her back and leaned her head against her boyfriend's jeans jacket, caressing its sleeve.

What's so special about that goddamn jeans jacket?

Meanwhile, some girl in a Led Zeppelin shirt was scouring the ground—evidently looking for her *Dibs.* Rook quickly slid it into his backpack, but couldn't manage to extricate himself from the quad just yet.

"What the hell are you doing out here anyway?" asked Jim. "Why would you—"

"You have a smoke?" Rook interrupted Jim.

"Sure," said Jim, surprised. "Here you go."

Rook delicately removed a Marlboro Red and inspected it.

"You put the filtered end in your mouth," said Jim.

"I know, I know," said Rook. He put it behind his ear for later. What he was going to do with it, he had no idea.

"You need a drink?" Rook heard a female voice ask. He was hoping it would be Hula, but when he looked up, he beheld Led Zeppelin girl.

"Sure," said Rook, gulping the Dr. Pepper she held out. "Thanks."

She stared at him and took a sip from the same can.

"This really is the best soda. Some people say it tastes like prune juice, but I don't care. I love the caffeine. I'm Lisa, by the way," she said, holding out her hand. "You're in my math class."

"Oh, right, right," said Rook, shaking her hand with both of his. Not knowing what else to do, he kept shaking her hand vigorously.

"Just started smoking?" Lisa asked, inspecting Rook and his spare coffin nail.

"I've never seen him smoke before," said Jim, inspecting Lisa.

Rook shot Jim a glance. "I've smoked a little. Little by little."

"Let's all go to the park," said Lisa.

Now Rook was accustomed to asking girls out, but he had never had the tables turned. Believe it or not, this future magazine-gracing idol, at this stage in the game, had never had any girl ask him out period.

He looked at Lisa. She was attractive, in a Winona wanna-be sort of way. *A little short, a little shabby, but not a bad-looking chick,* thought Rook.

"Sure," said Rook, succumbing to that Hydra of adolescence—peer pressure and impressing girls. "Where do we go?"

"I know a place," said Jim. "Follow me."

And so the three of them ambled towards the nearby park. Rook managed one more glance back at Hula. She wasn't even paying attention to him anymore; she was dancing to some Stevie Ray Vaughan coming from some boombox. Rook, Lisa, and Jim crossed the busy street and entered a muddy trail. They came to a heavily wooded area, and then Jim led them down a little ravine that was off the beaten path. He presented them with logs to sit on, and Lisa jumped up and down.

"Wee!" she yelled. "I'm freeeeeee!" Rook and Jim looked at each other and shrugged. "This is good stuff," said Lisa, as she got out a flask that she kept in her sock.

"Really," said Rook, wondering how anything that had been in somebody's smelly stocking all day could be "good." Then feeling a need to make conversation, he asked, "What is it?"

"Just some whisky from my p's liquor cabinet," said Lisa as she passed it to him. He was careful not to take too much. He felt a burning at the back of his throat, and almost coughed, but didn't. He quickly passed it on to Jim.

"That's good shit," said Jim, lighting up a cigarette and offering Lisa and Rook a jump start. Lisa took her smoke and lit it off Jim's. Rook tried to do the same, but had difficulty, and started coughing violently.

Lisa giggled. Jim said nothing, just sat there observing Rook. He patted him on the back.

"You okay, man?" asked Jim.

"Yeah, yeah," said Rook.

"I normally smoke lights," said Rook. They all laughed. But really all Rook could think about was his parents. Their stern faces hovered in his mind like the time he came out of the laughing gas at the dentist. *Man, I'm going to be in trouble!*

"Hey, you know this one?" asked Jim, holding up a CD of Black Sabbath's *Master of Reality*. "It kicks ass."

"Sure," Rook lied. "Put it on." Rook stared at some moss growing on the wet log.

Jim pulled his little stereo out and they continued to pass the afternoon like budding rockers, hanging out and listening to Ozzy. When Rook finally got home, much later than usual (he had to walk since he had missed the bus), his parents couldn't help but smell his new cologne.

"What are you doing with yourself?" his mom asked, on the verge of tears. "Don't you know I've sacrificed everything for you?" She grabbed him by the shoulders and examined his pupils. "Honey, wash your face and brush your teeth. Right now!"

"He's hanging out with the wrong crowd," said his dad, shaking his head and lighting up a cigarette. "You're grounded for a month! No allowance!"

Rook went to his room and slammed the door. He listened to the ticking of the clock, and the sound of his parents yelling downstairs.

Lisa, it turned out, liked Rook. But with him being in his group of hooligans, she didn't know how to approach him. She thought it a miracle that he would just so happen to be outside in the "grunge" quad that day. She did think it strange that he would even venture out there—all she could think of was that Jim was a neighbor, and maybe they were patching things up. If only she knew Rook's sights were set on Hula.

Hula, on the other hand, was into it hot and heavy with jeans jacket. His real name was pretty plain—Sam. He was a senior and in a heavy metal band called Mudfight (part of their gimmick during the finale of their show was to have a mud-wrestling match on stage with bikini-clad girls). Jim Jam, meanwhile, liked Lisa. Rook became friends again with Jim Jam just to get close to Hula—to hang out with that clique. Rook also started seeing Lisa (sort of), though he really wasn't interested in her; it was primarily to make Hula jealous. It didn't work. Hula continued to dismiss Rook—almost felt sorry for him.

So much of sophomore year went by in, well, sophomoric, soap-opera fashion. It was spring, and Rook was moping about one evening, grounded again—no longer close friends with most of his buddies—but not a full-fledged freak either—when he got a call from Jim Jam. Jim's older brother was getting married the next afternoon, and Jim wanted to invite Rook and Lisa. Jim, who was not so stupid, said that Hula would also be there—without Sam. Evidently, Hula was friends with the bride's sister, and Sam had a gig somewhere.

What was it with girls always going for the rock and roll guy? In pursuit of Hula, he had begun devoting most of his free time to learning guitar, writing lyrics, and singing along to a medley of music—Led Zeppelin, the Beatles, David Bowie, Queen, Prince, Billy Joel, Nirvana, Pearl Jam, U2, Michael Jackson, The Smiths, Soundgarden, and Judas Priest (though he could not fully hit Halford's notes).

The next afternoon, Rook glumly asked his parents if he could go to the wedding. After consulting with each other, surprisingly, they agreed. "It might do you some good!" said his dad. "Give you some direction," said his mom. "Remember," they said. "No drinking or smoking!"

"Okay, okay," said Rook. His dad actually went so far as to let him borrow his Porsche 944 (Rook now had his driver's permit), and the future idol drove himself to the church. His parents, smiling and waving in their flannels, watched their son disappear. They then disappeared into their quiet home, overlooking the Iowa River, where Mom began preparing supper (fish just caught and scaled from Dad's recent trip down the Mississippi), and Dad, seeing that the sun was peeking through the clouds, called his younger son, Harry, out into the backyard to play catch with the old, well-oiled mitts and grass-stained baseballs they would have to dig through boxes for to find in the musty garage that was crowded to the ceiling.

Ever optimistic, Rook had wanted a car for the wedding "just in case." He arrived early, and waited across the street for Hula. His mouth was overly dry, and he was sweating heavily, making his handsome suit unsightly. Suddenly, he saw her arrive and bells started to ring in his head. He quietly started up his old man's new Porsche (1991), then drove past Hula, as surreptitiously as possible, pretending not to see her, and pulled in a nearby spot. In the mirror, Rook noticed that Hula noticed. She and her friend (dressed like angels, or so thought Rook) were leaning against their old VW Beetle, smoking.

"Ladies! What a surprise!" said Rook, stopping to light up a smoke and join them.

"Daddy's car?" asked Hula.

"What, that old thing? It's mine. I mean, it will be mine as soon as I get my license."

"Uh-huh," said Hula, blowing smoke towards the heavens. "Rook, this is my friend, Joanna. Her sister's the bride."

"Right, right," said Rook, shaking Joanna's hand, all the while looking at Hula.

"You look very nice," said Joanna. "I love it when boys dress in suits and ties—it makes them seem so, so grown up."

"Daddy's suit?" asked Hula.

Rook's face turned sourpuss, as if he had eaten a lemon.

"Where's Lisa?" asked Hula.

"Oh, she'll be coming soon," said Rook. Actually, Jim had offered to pick her up, and Rook agreed. "Well, may I escort you two to the chapel?"

"Sure," said Joanna, taking Rook's arm.

Rook waited for Hula to take his other. Before she did, she leaned over and whispered: "Don't be so eager."

And then she locked her arm with his. As they walked to the church, though he had two ladies on his arms, Rook was aware of only one. He peeked at Hula's slender body, embroidered in white, against his black suit. Now she's got my sleeve.

He tried not to smile, but couldn't help it; her touch thrilled him to the core, and he felt a tingle go up his spine. He happened to glance at her face in the sunlight as they were approaching the massive wooden door, and there was the slightest hint of peach fuzz on her not-yet-tan cheek. As they entered the church, he imagined their own wedding.

***

Ah, the follies of youth. Rook laughed loudly and sent echoes of mirth through his Beverly Hills home. He was surprised at how vividly he recalled the sensation of her touch.

***

At the reception, Rook had no choice but to dance with Lisa. She kept dragging him behind a curtain to neck. There came a certain time, around 10 PM, when Rook intuited that if he didn't do something within the next few minutes, it would all be over—forever. He excused himself from Lisa, and went over to Jim, who was watching cautiously from the punch bowl.

"Listen, Jim," said Rook. "Let's help each other out. I want to dance with Hula, but haven't been able to get away from Lisa all night. I'll bring you over to her, and tell her I have to go to the bathroom or something. You make the moves, if you want—you like her right?"

"You know I do," said Jim.

"And you know I'm crazy about Hula. So let's go to work. Keep Lisa from noticing me and Hula. By the way, you have punch on your shirt."

Jim looked down at the sorry red stain against the white fabric.

"Yes, yes I know. I tried to get it out with an ice cube, but it didn't work so well. I feel like Hester Prynne. Only I haven't sinned yet."

"What the hell are you talkin' bout? Just appear really confident—even if you're not. She does like you, you know."

"She does?" asked Jim Jam, tjuzing his curly, strawberry hair in the silver punch ladle.

Rook nodded. He dragged Jim over to Lisa, and then really did go to the restroom. He splashed some water on his face and gave himself a pep talk in the mirror. "Now or never." Taking a deep breath, he stormed out, making his way toward Hula without Lisa seeing. Hula, however, saw Rook coming from a mile away.

"Oh no," she said to Joanna. "Here comes Romeo."

Rook stood before them and presented himself with his hands—*ta-da!*

Joanna laughed. Hula stared at the leftover green Jell-O on the table and wanted to throw it at him.

"Well, here we are again, ladies," said Rook, gesticulating far too much. "And being that it is getting late, I would love to ask you, Hula, for a dance before the night is gone. We are only young once."

"Yes, but you're a little too young for me," she said.

Rook gently pressed Hula's foot. She moved hers away.

"Come on, we're all dressed up and no place to go," said Rook. "Won't you dance?"

Joanna nudged Hula.

"Very well," Hula said. And she took Rook's outstretched hand.

It just so happened that the next song was a slow one, and Rook took advantage of it, placing his cheek next to Hula's. She did not move away. Rook felt like he was being lifted by balloons. Out of the corner of his eye, he couldn't help but notice what appeared to be a streak of mud on her temple. He wanted to wipe it and any trace of Sam away. But he didn't.

And then before he knew it, the dance was over.

"Thank you," said Hula. She walked back to her table and began chatting actively with Joanna. Jim meanwhile was still dancing with Lisa, who was looking around every now and then for Rook. Rook hid behind a pillar with his thoughts.

Okay, that was nice. But it wasn't enough. He looked over at Hula, then up at the band on stage, who were just finishing "1999." He danced up to the front.

"Hey," said Rook to the bandleader. "Would you mind if I sat in on the next one? I'd like to sing a song I wrote."

The rotund man in an ill-fitting tux rolled his eyes.

"I don't know, kid."

"It's for a girl—you see that beauty over there? With the wild hair?"

He looked where Rook was looking.

"She's out of your league, kid."

"But I at least have to try. I at least have to try."

The bandleader nodded his head.

"Okay. I can relate; I remember what it was like. What do you want to do?"

"It's simple: C-Am progression. Just follow along, you guys, with feeling. Improvise a lot on the keyboard."

The band looked at each other and shrugged. Rook borrowed a Les Paul and took the mike.

"This next one goes out to a very special lady," said Rook, looking at Hula. Lisa of course was looking now too. She jumped up and down, clapping, and pulled Jim closer to the stage with her. "She knows who she is. I wrote this to express things I just couldn't . . . express. I hope you'll understand."

Lisa was beaming with pride. Rook smiled at her—what else could he do? But before he began, he took another look at Hula. She was still sitting down next to Joanna, but her face assumed a quality he had never seen before—as if she were frozen—as if she were unsure whether to be embarrassed or flattered.

Rook took a deep breath, looked at the band, strummed the opening C, and sang his heart out:

"We start the day . . . on a good note. We carry through to a good note. Pianissimo. Pianissimo. Middle-C. We start the good day . . . on a good note. We carry through to a good note. We take the day—lightly—you and me. We dance through the cathedral, listening to the music that appears . . . from up on high . . . ."

As Rook sang, he closed his eyes. He couldn't connect emotionally with all those people staring at him, so he had to go within and pretend they weren't there. The only person who was there for him at that moment was Hula. As the band soloed, Rook snuck a look up at the audience. He couldn't believe it—but they were rapt with attention. He enjoyed this new power, this connection, this sublime feeling. The song then shifted and he raised his voice: "Sweep the leaves away from my grave—! I'm not dead yet. I want to see if anyone remembers me when I'm gone. Sweep the leaves away . . . sweep the leaves away. Hey! I'm still alive! I'm still alive!"

And the song picked up, ending on an upbeat tempo. When it was over, the audience began cheering madly. Rook shrugged.

"I just want to thank the band for giving me the chance to express myself—thank you guys."

The band nodded and the audience kept on clapping enthusiastically.

"Good job, kid," said the bandleader. "You really put your heart into it."

"I tried." Rook looked out into the crowd. They were staring at him strangely. He was not really aware of the affect that he had upon them. Of course, he realized the emotion he had poured into the song, but it was as if he were oblivious of his vocal gift and stage persona. His charisma was so contagious, so natural, so without contrivance, that it offered an immediate connection into something big.

Lisa tugged at his pants leg and wouldn't let go. "Thank you, honey," she said. "I, I . . . ."

Before he came down, Rook searched out Hula. She was still sitting at her table, though the frozen look was gone, replaced by another look Rook had never seen before. They locked eyes like Dante's Paolo and Francesca—their souls were one for a timeless moment.

Lisa reached forward to kiss him, but Rook turned his head and she ended up kissing his cheek.

"That was awesome, dude!" said Jim. "I really liked that—I'm not just saying that."

"Thanks," said Rook, noticing Hula getting up to leave.

"We should jam sometime, you know," said Jim Jam with the conviction of his intuition. "I play guitar pretty well. I just had no idea—"

"That's a good idea," said Rook, feeling as if Hula were about to walk out of his life permanently. "Let's talk about it later. I'm not feeling so well."

That was the truth. He felt like he was going to throw up.

"What's wrong honey?" asked Lisa. "Can I help?"

"No, I just need to go home and rest for a while."

"Okay, dear."

He kissed her on the cheek and hurried towards the door. Out in the parking lot, he grabbed Hula just before she was about to get in Joanna's Beetle.

"Listen," said Rook. "I'm not very good at this; I'm sorry. And I'll go away and never bother you again if you say so, but I have to at least try. I have to at least try."

Hula just looked at him. In the moonlight, her face was phantasmagoric—little angels seemed to be dancing about her, orbiting her head. Off in the distance, a moonbow subtly appeared against the canvas of the night.

"Let me give you a ride home," said Rook.

Hula kept looking at him, saying nothing. And then, after what seemed like the longest time, she took his hand. Rook led her to his car. Her arm felt different now. They said nothing on the way to her house. Not how to get there (Rook already knew), not how Rook already knew (he wanted to tell her he wasn't a stalker, but that would look bad!), not a word about Sam or Lisa or Joanna or school or typical teenage bullshit or anything else. They just held hands and shifted, listening to the gears of the Porsche, wondering where this road was taking them.

As Rook pulled into her driveway, he stepped on the brake, and turned to her.

"Well, here we are," he said.

"Here we are."

They looked at each other then simultaneously moved towards each other. As they kissed, Rook felt like he was on some other planet, defying gravity. He kept his eyes closed. It was his first real kiss and his most memorable one.

Hula felt like she were somewhere else too—but where she didn't know. She had never felt anything so intense and aching as this passion she suddenly held for Rook. She opened her eyes for a moment. She had had many kisses, but none quite as ethereal as this.

Suddenly, they both felt as if they were falling in love—literally—everything was moving! The car was rolling backwards down the driveway—their kiss broke—Rook slammed on the brake.

"Sorry!" he said.

"It would help if you put it in park," Hula said, beaming. They both laughed.

***

And Rook laughed again now in his twenty million-dollar mansion. If any of the people with the Star Maps were staring in, they would think he was some mad rock star-vampire, living in a gothic castle with a coffin next to his bed—raving to himself loudly in the middle of the night.

Goddamn lunatic rock star and his pathetic reveries. They're almost painful.

"Oh Hula, Hula, Hula, whatever became of you? Of us?" he spoke aloud. "How do I recapture that look? That kiss? How do I go back?"

He rubbed the tattoo of Hula he had gotten on his arm when he turned eighteen and remembered how his whole life had revolved around her.

They say you never love as deeply as you do with your first love. For Rook, this was true. But the current of time has a way of pushing people in different directions, and Rook, for a number of reasons, had long ago lost track of which shore Hula had landed upon. He had always thought that after leaving Iowa and moving to L.A. to seek fame and fortune that she would follow him out there. That was the plan. After a whirlwind relationship junior and senior years, he just assumed they would eventually get married. But that graduation day was the last time he had ever seen her, and God only knew where she had gone. He had talked to her mother several times on the phone, but all she said (she didn't much care for Rook or for men in general) was that Hula had "moved out" and that she would pass on his number to her. Throughout the years, he now and then thought of her, and occasionally would look out in the concert crowd for her, but she was never there. And he always thought she would call one day out of the blue, but that call never came.

How can I get a hold of her? "Never, I guess. Never."

He threw up his hands and went back to sleep. Being a rock star was tiring.

He awoke some time later as someone brushed up against him.

"Hula?" asked Rook, jumping up.

"Hula?" replied Monique. "Who's Hula?"

"Hey, gorgeous," said Rook, smiling and kissing this strange woman automatically.

"Who's Hula?" Monique repeated, withdrawing.

"Oh, teenage romance. I was dreaming of her."

"Oh, that's sweet. Oh, if only we could go back . . . ."

"If only . . . ."

Suddenly the door opened and a woman dressed like a French-maid appeared. Actually, it was a maid, but she was dressed as only maids for rock stars dress. Rook vaguely remembered her name.

"Hey, Monique," said Rook, "I don't remember ringing for you."

"I'm Monique," said rock star girl, pulling on Rook's chin.

"Then who's she?" asked Rook, shrugging with a grin.

The underdressed maid took off her cleaning outfit, setting it beside the bucket of 409 and sundry items, and walked the runway to the bed. Rook remembered red balloons from a childhood birthday party—rising against a magically blue sky. She tickled him with her feather duster.

"I'm Meriweather," she purred. "How could you have forgotten?" And the three of them went at it. Ducking, covering, and rolling, they forgot who they were for a moment. Opening their eyes, they collapsed on the Berber carpeting, which still had a new smell to it.

"Sing me a song," asked Monique, tracing Rook's bunny trail.

"I can't wait, to get married to you, to the both of you, we'll live in a tree that's what we'll do," sang Rook, pulling their hair. "And have beautiful babies."

Meriweather laughed. Naked she went to the kitchen to fix them all some energy shakes. She added protein, ginseng, and multi-vitamins. She admired the greenish color and thought of Ireland.

"Boy," said Monique, "that was interesting."

"Yeah," managed Rook, swigging Listerine as he tried to wake up. "For you, maybe. I feel like I'm stuck in a loop."

"Do you really mean to say that this is how most of your days start?"

"Sure, one way or another. Or two. Or three. After three I lose count. Sometimes I throw everyone out so I can get some sleep. Wake up around 2. Have some champagne brunch, coffee, and a smoke. Answer some phone calls, check my email, take a quick shower and before I know it my agent is carting me off on stage or to an interview somewhere. I pop some pharmaceuticals to keep going and sing and play and then we're on a plane and in another city for a retake."

Meriweather suddenly reappeared with the energy shakes, some champagne, coffee, and croissants.

Monique, pretending she was the only woman in the room, said, "Let me ask you a question--would you ever marry me?"

Rook played with his perm by the vanity. "No," he said.

"Why not?" asked Monique, watching the bubbles pop in the drinks.

"Because he's going to marry me," said Meriweather, "isn't that right, baby?"

"Do you have it in writing?" joked Rook. "Listen, no offense," said Rook, "but there's no point to marriage. The whole point to life is pleasure. What makes you feel good. I'll let you in on a little secret. To me, the whole pleasure of romance is the chase, and the sex. After it's over, it's sheer boredom. Blah-blah-blah, predictable soap-opera shit. Come on, change the channel! That's why I make it a rule to never sleep with the same woman twice." He gave them each a long look. "At least I try to make it a rule. But you're both so gorgeous!"

Neither lady spoke. They glanced at each other with feigned patience, wondering what the other had that they didn't.

"You're weird, " said Monique to Rook, feeling her future husband slipping away, and thinking of the Texas Panhandle. "I don't bore you, do I?"

"No," Rook said quickly. "But I don't even know you. I don't even know your name."

Meriweather sighed and began vacuuming up the dog hair. Rook observed her. *She's cutest when she's just herself, not trying so hard. Not acting. Why can't we all just stop the charade?* He threw some shorts on and went outside on the balcony. The sun was rising over the City of the Angels, the Entertainment Capital of the World! Rook watched all the cars heading towards the freeways. He was so glad he didn't have to commute to work. He was so glad that he did what he loved to do for a living—rock out. He was so glad he didn't have to make a résumé for that.

He lit up a Marlboro and searched the horizon for inspiration. The tour was now over. *But what now? What now? Oh, Hula.* And he felt silly and a little angry for thinking of her.

He tossed his smoke, which bounced off the diving board in a parabola, and quickly jumped off his balcony into the pool, trying to catch the cigarette in mid-air before it hit the water. He missed. He threw the soggy cig in the flowerbed, did some backstroke, and watched the clouds drift by. *They're mocking me.* One was in the shape of a camel.

"We brought you some refreshment," said the girls—apparently now friends—both suddenly appearing in their birthday suits at poolside with more energy shakes.

They're in league now, thought Rook. It always happens.

"What?" asked Rook, stopping his floating.

"More drinks."

"Thank you," said Rook. "Why don't you come in?"

They smiled and put their nineteen toes in the water.

"That's cold," one said.

"Just take a leap," Rook said.

They both did, and surfaced in each other's arms.

"How romantic," one said.

They all went at it again. Rook didn't like breaking his rules, but there was an ache deep down inside and it bothered him so much that he kept exploring. The three of them splashed about and then relaxed in a long embrace. Rook watched his little guys swimming without a clue— like a lost galaxy or primordial goo. They drifted frantically and aimlessly. *Where are you heading, my soldiers?* he thought.

"I have to go," said Rook after a while, getting out, looking for his shorts.

"What's wrong?" asked Monique.

"Nothing," said Rook. "I just need to take a walk—clear my head."

"Can I come?" asked Meriweather.

"No." He found his shorts near the juniper bush and wrung them out.

A tear rolled down Meriweather's face. "I should just leave," she said. She had been looking forward to seeing Rook for almost a year, and he barely remembered her.

"Go ahead," said Rook, not looking at either of them. He reached into his shorts and threw a handful of wet $100s into the air. "Leave the key if you don't plan on coming back." *All my help is leaving me now!*

"You're an asshole," said Monique as Rook disappeared inside the house. The two girls looked at each other, and felt they were gazing into a circus mirror. Slowly, they emerged from out of the water, dried off, then gathered up and flattened out the soggy bills. Meriweather looked up at the sky, and then placed the money in ideal sunlight. Monique sat, fuming, wondering who the fellow was on the bill, and wondering where she had left her clothes. Suddenly, a voice called to them from above and behind the twenty-five foot fence and hedge.

"Who's there?" they asked, covering themselves with their hands and towels and money. For a second, they both thought it was the voice of God.

"Aitchkiss Killawathy, reporter," managed a man in a British accent, his plump yet distinguished face sticking out from the leaves way up there. "Perhaps you've heard of me?" He was obviously struggling to hold on.

"I'm going to call the police," said Monique, walking away determinedly.

"No need, no need! I'm with the *Interloper*. I overheard everything, and caught a few photos. My paper would be happy to pay you both for an interview."

Monique looked over at Meriweather, then back up at the man.

"Okay," they said. "We'll meet you outside the gate in ten minutes."

"Okay!" piped Aitchkiss, slipping. "Okay!" Then there was a dreadful yell, and a long, trailing fall and crash. "Okay!" came one more, a bit too enthusiastically.

Meriweather set the leftover drinks on top of the drying bills. A cigarette smoldered. The two girls walked inside to gather their things. Meriweather thought of saying goodbye to Gary (she didn't), and shortly, with a slam of the door, she exited Rook's mansion and was standing outside the gate at exactly the ten minute-mark. Monique was already outside, and thinking about how much she missed Texas and her dreams (which seemed to her to be going up in smoke). She gazed down at a four-leaf clover growing in the St. Augustine. Suddenly, a long black limo pulled up, the tinted window rolled down, and a gentleman in a very proper black suit, but with rather grotesque-looking boils on his face, a bloody nose, and rotting teeth said: "Come on, come on, we haven't got all day."

"Aitchkiss?" asked Monique, standing back. *He looks different close-up. I could help him.*

"The one and only."

"What's wrong with your face?" asked Meriweather.

"Nothing! I just fell off a gate, goddamit! Now I'm trying to get a story, and I need your assistance. I have some very specific questions, and some very specific instructions. You both seem like very reliable ladies, huh?"

"How much are you willing to pay me?" asked Meriweather, wondering how she was going to make it through the next month.

"How's $10,000 each sound?"

They both frowned.

"Okay, $20,000. Half now, half when the mission's over."

They both smiled. They would have both taken the $10,000; they had looked askance because a particularly heinous boil of Killawathy's was oozing pus.

"I want it in writing before the interview," said Monique.

"As long as we don't have to sleep with you," said Meriweather.

"Of course, of course," said Aitchkiss, eyeing their bare knees. "Let's go already." And he couldn't look at their stunning faces for the tears that were welling up from behind the cataracts in both his eyes. "Even though I'm an entertainment reporter," he went on, confiding, "I am a respected professional, striving always for veridicality."

The ladies both shrugged glitter and hopped into the limo. As it lurched away towards the Wilshire office of the publisher, a police car pulled out of Greystone Park to follow it.

"Have a possible 647b," said the officer over the radio, citing the code for prostitution. "Following a black limo, license plate . . . ."

***

Rook had taken a quick shower, and was throwing on some jeans and a T-shirt. *Why am I such an asshole sometimes? I really am.* He stared blankly at the platinum-certified album plaques on the wall. *Did I do that? I don't remember. I don't remember the last time I was clean and sober.* In the background, he heard on the TV his interview, or altercation, with Mindy Mountain from the night before. He ran to check it out. *Oh, Christ.* They kept replaying her slap across his face. *At least I look good.*

He went to his main travel bag and dug out his little black book. This is where he recorded his escapades, and kept track of his lady friends. He made a notation for Girl #8 (Monique), and Girl #9 (Meriweather) of the month, while their names were still fresh, and made a brief annotation so that he would remember their ménage à trois. Normally, he would print out a photo with his Polaroid or snap one with his iPhone so he could envision their faces when he was old and crippled, but in all the excitement they had run off prematurely. He flipped back to the previous year, and found a photo of Meriweather from last June—the last time he had been with her. He smiled at his old notations, and noted that she had become more adventurous as of late. Rook then went on to detail the types of alcohol and drugs he had taken yesterday (Doctor Vilhelm was making him keep track), as well as what he had eaten, and couldn't help but notice that it was almost the same pathetic intake as this time last year. *I need to get in shape*, he told himself. He thought of his parents and how disappointed they would have been. *They deserve better.*

But he couldn't bring himself to think about them now on this happy occasion of his birthday and so he got up quickly and went to his computer, deciding to check his email before he went on a much-needed walk. He came across an ad from one of those schoolmate sites. Not capriciously, recalling his dream, he decided to look up Hula Kentucky: she was listed. *That's weird. All these years and I find her just like that.* He reflected on the visions he had last night that had stirred from within his sarcophagus.

What the hell. Rook began writing her a letter:

Date:

Tues, 16 Jun 2009 12:25:20 -0700 (PDT)

From:

"Rook Heisenberg" <undisclosed@yahoo.com>* | This is spam | Add to Address Book

Subject:

Is there anybody out there?

To:

"Hula Kentucky" <undisclosed recipient>

---

* It is unclear how the author obtained these email correspondences. Verification was attempted, but rejected by no less than seven separate entities. This editor was also warned not to disclose the actual addresses; hence, they appear as "undisclosed."

Hula,

I was thinking about yous last night from within my coffin. Maybe that means something—near death and regrets and all that. I know we had a strange relationship in high school. And I realize you're probably freaked out to be getting this—me being a rock star and all now. I dreamt that you were in London. I'm still living in L.A.—home after a long tour. Sometimes I think I'll see your face in the crowd, but I never do. You know, you were the reason I learned to play, and that song I sang at the wedding was the first performance I ever gave. Anyway, I don't know whatever happened to us, but it doesn't matter now. Feel free to tell me to fuk off. No prob. But if u like to get together, perhaps we could recapture something I haven't felt in a long time. I'm goin' so fast with this kwazy lifestle somtimes I can't remember who I am. Help me remember and find my footing. This sounds stupid because I'm wasted 23/7. Hope to hear from u.

Rook

Rook realized the irony that he was going to Hula Kentucky to regain his innocence—Hula, probably the least innocent girl in high school. But she felt like his only link to a past where he could feel, and he had to open that door.

Rook sighed and squinted as he headed out, like a strange lizard that has been in a dark cave for far too long. The sun was blinding, and his hangover was making him a little disoriented. It had been years since he had walked the neighborhood. He stumbled and strolled past the park, descended the hill, and eventually meandered his way over to his old hangout—the classic Rainbow Bar & Grill on Sunset. He sat down at the cozy outside bar in back, ordered a cappuccino from behind his Versace glasses, lit up a cigarette, and asked for some spinach tortellini.

"So. How ya' been?" asked the barmaid, her cleavage on display to movie moguls everywhere. She smiled, looking at Rook's long and bare fingers.

"Yeah," said Rook.

She raised a black, velvety eyebrow. "You okay?" she asked. "It's really early for you."

"Yeah," said Rook, his eyes riveted to her and her nametag. *Marissa. Girl #10?* thought Rook. "Sometimes I'm just leaving upstairs about now." "Upstairs" referred to the private club at the Rainbow—called Over the Rainbow—where celebrities would come and play in privacy. "I'm just tired, girl. Tired of being on the road. Tired of no personal space. Tired of the rock and roll routine marketing machine. Tired of—"

"Shut up! I can't believe you're complaining! If you're not happy, then change things, you idiot!"

Rook dropped his cigarette. It was rare for a woman to speak honestly to him. "I like you," he said. "And I love this place! And you're exactly right! You know, I was sitting here fifteen years ago, when I was eighteen and new to L.A., and I feel like I was a lot happier then. A lot more naïve, but a lot happier. Hell, I love my work, but it's walking the treadmill now. I need to do something entirely different for a while, then maybe I can go back and play music with renewed inspiration and, and purpose."

"Sounds like a bunch of shit to me," said Marissa, wiping the bar and bending over more than necessary. "Hell, you've got it made. You're richer than 99% of the population! Buy some new toys."

"Like what? Another Enzo Ferrari? No, I think I need to experience some real hell so I'll have something real to write about. I think that's the problem: I can't relate to my fans anymore, and they can't relate to me. What's that they say—great art comes only through great suffering?"

"I suppose, but don't go getting masochistic on us now. Why are you talking crazy? Try and find some sort of normal motivation—like to impress girls." And she winked at him.

"That's what it was at first. It's funny you should mention this; I just dreamed about it. In high school, when I started—the only reason I started was to impress this girl. Not just to impress her—I was in love with her and the only way I knew how to win her was through music."

"Did it work?"

"For a while. But things happened . . . ."

Marissa picked up Rook's left hand and began massaging it, starting with his thumb, slowly caressing it. She stared intently into his dark, giddy eyes. Just as she got to his ring finger, the roar of a Harley interrupted her. In walked a couple—some young heavy metallers in biker regalia. The guy stopped dead in his tracks when he saw Rook. The look of shock and awe in his eyes was unmistakable.

"You're Rook!" cried the young man, hesitating to approach.

"And you're not," said Rook, letting Marissa's hand drop.

"Jesus Christ, Ray—are you hypnotized?" the lady biker asked her boyfriend. "Great concert last night," she said to Rook, pulling Ray towards the bar. They plopped down next to the rock god, leaving one seat in between.

"It was okay. What song did you like the best?" asked Rook, genuinely interested. Marissa, genuinely disinterested, pretended to be busy suddenly behind the bar.

"Surprisingly, the mellow one—'A Good Note,'" said biker girl.

"Believe it or not," said Rook, giving her the once-over twice, "'A Good Note' was the first song I ever wrote. Sang it at a wedding," he wisped, following the steam from his pasta brunch as it was served by a busboy in white who disappeared just as fast as the steam.

"Yeah, I heard that somewhere," said the girl, inspecting Rook closely.

Marissa rolled her eyes. "You two want something?" she asked the bikers.

"Yeah, give me a bourbon," said Ray, scowling, fidgeting with a coaster.

"Mojito Bartles and Jaymes," said the girl, smiling at Rook.

"Now, Reba, why do you have to go and order that fruity drink?" asked Ray.

"It's not, Ray. It's named after two Shakespeare characters, I'll have you know. You look different in person, you know. Not so much of a bad boy."

Rook shrugged. "Bartles and Jaymes," was all he said. He couldn't remember any such characters. He did remember visiting Shakespeare's grave in Stratford last time the band was in London, and how he was overwhelmed by the sense of how one day none of this would matter. He felt similar ennui at Jim Morrison's grave in Paris. There was still something in the back of his mind that said that Jim had just faked his death to escape from this circus—something he had thought of doing now and then himself.

"Let me ask you a question," said Rook to the couple. "Are you two happy? Are you in love?"

"You ask hard questions," said Reba, laughing nervously.

"I don't know, you can't really explain love," said Ray, lighting up a cigarette with trembling hands and downing his bourbon.

"That's true," said Rook. "But you two seem to be together—to have a connection. You're starting out, and have a promising road ahead."

"So," said Ray. "What are you trying to say?"

"Let me tell you a story," said Rook. "I first moved out here to California from Iowa some fifteen years ago—when I was eighteen. I had just finished high school, and arrived here in June—on my birthday. All I knew was that I wanted some excitement. I wanted to get away from everything—family, friends, the snow. I wanted to forget everything—almost everything—and start new. So I had this friend in Santa Barbara who was a year older. He had moved out a year earlier, was working some odd jobs, but really wanted to start a band."

"Jim Jam," said Ray, playing with his drink, rearranging the ice cubes in an attempt to find a subliminal message.

"Yes. Anyway, the first day I get out here, I thought, my God, California, Santa Barbara, palm trees, the sunshine, the beach, the mountains—beautiful. When I walk in his place—and he was staying at an extra home of his parents, there was a party going on. I was down with that. I had a beer. Then someone had cocaine. I had never done cocaine before, and so was hesitant. I kept saying no thanks. Then, I don't know why, I gave in and tooted up. Toot toot. I felt euphoric. I felt like I could do anything. All the problems melted away. Then in walks this typical California blonde bombshell—wow. I told her it was my first day in California, and she says welcome to California and kisses me on the lips! I'm thinking, what the hell sort of place is this? And so the party went on for years like that, lots of excitement, I was doing cocaine all the time to keep up the euphoria, or to try and reach that original state of euphoria that I felt the first time. But I never again hit that peak. Meanwhile, Jim Jam and I had started the Little Bang—our first shows were those pay to play gigs you have here on the strip. Eventually, we attracted a following. So our careers were taking off, our success fed the drug problems and constant partying, and I was just caught up in this whirlwind. Constant excitement—but try and keep that up for years. Then one day, after an all-night binge, I got up and attempted to work out—stay in shape—you know. But after only eight bench presses, I felt like I was having a heart attack. All I could think of was that basketball star—who had died from cocaine. I stepped outside for some fresh air, really thinking I might die. I just sat there on the steps of my goddamn mansion, wondering why the hell I was killing myself like that. So I got myself a doctor. Great guy—Doctor Vilhelm. He takes care of me and the band. Monitors us so we can still party but don't overdo it. Too many people's wallets are depending on us now. But I'm getting tired of the whole machine that doesn't stop. I need to stop for a while. And there's nothing the good doc can give me for that. I'm burned out with the Bang. You know, today I turned thirty-three years old, and I was lying in my coffin thinking—thirty-three and what have I accomplished? Five multi-platinum records? Who cares."

There was a long silence. Then Marissa said, "Let's have you a birthday party tonight!"

"Yeah!" said the couple.

"Don't worry about a thing," said Marissa. "The restaurant will call your agent and we'll organize it. It's the least we can do for one of our best customers! We'll close the place down just for you and your friends!"

"Awesome!" said the couple.

"Well thanks for listening to my ramblings," Rook said, wiping his plate with garlic bread and downing his third cappuccino.

"No problem," said Reba. "Anytime." She placed her hand on his knee.

Rook nearly spit out his coffee. "I've gotta go," he said, getting up.

"Can I have your autograph first?" asked Reba, getting up also.

"No problem," said Rook, getting out his wallet. He removed a crisp $100 bill and signed his name across Ben's forehead.

"Wow !" she said. "Thank you!" And she kissed Rook on the lips before he could turn away. Rook took out another bill and signed it for Ray.

"Ask and you shall receive," said Rook, handing it to Ray. Ray wanted to set it on fire. Instead, he just set it on the bar.

"And here you go, Marissa," said Rook, tossing a couple of hundreds at her. "That should help cover any more boob jobs." He gave her a wink.

"They're real," said Marissa, letting the money fall to the floor.

"Then they're the only ones in this town that are. Take care," said Rook. And he put on his dark sunglasses and walked out again, rejuvenated, into the bright sunshine.

"Happy birthday!" called Marissa. "See you tonight!"

Rook waved goodbye without looking back.

"I hate that guy," said Ray, staring at the signed $100 bill on the bar.

"Oh Ray," said Reba. "Stop it. He's on a whole 'nother level."

On the way home, Rook stopped at Book Soup—across the street on Sunset. *Wow! What a fantastic place! If only I could through osmosis acquire all the knowledge in these books.* He picked up the local newspaper. In the entertainment section headline it read:

Local Boys Do Good—the Little Bang Lights up the Night!

It went on to give a favorable review of their show last night, but Rook could never bring himself to read reviews in their entirety—good or bad. "I need inspiration." He hid himself behind the paper and sauntered about the store.

Noticing all the dead celebrity icons littering the aisles in cardboard standups, Rook felt like just one more of them, although they seemed more alive than he felt. *Hi, James Dean! Hi, Elvis! Hi, Marilyn Monroe! Hi, Kurt Cobain!*

While finding an inconspicuous corner, Rook came across a book that caught his eye—*Either/Or*—and flipped through it.

On the opening page, he read:

> What is a poet? An unhappy man who hides deep anguish in his heart, but whose mouth is so formed that when the sigh and cry pass through it, it sounds like beautiful music . . . People gather around this artist and say: 'Sing again soon' — that is, 'May new sufferings torment your soul, but your mouth be fashioned as before, for the cry would only terrify us, but the music, that is amazing . . . .'

"That's me," said Rook, aloud, looking about to see if anyone had overheard him. *That's me exactly,* he thought. *Who is this guy? Kierkegaard? Never heard of him. Either I buy it, or I don't.* Rook walked right up to the counter and purchased the classic—exchanging knowing nods with the clerk—who kindly did not call attention to him. As he walked home, nearing Greystone Park, he sat down and opened to a page at random—Literary Russian Roulette.

It read: "I feel as if I am a piece in a game of chess, and my opponent says: That piece can't be moved."

"This book was written with me in mind!" Rook said aloud.

"Who's that? Well, hi Rook! Welcome home! How are you?"

It was Rook's neighbor Mr. Josephine, who was in the fashion business. He ambled up in a thoughtful design yet awkward gait, walking his German Shepard. The dog was barking, or attempting to bark, but only raspy sounds came out; Josephine had a vet surgically cut the dog's vocal cords so as not to disturb the neighbors.

"I'm okay," said Rook, setting his book down and reaching out to pet the animal. "Hi Princess, how ya' doin?"

"She's fine. Just getting older, like all of us. Just faster! Word has it that you're becoming involved in the fashion world!" said Josephine.

"Yeah," said Rook. "I don't know much about it though. Did some shoots." He recalled the hours of posing in clothing that looked beautiful but felt uncomfortable.

Rook focused on projecting good-will towards the dog . Princess seemed to appreciate it, licking Rook's face. More difficult was projecting positive thoughts towards Mr. Josephine. He found his empathy targeted his light blue sweater and the unfortunate monogram of "BJ" rather than the man himself.

"Jo', how would you feel if someone cut your vocal cords?" Rook asked.

Josephine said nothing.

Princess licked Rook some more, then Mr. Josephine pulled her away. "Come Princess, let's leave the nice man alone. Good day, Mr. Heisenberg."

"Good day," said Rook. "It's great to come home to Beverly Hills, isn't it?"

"You'll get no argument from me there!" replied Josephine. "No place like it!"

He watched Josephine and Princess walk across the way and disappear behind the tall gate of their estate. As Rook was wondering what went on behind that big hedge, an officer pulled up, and upon noticing Rook, did a U-turn and pulled over near his park bench.

"Hey Rook," said the officer. Rook had seen him before, but couldn't remember his name. He was tall and lanky and walked like he had forgotten something.

"Hey," said Rook. "Am I in trouble?" He laughed nervously.

"No, no," the officer guffawed, taking off his shades. "I just wanted to say that I was at your show last night—my wife and I really enjoyed it."

"Why thank you. I'm sorry, what's your name again?"

"Kerry. Kerry Daniels." The officer smiled like he had accomplished something.

Rook took off his shades and put out his hand. "Nice to see you again, Kerry. Hey, aren't you the one who acts in his spare time?"

"Yeah, what little spare time I have," said Kerry, embarrassed. "Hey, I just want you to know that we kept a close eye on your place while you were gone."

"Thanks," said Rook. "Any problems?"

"Not really. Though this morning I was making my usual stop—wasn't sure if you were back for good yet, and saw this limo picking up two women in rather racy outfits."

"Hmmm," said Rook. "What was it?"

"Well, I followed them, thinking it was prostitution, but they went right to the *Interloper* office. I questioned them when they got out, and they said they were doing an interview."

"Did you get their names?"

"Aitchkiss Killawathy and Monique and Meriweather. They said they knew you."

" Yeah, I know them too. Hell—that damn tabloid may as well be prostitution."

"I understand, sir," said Kerry. Kerry dawdled. He looked up with the practiced air of one who had posed for too many 8x10 glossies.

"Is there something else?" asked Rook.

"You know, I hate to ask, but my wife's dying to go to some big party here. Would you mind letting me know the next time you have one? Hate to be an asshole, but just trying to please the old lady." He handed Rook his card.

Rook smiled. "I understand. No problem. I'm actually having a birthday bash tonight at the Rainbow. It'll probably end up here late."

"Sounds great," said Kerry, shaking Rook's hand too vigorously. "We'll see you then!"

"Sure," said Rook, making his way back to his castle. Once inside, he relaxed, trying to catch his breath. *I'm not as young as I use to be.* Rook stared out his fortified window at the city below. *Where is my angel? Where is my little angel?* He sludged his way to his computer. Checking his email, his face froze when he saw a response from Hula. At first, he was afraid to check it. *Do I really want to open this door?*

*Who knows where it might lead? I never thought she would
actually get it, let alone respond. But I've got to open it.*

Date:

Tues, 16 Jun 2009 15:07:03 -0700 (PDT)

From:

"Hula Kentucky" <undisclosed@yahoo.com> | This is spam | Add
to Address Book

Subject:

Re: Is there anybody out there?

To:

"Rook Heisenberg" <undisclosed@yahoo.com>

Rook,

It was soooooo great hearing from you! And so unexpected! I
apologize for not keeping in tocuh after high schhol, bt I got caught up
in this quest to find my dad. Long story! Led me to London—lived there
for a while. That's weird you had that dream! Now I'm in Amsterdam.
I'd luv to see you! We need to talk abot some things. Plzz cum vistit.
Gotta go to wrok...;)

Hula

P>s> Happy Birthdayyyyyy! Are you really in your dyin coffin?

Rook just stared blindly at the computer. Her father?
Rook couldn't remember one. Then he recalled something
of how she never knew her dad—her mom, who was a
writer/professor at the University of Iowa, had had an

affair while young and in Europe, but never married the guy. Amsterdam! Rook had been there many times on tour, and now it looked as if he would soon be going again. He read the email over and over again, trying to piece it together. He kept analyzing it—overanalyzing it, ad nauseam: *It looks like it took her, what almost three hours or so to respond. Does that mean she got it earlier, and waited? Did she write right away? There's no way to tell. And London— weird. But why doesn't she mention my music? It's as if that doesn't matter to her. I wonder if she's even heard of me? How ironic! I get into the business because of her, and she's completely oblivious of it. Or maybe she purposely doesn't mention it because she figures I get too much of that already. Hmm. And she remembered my birthday! That's a good sign! That's got to be a good sign!*

Rook picked up the phone and dialed Southhampton.

"Southhampton here," said a gruff voice.

"It's Rook."

"Rook! Hi! How are you enjoying your first day back home? We're in the middle of organizing your birthday, you know."

"Great. Listen, I need you to set up a flight for me to Amsterdam. Tomorrow. Then book my usual room at the Genteel."

"Amsterdam? What are you going there for?'

"To meet an old friend."

Silence.

"How long do you want me to book the room for?"

"I don't know. A week. Maybe two. Leave it open."

More silence.

"Do you want me to go with you?"

"No."

"How 'bout a bodyguard? I'd feel more comfortable if you took Gary."

"Gary quit—moved to Omaha. Listen, if I feel the need for one, I'll let you know."

"Okay. Hey, I'll talk to you at the party. And for my sake, let me call a few folks and see if I can line up at least a temporary security for you while you're in Europe. And listen, Rook, we need to talk about the next studio session."

"Not now. Jesus, SH, I just started my vacation."

Rook hung up. He then typed a response back to Hula.

Date:

Tues, 16 Jun 2009 16:28:32 -0700 (PDT)

From:

"Rook Heisenberg" <undisclosed@yahoo.com> | This is spam | Add to Address Book

Subject:

On my way

To:

"Hula Kentucky" <undisclosed@yahoo.com>

Hula,

So we're both a bunch of yahoos. I always thought as much. I'll be in Amsterdam in a few days. I'll be staying at the Genteel. I won't howevr be under my name—ask for Piliper Grits. I look forward to seeing you soon. We have a lot to catch up on.

Rook

Rook got up and began pacing about the house. He stared at his sticker-littered suitcases. *No need to unpack!* His eyes landed upon some old family photographs and he sighed. He didn't know why he kept them out; every time he saw them he felt only sadness. He picked one up—it was of him (he must have been about ten), his parents, and his only other sibling—his younger brother Harry. They were standing in front of their pool in Iowa, smiling at the promise of the summer ahead. The grass looked so green in the background. He recalled how he had to step in a plastic tub full of water to clean the blades off his feet before he dove in. Who took the picture?

Rook studied the photo, trying to find signs of foreboding amidst the surface joy. There was no evidence of foreshadowing, no hints of the future tragedy. He put his hands to his head. He could barely stand remembering.

***

Some eleven years after the snapshot, his parents and brother had run out of time. They were making a pilgrimage to the Holy Land. They were in Jerusalem, touring the places Christ had walked. Rook had planned to join them, for a long-postponed reunion, but had to postpone it again due to an additional touring commitment that Ted had booked without his knowledge. He couldn't get out of it, and besides, he thought there would always be another time. That is, until a suicide bomber stepped on the bus his family was on and blew everyone to pieces. When Rook got the call, he was in a drunken stupor. The band was starting to get big, and had just played in San Antonio.

Rook was celebrating his 21st birthday. It was after the show, and the band was partying at the famous Ranger Hotel. When he was handed the phone, and listened to the strange voice impart the terrible news, he felt like someone had poured mercury into his ear. He stormed out of the hotel and wandered around the Alamo. He collapsed on the ground and stared up at the stars. He heard people talking and pointing at him. "Is that him?" Footsteps approached and someone asked him for his autograph and took a photo—posing with him insanely in the mud. "Happy birthday, Rook! Wanna' blow out some candles?" giggled some heavenly, carnation-scented ladies dabbed in Caron's Poivre.

"Fuck off," Rook swore. He wanted the earth to swallow him up. Instead, he fell asleep.

The triple funeral, a week later in Iowa City, was closed caskets. He stood so nicely in his Armani suit, trying to remember the last time he had seen them all alive. He couldn't—his life had been such a constant rave, everything was a fog.

***

Rook set the picture down and turned off the memories, shrugging. He began wandering again throughout the house. He stared at his slippered feet flopping about— again they seemed like they didn't belong to him. He found himself back in the kitchen, next to Kierkegaard. He picked it up and turned to another page at random. It said something about the character's soul being so heavy that it was like the flight of birds low to the ground before a storm. *That's me.*

He set the book down and made his way upstairs. He collapsed in his coffin, and thought about how much time he had until he was really lying in the good earth. He thought of all the things he wanted to do . . . needed to do. And despite the wisdom of the ages calling to him, and all manner of other important matters, Rook allowed his predominant thoughts to be of Hula. Images of her blazed through his mind. He could see her there with her ripped jeans at the knees and the rosebud tattoo calling to him like the Tao from the deep end of Coralville Lake.

Corresponding Map of Coralville Lake and Iowa City, also Holywood and Beverly Hills and more?[*]

---

[*] At this point in the manuscript the above notation was slapdashedly scribbled, along with some even more indefinite, abbreviated directions. A possible intent of the author was to draw out the various locales described herein to give readers some sense of scope of the characters' environments.

3

BEDROOM 8.5

What if things had turned out differently? What if there were a parallel universe where they did? There were so many things Rook would have changed—his family's tragedy, the Hula ordeal, Jim Jam's death. But there was no magic time machine, no Dr. Heidegger's elixir. *Be stoical,* thought Rook.

He had to stop blaming himself for the death of Jim Jam. When it occurred, the Little Bang had been expanding for a little over four years. They were making money— more than ever before. "Los Angeles" had just made it to #1, and they were living it up (Rook was also trying to erase his loss—his family had passed just a few months back, and he was drowning himself in a pharmacy of forgetfulness). They had been partying all day at Venice Beach, and as night fell the band and friends lit a bonfire and sang songs—people just started gathering—word got out that there was an impromptu concert—and the media and paparazzi soon showed up. They decided to high-tail it out of there when the flash bulbs began going off. They ran to Rook's Mercedes. Rook remembered he felt like the Beatles—in all those girls-chasing-them scenes. Rook and Jim got in and began to speed away towards a party in Malibu. They were on their way down PCH when an SUV

of paparazzi began following them. Rook, feeling happy—
a little too happy—put his foot to the floor. They wove in
and out of traffic, and were about to lose the chasers, when
a car in front of them put on its brake lights. Going too fast
to stop, Rook swerved instead, heading into oncoming
traffic. His whole life did flash by—like a horribly melodramatic movie. He was able to avoid the first car that
came towards them, but another one clipped them on the
passenger side. He heard Jim scream—but he was blood-
curdling himself. They were spinning out of control. Next
thing he knew, there was a huge crash, and then he
blacked out for a minute or so. He came to to the sound of
approaching sirens. They were in the living room of some
house. An older couple was peering in at them from a safe
distance, asking if they were okay as the car smoked and
burned.

"Yeah, yeah, I think so," said Rook, though the airbag
was smooshing him so he couldn't move much. He looked
over at Jim and almost threw up—his best friend was a
frightful mess: his legs embedded into the dashboard, his
head turned unnaturally, blood pouring bright red from
out his mouth.

"I'm so cold—" said Jim, his eyes blinking rapidly then
glazing over.

"It'll be okay," said Rook, lying and he knew he was
lying but what could he do? He reached out to Jim, but his
hand was stuck. "Call an ambulance!"

"Help is on the way," the old couple insisted. The
woman inched closer, but the man held her back. They
sported black silk pajamas, reminding Rook of art critics on
holiday.

"I never thought it would be like this," said Jim. "I had so much I wanted . . . what happened?" He stared at his blood flowing out, soaking into the plush upholstery.

"I don't know," said Rook. "I don't know."

Jim's attention suddenly came alive—seized by something else.

"The TV. I remember that show," laughed Jim. An old episode of *Lost in Space* was playing on a large flat-screen just beyond the cindered wreckage.

Rook forced a smile. "Save your strength. They'll be here soon. They'll take care of you."

"I'm fucked," said Jim. "I'm really fucked." Jim then felt a strange desire for a cup of coffee and a cigarette, yet didn't have the energy to ask and just went "Hummpf."

"I'm sorry," said Rook. "I fucked up."

"No you didn't. It was an accident. It was just an accident . . . ." Jim's voice began to fade away like a mantra. In his mind, he saw coffee steam and cigarette smoke floating towards the sea; he followed them.

"Don't go to sleep on me!" shouted Rook. "They're almost here!" Red, white, and blue lights cascaded upon the white minimalist look the aging mod couple was going for. Then all manner of commotion scrambled towards them.

"Tell Lisa, tell Lisa—I love . . . ." managed Jim. And he checked out.

"I love you," said Rook. Whether Jim heard it or not was unclear, but the fireman certainly did (and he told as much to the press) as he struggled to free the smoldering rocker whose first CD he had just listened to that morning while jogging at the fitness club.

Rook didn't say a word for four days. At UCLA Hospital, wrapped in gauze and hooked up to an IV, he rested and gradually regained his strength. But he could not bring himself to speak. Whenever someone asked a question, he'd just stare forlornly out the window. He kept reliving the accident and pictured them working on Jim. He recalled with painful clarity how they shook their heads when they saw him and he knew then it was hopeless. Later, he heard that it took them almost an hour to extricate him from the car. By then, Rook hoped to think, Jim was enjoying his coffee and cigarette at the café in the sky.

It wasn't until Lisa visited that Rook opened his mouth. She entered the room with a manic expression on her red and tear-worn face.

"How could you? How could you let this happen?" she asked.

Rook didn't know what to say. He couldn't even look into her eyes.

"You fuck!" shouted Lisa. "You miserable fuck!"

Rook's eyes began to well up. He forced himself to stare at the starched white sheet—*it will help me keep my emotions under control,* he thought.

Lisa grabbed his backless, standard-issue pajamas and pulled his face towards hers.

"Do you realize I'm pregnant? Did he ever tell you that? Now who's going to be the father?"

Rook automatically began forming some song-like response, but quit.

"I'm sorry, I'm so sorry, Lisa. I am a miserable fuck. It was an accident—it was an accident. I had had a little to drink, but . . . ."

"No, you shithead. You can go to hell for all I care. Jim was a good man. I loved him. It wasn't bullshit like you. It was real."

"I loved him too," said Rook. "He was my best friend. And before he died, before he died, the last thing he said was to 'tell Lisa—I love.'"

"'I love'?"

Rook nodded.

"Don't we all," said Lisa, closing her eyes. Rook reached out his IV-laden hand and took hers. He felt her wedding ring, and almost let go, but instead squeezed it tighter.

After a mountain of silence, Lisa asked, "How are you? Are you gonna be okay?"

"I guess so," said Rook. "They said I'll probably be in here another day or two. I had shock, a minor concussion, chronic subdural hematoma, broken feet, broken ribs. I'll be out of commission for a while, but I'll be okay. I've been watching old episodes of *Lost In Space* to get my spirits up."

They almost laughed.

"You always were the strange one," she said. And then she started crying softly.

"Listen, I'm really sorry about this whole thing. I wish I were the one who were dead, and Jim had lived. But what am I supposed to do? I can't bring him back. Do you want me to kill myself? Go to jail? Cause I'll do it if you say so, I don't give a fuck, just give the word and I'll be gone."

"No, no," said Lisa. "I'm sorry." And she went to the window and looked at life continuing to stream by on the streets below. Paparazzi were staked outside the hospital;

they looked to her like ants swarming and feeding upon a dead bumblebee.

"I didn't know you two were having a child," said Rook in a voice that sounded like he was having lines fed to him. "Congratulations."

Lisa nodded, and with her finger, slowly smudged a heart with her and Jim's names on the glass.

"I'll help out with the kid any way I can," said Rook. "Boy or girl?"

"We wanted to keep that a surprise." And she turned to Rook, kissed him on the cheek, and was gone. Rook looked toward the window, and observed the heart that she left there, an arrow pointing beyond the sun.

Two days later, Rook was well enough to make it to Jim Jam's wake and funeral. He walked in on crutches. He was also on emotional crutches—Prozac, and some combo cocktail—for the depression and guilt he was feeling. He wanted to say something that would make everything all right, but he couldn't find the words. All he could manage at the wake was a little speech: "I've known Jim ever since we were kids. I never could have predicted as we were growing up that we'd be in a band together, and that band would be successful. And I never could have predicted that it would have ended up like this. I'm sorry. I'm so sorry. I loved him. I don't know what else to say."

Rook ended up being booked for vehicular manslaughter. His blood-alcohol level was 0.07, just below the legal limit. He hired some high-priced lawyers, had to pay a large settlement to the Jam family, Lisa, the female driver in the other car who suffered a broken nose and cracked ribs, the owners of the house he had crashed into, and other miscellaneous costs, which when added up, weren't so miscellaneous. He also agreed to child support for Lisa and Jim's child (a girl she named Dawn). He and Lisa then sued the paparazzi, along with their tabloid—*The Interloper*—settling out of court. Rook ended up being sentenced to thirty days in rehab, 100 hours of community service, and two years probation. The rehab was a famous, country-club type place for the well-to-do star/criminal. For service, he worked at a homeless shelter in East L.A., where he feared a drive-by shooting as he helped to check in the line of guys outside. It never happened, but he turned it into a song called "Waiting." At first listen, the catchy song seems to be about some guy waiting for his girl to come home, but upon a closer reading, it's apparent that the crooner is waiting just to get inside for a nice meal and comfy bed where he won't have to worry about getting whacked.

Rook also feared death in the minimum-security rehab center, but only before he entered. Once in, in his own room, he was relieved to see he was dealing with a lot of the same people he already had experience with—the rich, the corrupt, and the drug dealers. Instead of fearing violence or rape or death, he actually began to ponder his inevitable death, read some books, and ended up buying a coffin to do spiritual exercises in on the advice of a counselor with shamanistic inclinations. It was delivered to his house in Beverly Hills the day he got out. He also bought some real skulls to make it more visceral—to experience death as closely as possible so that one might truly live—*carpe diem!* Friends and family thought he had flipped, but they let it go. He was at least functioning now, albeit awkwardly on a walking cast. He eased off the Prozac, but became addicted to a plethora of painkillers, and was seeing a therapist once a week. He started spending time with Lisa, and was there when the baby came. After Dawn was born, he tried to play father. He enjoyed it. But it became weird when he and Lisa tried dating again. Though they had never consummated their awkward relationship in school, their whole past history, and the remembrance of Jim Jam every moment made it even more awkward to make love now. Still, they remained friends, and Rook would come to see her and Dawn once a week when he was in Los Angeles.

The Little Bang never replaced the Jam (as he was affectionately called) with another guitar player. It just didn't feel right. Instead, Rook tried to create more of a guitar sound himself, quadruple-tracking songs, and while live, using all sorts of effects pedals. Their next album, which was released about two years after the whole incident, was their biggest one yet. It was a heartfelt collection of songs penned by Rook about all matters of love and loss. It was called *Free Fall*. Rook almost regretted naming it that: during interviews he would have to tell the reason behind it, reliving Jim's passing, and reliving himself lying at the Alamo, looking up at the stars, pondering the news of his family's death. Eventually, Rook just wouldn't answer that question.

And now lying here in his box in Beverly Hills on his birthday, there were a lot of questions that Rook couldn't answer, try as he might. *Why Jim, not me? Jesus, he has a kid—he should have been allowed to be with her and Lisa. I'm just a goddamn asshole.*

He tried to exhale all his problems and all his past that he couldn't change. "I've got to get it together," he said aloud.

He dozed off to sleep. His cell phone woke him some time later. He momentarily forgot where he was. "Hello?" he answered.

"Hello, Rook. It's me," said Southhampton. What are you doing?"

"Oh, lying in my coffin."

"Oh yes. Well, I hope that's going well for you. But don't check out yet—we have a long career ahead of us still! Anyway, listen, Rich will be there in a few minutes to pick you up."

"Why?"

"Have you forgotten? It's your birthday! And then you're leaving tomorrow for Amsterdam—so make sure you're ready."

"Ready? I was born ready," said Rook, coughing.

"Funny, I don't hear any conviction. You know as well as I you have to do everything with conviction." And Southhampton hung up the phone.

Rook coughed and rose from the dead. He wandered downstairs in his flip-flops, and decided he had to convince himself the whole correspondence was real again. *Maybe I'm just imagining the whole Hula thing. Or maybe it's an imposter.* He went downstairs to his computer and looked at her message again.

I guess the only way to know is to go and meet her—if it is her. If it is just some scam, what do I do? I don't know how it can be fake, but you never know. But why would someone fake this?

Lots of crazy fans out there. Chances are it's really her. I should ask her some question that only she would know.

Rook was thinking about what to ask, when he noticed that Hula was online. He typed her an instant message:

Hula, sorry for being an asshole, but being a celebrity you get a lot of phonies trying to approach you. That's the first thing I think when a stranger walks up—what do you want? Well, what do you want? Do you remember our conversations in high school with your grandfather? Please, let me know it's really you.

No instant reply. Rook put his head down on the desk. *Another scam. Always disappointed. It's better to have no hope at all, that way anytime things go right it's a pleasant surprise.*

Suddenly, a message shot back:

Rook, I understand completely. How do you know who I say I am? How do I even know who I say I am? Isn't that the pernial questioon? Who am I? You know I've always been interested in the mysteries in life...and still am. Of course I rememberwhat we talked about with grandfather. It was after he was showing us his Masonic texts and I was upset that the pyramid info wasn't there. He said it didn't matter, and that the necessary info for life was here—and he pointed to his heart. And then I said something like what I really wanted in life was to follow my heart—wherever it took me. I think that's what I've done. Sort of. We never live up to our expectations, do we?

Rook replied:

No, we don't. I'll be leaving in the morning. See you soon. Piliper Grits.

Her reply raised some sort of compassion in him. Was chivalry dead? Was it sentimental nonsense? Rook decided he would soon find out. He went out on his balcony and looked at the city lights. Off in the distance, he could hear the partiers echoing very faintly from down on the Sunset Strip and smiled as he imagined a sick shindig at the Rainbow.

Aitchkiss, Monique, and Meriweather were among the crowd waiting outside the Rainbow to get in. Aitchkiss was wearing a disguise (a long, black wig and shades) to make sure he was not seen (there was still a restraining order on him and *The Interloper* not to get close to Rook).* The inveterate reporter had been talking to M and M for a good part of the day, trying to get the latest on the reclusive celebrity. Now, he was having them get even closer, doing the detailed work that he by law could no longer do, getting a fly-on-the-wall insight into what went on in this superstar's life.

---

* Editor's Note: There was a brief parenthetical notation here with a phone number: "Include? Check w/legal. --- - ----." It is a working number. It has been verified, but legal action was threatened, so I am not at liberty to say more. Please pardon these occasional footnotes. Limited use will be made of them—only when necessary for clarification or postulation. The original manuscript is on file with the Library of Congress for those researchers curious as to all of the anonymous author's addendums, which for narrative purposes cannot be included here.

"Remember," said Aitchkiss. "Make up with him. Give him those pendants as a gift. But make sure he wears them!"

"Sure, Kisser," said Monique, a nickname she gave him to lighten his unattractive load.

"Monique and I are good kissers, Kisser," said Meriweather, leaning over and giving rock star girl a twirl of the tongue. The two ladies had grown closer throughout the course of the day, especially over a late lunch, talking and confiding for hours, and afterwards making an impromptu visit to a well-known psychic in Beverly Hills to seek some much-needed guidance.

Aitchkiss felt biologically compelled to stand on his tiptoes and kiss them—dreaming of their six lips merging in steps—he pictured the locks of the Panama Canal lifting and churling and rolling along. But instead, Aitchkiss wrote something on a yellow pad.

Kerry the officer, off-duty, his long gangly arm wrapped around his beaming wife who so wanted to mingle with the pretty people, noticed the threesome he had pulled over earlier in the day and shook his head, thinking he would mention it to Rook later.

Suddenly a white leviathan of a limo pulled up and out scuttlebutted Rook. He was snapped and flashed and escorted upstairs by Marissa (who by the way was looking brilliant) to the top of the club, climbing the little ladder to the little red room at the very top and receiving guests cordially like a king.

A giant cake shaped in the form of a guitar materialized, and the entire band (Chop-Shop who was shopping for the ladies, Billy Razor who was floating out in la-la land

and talking of surfing, and Shitfaced who was barely managing to hang on to the bar), as well as their manager, Southhampton, posed for the media. Rook made a wish, and blew out the 33 candles.

Suddenly, Lisa appeared at the front of the crowd.

"Hey," said Rook. "How are you?" He was stretching out on a flutaki rug Marissa had set up for him to receive the women. "Just got back yesterday."

"I'm sorry I missed the show, I just . . . ."

"Don't worry about it. How's Dawn?"

"She's getting smarter day by day. She's learned some Beethoven!"

"Amazing! What is she, ten now?"

"Eleven."

"Wow! I can't believe it! Listen, Lisa, I'll be leaving tomorrow for Amsterdam."

"Amsterdam? You just got back."

"I know, but I heard from someone—you'll never guess who."

There was a short pause, then a laugh.

"Hula."

"Yeah, how'd you know?"

"There's no one else you would say that about."

"That's probably true. Anyway, she's over there and so I'm gonna catch up on old times with her."

Lisa laughed.

"Same old Rook. Just be careful not to catch something from her."

"Ha! Well, you know they say—you never love like your first love."

Lisa gave a long pause.

"Hey, I'd love to see Dawn sometime," said Rook, pushing a blonde's long hair away. "I really miss her."

"Okay. Say hello to Hula for me. I wonder if she's as pretty as she used to be."

"Nobody can be that pretty," said Rook. And he got up and kissed Lisa on the cheek and felt like he was back in high school, at that wedding, and he felt incredibly happy.

Before he could enjoy the moment and let it linger, Marissa began parading 100 women she had pre-selected for Rook. They shimmied and shined by in all sorts of sexy leggings; Rook selected nine women and gave them each a pink stickie with a number on it. With a few curt commands from Southhampton, Rook was carried off on the shoulders of his entourage down to the limo, to bring the party back to his estate.

Back home, as he went from Bedroom #1 to Bedroom #8 (master), he carried his little black book along and made brief notations and took photos.

As he majestically entered Bedroom #8, he experienced déjà vu. It was Monique and Meriweather.

"Did you like those presents we gave you?" they asked of the gold and silver pendants.

"Like them? I love them!" And he displayed and played with the medallions they had hung around his neck earlier at the Rainbow. "Well, we started the day here in Bedroom #8, and we end it here," he laughed. And they rolled and tumbled with awkward gymnastics.

At about 3AM Rook awoke to someone whispering. It was Meriweather.

"Well?" she asked, wrinkling up her nose.

"What?"

"In all the time I've worked here, I always hear you say 8.5 bedrooms. But where's the .5?"

"Well, right there!" Rook laughed, nodding towards the mahogany veneer coffin.

"That old thing? It smells like mothballs! I hate dusting it!"

"Well, please be careful. I'll be spending a lot of time there. I consider it my most exquisitely furnished bedroom, although the quarters are a bit tight! Look at all those delicate, painstaking engravings the next time you get a chance. Hieroglyphics!"

And Rook got up, took a shot of Everclear, lit up a smoke, and collapsed into Bedroom 8.5, feeling like he was breathing fire. And it occurred to him that this abode was the only one of his bedrooms he had not had sex in. He blew some smoke rings and toyed with the idea.

"Ladies?" he called. And with some convincing, Monique and Meriweather managed to position themselves within the sarcophagus.

"Happy birthday!" they murmured.

"Hmmm," mumbled Rook, falling asleep before they could finish.

***

Over in Hollywood, Aitchkiss turned up his little receiver, trying to ascertain what exactly was going on. Smiling gleefully, he wrote some acronyms on a legal pad, controlling the shaking of one hand by steadying it with the other. He peered at the image from the camera, but even with the infrared it was such an extreme close-up that it was impossible to see anything clearly. *That's okay,* he thought. *I connect the dots. My foundation is the facts, and then I connect the dots. I make it more interesting that way anyway.*

***

Meanwhile, on the other side of town, in Malibu, Lisa looked out at the ocean waves splashing against the shore, and the moon shining bright, casting a very light moonbow. She wiped her tears and stared at a picture of her and Jim, which hung upon her western wall. And thinking of Rook: *Stupid fuck. Goddamn stupid fuck. What about my dreams?* And a tear ran down her cheek, which reflected an authentic Waterhouse painting that hung upon her lonely bedroom wall. She suddenly got up and went to check on Dawn. Dawn was sleeping, curled up with an old teddy bear that use to belong to her father. Lisa sat very quietly on the edge of the bed next to her and hoped all her daughter's dreams would indeed someday come true.

4

KEEPIN' IT REAL

Rook put on his white Versace shades, grabbed a newspaper, and tried to hide behind it in the first-class section of the plane. Stretching out his legs, an article about a pop icon's new look caught his attention. *She's lost. They're repackaging her. She needs to just be real. But what is reality?*

Rook recalled when he first began asking this perennial question. It was upon meeting Hula's grandfather, Dr. Louis Kentucky. He was a retired family practitioner, but the study of life and achieving one's maximum potential was still his passion. His hero was the Swiss psychologist, Dr. Carl Jung. He followed in his footsteps, studying much of the same esoteric literature. Sometimes Rook came over just to talk to Dr. Louis about the peculiarity of existence. The future rocker would roll through the doctor's library, pull a book down on any number of subjects—from Agrippa to Zoroastrianism—and ask him to explain them. Rook, Hula, and Grandfather would have long conversations into the night about synchronicity, yoga, dreams, and the nature of life itself. Hula's mom rarely joined them— she considered herself an "academic" and preferred not to talk about such "castles in the air."

One night, shortly after their disappointment with not finding out how the pyramids were built (that supposedly was reserved for 33° Masons, and Louis had left shortly before he reached that level due to unknown reasons), Rook pulled down a book about holographic universes.

"What the hell's this all about?" he asked the doctor.

"Well, you know what a hologram is, don't you? This book posits that the universe is itself a hologram, that there are many more universes—in fact, an infinite number, where an infinite number of possibilities are played out. Time and space are illusions—everything is intricately connected to everything else. There's a Buddhist analogy," continued the doctor, lighting up a Romeo y Julieta, "called Indra's Net. It concerns an endless web of threads that runs hither and yon—all across the chessboard of life. Let's say the chess pieces are made of precious jewels, and each piece is reflected in every other piece, and so on. It's an endless process of interconnections. Extend this to the quantum levels, and the implications are profound. But to put it simply, let's just say that every move you make, dear boy, impacts every other piece on the board, as well as the outcome of the game."

"But what's the purpose of the game in the first place?" asked Hula.

"That I don't know, Hula hoop. But I do know that it's a lot more fun if you play—if you really try to win."

Dr. Lewis finally stopped blabbering, puffed at his cigar, and assessed Rook and Hula's understanding, or lack of it, with a glance.

Rook stared out at the Iowa cornfields and watched Hula's puppy, a collie named Kali, run by. It started chasing its tail, gave up, and laid down to rest in the dirt—panting—smiling effortlessly.

"All I can say is now I know where Hula gets all her wacky ideas, sir," Rook said, smiling as easily as the dog.

"William Blake! He expressed similar ideas—way ahead of his time!" said the doctor, with a slight Southern accent, slapping his knee. It made a hollow sound, which he quickly tried to cover up by coughing.

"Yes, Grandpa," said Hula, wiggling her toes which glittered with red nail polish. "We all know that Milton lived in Blake's foot for a while until that young girl who flew down needed him."

Grandpa took off his glasses and gazed forlornly at all of his books, as if trying to remember every idea offered in each of them. "Well, it's a very complex mythology. But then, life is complex. Sometimes symbols better convey ideas than words. And sometimes action is necessary. And assistance. No one can do everything alone. Isn't there a time when we all need a hero to arise and assist us? Often they emerge from unusual places."

"And give hope," said Hula, winking at Rook and extending her foot for him to massage. He began with her toes, his guitar fingers working at them briskly.

"How do you know Blake wasn't just mad?" asked Rook, making the cuckoo sign behind the doctor's back and giggling.

There was a long silence. "Well, we don't, for sure," said the doctor, contemplating his cloud of smoke which had assumed the form of a small galaxy as a beam of sunlight hit some dust at just the right angle. "It's hard to put someone on the couch when they've been dead for some 200 years. The link between madness and genius has been the subject of several fascinating studies. You're welcome to peruse them. But let me quote you my favorite Blake. I learned it as a child in grammar school:

> To see a world in a grain of sand,
> And a heaven in a wild flower,
> Hold infinity in the palm of your hand,
> And eternity in an hour . . . .

"I'm sorry, but I forget the rest," said Grandpa.

"Well, I'll help you remember it then, Father," said Hula's mother, bringing them tea and cookies on a silver tray. She kept one eye on the cups, careful not to spill them, the other studying her distorted reflection. She set the tray down and kissed her daddy on the cheek, waving the smoke away. "I hope you're not filling their heads with guano," said Professor Kentucky.

Grandpa laughed. "Of course not, dear. Now, guano, that's another—"

"Will you let me?" Professor asked. "It really bothers me that no one ever recites the whole poem—'Auguries of Innocence.' But that's the world we live in, condensed version, CliffNotes! Bullshit!" She looked somewhere far away, then:

> A robin redbreast in a cage
> Puts all heaven in a rage.
> A dove-house fill'd with doves and pigeons
> Shudders hell thro' all its regions.

A dog starv'd at his master's gate
Predicts the ruin of the state.
A horse misused upon the road
Calls to heaven for human blood.
Each outcry of the hunted hare
A fibre from the brain does tear.
A skylark wounded in the wing,
A cherubim does cease to sing.
The game-cock clipt and arm'd for fight
Does the rising sun affright.
Every wolf's and lion's howl
Raises from hell a human soul.
The wild deer, wand'ring here and there,
Keeps the human soul from care . . . .

And as the good professor continued, reciting verbatim, her eyes flitted elsewhere, recalling a youth slipping out from beneath her bare, unpedicured feet like the sand and waves at the shore: *What happened to my innocence? Where on earth did it go? What happened to that child who trusted with no doubts and dejection? I trusted completely, and now that is completely gone.* And then came a most strange and sudden feeling—*in medias res*—hiding as a girl in a game of hide and seek—and now FLASH she was talking to her daughter and father and this Rook character and her lips were moving but she was an etheric double. *Was this possible? Was it possible to be in two places at one time?*

Oh yes, always the questions, the mind constantly questioning and hitting a wall. But why does the One become the many and then return to Its beginning in the first place? For the experience?

And then the professor's thoughts took a sudden turn, and fell towards an old love—towards London. Ah, that precious jewel, and now staring at Hula, she thought of the man she came from. What a peculiar fellow! What a terrible man! What a man she loved once with what she knew of love.

How did they meet? Leaning over a stack of books at the British Library, perhaps near where Marx had once stood, she noticed a man in a grenadine business suit speaking in Russian. She had learned a little Russian while studying Tolstoy and Dostoevsky, and caught a few key phrases. She attempted a joke:

"Ah, drakshay qua!"

The two men turned and looked at her with wide, dark eyes. They looked as if they might utter something, but didn't.

"No, I'm not out of my mind," said Professor. "I'm just trying to make small talk."

"By saying there's a stone up my ass? That's Georgian, not Russian." The alpha moved a little closer to the professor.

"Well, why are you wasting my time then?" asked the professor. She turned away, but the enigmatic grenadine was now hooked upon this strange American professor who outdid his style and *spreezatura*, so he prepared a syrupy line.

"Who and what are you and where do you come from?" he asked a little too gruffly.

Words came out of the professor mysteriously. "I am the one who comes into your life and then leaves it. I am the one whom you will always miss. I am the one you will always think of, no matter how many lovers you take. I am the one. I am the one to kiss your dead lips. I am the one to nurse our child. I am the one to visit your mother when we all know the bad jokes. I am the one to be a good mother to your child, even if you are absent. I am the crazy bitch you'll always wonder about whether you should have slept with or not. Well, you'll never know unless we do it, huh? I am the one you'll love and hate, want to kiss and kill, spit out of your mouth cause I'm too cold or too hot, but never lukewarm. That is one voter—I'm definitely different from all the other women—smarter than you and never lukewarm. So consider carefully. I come from somewhere far away and soon will be going back there."

Grenadine grabbed her then and kissed her there and a logical and illogical chain of events followed . . . .

Some are born to sweet delight.
Some are born to sweet delight,
Some are born to endless night.
We are led to believe a lie
When we see not thro' the eye,
Which was born in a night to perish in a night,
When the soul slept in beams of light.
God appears, and God is light,
To those poor souls who dwell in night;
But does a human form display
To those who dwell in realms of day . . . .

Professor Kentucky finished, coming back to earth from wherever she had flown, and looked at them as if they were strangers and she had revealed something she didn't wish shown. She sniffled and quickly took a sip of tea.

"That was lovely, dear," said the doctor, admiring his daughter. "I remember when you used to recite poetry as a young girl."

"You're to blame," she laughed. "You'd always go about bowdlerizing poems, so I made it my business to learn them properly."

"And now it is your business," joked the doctor, inspecting his cigar, and taking a bit of tobacco off his tongue. "Although I wish you'd finish that damn book of yours."

"Oh—can we read from your new novel?" Rook asked Professor Kentucky, snatching a pecan cookie. He would make this request every time he visited, like a child asking for a favorite bedtime story—he always got the same response.

Professor rolled her eyes, as she would often do at exasperating students, and sat down on the radiator. "It's not done yet. And you know, Rookie, that I don't show it to anyone before it's done. Anyway, great works of art are never finished—they're only abandoned."

"What about Hula? She's a great work of art, isn't she?" asked Rook.

"Yes, but unfortunately she was abandoned by her co-author—her father—goddamn asshole good-for-nothing."

"Some would say that we've all been abandoned," said Grandpa.

"I'd have to concur with that," said Mrs. Kentucky, leaving the room. "I'll be writing upstairs. I'm not to be disturbed."

The three of them sat listening to her walk away, the floor squeaking, saying nothing. Rook chewed his cookie as quietly as he could.

Hula's mother, April Kentucky, had been working on her new novel for some thirty-three years now, and Rook had still not seen it hit the presses. Some likened her to a female J.D. Salinger. She had had much success in her mid-twenties, with a couple of novels about girls coming of age in the turbulent 1960s. But then, on a book tour in Europe, she had a stormy summer affair with a businessman from London, who evidently wanted nothing more than to deposit his check. Coming back to Iowa to teach in the fall, she was preparing a lecture on *Crime and Punishment* one morning when she threw up. At first, she thought it was her oversensitivity to the ax scene. When she tossed her cookies a second time, she went to the doctor. Much to her astonishment, she was pregnant. Leaving the office, she sat in her car a long time and stared vacantly at the rain lightly falling upon the windshield.

She refused to track down the father. She wouldn't even speak his name. Apparently, he had humiliated her in some fashion, and so April pretended like he didn't even exist. Hula grew up an only child, without a dad, and with a mother whom, despite her love, always considered Hula a constant reminder of a past she wished to forget. When April's mother passed, Grandpa Louis moved in with them. He treated Hula like a daughter, and April was thankful for that. She would watch them play and read together, and then she'd go in her den and resume writing, only to throw it away the next day. After five years, her publisher had given up on her galleys. The Kentuckys lived mostly off her professorship and the royalty money that still flowed in, and April eventually only taught one class per year, usually in the spring (she had been diagnosed with Seasonal Affective Disorder, which despite the ultraviolet lights, caused a lingering cloud of melancholy to hang about her during fall and winter). She would teach Creative Writing in the Workshop, becoming more and more animated as the weather blossomed. Many questioned how she could lead the class, when she herself hadn't published anything in so long. She would counter with: "Publishing is not writing. I write every day. I will not, however, succumb to pressure to show my work before it is finished. I would rather perish."

Had she not been so successful with her oeuvre so far, she would have indeed perished. She came to develop a certain reputation around the department as a live wire: you never knew when she was going to snap at you. She would grade papers in her tiny office (she never took classwork home) behind a locked door. If anyone knocked, she usually pretended that no one was there. She would listen as whomever had knocked listened. Sometimes, the ruffling of papers or the rumbling of her stomach or the sound of her swallowing would betray her. People would knock again, and listen to the odd silence. Usually they gave up, settling for shoving something under the door. She wouldn't even look at the delivery until she was leaving. One time, however, a distinct odor caught her attention. She looked down, and saw that someone had shoved in a still-steaming pile of shit upon a newspaper. She burst up, flung open the door, and ran towards the staircase to catch the perpetrator. As she came around the last bend to the first floor, she heard the sound of laughter fleeing. She rested at the entranceway to EPB (English-Philosophy Building), huffing and puffing and looking out at the crowd of students on their way to classes; they stared at her like she was out of her mind.

She walked outside, unsure of where she was going. She ambled towards the river, and sat down on its bank. She watched the muddy-colored water flow by. *I should just throw myself in.* Then she thought of Hula, who was in tenth-grade at the time. She began crying.

"I can't leave her alone," she mumbled. "I can't leave her alone." She got up, brushed herself off, and made a beeline towards her office.

"What is this shit?" she hollered, picking up the organic editorial. She went and opened up the men's room door. "Incoming!" And she hurled the crap in.

She thought she had an idea of who was responsible. About a week earlier, a student of hers came to workshop without a draft of a story. It was his turn that day, and so the group was stuck without having anyone to critique. At first, he claimed that he didn't want to show an unfinished work. April asked him if that was the real reason (if he was pulling a "Kentucky"), or if he was just lazy.

"Okay, I'll tell you the truth," he said. "Truth is what matters in writing, and in life, isn't it? I went out to the Vine last night, played pool, got drunk, and took home this girl who was a little overweight, but we both liked the Steelers."

"Well, let me tell you the truth, young man," Professor Kentucky said, slowly and deliberately straightening out the blank notepaper she had in front of her. "You'll never be successful unless you discipline yourself. Lazy, sloppy drinking and sloppier sex is indicative of lazy, sloppy writing. You've let down our entire workshop, and you lied about it at the start. Get out."

The young man stared at her incredulously.

"Are you deaf as well as impotent?" asked Professor Kentucky.

"Don't you mean incompetent?" asked the student, smirking. He looked around to get some idea as to what to do. Most students just kept their heads down. A few people were trying to repress laughter.

"No, I meant impotent—as in lacking in power to act effectively, from the Latin *impotens*. Whether you're incapable of sexual intercourse, I do not know. Nor do I wish to."

The class laughed heartily.

"I've already paid for the course," he said, throwing up his hands.

"And so has everyone else," said Professor, throwing up her hands. "Goodbye."

The young man got up, grabbed his stuff with much commotion, and left, mumbling "bitch" under his breath.

"Very impressive," said Professor. "He can do dialogue!"

Everyone chuckled.

As soon as the young man was gone, Professor Kentucky instructed: "I want you to imagine that our young friend who just exited is a character in a story of yours. Change him around, transmute, transform him, but use this real life contact to springboard into fiction. Remember, you're not drawing from a vacuum; you have to take something with substance, and run it through your creative engine. Now picture this character thirty years from now. Chart the course of his life. How does he turn out? On a psychiatrist's sofa? Or mine?"

Most of her students loved April Kentucky as a professor. Many were scared of her. Some had complained to the university, and there were meetings with the higher-ups as to whether and how to get rid of her (she had tenure). It was decided that although she was a bit of a thorn in their side, April did, at least on the surface, provide a rosy attraction to all sorts of wanna-be writers out there. Many talented young graduates applied to the MFA program just in the hope of working with this famous, eccentric, and demanding author.

She was good for business, and as long as she didn't push the envelope too far, the university thought it would be best and easiest to keep her. They were actually glad that she only taught one class per year.

So was her publisher. They hoped the extra time off from teaching would give her freedom to write. They did not know that in the fall and winter she accomplished little. April was fully aware of her SAD's impact on her writing; the little she got done during those months only added to her melancholy. She often thought: *writing is a recursive process, but my book is vanishing, and so am I.*

If her publisher were aware of her seasonal difficulties, perhaps they would have found some creative way to help her. As it stood, however, they didn't want to bother her with more demands. They knew her well enough to know that pressuring her might send her in another direction—to another publisher—or she might never finish the book at all. Year after year went by, and they basically had given up all hope of seeing the tentatively titled *Boudicca* (Boudicca, meaning "victory," was an ancient woman warrior/druidess in Britain who fought the Romans successfully for a long time until, some say, she was betrayed).

In spring and summer, April was quite productive. So much so, that her mania almost made up for her hibernation periods. However, as each year went by, she felt more and more pressure to deliver a masterpiece. She would make continual changes, and create complex contingencies, until it became a sprawling historical novel out of control, as were her spring flings with graduate students.

Rook now wondered how all this had affected Hula. He had never really thought about it before, when they were young, because all he had on his mind were sex and music—in that order. And to tell the truth, sex, drugs, and rock and roll were all that he had on his mind to this day. But now that he cast a look backwards through the looking glass, he could understand why Hula had wanted to go seek her father. A strange recluse writer as a mother and a dear old grandfather preoccupied with the esoteric were not the realities a young woman wants to deal with. So

Hula followed her heart like a modern Boudicca to find her origins. Rook wondered if she were successful. *I'm not sure how to feel about all this,* he thought. *What am I getting myself into?*

"Excuse me," said a young woman, tapping Rook on the shoulder.

"Huh?" said Rook, snapping out of his reveries.

"You're Rook, aren't you?" asked a pretty, blue-eyed blonde with a mole.

"I don't know who I am anymore." He put down the newspaper and pictured himself being knocked off a chessboard.

"I'm in love with you," said the girl, blowing a bubble that went POP! "I've been in love with you ever since I can remember." She rubbed his sleeve.

"Oh, come on," said Rook, "You don't even know me. You listen to my music, you look at the videos, you go to the shows, you put up a poster, but everything you see is a projection—it's not real. The real me is the same as the real you. I don't mean to be an asshole, but if you were me, what would you say?"

"That you're an asshole," she said, almost crying.

"Okay, I'm sorry," said Rook. "Come on, sit next to me here."

She plopped down into the large, empty and blue seat next to him that he had bought specifically for the purpose of keeping people away from him.

"Oh, this is cozy," she said, massaging his sleeve with a nostalgic connection she was unaware of. Her eyes looked at him frenetically.

"What's your name?"

"Bridget."

"Well, Bridget, let me give you the facts. When this plane lands in Amsterdam, I'll probably never see you again. But we have quite a bit of time to kill before then. What would you like to do? Give your friends a story to tell?"

"Why not?" said Bridget, reaching under Rook's blanket.

A slightly plump stewardess with a Suzy-Q peeping from her pocket passed by—noticing their touchy-feely. She gave them the lollipop eye and said: "That will not do. I don't care who you are."

"Okay, okay," said Rook. "No problem." And then he whispered in Bridget's ear: "I'm going into the bathroom. Meet me in there when the coast is clear."

Rook got up and headed towards the restroom, taking the paper with him as if he'd be in there a while. He left the door unlatched, sat on the toilet, and glanced more closely at the front page, which he hadn't really been reading up to this point. He recognized someone familiar, in an all-too familiar situation. It was him! Naked with his wee-wee blacked-out. Swimming and copulating with two gorgeous women. This was yesterday! My birthday! He looked at the headline of *The Interloper* article: **Birthday Boy Up To His Old Tricks!** *I can't believe it. In my own backyard. Damn Interloper! I'll sue them again!*

There was also an interview with Monique and Meriweather, who said Rook had fired her that day after they had sex—after over a year of faithful service. Rook couldn't believe that he had slept with both of them again afterwards—and in his personal coffin at that!

"God, what a mess," said Rook, aloud. The lavatory door suddenly swung open, and Bridget entered, securing it.

"Did anyone see you?" asked Rook.

"No."

"Listen, I've done this before, but usually the bathrooms are a little bigger."

Rook set *The Interloper* down as he fished in his wallet for a condom.

"That's you!" shouted Bridget, eyeing the paper as she was wiggling around. "Let me see!"

Rook instinctively reached to grab the tabloid, but then let go as she yanked it most interestedly. Rook shrugged as she read.

"Oh my God," she said. "Oh my God!"

Rook sat back down on the toilet and flushed it so as to keep up appearances. He then unrolled some toilet paper and made sundry other bathroom noises. He signed his autograph on the tissue and handed it to Bridget. She took it without looking and just held it.

"I can't believe you fired her!"

"I can't believe they snuck in my backyard and took photos of me on my birthday. Can't I have some privacy? Is nothing sacred?"

"Apparently not your bum-bum." Bridget sighed and looked down at Rook.

"What?" he asked. "You're making me feel all guilty or something."

"Aren't we all? Hey, you know, I feel all weird now. Do you mind if we not have sex?"

"Whatever you want."

"It's just, if you were me, how would you feel?"

"Weird. I feel weird as me!" Rook grabbed *The Interloper* and looked at the photos again. *At least I look good.*

Bridget shook her head and put back on her soft, cottony clothing that still smelled of flowery dryer sheets. "I never realized how vain celebrities are," she said, turning and checking herself in the mirror, and then leaving the lavatory. When she got to her seat, she realized she was holding Rook's autographed toilet paper. She traced the pattern of his signature gently with her fingertip. She felt as if she could somehow enter his spirit by doing so. She repeated this action several times, carefully folded the toiletry collectible, placed it within her lock and key diary under the day's date—June 17, 2009—and secured it within a secret compartment in her carry-on. *Someday it might be valuable,* she thought.

Rook watched the blue water go round and round in the toilet. *I must be losing my touch.* Collar up, tabloid under his arm, he put his shades on, inspected the veneers on his snowcapped teeth, and left the restroom. Much to his relief, most of the passengers were sleeping and had not noticed anything. He waved at Bridget in coach and stretched his legs across his two first-class seats. Throwing the woolen blanket over his head, he felt little security, and even less optimism about the future. He slid off into slumber as the plane hurtled through space, above a world hurtling through the cosmos.

Rook awoke to the plane touching down at Amsterdam Schiphol. He made his way off as quickly as possible and towards customs. He used to be in shape, years ago, but the rock star lifestyle had extracted its toll. Lugging his two bags, he took deep breaths as he rested on the moving walkway. He hadn't carried his own weight in quite a while.

Most of us are on treadmills and we don't even know it. Treadmills to where? We're stuck going somewhere we don't want to go and we don't know how to get off. We're automatons.

"Mind your step," said the female voice over the intercom in a most pleasant manner. "Mind your step."

Rook walked forward and made his way towards Immigration. He took off his bulletproof sunglasses and handed his passport to the Dutch officer. He watched the young man's eyes grow in astonishment.

"Rook! It really is you! Wow. Wow. I have lots of famous people come through here, but I'm such a fan of yours..."

"Thanks," said Rook, eying the officer's gun. *I could take that and run around shooting it in the air and the papers would read*: **Rock Star Goes Gun-Crazy in Amsterdam!**

The officer stared at him, as Rook was accustomed to people doing. They just were trying to match the image they had in their heads from TV and God knows where else with the living reality in front of them.

"You look different in person," said the officer.

"Better or worse?" asked Rook, smiling.

"Worse," he said. "But that's to be understood—you just had a long flight—where are my manners? I'm sorry, Mr. Heisenberg. What's the purpose of your visit here in the Netherlands? Business or pleasure?"

"Pleasure, I guess. I'm meeting an old friend." *Is that a Glock?*

"Well, enjoy your stay." He stamped Rook's passport and passed it back. "You keep staring at my gun. Would you like to see it? Let me show it to you."

"That's okay," said Rook, holding up his hands.

"No, really. It's quite an impressive weapon."

"Is it a Glock?"

"Why yes, it is. The law enforcement and military issue Glock 18 select-fire machine pistol--virtually identical to the full-size Glock 17, but with the addition of a selector switch on the left rear of the slide that allows fully auto-matic fire. See?" said the officer, moving the switch quickly and expertly. "Wanna try it?"

"I don't know."

"What are you, chicken? Jesus Christ, you're a rock star. Live it up a little!"

"Okay, let me see." Rook held the pistol in his hand, carefully caressing the cold polymer. He had held a pistol just once before. He was being harassed for months by a stalker, and decided to take a self-defense course. The last day of the week-long program involved the use of various weapons. They began with knives and swords. Then bow and arrows. Then guns. He enjoyed the power he felt firing the weapon, but decided he already had enough power and did not want one in his house. He settled for a bow and arrows; he was quite good at archery, he found, much to his amazement. He became even better after reading some books on zen. He kept a quiver (given by Anatoli Anti off one of his futuristic spaghetti westerns) in his master bedroom (underneath the bed), as well as a samurai sword in the kitchen. He enjoyed cutting up vegetables with the medieval, $25,000 relic from Japan.

Unfortunately, when he needed these weapons, he was not at home. The same crazed fan who had been stalking him found it convenient to get a little closer at a 7-11. Rook was buying a Hostess blueberry pie, reading the wrapper, shaking his head at the ingredient of lard, when someone tapped him on the shoulder.

"Excuse me, are you Rook?" asked a young woman in a blue babushka.

"Yes."

"Would you mind?" she asked, holding out a card to sign, covering up the sentiments. Rook automatically scribbled away, thinking about the consistency of the blueberries in the pie. He remembered he was about to eat such a pie long ago, when Hula tugged on his arm. He never finished the pie.

"You're too pretty," Babushka mumbled, obsessively. "Too pretty."

Before Rook even finished signing the card, he recalled the strange line from the stalker's letters. **You're too pretty for this world.**

Rook completed his best wishes and autograph, and handed the card carefully back to the lady. He noticed it was a wedding card.

"Going to a wedding?" Rook asked her, inspecting her stained raincoat.

"We two," she said, making a sudden movement and tossing something towards Rook's face. Rook, on guard, ducked, and whatever liquid was thrown sizzled on the boxes of Kleenex behind him. He football blocked the woman, who crashed into the candy rack with a howl. He sped towards the door as a gunshot exploded. Bursting out the door, pie flying through the air, he kept running, looking back, looking down to see if he was hit. He ducked behind a car at the end of the block, peeping out. Lungs heaving, head tingling, he tried to calm himself. A minute later, the 7-11 clerk came out, waving him down.

"It's okay," he yelled, holding a gun. "She's incapacitated."

What the hell does that mean? Rook stayed behind the Chevy Malibu a moment longer, decided he didn't like that goddamn car, and began walking furtively back to the store, noticing his smashed pie. He stood outside, watching the police and ambulance pull up. They took away the crazy woman, who noticed Rook with the wild eye of a hovering bird. "Come darling, let us honeymoon by the Seine," she yelled out. After she recovered from her gunshot wound, she was locked up in an asylum in the desert of California. She would comfort herself that an underground river flowed somewhere nearby, and that Rook would one day appear in shining armor that could contain his beauty.

Rook handed the gun back to the officer very carefully.

"Nice weapon," Rook said. "Bet it comes in handy in a crunch."

"That's for sure," said the blonde Dutchman. He scrambled for something in his drawer, and pulled out an issue of *Rolling Stone* with Rook on the cover. "Would you mind?" he asked, handing Rook a pen.

"No problem," said Rook, signing away.

Rook put his shades back on, heard people muttering— "Why'd he let that guy play with his gun?"—passed through the area, and waited for his baggage to come around. *Everyone always wants something from me. Why do people have to be so needy? Why do they have to grab on to everything, as if to convince themselves of the validity of their existence? Why can't people just keep it real and act normal? Then again, if they did, I wouldn't have a career. Nobody would care. They want a show. Well, I'll give them a show . . . .*

Rook grabbed his luggage, tossed it on a cart, and wheeled it through customs, declaring nothing. As soon as he walked through, he noticed a man wearing a black chauffeur's outfit holding up a sign with a drawing of a chess rook on it. He nodded at the man and pointed at all of his stuff to be carried.

"I've had a long flight and would like some blueberry pie," said Rook.

"Are you for real?" asked the driver, struggling with the baggage.

"I don't know what's real anymore," and Rook lit up the smoke that he had been dying for when suddenly out of nowhere a swarm of paparazzi appeared, and consequently, some fans perked up to who this guy behind the oversized shades really was.

"Who's that?" Rook overheard someone passing by say.

"Oh, I think it is chess piece—that Rook."

Yes, I am a chess piece, thought Rook, abruptly being squashed, *and I want to play.*

Airline Tickets and Itinerary[*]

---

[*] Attached here were the rock star's airline ticket stubs, along with other detailed travel information regarding his stay in Amsterdam and elsewhere. Due to ongoing criminal and civil investigations, both nationally and internationally, I am forbidden to reproduce these documents here at this time.

5

STRANGE REUNION

"I understand," said the driver, whom upon closer examination was absolutely fastidious—from his dapper cap to his exfoliated face to his pressed and creased Valentino Newman suit to his high sheen shoes. He honked the horn and slipped the star from out of the black hole of mayhem that had just erupted. "I have a penchant for blueberry pie myself."

"Just so you know, I'm going by Piliper Grits," said Rook, under his breath.

"I understand completely! And I am going by Aert Spanbroek," said the driver as they exited the airport. The morning sun sparkled off the white Rolls as they headed towards the city center.

"That's an odd name."

The chauffeur nodded sadly. "Arthur of the Tight Pants."

Rook laughed more loudly than he intended. "I'm sorry."

"It's okay," said Aert. "I just blame it on Napoleon."

"That's a good one."

"No really," said Aert, as he ushered Rook into the car. "Just before Napoleon was defeated, he forced the Dutch to register our names for a number of reasons—including so we could not, how you say, escape military service. So many of us came up with some quite silly names which the French would not realize was joke. Unfortunately, the names stuck. Of course, I could pay to change my name, but why waste the money at this point?"

"Indeed," said Rook, calculating how much Aert's suit cost. "And I'm sure by this time there's some sort of pride associated with your family name."

"Oh you can be sure of that, Mr. Grits. You can be sure of that."

Rook had been to Amsterdam twice before on tour, and enjoyed it tremendously. He never seemed to have enough free time to explore all of it, however. This holiday, he looked forward to wandering. Perhaps Hula could show him around. Perhaps she could show him a lot of things.

As they drove the thirty-minute drive to the hotel, Rook lost himself in the countryside. Near the airport, industry, factories, and warehouses sprouted up, but there were also farms with multi-colored tulips, cattle, sheep, windmills and an ingenious checkered polder landscape of reclaimed land whose controlled, pumped waters flowed into canals and the curvaceous Amstel River and lakes and towards the sea.

As they neared the city, Rook smiled as he watched trains gliding quietly by, cyclists riding old bikes, businessmen busking briskly to work, and children heading drudgingly to summer school. At a stoplight, he stared out the tinted window at a bum on the street. The bum waved at him as if he could see inside.

Aert stopped next to the Crowne Plaza Hotel—near Centraal Station on Nieuwezijds Voorburgwal. "There's a little coffee shop right down there," he said, motioning towards a very narrow alley. "You should be able to get some pie there. Sorry, I can't drive down—*je kunt*."

"It's okay," said Rook. "I think I've been there before. Just wait."

Rook got out and walked swiftly towards the shop. The girl was just opening up, watering the bright flowers.

"Hey," said Rook, sitting on a bench and lighting up a smoke.

"Hey yourself," she said, now taking down the patio chairs that had been chained up over night. "Wake up!" she insisted, smiling like the Vermeer girl.

"I'm sorry. Long flight." He tried to shake himself awake.

She laughed openly. "I had a party last night. I'm so—tired. I don't usually work morning shifts, but here I am. Bright eyed and the bushy tail!"

"I can't believe I'm here," mumbled Rook, watching her brush off the rain from the furniture.

"What?" When Rook did not respond, she mumbled: "*Een suffe knor!*" Although he did not understand, he sensed it to be pejorative. Rook got up to help her arrange the tables and chairs. "Where do you come from?" she asked.

"California. And you? Are you native?"

"I'm Dutch. Though I grew up in Haarlem, not here."

They finished their design and inspected it. The streets were still empty, save for the straggling tourist or garbage truck. Things were always neat at the start.

"I'll have a blueberry pie please and a cappuccino."

She nodded pleasantly. "So what are you here for?"

"I don't know. What are any of us here for? I'm supposed to meet up with an old girlfriend. But suddenly I'm very nervous."

"It happens. I'm Betty," she said. Rook watched her operate the machine. He smiled at the satisfying sounds, and the steam rising. "Would you like something special on top of your coffee?" she asked, matter-of-factly.

"No thanks," said Rook. "I want to be sober when I meet her." Rook stirred the coffee carefully and added some cinnamon. He watched the brown spirals whirl like a mini-cosmos. He hoped his fear would dissolve in its quantum sea. He wondered if Hula were the other particle that appeared suddenly.

"Well, I need to wake up and sell the coffee," said Betty, primping her hair in the tarnished mirror and putting on her best exploding pink glittering lipstick.

Rook looked out the window. Across the street, a man with a dog sat on a crumbling step, asking for handouts. "Do you speak English? *Sprichst Du Deutsch?*" he would try on various passersby depending on what they looked like.

Rook lit up another Marlboro Red and blew the smoke out towards the sky. It blended in with the clouds. The day reminded him of a painting by Van Gogh.

"Let me ask you something. If you were me, and hadn't seen an old flame in some fifteen years, what would you bring her on your reunion?"

Betty looked at him hard.

"I'm not you. But perhaps flowers would be nice. And chocolates. I don't know, what does she like?"

"I don't know anymore. I don't even know how I feel."

Rook was about to take his long-awaited bite of pie when one of his songs off the *Free Fall* CD—"Art Critics on Holiday"—came on the radio.

"I hate this song," said Betty, wiping the counter and accidentally knocking some glasses to the floor; they shattered every which way, leaving jagged pieces upturned sharply.

"Oh, I'm sorry," said Betty. She went to get a broom to clean it up. Rook listened to his song and relived it all over again—the crash, the nightmare.

He left $100 without tasting his pie or finishing his coffee and wandered back onto the street. He heard Betty calling after him, but kept walking briskly, trying to forget. He had his mirrored shades on and winded his way down the cobblestone streets and alleyways as it was coming to life with shoppers and partiers and tourists hungry for brunch and godknowswhatelse. He passed a coffeeshop with hookah smokers sitting outside toking, but Rook kept going, finding himself by Centraal Train Station—staring out at a sea of bicycles—some of them leftover from a thirty-five year old experiment where utopian-minded students painted bikes white and set them free, with the understanding that people would ride them as need be, then leave them for the next person coming along to use. It worked for a while, but greed halted the dream.

Rook watched a tram drive alongside, ringing its bell as it approached a busy intersection. He looked at all the phallic streetposts, with XXX on them. Like many people, he thought they stood for the hedonistic. And of course with Amsterdam's reputation, they did have that connotation. But supposedly, they originally symbolized the cross

of St. Andrew and three values declared by Queen Wil-
helmina back in the 1940s: compassion, resolution, and
heroism.

Rook loved the Dutch architecture—the buildings leaning slightly forward, the character of the city—everything
being so old—he remembered hearing somewhere that
Amsterdam was one of the oldest still relatively intact city
centres.

Unfortunately, despite the magnificent architecture,
Rook still couldn't get the image of the bleeding and
gasping and dying Jim Jam out of his head. Or of Lisa
blaming him. Or of their daughter Dawn growing up
without a father. Or of his upcoming encounter with Hula.
Suddenly, he felt the nausea coming and ran to an alleyway, bent over, and threw up. He noticed some undigested
creamed corn from the flight. Airplane food—what an
oxymoron! Eventually, he caught his breath, wiped his
chin, and felt a sweat breaking out on his brow. He dabbed
his ruddy face with his soft, baby blue Brooks Brothers
shirt and kept on moving; he winded his way towards the
Red-Light District. He had been here before, with the rest
of the Little Bang while they were on tour. They had all
taken crazy walks together and partied all night long with
the ladies. But he had never been here by himself. Suddenly, he was in Dam Square. He stood in front of the
Grand Kranapolsky Hotel, and looked around.

"Looking for something?" asked a bellman in dignified
regalia.

"Uh, I always forget, which way towards the Red
Light?"

"Ya-ya. Just turn around and go down that street there. Then hook a right. About a five minute walk."

Rook began walking confidently. He made a right turn where the man said—straight would have led him to a gay area—and walked past some shops selling falafel and ice cream and cigarettes. He came out into the Oedesplein, an open area where the old church was, and gazed about.

All of a sudden he felt someone looking at him—it was unnerving how his sixth sense had been refined due to his fame. He could feel someone stalking him a mile away. He turned—someone was filming him. He simply waved at the camcorder and continued ambling.

Right outside the Oede Church, in the ground, was a little bronze sculpture: a woman's breast and a hand cupping it. Rook still felt uneasy—out of the corner of his eye he saw the cameraperson now talking to someone else. Rook ducked into the old church.

He paid the four euro to get in, then began to wander. According to the brochure, this was the center of old Amsterdam. This was where the city started back in 1250, and it fanned out from there, expanding in concentric circles. People would come to worship at the church, which was once Catholic but now Protestant. They would also sleep here with their animals! Rook listened to some invisible person play the old grand organ. It resounded marvelously.

In the cobblestone floor, there were the resting places of many old parishioners, one of them being Rembrandt's wife, Saskia. He read about the city expanding during the Dutch Golden Age, and how prostitution had been legal for some time now. The Dutch attitude was that it had always been around, it will always be around, why not at least make it safer? Guns, on the other hand, were illegal; it was very difficult to get one. Police had them, some criminals had them, but still, even being a criminal it was difficult to acquire. Soft drugs, such as marijuana, were not legal, but tolerated in small quantities. Rook was amazed to find that the violent crime statistics were quite low for such a large city; perhaps the scarcity of arms and the ease of sexual satisfaction made a good mix. *Make love, not war,* thought Rook, as if he were back in the '60s.

It seemed to Rook that the Dutch attitude was very progressive. He figured that all nations at some point would have to legalize marijuana. To spend billions on fighting it just didn't make any sense. He always felt like it was the alcohol companies that fought off the legalization—that they would lose profits if people turned to another form of relaxation. But look, people still bought Heineken in Holland! The Dutch seemed to realize that, just like letting in a little sea water so the whole country didn't flood over, that it was better to let in a little sin than let a whole nation be inundated by corruption.

Rook exited Oede Church, made sure he had lost the camera crew, and headed towards Sexy Land—right across the square. He smiled. It always amused him how casually sex was marketed here as if it were like going to the local strip mall. The ladies in the windows waved at him. It was still early, so many of the little rooms were vacant. There was the usual mix as he walked the District—some very unattractive ladies that he couldn't imagine being paid to have sex with, some fairly attractive dames who just weren't worth the money or risk, and some drop-dead

gorgeous girls who he just shook his head at and wondered *they're so beautiful, like they stepped out of a magazine.*
What are they doing here? Who knows?

One in particular caught his fancy. She worked in a
narrowing alleyway, that as it shrank and the windows
disappeared, it also began to smell worse. He came out the
other end and decided to walk around to see her again. The
second pass he was equally pleased by her. Upon emerging
from the alley, he lit up a smoke and paced about, trying to
decide what to do. He used the green spiral outdoor urinal,
standing as far away from the smelly puddle of aggregate
piss as he could. As he emerged, someone snapped his
picture.

"You're Rook!" shouted an eager fan.

"Who?"

"Don't act like that—the shades doesn't fool me. Can I
have an autograph?"

"Sure."

Rook signed the back of a brochure from the Prostitution Information Center on preventing AIDS, wished the
fan well, and walked once again towards the pretty lady.
He tried to get his courage up. He tried to decide what he
wanted to do. *I want to forget. I need to forget! I hate myself.*
Rook walked down the alley once more. This time, however, when he passed his favorite, she opened her door and
reeled him in. As he tried to resist, she smiled and hooked
Rook close to her chest. She was wearing a gold lame bikini
and smelled of the sea; Rook drowned. She shut and
locked the door.

"You've done enough window shopping. Fifty euro,"
she stated, no longer smiling, all business. "Yes or no?"

"Okay. High-pressure sales tactics, huh?"

She drew the red velvet curtain shut. *What the hell am I doing?* thought Rook.

"It's fifty more if you want extra," she said, not looking at him.

"Yeah, yeah," said Rook. "Can I kiss you?"

She smiled coyly. "No—unless you pay more . . . ."

Rook paid her 100 euro. *What am I getting myself into?*

"You can put your clothes there," she said, nodding to a hook on the wall. It was a miniature version of the grapnels on Dutch buildings that were used to haul up furniture that couldn't be maneuvered through the narrow hallways.

Rook hung up his outfit, and hid his wallet as best he could.

"Now what? Shall I warm up?" he asked, trying to lighten the conversation. He began stretching as if he were about to run a marathon. The girl laughed.

"My name is Mandy," she said, shooting out her hand.

"Piliper," he said, shaking it firmly. It was a pleasant surprise when people didn't recognize him. He examined her ringless fingers and kissed them cavalierly.

"You're silly," laughed Mandy. "Come, lay here," she said. "And take off those ridiculous shades. Where are you from?"

"Don't know," said Rook, throwing his glasses in the sink. "I don't know anything anymore. I don't want to. Can you help me forget? Can you help me forget everything?"

"I can try," she replied, putting on a condom and going to work.

Rook was particularly captivated by the beauty of her face. She had tiny freckles by her nose, and the most beautiful Saharan eyes.

"You have such a pretty face," he said.

"Thank you," she whispered, and for the first time, really looked at Rook's mug. "Oh my God!" gasped Mandy. "You're him! You're him!" And she sat up straight and covered herself and put her hands to her head as if she couldn't believe this rocker who had been on her iPod forever was now in her bed. "I can't believe it! Now that I know who you are, you're making me nervous."

"There's no need to be nervous," said Rook. "We've both done this hundreds of times." He massaged her sandy brown hair, letting it fall through his fingers like so much golden sand. "I just need you to help me forget."

"Forget what? This tattoo?" She felt the old scar of Hula.

"No, yes, I don't know. I think I'm losing my mind."

"It's okay," said Mandy. "It's okay." She held him . . . later, she mumbled something in Dutch—*"Een beurt geven!"* At first, it seemed like Mandy was trying to avoid his eyes, but then they locked orbs, and were somewhere else entirely together—forgetting everything for a moment.

When they were finished, Mandy gave Rook a paper towel to clean up with. He threw it in the trash, and noticed the other ones already there.

"What are your plans?" asked Rook as they both got dressed.

Mandy, looking in the mirror and tousling her flaxen hair, said, "I'm going to school. I'm studying to be a doctor. I want to make my parents proud."

"A doctor, wow," said Rook. "Does this help pay the bills, then?"

"Yes," she said, somewhat pensively.

"Here, let me give you a little tip," and Rook gave her another 100 euro.

"Thank you," she said. And she kissed Rook on the cheek.

"Hey now," said Rook, "No kissing. Thank you for taking care of me. Thank you for being my doctor."

"Ha! I work only da weekends. If you want to see me again, I'd enjoy company."

Rook threw a few more hundred euro at her. He smiled as she bent down to gather them up.

The rock star then attempted to exit stage left as gracefully as possible, but there was a ferocious pitbull right outside the window.

"It's okay," said Mandy, "he won't hurt you."

"He doesn't look like he likes me."

"You make it hard to sometimes," said Mandy, picking up the last 100 euro from inside the foul garbage can.

The pitbull was pulled away by its owner, a neighborhood *engerd*, or geek, who looked at Rook with disgust as he stumbled out the door.

"*De ballen!* Goodbye! Be careful," Mandy said as the rock star tried to steer clear of the dog, who was now shitting. The owner suddenly recognized Rook and put his hand over his mouth. Rook nodded at him and walked away.

"*Gadverdamme!*" said the owner, having stepped in the fresh pile of turds.

What has my life become? thought Rook. *I lose myself in sex. I want to forget everything. But I can't forget. Everywhere I turn, I'm there. Lose myself in work, I must do something heroic to rise above all this madness.*

Rook ambled back towards the Rolls. He let the image of Mandy replay through his mind, but already he was forgetting what her face looked like. He got out his phone to make sure he had a good photo of her. *I'll make my notations later,* he thought, wondering where his little black book was. The photo already did not match his recollection—in his memory she looked better. *What's wrong with me? Am I going downhill that fast already?* He tried to remember Hula's countenance. Her cherubic face floated in his head, impish grin and all, but then dispersed like a summer cloud. He wondered how she presented herself now. He wondered if she were a cow.

He reached the Rolls and found Arthur of the Tight Pants asleep. He knocked on the window.

"Pardon me, sir," said Aert, jolting. "I haven't been able to get any sleep lately—new baby at home."

"Who cares," said Rook. "Just drive." Rook nodded off and on. He stared out at an old bar, De Druif, which sported a sign that it had been there since 1631.

They soon arrived at the Genteel Hotel. A doorman greeted him, opening the limo door, while another opened up the lobby. He was ushered into a magnificent, marbled foyer, with a long red carpet, golden lighting, and employees ready to help at a moment's notice.

"Welcome, Mr. Grits," said the manager, with incredible style.

Rook looked at his nametag. "Mr. Vruchtwater, remember you well. How are you?"

"Fine. Fine. You have the Royal Suite, as usual, and the Rolls at your disposal."

"Thank you," said Rook, eying the Delft lamps and matching oriental rugs.

Rook always enjoyed the Genteel. Before the Little Bang was big, and they played in Amsterdam on their European tour, they had stayed near the Palladium Club—at the Quentin Hotel. But once they had moved up in the world, they decided to go in class. The Genteel was a five-star hotel and very chic, or *grachtengordel*, as the Dutch say.

Rook stared at the calendar on the desk.

"Is there something wrong, sir?" asked the manager.

"Oh no, it's just that the other day was my birthday, and I'm feeling my age."

"Your birthday? You? Unbelievable. You know here in the Netherlands birthdays are of utmost importance, and celebrated with much hoorah. We will have to make you feel better!"

"Well, thank you," said Rook. "But right now I'd just like to relax in my room. Maybe go for a swim."

Vruchtwater snapped his fingers and a bellhop with an apoplectic eye suddenly appeared and grabbed Rook's luggage.

"If a woman named Hula Kentucky comes to see me, send her up," Rook told the manager.

"Of course, sir."

They walked towards the elevator. Rook admired the staircase in the center of the lobby, with the sunflowers at the top. *I should have been a painter.*

As he entered his room, Rook got out some euros to pay the bellhop. He liked the look of the old guilders better, with the sunflowers. As he made himself comfortable in his room, a message came on the TV. It sang: "Hotel Sex, okay now, Hotel Sex!" *Sex and money sex and money.*

Rook splashed some water on his face and felt newbaptized.

After cleaning up, he went down to the pool for a swim. He did the backstroke, staring up at the sky-painted ceiling, and felt transported back to his childhood.

As he got out of the warm water, and went to relax on one of the chairs, a man in gold chains and gold watches—one on each wrist, began to strike up a conversation.

"Rook, hey how's it goin'?"

"Okay."

"Hey, don't you remember me? Hay?"

Rook examined the man. He had the appearance of someone who wanted to look wealthy, but really was just struggling to get by.

"I'm sorry, should I?'

"The mayor's race in L.A. Remember, I was running ten years ago? You came to one of my fundraisers."

"That rings a bell. You'll have to forgive me, ten years ago is I was in my cocaine spiral."

"So was I! Why do you think I lost the race?"

They both laughed.

"What's your name again?" asked Rook.

"Billy Todd. Remember how all the pundits said I should change my name cause I shouldn't be running with two first names?"

"Oh yeah. So what are you doing here?"

"Vacation. Getting away from my fourth wife, if you know what I mean. And you?"

"Vacation. Getting away from my wives—the band," laughed Rook. "We just finished a long tour."

"Man, that must be something, traveling the world, partying, playing, what fun!"

"It's fun, but it can kill you too." Rook tried to catch his breath.

"Waiter, can't you see this man needs a drink?"

"No, no, it's okay," said Rook. "It's too early."

"What do you want then, a coffee?"

"Coffee's good. And a blueberry pie." Rook laughed and admired his own designer trunks. They were a light chocolate color with green trim—a latte would go well with them. And before he knew it one was beside him.

"Sir," said the waiter to Rook, "I regret to inform you that the kitchen is out of blueberry pie. Perhaps a bit later today, I apologize." And he bowed and disappeared.

"Listen," said Billy. "I have a business proposition for you. How would you like to be the spokesperson for a new clothing line? It's something I'm working on, but I need a face . . . a respected, handsome face to help me launch it. Interested?"

"Maybe. My manager's already working on something. You're welcome to join in and partner with us. Kind of a retro style—60's, 70's stuff. Sort of where my music is inspired from. Call my manager—Ted Southhampton."

"I've done business with that fellow before," said Billy Todd, rolling his eyes. "He's exasperating."

"Yes, but he makes us money."

"Yes," was all Billy had to say. He stirred his Scotch.

"Well, maybe we can have a drink and talk again later," said Rook.

"Sure," said Billy. "Are you in town for business?"

"Old business," said Rook. "Old business."

"What the hells the Little Bang mean anyway?" Billy asked suddenly.

"Well, Jim Jam and I, the original founders of the band, were hanging out at the beach in Santa Barbara. We were tossing around names, but didn't really like any of them. I was listening to the sound of the waves crashing, and thought I wanted something explosive—but not pretentious. Something funny too. Explosive? What's more explosive than the big bang, I thought. But of course that would have been ridiculous. So I just thought of the Little Bang. Funny, original, and as a rock band the sexual innuendo is helpful."

"Yes!" said Billy Todd, comparing the time zones on each of his watches.

"But then a couple of years ago, scientists were duplicating processes that occurred in the early universe—just after the big bang. They called it the little bang; they made matter that hasn't existed in a very long time—quark gluon plasma. Quarks today are normally joined together in twos or threes, but the theory is in the early days, they roamed free, acting as building blocks of matter and helping to create the universe as we know it."

"Wow, that's some smart shit. But what about makin' some bread? What about the campaign for our clothing line?" asked Billy Todd. "Time is money and money is time and you know what—we're running out of time every goddamn second!"

"I don't know, dude. Listen, I'm on vacation. But I think something's in the works. I remember seeing some print ads being drawn up. Ted showed me thum."

Billy was trying to synchronize his watches, and noticed Rook's puzzled expression.

"Hey, I'm a good business partner. I'm very detail-oriented. My left hand, Amsterdam time, knows what my right hand, LA time, is doing. I got a lot goin' on, so if you want in on this, let's get goin'. Wait, I's got a phone." And he answered: "Talk to me, baby . . . uh-huh. No, no, sell, sell!"

When he was done, Rook said, "You're an odd sort, you know that?"

"Ain't that the kettle calling the pot square. Sounds like you're barely aware of any of your business ventures," said Billy, looking at his empty glass.

"I don't need to be, I just lend my face and my music. Listen—see my manager when you're back in LA, and he'll put you in touch with my lawyer to draw up the necessary paperwork. Now as far as investors, who do you have?"

"Uh . . . I have some money coming from a Dutch firm—that's why I'm here. And some meager funds of my own."

"Show Southhampton some of your designs too as well as the money. That might help you aboard. Good luck."

"I'll wire it to him today. I have a great marketing idea for developing countries too! I figure if we can combine your clothing line with the desire for strength and machismo, that that will attract the younger crowd. They will feel like they must pay a little more to look like a rock star and impress their woman. And if you sing in the local language, it will appeal all that much more!"

"Great, great," said Rook, staring at his cup of coffee swirling about. "The machine keeps going. Spin those wheels, raise the curtain, and let's make these clothes off the hook!"

And Rook dove into the pool.

He swam underwater the entire length. He remembered as a child he would do the same—seeing how long he could hold his breath. But with smoking and age, what use to be easy had now become demanding. He spewed water like some ancient sea creature surfacing, and rested on the edge, huffing and puffing.

He got out and sat down, dangling his feet in the blue man-made sea. *I should put a dam around them.* He laughed and inspected his body: he was still incredibly attractive, but the tattoos on his arms and chest were now embarrassing. Not only of Hula, but of a dragon and a flying-V guitar. He made a promise to himself to do something about them—and to work out so as to define himself more.

"Drop off your card," Rook said as Billy went to leave.

"Will do," said Billy, his voice echoing, staring out the window as if waiting for something inspirational to say, then disappearing without a word.

After a few more laps, Rook retired upstairs to take a nap. Upon waking, he felt a sense of dread. He gazed out the large window at the majestic Amstel River flowing by. There was an old, upturned bicycle along its bank; it's wheel spun round and round, propelled by the wind.

Rook freshened up, then wandered his way down to La Riviera, the five-star restaurant in the hotel. Gold sparkled from the vaulted ceilings, and so did the teeth of a famous rapper, Bling Blam, who was lounging by the window overlooking the river. Rook nodded to him, and he to Rook.

"We'll have to get together on an album sometime!" Bling said.

"I'd like that. That'd be unexpected, wouldn't it?" asked Rook.

"Sure thing," said Bling, throwing out his signs.

Rook marveled at the old-world luxury of the restaurant. A pianist was tinkling the ivories in the corner—classical—Beethoven, Brahms, Chopin. Rook reviewed his early piano lessons—John Thompson. The only time his teacher ever took any interest in him was when he actually made something up on his own. Rook didn't have the technical talent in piano, nor was he the most proficient at guitar, but he played with much soul and imagination, and the creativity he allowed to pass through him made up for the lack of virtuousity.

"May I get you a drink, sir?" asked the waiter, holding his pad a little too formally, even for a place like this.

"Yeah, Heineken," said Rook, now wanting to take the edge off. "And bring me a Cuban."

"Of course," said the waiter. "Here's a menu, the special tonight is *Aile de Raie aux Câpres - Pommes vapeur*—Skate Wing with Capers and Steamed Potatoes."

"Very well," said Rook, too embarrassed to ask what Skate Wing was.

Rook watched the boats up and down the Amstel River. They pushed their way against the current as the lights twinkled off the water.

"Here's your beer, sir," said the waiter, returning with a frosty pint. "And your Cohiba. Are you ready to order, sir?"

"Yes, I'll take your special, please."

"A wise choice. It's so fashionable this time of year."

Rook's spidy sense began to tingle—he noticed two girls—a blonde and a brunette whispering and giggling and having a conference--probably about whether to approach him. He took a sip from his beer—Heineken always tasted so much better—fresher—here in Amsterdam, where it was brewed. Suddenly, the girls were walking determinedly his way.

"Hallo, ladies," said Rook. "Looking beautiful."

"Are you him?" asked the brunette, dressed to the nines in Giordano Bruno.

"I don't know. Who's him?" asked Rook, smiling.

"You know, the Rooks," said the blonde in fire-engine red. Somewhere, sirens started sounding.

"Well, I'm actually trying to find out who I am. In search of myself, you know? Come back later," said Rook.

"Can you sign me?" asked the blonde. "Do a Picasso."

"I don't know what you mean," said Rook. "But it sounds fun."

As she leaned towards Rook, she let her long golden hair tickle his cheek.

"Uh, do you have a pen?" Rook asked. "And remember, this is a family establishment." The waiter suddenly appeared and handed a Sharpie to Rook. "There you go," Rook said, autographing her bosom. "Now if you'll excuse me, I gotta eat."

"You heard de man," said the waiter, shooing them off as if they were pigeons. *"De ballen, de draaikont!"* They skittled off, back to their table, blowing kisses all the while, motioning for Rook to call them.

Rook wondered why so many ladies wanted to be treated like crap. That is, it seemed certain women were attracted to men who treated them like they were whores. Why were they attracted to "bad boys?" Why did the nice, innocent farm girl always seem to end up with the motor-cycle, rock star rebel?

As Rook meandered in reverie land, sipping his cold beer, he noticed a rather large gentleman in an impeccable Savile Row custom-tailored suit enter the room with an entourage of some ten people. There were some pretty tough guys with him—obviously bodyguards—and a really hot lady on his arm. The entire restaurant turned deadly quiet—people stopped eating. The man paid no heed and sat so he could see the entrance, while his crew canvassed the diners. They evidently took Rook as some harmless chap, but the rapper, who was now with a lady friend, attracted their attention. Two of the bodyguards—twins—took up positions by each side of the foyer, standing, with hands folded but at the ready.

The man in the suit and hat folded his Super 220 me-rino wool jacket carefully and handed it to one of his assistants—a scrawny little guy with glasses who seemed to have more going on than appeared. Some three or four waiters suddenly materialized, as if summoned by the change of atmosphere in the room. The pianist began playing again—but now Wagner—and just a little too fast and violently. Vruchtwater surfaced, snapping a command in Dutch—*"Buffelen! Op z'n sodemieter geven!"*—and the restaurant lights were dimmed and candles were lit. Rook lit his cigar and blew a cloud of smoke, which drifted away and then seemed as ethereal as this tableau vivant.

Bling Blam's girl was talking animatedly to him, but he didn't seem to be paying attention. He was very intent on the gang that had just exploded into the room. *Now just what's their scene?* he thought.

"Another Heineken, sir?" whispered the waiter to Rook.

"Yeah," said Rook. "Hey, who is that guy?"

"Oh, him. Svidrigailov—a powerful businessman." And then leaning over, confidentially: "Mafiya."

Rook had intuited as much. The gentleman in question was now making a big motion and commotion—ordering drinks for everyone in the room. A bell rang somewhere. People clapped. They held up their glasses in appreciation. Rook held up his too. Bling Blam did not hold his up immediately, but when Svidrigailov turned round to look, he made quick to.

Svidrigailov then began conversing with the members at his table—it appeared he was telling a funny tale, for after a minute or two, everyone laughed and shook their heads as if they couldn't believe the wit of this portly fellow. The knock-out girl grabbed onto Svidrigailov's exorbitant suit-sleeve.

Rook began chugging his second beer when through the frosty mug he thought he noticed Mafiya's girl waving at him. He looked over again, and sure enough, she offered a minute gesture with her pinky, as if she wanted tea. He nodded at her, but felt that an imbroglio with this underworld boss was something to be avoided most definitely. *Fans everywhere,* thought Rook. He shook his head.

As it was, Svidrigailov appeared not to notice, but one of his guards at the door seemed to have caught the exchange, and was now eyeing Rook more closely than Bling Blam, who was busy looking out the window at the lights reflecting upon the river as his girl played footsy with him beneath the table with the long cloth that covered its too suggestive legs.

Rook lost himself in the bottom of his mug. *Avoid a scene, avoid a scene . . . I wish Gary were here now.* He recalled how Southhampton was going to try and arrange a temporary bodyguard for him, and wondered where this guy might be. The waiter approached him again.

"Another beer, sir?"

"Yeah, yeah," still unable to shake his nerves.

"This is from the lady across the room," whispered the waiter, surreptitiously slipping Rook a note as he removed his empty flagon.

Rook tried to appear casual, then read it:

I'm not waving, but drowning in Coralville Lake. Hula.

Rook looked up at the woman again. *Hula?*

She waved. This time, however, Rook saw the girl beneath the costume. She was on the Titanic and she was sinking.

Rook's new beer arrived promptly and he tried to muster up his courage by downing it. *But courage for what? I can't believe she's sitting right there across the room. Christ, I can't look at her! I really can't look at her!* Hula obviously had requested his help, but what sort of trouble was she into? How could he possibly help her? *How could she possibly be mixed up with this mafioso?*

He decided he would at least introduce himself to Svidrigailov. Finishing his drink, telling the waiter to put it on his room, he headed towards the boss. The waiter sensed what Rook was doing, started to reach out to restrain him, but then thought better of it. The bodyguards stepped in closely as the rocker approached.

"Excuse me," said Rook. "I don't mean to interrupt, but it's come to my attention that you are a powerful businessman here in town."

Svidrigailov slowly turned around. His five bodyguards gauged his reaction from behind their mirrored shades, which glinted from the lights and bounced off the mirrors in the room.

"Who are you?" asked Svidrigailov, warily, with a voice that seemed to come from under water. Rook recognized that look. He had exhibited it many times himself when unknown people approached him.

"Rook Heisenberg," he said. "You know, from the Little Bang."

"Oh yes, I've heard your music. Once."

There was a collective smattering of appreciative laughter.

Rook, undaunted, began to sing: "We start the day—on a good note—we carry through—to a good note. Pianissimo, pianissimo. We take the day—lightly . . . Sweep the leaves away from my grave! I'm not dead yet! I want to see if anybody remembers me, when I'm gone—sweep the leaves away . . . sweep the leaves away . . . sweep the leaves away . . . ."

Rook bowed and smiled. No one said anything for a long moment.

"You're a lucky son of a bitch," said Svidrigailov, chortling. "I was going to shoot you, just now, but boy, you can sing!"

Rook kept smiling, doing his best not to look at Hula, but instead at the blonde and brunette across the way—who blew kisses. "Thank you, Mr. Svid-ri-gai-lov," Rook mangled.

"Call me S. The name's a fiction anyway—after my favorite literary character. You really do have to be theatrical these days. Please, sit down."

One of S's henchmen, with an odd gentility, patted down Rook as he pulled out a chair for him. Rook shook the henchman's hand and smiled like a moron.

"You know," continued S, "I thought you were just one of those rock and roll thugs. But you touched upon my secret passion—a heartfelt song. I wish I could sing! But I can't, so I do other . . . things."

"Well, whatever you do, you're sure sitting pretty. Boy, and I thought I traveled in style," said Rook, motioning for the waiter. "Cristal," he whispered.

The waiter disappeared as quickly as the puff of cigar smoke Rook blew.

"I never sit pretty," said S. "That's her job." And he nodded at Hula, laughing. There was forced ha-hawing from the rest of the entourage.

"I'm sorry, ma'am," said Rook, addressing Hula just like he addressed an actress in the Anatoli movie he had been in. "I didn't mean to detract from your beauty. Rook Heisenberg." He shot out his hand, a tad too eagerly.

"Hula Kentucky," she said, holding it. Suddenly Rook was back in high school—at the wedding—at that church—touching Hula again for the very first time. He took a photographic memory of their hands and felt like time had stood still, or come full-circle.

Hula almost peed in her dress as she saw Rook approaching. Yes, she wanted to get his attention, but she never thought in a million years he would just up and saunter over. *Was he completely clueless? Dombo? Well, yes. Still* . . . thought Hula.

It was Rook's blind luck that proved his savior once again. She had seen S shoot people before in restaurants—just to see if his gun worked. How Rook suddenly began to sing—and sing with true emotion—and hit S's soft spot—was a miracle. Not only had he gotten himself unwittingly out of a dangerous morass, he had now somehow ingratiated himself with the boss.

"Here's my business card," said S to Rook. "Why don't you drop by sometime and we'll have a drink and talk about your so-called country. I would like to go to America someday. If they'll let me in." He howled.

"And perhaps we could even do some business together. I could use some stronger promotion in Europe and I take it you also have Russian connections?" asked Rook.

S convulsed in a paroxysm of laughter as if that was the funniest thing he'd ever heard. The rest of his group, even Hula, joined in.

"What?" asked Rook, sheepishly.

"Mr. Heisenberg," said S, coughing and pounding a shot of Stoli's, "*I am* the Russian connection." And he popped an olive, spitting out the pit into a glass and breaking it.

Rook winced at his own stupidity. *Of course. Leave it to Hula to make everything so complicated. I'm back in high school all over again!*

"I'm sorry," said Rook. "How foolish of me. Of course. Now if you'll excuse me, I have some work to do. Please enjoy the Cristal, my compliments."

"Ya, ya," said S, nodding. "And by all means drop by my club. I'll set you up while you're in town."

"Great," said Rook, shaking S's hand a little too firmly and bowing once more. "I look forward to doing business with you."

"Not everyone looks forward to doing business with me," said S, "but some do nevertheless!" And he let out a hearty guffaw, handing Rook a business card. It was simple, yet mysterious, white with raised black glossy lettering:

S

The Capri Club
Raadhuistraat 51
Amsterdam, NL
020 112 333 55

Rook placed the card in his hip pocket and turned to Hula.

Oh my God he's gonna get us both killed, thought Hula.

"Madame," said Rook, bowing and kissing what he excitedly noticed to be a ringless hand.

Hula nodded ever so delicately. S did not notice—he was checking the bottom of the Cristal bottle, perhaps reliving the fears of Alexander II.

And just like that—Rook exited, trembling. Feeling a little nauseous again, he felt like he was skating. Darting a quick glance at Hula as he left the room, he concluded that she was almost unrecognizable. *Has she really changed that much—or is my memory shit? Or do we only remember things the way we want them to be? If it weren't for her eyes, and the old familiar stare, I don't think I'd know her. Dressed so elegantly, decked out in a designer dress and diamonds, her reddish hair now dyed classy blonde. She looks like one of those women in Beverly Hills who spend all day shopping on Rodeo Drive. Jesus Christ, Hula, what have you gotten yourself into?*

Before going up to his room, Rook pulled Vruchtwater aside.

"Listen, I told you before if a Hula Kentucky came up to send her up. Forget that request. It never happened. Erase any record of it."

"No problem, sir."

"Send my meal up to my room. Along with a bottle of Stoli and some olives."

"Not an outrageous request. Don't worry about it," Vruchtwater comforted Rook, patting his shoulder.

"And what is with that Mr. S guy? He's like something out of some movie."

"People are afraid of him. He's very powerful and very dangerous. But he seems to have taken a liking to you. Beware of the crocodile's smile."

And Vruchtwater smiled and disappeared into a back office.

Rook made his way towards the elevator, narrowly escaping the blonde and brunette autograph-seekers as they came scuffling after him in their high heels. Ducking into the golden solitude of the lift and manically banging the buttons, he breathed a sigh of relief as the doors closed, whisking him away. An hour ago, he would have loved another *ménage à trios*; but now he wished to be alone with his thoughts and his reflection. He surveyed himself in the mirror. "What have you been doing with your life? What have you got to show for yourself? What the hell's going on, dude?" He played with the gold and silver pendants that hung around his neck. He noticed they had little clasps that could be opened. He unlocked one of them; inside was a little piece of paper, folded up in a pyramid-shaped football. Opening it, he thought of his childhood. And then, there was a square, with numbers:

16	3	2	13
5	10	11	8
9	6	7	12
4	15	14	1

"What?" Rook said. He hadn't thought of math in so long, and couldn't be troubled to think about it now. He put the paper back in the locket and locked it, thinking it might be some model number that he might need in the future. As the egress slid silently open, the aging rocker trod his way towards the Royal Suite, holding the wall for support. *But I don't feel like the king. How do I play this game?* Unlocking the door and collapsing on the edge of the stately bed, Rook looked outside. A wind began to howl, and a tree branch tapped against the window. Lightning flashed wildly in the distance, and thunder soon followed, rumbling. A moonbow cast a strange glow across the dark room. Almost unable to lift his head up, he noticed his pale, forlorn shape in the antique mirror on the other side, saw himself as a child, and suddenly knew what he had to do.

Frenziedly, Rook began composing a new song for Hula.

"Song to Save the World"[*]

---

[*] Paper clipped here was a facsimile of this new, unpublished song that Rook reportedly penned in Amsterdam, on hotel stationery. I have had the handwriting authenticated, but am unable to reproduce the composition, having been denied permission due to copyright restrictions. This refusal would seem to affirm the legitimacy and value of the document. Hopefully, this masterpiece will soon see the light of day; it may be the rock star's greatest work yet. But of course, I have not heard it. But then, what was it that Keats said?

6

THE CAPRI CLUB

The next morning, after a breakfast of sweets but still no blueberry pie, Rook leaned across the front desk confidentially and cleared his throat.

"The man in the restaurant gave me this," he said, showing Diederik, the concierge, the card. Diederik looked at it then pretended as if something important were going on across the lobby.

"Yes, Mr. Grits, that's S's main club."

"Main club?"

"Brothel. It's the most exclusive, expensive one here in town. The finest wine, women, and song are yours for a price, along with a casino. Other pleasures and games are available as well; it caters to all sorts of clientele. Celebrities like yourself, politicians, criminals. Ha, sometimes you have all three in one! It can be a rather bizarre place, but that should come as no surprise. After all, it is named after the Roman emperors' island of retreat."

"Great," said Rook. "I'm dealing with Caligula."

"More or less," said Diederik. "What's this all about, anyway?"

"What else? A girl. Isn't it always? Listen, I plan on visiting there later tonight. Can you have the Rolls ready?"

"Of course," said Diederik, frowning, wanting to wipe the powdered donut remains from Rook's precious, underinsured mouth. "Just be careful about getting involved with him."

"Is he really mafiya?"

Diederik's perpetual frown worsened. "You've heard that already, have you? Well, I guess you'd call it that. He is a very powerful businessman. Many ties with organized crime. They call him the Octopus of Despair—he has many tentacles or branches of businesses, some legit, some not, and they reach far, in the Netherlands and beyond, making many unhappy. A real nihilist!"

"And that makes him tough? What else can you tell me?" asked Rook, lighting up a smoke with a flip-top lighter as coolly as he could. "I'm thinking of doing business with him managing our European/Russian tours."

Diederik shook his head. "Crazy boy. *Ik voel me afgezeken.*"

"What?"

"You shit on my intelligence. Are you crazy? Sure, Svidrigailov will be able to use his contacts to get you a higher take and he'll do a great job of promoting, but once you get into business with him, it's hard to get out."

"What do you mean?"

"Well," Diederik looked about, then lowered his voice. "Let's say you want someone else to manage a future tour, he might choose to make that very difficult for you and others might be intimidated, or an unfortunate accident might take place at one of the venues—you get my drift—he doesn't like things that are under his control to escape from his control."

"I understand," said Rook, nodding. "What are some of his holdings?"

"Well, the sex clubs, which bring in a lot of money—not just through the girls, but the partying—the liquor, caviar, the casino, internet site, porn videos. He also is known to deal in illegal drugs—cocaine, heroin. Diamond Market, other business—some legit, some not. Money laundering. Human trafficking, body parts. Art—stolen, forged. Internet fraud. Perhaps old Soviet nukes. Who knows what else?" Diederik put his right hand out and looked at the fingernails on his left. Rook shook them both.

"No, you dombo! Euros!"

"Just teasing," laughed Rook, scrounging. "Here you go," he said, giving him a handful of crumpled notes, letting them drop on the ground.

He is delicious, but I hate him, thought Diederik, waiting until Rook left before he picked up the cash.

Rook took the lift up to his suite and picked up his guitar. He was reworking his new masterpiece that he had started on the evening before—"Song to Save the World." He allowed the high school feeling to wash ashore all over again, letting it swim over him, with Hula and Jeans Jacket and all that adolescent torment. Now, all these years later, it was the same, just the players and stakes had changed.

He worked for several hours, then cleaned up real pretty-like, putting on just a shade of make-up. He had gotten so accustomed to wearing it over the years, especially while performing, that now, almost every time he went out, he felt naked without it (just the slightest bit would make him look better for the cameras). He practiced a grimace in the mirror. Again. Again. It wasn't so believable. He thought of Hula dying. He tried again. He picked up an olive and tried breaking a glass by spitting out the pit. It didn't work.

Rook threw on a nondescript jacket, a 1950s tweed hat, and a pair of mirrored shades. He wished he had a Glock. He didn't know what would happen, but he wanted to be ready. He called downstairs, and as he let the phone ring, looked at himself in the mirror. He adjusted the light so he looked like he was in a movie.

"Mr. Grits?" answered Diederik.

"Yes, I need a gun. A Glock, if possible."

After a pause, Diederik replied: "Let me see what I can do. Also, if I may suggest, I would think it best if you took a bodyguard. Your manager already called ahead, and we have arranged one."

"Okay," said Rook. "Send up a bottle of Everclear. Have the Rolls and everything else ready in half-an-hour. Send the guard up to get me." Rook hung up the phone and stared at himself in the mirror. *What am I doing?*

He turned off the light and waited in the dark for what he didn't know.

Twenty minutes later, there was a knock upon the door. Rook opened it and a slender Cantonese woman carrying an Everclear bottle entered. She set it down, and as Rook was getting out money to tip her, she suddenly did a flip and was behind him with a gun to his temple.

"What the hell?" shouted Rook. "What are you doing?"

She breathed warmly into his ear as she pressed the cold polymer against his skull, tracing its outline.

"Am I moving too fast for you?" she whispered.

And then suddenly the gun was gone and she was in front of Rook, smiling and making him a drink.

"How thoughtful of me, huh?" she asked. "But then again, I'm at your service. Allow me to introduce myself: I am Pui-Pui Poon, your bodyguard for the night. But you can call me triple-P or just P. This is your Glock," she said, spinning it on the table, then stopping it so it pointed at Rook. "I get to kiss you!" And she did, then stepping back: "I suggest you let me handle the pistola and everything else." And as if to further inspire Rook's confidence, Pui-Pui smashed the table, caught the weapon in mid-air, shot the cork off a bottle in the mini-bar, and poured it into a goblet without even making an excess of foam. A trace of gun smoke and Belgian vapors lingered in the air. She blew the hot barrel with her pursed wet lips.

"Jesus Christ," said Rook, "are you for real? You really gave me a scare!"

"Well, just imagine what I do to the bad guy."

"How do you know I'm not the bad guy?"

"How do you know I'm not a bad girl?"

"I don't. You're crazy though."

"Yes, but that's a pre-req. Let me assure you," she whispered to Rook, standing behind him again, "I'm a black-belt, and can take on the biggest of men."

"That," said Rook, "could be taken two ways."

"Exactly," she said. "But my word can be taken only one way. I will keep you safe."

Rook laughed. "Listen, I have a lot goin' on…"

Pui-Pui smiled without showing her teeth and blew her dark hair from her green onyx eyes. "Don't worry about a thing," she said, almost kissing him again, but then turning away, holding out the Glock. "Do you want it or not?"

"You better keep that," said Rook, holding up his hands in surrender. She turned, and he took a sip of the Everclear mix and followed her out the door, staring at her. Though she was dressed in a black business suit, he imagined her toned body.

Pui-Pui was from the Panyu District of Guangzhou, the current Chinese name for the old French misnomer of Canton. When she was three, her parents were killed in a typhoon. The only way she had survived was because they, quickly thinking or not thinking at all, placed her in the money hole under a large brick in the floor. She was too weak to move the brick when it was all over, and so was forced to wait until rescuers came; they heard her screams. This was her first memory, arising from out of the muddy, soaked earth, an RMB 100 note stuck to her foot, to the sight of her dead parents who had been crushed when the roof fell in. The money, some 8300 yuan RMB, was stolen by one of the authorities.

Pui-Pui was raised by her Uncle Au Xian Sheng, a sensei of Shaolin kung fu, specifically of the Choy Lay Fut style. He taught her very well the technical aspects of the arts, but was unable to help her with reining in her anger. Uncle decided he must assist her to at least transform it into a useful power, but it became a force that could not be relied upon or controlled. Hence, when she was at the height of her fury, they developed a twirling insane dragon move they called what else—the *tai-fung* (great wind). Pui-Pui would always practice it at the end of her morning workout—a sort of cathartic climax. She had only had the chance to use it once so far, however, in her line of work, which for the last year, since she had turned twenty-one, had been serving as a bodyguard for various dignitaries. She was on a delicate assignment in Bern guarding a political figure in exile. The two of them were returning to the hotel after a heavy dinner and one mojito each, exiting the elevator, when suddenly they were surrounded by assassins. Before she knew it, her client was dead—his brains splattered on a sign which read: IN CASE OF EMERGENCY, EXIT LEFT.

Out of her mind with rage, she flew into the *tai-fung*. She killed all seven of the attackers, but in the process also eliminated an old man whose decision to take the stairs instead of waiting for the next lift had been quite inauspicious.

Despite the disaster, and the deleterious effects it had upon a myriad of people, politicians, and countries, her agency was still sanguine about her prospects and hence "transferred" her as quietly as possible to another city— one where her wildness and live-wire lifestyle might blend in more easily.

Her first week in Amsterdam was filled with people-watching. She even hired a prostitute, but not for sex. She wished to sit in her window and watch the clients go by. She sat and stared at them, and enjoyed tremendously shaking her head and turning them away.

The second week she watched the river and the wheels of the town turn. She rented a yellow bicycle and took a tour out to Waterland. She painted tulips, though she was not a painter. And although she scoffed at her canvas, she had the natural ability of many a martial artist to create kinetic feng-shui triptychs.

The third week Pui-Pui hung out at Rembrandt's house, the Van Gogh Museum, and the coffee shops near them. She was trying to forget and she was trying to remember. She watched the steam appear and rise from her coffee and disappear as mysteriously as she would one day.

The fourth week she sat in her loft with the window cranked open and worked on a self-portrait. By Friday, she was done, and she smiled a contented smile, feeling that if she died now, it would be okay; she had played her "music."

She sat and meditated in her room, waiting for something to happen.

A few days hence, which was today, the phone rang. It was the first time in almost a month. Pui-Pui stared at it, and with not inconsiderable difficulty, unlocked her limbs from the lotus posture, caught the call on the seventh ring, and listened to her new assignment without saying a word. *A rock star! A rock star! Wa! Okay, I'm a little bit too excited. Calm—siu sam!*

She took a look at her self-portrait before she left. A truer mirror than any other, she thought. She threw on the standard business bitch wardrobe and walked down the hallway of the Genteel to the elevator and up to the Royal Suite. Surprise and shock your opponent, then surprise and shock yourself. And surprise Rook she did.

"Listen," said Pui-Pui to Rook as Aert skippered the white Rolls like a dying Moby Dick through the elongated streets with phallic posts pointing towards the sky shooting clouds of birth and expansion. "I'm going to have to kiss you and all that stuff to make it look believable in there. I just wanted you to know. I don't want them to know that I'm working. Also, when we're in there, I'll go by Ming Dynasty. I don't want them to know my real name. Come to think of it, there are a lot of things I don't want people to know about me." Rook cast a furtive glance at Pui-Pui's jade onyx eyes as they sat in the backseat together.

"Of course," said Rook. "Well, shall we practice?" He took her hand.

"Why not?" she said, smiling not too shyly.

He leaned over to kiss her, and felt the sultriness of her feelings a little too strongly. He broke and looked out past her—out the window at the Amstel flowing, wondering if he could step forth into the same river twice with Hula. *Or was it a completely different river? And is it a completely different Hula? Different me? Who are we anymore?* And then he asked P: "Are those contacts?"

He's a strange chap, thought Pui-Pui, contemplating the aftertaste of Rook's smooch; it reminded her of cotton candy.

Aert negotiated the gas-guzzler tightly through the streets towards the Capri Club. It was located outside of the main Red Light, within sight of the Royal Palace and about a five-minute walk to the Anne Frank House. Aert glided the white steed down a narrow alley nearby, much to the gawks of ambling onlookers trying to peer and stare at just who might be inside.

"I'll wait here," said Aert. "If you need me, here is where I'll be. Would you like to see photos of my new baby?"

"Maybe later," said Rook, helping Pui-Pui out by the small of her delicate back. They walked briskly towards the club, and up the steps. Two big bouncers stopped them, padding them down. As P was about to be searched, she handed the man 100 euro.

"That's for you," she said, cracking her best smile and wink. "This man's a rock star and should be treated as such." She reached up to kiss Rook, and their lips met.

"Of course," said the blonde-haired, blue-eyed, 275-pound bouncer. "I met him the other night! I could barely believe it! We'll keep an eye out for him."

"Yes," said the other bouncer—his identical twin. "We will keep an out for him. There are no two ways about it."

As Rook held their attention, with his charisma and money, counting out the hefty entrance fee of 300 euro, Pui-Pui clandestinely threw the Glock into a bed of flowers on a little ledge above the entrance door.

The bouncer brothers simultaneously ushered them inside, escorting them into a world where red velvet carpeted a plush, opulent, epicurean room. Gold chandeliers hung from the vaulted and gilded ceiling. The walls were of solid oak, and a bar of mahogany and old-world cabinetry lent an air of *gezilleg* or coziness to the place. Softly lit, the smell of freshly-baked bread in the air, Rook and Pui-Pui allowed their eyes to adjust, bypassed the dining section, and made their way up to the bar as P undid a button on her white blouse. Rook drooled like a baby.

"It's okay," she said. "I want you to know I saw that. But that's my job—I have to see everything." And she placed her hand on Rook's thigh and reached over and kissed him violently, biting his lower lip.

"Ow!" cried Rook.

"No, that's my Uncle's name—Au," joked Pui-Pui.

"Jesus!"

"No," said a pretty barmaid, approaching in a scandalous fishnet outfit. "I'm afraid I'm not him. I'm afraid I can't change water into wine. But I can ask myself 'what would Jesus do in this situation?' The answer is that he would never ask himself that question in the first place. He would just be."

Has the world gone crazy? thought Rook. *Where are the normal people?*

"Could I get a Heineken?" asked Rook, casting an eye towards the stage.

"Mai tai," ordered Pui-Pui, with a look at the barmaid that sent her searching for Christ and fishing for a cigarette.

On the stage, two Hungarian blondes were simulating a lesbian show; one was disrobing from a gorilla suit, and about to do something titillating with a banana to her fellow Magyar. Suddenly someone placed their hand on Rook's shoulder, causing him to jump and find a beautiful brunette licking her luscious silvery lips.

"Hi," she said. "What's your name?"

"It doesn't matter," said Rook. "I want to forget my name for a while."

"I can help you with that," she said, blowing on his neck feebly.

"Maybe later," said Rook. "We just got here." And he placed his hand on triple-P's knee, with thoughts of getting to third base. The brunette walked away.

"Hope you don't mind," Rook whispered to Pui-Pui. "Must keep up appearances." She giggled like a schoolgirl and placed her hand on top of Rook's.

Rook looked back at the stage, disappointed that he had missed the banana split, then scanned the room, trying to catch a glimpse of Hula.

"Excuse me," said Rook to the Christian barmaid. "Do you know a girl named Hula?"

"Sure," she said. "She's about somewhere. Probably with the boss, but she'll be out soon."

"Do you mean Mr. Svidrigailov?" asked Rook. She nodded, carefully. "Can you tell him that Rook is here and would like to see him?" She picked up the bar phone and dialed three digits. Rook tried to make out what she was saying, but couldn't amidst the din. Then he laughed, because he realized that part of the din was one of his songs playing through the PA.

"He'll be down in a little while," said the Benedictine barmaid, who had left the convent last year. "He said in the meantime, 'make yourself at home.'"

"Will do," said Rook. And he kissed Pui-Pui with gusto.

Suddenly, the emcee came over the microphone: "Ladies and gentlemen, welcome to the Capri Club. We hope you are enjoying yourselves. In a few moments, we're going to have a little game—a little game of bows and arrows. Now this is not your usual type of archery, but a, shall we say, game of love—affair of the heart—and the body. Now I'm going to be asking for volunteers, but before I do, let me explain further: it costs 100 euro to enter the game. After you've put your money in, a dozen women will line up in front of you. The first one to hit the target, so to speak, is the winner and gets the pot of money, plus a little trip upstairs to one of our twelve rooms with one of the ladies—if he's still up to it. Any questions? No? Okay, who'd like to play?"

At first no one seemed willing, but then one college-aged guy, urged on by his friends, raised his hand, and then one of his friends joined, then some guy in a navy uniform, then some old Italian guy, and a middle-aged Rastafarian.

Rook squirmed and Pui-Pui rubbed his hand. He coughed as a parade of women began to come out of the back room. One of them was Hula.

My worst nightmare is coming true! Rook grabbed onto the bar for support, but it didn't help much. The veins in Rook's forehead began to show, and the room began to spin; he wondered if he should join the game, to somehow help Hula, but thought: *No way. There's no way I'm doing that. What good would it do anyway?* He tried however to catch her attention by passionately kissing Pui-Pui. With one eye open, Rook gauged Hula's reaction. Nothing. Straight-faced and straight-laced—*comme il faut*. She didn't even look at him as she joined the rest of the girls in lining up.

"Okay, gentlemen," said the emcee. "Get ready. Don't be nervous. Come on guys, pick your girl—pick your target. Okay, ready, set, go!"

Cheers and a heavy bass beat erupted. The two college boys at first had a little trouble—perhaps they were two sheets to the wind. Some people in the club snickered and laughed, which made it even more difficult for one of them. The Rastafarian fellow was going strong, the Italian guy was fiercely determined, and the navy chap—from the Royal British Navy—was on a mission that would likely distress his hero—Admiral Nelson.

Rook's heart was distressed; as the thunderous bass beat got louder and Hula smiled and danced, he felt like his heart was going to explode. But it didn't. The atrocity continued. Rook remembered the carnival from when he was a child, getting dizzy and sick after so many rides, then sitting down to pop the balloons with darts and missing and winning nothing. Now, so many ups and downs all these years later . . . . Eventually, the competition began to flounder—it was down to Navy and Rastafarian. Rastafarian missed his target. Navy shuffled his step, aimed at and hit Hula squarely. As his "arrow" ran down her gentle derrière, a tear ran down Rook's pale, horrified face. For the first time in years he was suddenly and completely sober and shocked into disbelief.

There was wild applause; Navy bowed and smiled, Hula cleaned herself up, and the emcee gave the Brit the money.

"You now get to make your selection—which girl would you like to go upstairs with?" asked the emcee, illustrating the question with a gesture of his white-gloved hand which glowed a little purplish in the black light. Navy wrapped an arm around Hula. "Hula! Of course!

Congratulations!" Hula leaned over and kissed Navy on his wind-chapped lips much to his and Rook's amazement.

As Hula and the Brit snaked upstairs, Rook crunched the napkin in front of him.

"It's okay," said Pui-Pui. "There are ways to channel your anger."

Rook looked about the room at the various frescoes and friezes. One of the Roman emperors stared out at him with a harem of young men and women at his feet as Dionysius frolicked in the background. Uncrumpling the serviette, Rook wiped the cold sweat from his famous face. Suddenly, he felt an arm around him.

"Well, my rocker friend, are you enjoying yourself?" S asked with a big grin, swanking up to them.

Rook began crunching the napkin again. "Sure," said Rook. "Quite a place you have here. You have any olives?"

S raised his dark unibrow in surprise. "Sure, sure," and he motioned to the barmaid. "I'm glad you like my establishment. Most people don't know what to make of it at first, but once they get acclimated, they relax. Even the old Roman emperors would feel at home. Can you imagine entertaining Tiberius? Caligula? Nero? Ha! That's my business vision statement—a bar and brothel that would please Caesar! This place used to be considered *zapodlo*—shady—but you throw enough money in and it's funny how perception changes! Let me buy you both a drink." S snapped his fingers and momentarily two *Medovukhas* appeared.

"Who is your lovely friend?" S asked of Pui-Pui, who was massaging Rook's tense hand.

"My name is Ming, like the Dynasty," she quickly said, extending her petite face for S to kiss. He licked it and pinched her cheek.

"Well, I dare say, you look as fragile and as priceless as a Ming vase. If you'd ever like to join my harem here, feel free. And if either of you ever need a favor or help—*poblatu* as they say in Russian—you just let me know."

"Thank you," said Pui-Pui. "But I can't imagine doing all that."

"That's what they all say, at first. Anyway, Rook, I assume you've looked into my dealings, as any good businessman would. And I yours. To tell you the truth, I didn't realize your band was so successful. Of course, I've heard of you before, but I don't really follow the music scene all that closely."

"Yes. Well, you don't look like the rock and roll type," said Rook.

"No? What do I look like, then?" asked Svidrigailov seriously.

"Uh, jazz?"

"Jazz! Ha! That's a good one! Actually, I prefer opera. I wish I could sing; as a child I tried, but alas I was not cut out for it. And now I cut out things I need and take my cut! Heisenberg, my well-sung friend, I want to be straight with you. I have not promoted a concert before, but I want to assure you that I'm more than able to do so. As an *avtoritet*--leader of this *tusovka*—this slice of the pie, so to speak, I have the means to get the job done, turning us both a handsome profit. I can also offer, how you say—*po ponyati-yam*—security services. I ask you, as a wealthy man yourself, is that what you live for? More security? More money? More toys? More sex?"

"I don't know," said Rook, honestly. "I was trying to think of what I wanted for my birthday recently, and I couldn't come up with a damn thing."

S laughed his head off. "Are you for real? I don't have time for such melancholy! Come now! Another drink!"

After another round, and after Rook tried, unsuccessfully, to spit his olive and break his glass, S, for a moment, smiled like a normal person.

"You're alright," said S to Rook while nonchalantly placing his hand on Pui-Pui's knee. "Money does bring a certain concern about its loss—almost a preoccupation— my God, what if I lose it all? I couldn't possibly go back to how I was living before! And I know speaking for myself, that I therefore put my utmost concern on preserving and building my fortune, my empire, and make sure nothing gets in my way. Nothing. I don't like to lose, and I *uryt*— bury whoever interferes. But besides the money, there's the power, and surely you must know that to some extent. The power of *nomenklatura* I feel from my wealth and the accords it brings, also the reputation. Sometimes it's good to have a rep, it gets you things—respect, the best table in town. Fear can be a good thing to keep your rivals intimidated." And he edged his hand up Pui-Pui's thigh; she allowed him to do so, although she now was forming the iron wire fist.

"I can see what you're saying," said Rook, forgetting whom he was talking to for a moment (it might as well have been Southhampton or some other fancy suit). "It's somewhat satisfying to have power—on stage knowing you have thousands of people under your control—you almost feel like Alexander the Great. But in my business, fear and intimidation don't get one very far. Talent, creativity, keeping your image new, marketing, but more than anything else I've found that I have to make music I like, disregarding any market niche. I have to like it. If others do too, that's fine, but my audience is myself. One can tell if the artist is really into the work, heart and soul, or not. One can tell if the art was inspired, or just a chore. If it flows and you can tell it was a labor of love for the artist, chances are people will connect to that."

"Yes," said S, turning over Rook's philosophy as if looking for a bug beneath it. "And I'd have to say if I were in your position, I'd agree with you. But think of my line of work. It's a little different; I'm not an artist. I have to be a larger-than-life character. And as *vor*—lord of crime—in *vorovsko mir*—a thieves' world—I have a certain image to maintain."

"Exactly, as do I, but I also have to change it now and then so people don't get bored. Remember, the public has a short attention span. I stay true to myself, but mix it up a bit—surprise them."

"Very wise," said S, suddenly kissing Pui-Pui on the lips.

Pui-Pui pulled away, then slapped S across the face. S just laughed. Rook looked at her, trying to gauge her expression. It was unreadable, as if she were at a game of poker. Rook then looked upstairs at the privates, hoping Hula would emerge and they could just leave this place. *But that hope is absurd.*

P followed Rook's gaze up and into the little villas of lust. *He is so predictable,* she thought. She could feel the typhoon rising inside her. *I wish I were telekinetic so I could just blow this place to hell. Okay, breathe . . . calm.* She looked back at Rook, placed her hand on his, then looked at S and smiled, trying to convey a look of lust. *I am going to kill you, you bastard. Justice will be ser-ved.* He returned her look with a wiggle of his unibrow. P wiggled her nose.

"But even in your line of work," continued Rook to S, "you are an artist. You're an actor of sorts, portraying this larger-than-life character, and I'm sure much of this you get from Hollywood movies. But nonetheless, it's a role you're playing. We're all playing a role in life, though most of us are unaware of it."

"And so we all play our roles," agreed S. "And mine now consists of being frank with you: what do you want?"

"Huh?"

"What do you want?"

"What do you mean?" asked Rook, casting a glance at Pui-Pui; she just pulled out her cell phone.

"You know exactly what I mean. I didn't get to where I am by being stupid. Why did you come to me? To promote your next tour? Why? I've never done it before. Why did you approach my table, singing? It's just too bullshit, like you're up to something. Sure, we probably could have a profitable relationship, but you better lay it all out on the table—now."

Rook reached for a cigarette, and after lighting up, tried to leisurely sip his mead.

"Fair enough," Rook belched. "I too think in the same way: what does this person want from me? I'm so used to scam artists and hangers-on and gold-diggers, that's my immediate thought when a stranger approaches."

Hula and the Navy man suddenly appeared at the top of the winding stairs. She took a quick, discerning look at them, but neither Rook nor S saw it. P did, however. The Navy man tried to kiss Hula goodbye; she turned her cheek and let him. She disappeared somewhere—back to where the red lights faded into black. Navy then bumbled down the stairs, as if he had forgotten where he was going. Suddenly, he became transformed and skipped confidently towards the men's room, which was indicated by a neon arrow.

"It's really very simple, Mr. Svidrigailov," said Rook as a blonde girl neared. "It sounds silly, but after I get my fill, what I want to do is take my extra proceeds from our Eurasian tour and donate it to charity."

Svidrigailov began to grunt and guffaw. He started coughing, then laughed some more.

"You're funny," said S. "You're very funny. I really need to go to America someday."

The blonde started massaging S's neck with wild spider fingers. She simpered at Rook and Pui-Pui, then went back to spinning her invisible web.

"Ashley, honey, why don't you treat Rook to a visit to the Blue Grotto," suggested S. Ashley sighed then raised her eyebrows and moved over to Rook.

"Only if I can come too, honey," said P.

Rook looked absent-mindedly at his drink, then around the room, and not seeing Hula, said, "Sure, dear, sure."

"Enjoy yourself, my friends," said S. "We will talk more later, after you've had a chance to relax." And S suddenly breezed away past a door that read:

ABSOLUTELY NO ADMITTANCE.

Ashley led Rook by the hand, who in turn led P. They wandered upstairs like a slinky in reverse. *Hot damn!* thought Rook. *But what else can I do?* He peered into the open rooms, trying to find Hula. *Where on earth is she? Why invite me here to Amsterdam?*

"Now, duck your head," said Ashley as they seemed to come to the end of the hallway. "We are about to enter the Blue Grotto—nicknamed after the famous site on the island of Capri."

They plunged underneath a crag of rock and plaster, brushed aside a curtain from beneath which blue light emanated, and suddenly found themselves in a large, vaulted room, with blue crystals sparkling and a strange glowing light cascading up from beneath a pond-like fountain.

"S treats only his very favorite clients here," said Ashley. "You can't even pay to enter this room—it's for guests of only S's choosing. He must really like you."

"That," said Rook, "is what worries me."

Ashley laughed and squeezed Rook's hand, letting her cowboy rope loose from her belt.

"Come on, big rock star," said Ashley. "I'm expecting a whirlwind performance from you. Will you sing me that song 'Black Widow'?"

Rook frowned. "Maybe later." The sort of comment she made about great expectations always worried him. How could he possibly live up to the standards of his Don Juanic reputation? Especially when all he wanted to do now was help Hula. *But how, exactly? How to help?*

"Yeah," echoed P, as both she and Ashley slid the rope around him, tightening it. "We're both expecting a lot, honey!"

"Now. We have to get in this little gondola and row our way across the pond," said Ashley. "Careful! Put the prisoner in the back—dead-weight!"

They steadied themselves on the boat as they gingerly got in. Upon reaching the other shore, they disembarked and Ashley led them to a hidden garden—complete with a bed garlanded with rose petals.

"Take me, I'm yours," mocked Ashley, throwing herself back and opening her arms wide. She began giggling and kicked her feet in the air giddily.

Rook and P looked at each other.

"Well?" asked Rook. "What does your training say about this?"

"Go with the flow," said P, and taking Rook's roped body, they tumbled into Twister-positions. After a while, Rook turned over and laid on his back, looking at the ceiling. The whole bedside was painted with various lovers and their escapades in the style of Caravaggio.

"Um, I'll try one of those," said Rook, pointing to an exotic and kama sutra-looking pose.

Ashley giggled again and the three of them did their routine as the birds at the top of the "cave" looked on. They chirped appreciatively and pooped their sentiments and waited for their mother to return with food.

Meanwhile, Hula was cleaning up upstairs in her very private, marbled bathroom. She methodically showered off the sex of Navy, and then lay down on an Italian couch beneath the open window to catch her breath. As she relaxed on the red velvet, she absently looked at the little nymphs frolicking through the forest in the fresco above her.

What am I waiting for? Why don't I just get out and go? But I can't . . . I'm caught in this circle, fucking for S while he fucks me over. And Rook, God, I don't see how he's going to help anything—it'll probably just make it worse. I give up. I don't trust anybody. Not even Rook. I don't even know him anymore. He's just some famous-ass rock star who's probably sleeping with someone right this second. I don't know. Worst-case scenario? Best-case scenario? I should call my mother.

Hula got up suddenly and splashed some water on her face. Then with a spritzer of her favorite Chanel, she fluffed her boobs like they were stuffed with expensive down (they were) and made her way downstairs to the old-world bar.

When Rook, Pui-Pui, and Ashley finally finished their extended ménage à trois, they bumbled downstairs, not unlike the British sailor, as if stunned by their existence. Rook came to life when he saw Hula standing across the crowded room, drinking vermouth with an olive and caressing S's shoulders. She turned and inspected the rock star descending—sashaying across the red carpet. Rook stopped in his tracks as something strange went through the air. The music was now classical—Haydn—and Rook tried to waltz towards his love, but didn't know how. He stumbled over the last stair and his words got tripped up.

"Uh," said Rook, stuttering.

"Is that the best you can do?" S asked, raising his glass and squeezing Hula's horn. "Honk honk!" And he leaned over and kissed Hula, downing his bourbon as an antiseptic chaser. Hula finished her drink too, then twirled and sucked the ice cube expertly with her tongue.

Ice queen, thought Rook, feeling as if someone had just boxed his ears. He looked down at the bar at the wheat crackers with beluga, then at Hula's hand, which was tugging on the Italian silk sleeve of the S-man.

"I'm sorry, Mr. Svidrigailov, but I can't pretend any longer," said Rook.

Okay, thought Hula. *Here he goes. Be ready for anything.*

Tsai gwai lou! (stupid white guy) thought P, pulling out her cell phone. *Patience, patience, be ready to spring.*

"I've never been a very good actor," said Rook. "My last movie will attest to that. So allow me to sing. I have a new song."

"Great! By the way, I saw that film!" shouted S, surprised at the accuracy of his memory of the Anatoli Anti film, recalling a melodramatic scene not unlike this one at a bar where the hero—Rook—smashed a bottle over his head and then used the broken glass to commit suicide since his girl was now married to someone else.

"Please don't say that. You're embarrassing me," said Rook.

"Well, it's true. But why did you do yourself in at the end? There's plenty of fish in the sea!"

"The script," said Rook. "I just did the film as a favor for Anti."

"Why didn't you say you were friends with Anti? We go way back; I helped him get his start!" explained S.

"Why does that not surprise me?" asked Rook.

S pinched Rook's cheeks. "I like this boy! Entertain us!"

"Fine, Nero, but I can't go on with this charade. The reason I'm here," said Rook, looking at Hula closely and honestly for the first time since high school graduation, "is because of her."

"What?" S leaned closer. "*Brat na pont!* Surely, you are bluffing."

"Why? This lady you so conveniently drape over your shoulder is my first love. We've known each other since high school."

S began to laugh again, but stopped.

"Is this true, darling?" he asked her sternly.

Hula nodded. "It was a long time ago." She massaged S's hand, which was growing tense.

"And so now you've come to her knight in shining armor after all these years?"

"Something like that. So let me sing." Rook began snapping his fingers. "Sitting outside on the steps, sitting outside I see how you're dressed, sitting outside I watch you go by, sitting outside I give you the eye. You go by and you let me go. You go by and you leave me be, you go by and you leave me alone. You go by, I can hardly now see."

S was about to punch him, but Rook only paused for a moment. *I can't believe this fucking guy! But I want to see what he does next!* thought S.

Rook continued: "I gave you my eye so you could live, and now I just can't take it back. I gave you my eye so just kiss me or let me be, cause if this keeps up, I'm gonna have a heart attack."

Rook finished and looked into Hula's eyes for approval. She cast them downwards.

S began to clap. "That was a performance to be treasured! I should lock it and you in my vault—worst acting than in your movie. Hula, don't you agree?"

"It's not what it used to be," she said, and finished off her ice cube.

S studied Hula and Rook, then raised his finger for another bourbon; Pui-Pui studied S's right hand and the way that it moved.

"Let me tell you something," said S, now speaking confidentially to Rook in exactly the same manner that Rook had spoken that morning to Diederik the desk clerk. "Time changes people. The girl you knew in high school is someone else now. She is mine, and I have told you how I don't like to give up things that are mine. What do you care? You're a rock star. You can have any girl you want. But you can't have her. I like to think of Hula as, shall we say, my personal trophy. Every wealthy man needs an attractive woman on his arm, doesn't he? Well, Hula has been mine for the past ten years now, and I don't plan on that changing. It would make me look foolish. And that I can't allow."

Rook ran his hand back and forth along the smooth, polished bar.

"You know, you're lucky," said Rook. "Real lucky. I wish I could change things, Hula, but I can't."

"No, you can't," said S. "Did Hula ever tell you how we met? No? She was twenty-two, tending bar in London. I was building up my holdings in real estate at the time. We started going out, and she expressed to me how she had difficulty in affording a nice flat for her and her daughter."

"Daughter?" asked Rook. "Daughter?"

Hula nodded.

"So, being the gentleman that I am, I let her live in one of my properties. Oh, to be sure, I gave her one of the very best—near Harrod's—to impress her. I also began buying her gifts—clothes, a Ferrari, diamonds, and eventually began to pay for her daughter to attend a very good school. About this time, I had decided to expand my holdings: with the fall of the Soviet Union, many business opportunities presented themselves. With the proceeds from one particularly lucrative investment, I returned to my Dutch roots (I am half-Dutch) and opened up a brothel here in Amsterdam, which over the years has grown quite popular. I needed girls to help attract elite clientele, and I, shall we say, persuaded Hula to help out on that end. Oh sure, of course she was shy, like all the girls are, but now she is one of the elite's favorites."

"But, but how could you subject someone you love to all that?" asked Rook.

"Love? Who said anything about love? I put my properties to use as I best see fit," said S. "Strictly business." And he moved his hand towards Hula's derrière. "Mostly business, anyway." He laughed. "Hell, get over it man. She's done a lot more famous and powerful people than you."

Rook looked at Hula. She smiled at him condescendingly as S rubbed her ass. "Why not let her decide then?" Rook managed. "Hasn't she paid her dues? Why not let her do what she wants?"

"Does an owner let his dog go out and do whatever it wants?" asked S, playing with his bourbon. "Tell you what, I feel for you, kid. I'll let you two catch up on old times; you can even screw her if you want—but you'll have to pay for it. I'm not running a charity around here, huh? You already got one free trip up to the grotto anyway. Listen, I don't keep Hula on a leash. She can leave anytime. But she's smarter than that, aren't you dear? Now, if you'll excuse me, I have some things to do. If you still want to do business, Heisenberg, I'm more than happy. Ciao!" S kissed Hula on the lips, finished his bourbon chaser, and with a flourish, popped an olive, spit the pit, and broke a glass that was teetering on the edge of the bar. He then disappeared behind the NO ADMITTANCE door with two of his men following him.

Rook looked again into Hula's eyes, hoping they would look different now with S gone, but they were the same—cold and distant.

"Pui-Pui," was all Rook could say. She was standing nearby, her back to them, canvassing the room and playing a game on her cell.

"Yes?"

"Will you translate for me?"

"What?"

"I just give up," said Rook. "I don't understand anything anymore." He turned to go, reaching out for Pui-Pui, but Hula's hand caught him by the sleeve.

"Wait," said Hula. Rook stopped and turned.

"I wanted to tell you everything in email," she continued, now whispering. "But I wasn't sure if it was safe."

"Jesus Christ, Hula. Couldn't you have given me a little heads-up? What am I supposed to do? How'd you get yourself into this? It's insane! What does your mother and grandfather say about what you do?"

"Whenever they visit, I simply let them see my modeling. They see me in a photo shoot, or in some magazine, I put them up at some swanky hotel, they see my amazing flat on the other side of the city, my even more amazing daughter, and think all is well."

"Hula! And I thought I was sneaky."

"I'm sorry," she said, leaning her head against Rook's. "Things happen. I just got involved with him; I didn't foresee it turning out this way."

"What happened to you after high school?" Rook asked. "When I moved out to Los Angeles, I tried to get a hold of you, but your family didn't even know where you had gone."

"I moved to London. I was pregnant and didn't want my Mom, Grandpa, anyone to find out. I wasn't sure if I wanted the baby or not, so I just ran away, literally—I had to get away from everything—including you."

"Why?"

"I didn't know if we had a future or not, I don't know, I was just so confused Rook, I needed some distance from everything, a different perspective."

"So you had the baby, huh?"

"Your baby."

"What?"

"Oh boy," said P.

"No," corrected Hula. "A girl. And it's your baby, Rook."

Rook watched the drink go to his lips and then tasted it flow down quickly and lit up a smoke with a long exhale to try and rebalance his universe.

"Are you sure?" asked Rook, his hand trembling. *It'd be hard to play guitar now,* he thought.

Hula nodded. "You were the only person I had been with at the time."

Rook studied his smoke disappearing. "Why didn't you tell me?"

"I wanted to, but wasn't sure what I wanted to do—abort it or keep it. It could have gone either way—I don't know why I chose the way I did. I think I just didn't choose at all, and let things take their course. Oh Rook, you'd love her; she's such a wonderful girl."

"I'm sorry, this is going to take me a little getting used to," said Rook. "I'm a father! You're the mother! Oh Hula, I'm actually happy!"

They hugged and kissed. And then Rook kissed Hula again to remember and so he wouldn't forget. P almost frowned but yawned instead.

"So she must be, what about fifteen?" asked Rook.

"Yes," said Hula. "Her name is Boudicca. After the famous woman warrior, after the book my mother can't seem to finish."

"You finished it. We finished it! Boudicca!" echoed Rook. "Beautiful. Well when can I see her? Does she know I'm her daddy?"

"I haven't told her. She's asked many times, and I said one day I would tell her, but not yet. She thinks S might be her father, but I haven't said one way or the other."

"Geez, let me see her; we can tell her together that I'm her father."

Hula looked at an ice cube in her drink, trying to ascertain any subliminal messages.

"I wish it were that easy."

"It is. You just say, 'Boudicca, we have something to tell you . . .'"

"She's not here, Rook."

"Well where is she?"

"Mumbai."

"Mumbai? You mean, Bombay? What the hell is she doing there?"

"I'd rather not think about it. Listen, about a year ago, I started discussing my desire to get out of this business, to leave, to S. At first, I thought he would be reasonable about it; I should have known better. He called me an ungrateful bitch and beat me, and said he would kill me if I ever left. He said he needed me. The next day, as a sort of insurance policy, he took Boudicca from me, and said if I wanted her back, I'd have to stay by his side."

"Mumbai?"

Hula nodded. She caught her reflection in the mirror behind the bar between bottles of Barrique Tequila and snapped awake.

"It happened so fast. S had some business acquaintances from the Mumbai mafia visiting. And while I was entertaining one, the others took Boudicca. I'm not sure if they're using her for prostitution or not."

Rook gripped his beer mug quite tightly and looked at the flame grow in the candle jar in front of him.

"Okay, you've got to put the sudden father-anger aside, Rook, and actually do something to help. That's why I called you."

"Tell me what to do, Hula."

"You have to go to Mumbai," said P, her eyes barely visible behind her dark hair. "It's your duty as a father."

Rook had forgotten she was even there.

"What other choice do you have?" continued P, looking into a memory. "Hula, of course, would have to stay here, but Rook, you'd go and find your baby. You have to. You know it. I could come and help."

Hula laughed. Rook shook his head.

"It is not like that Hula, you don't understand, Pui, Ming, is a black belt—my bodyguard."

"Really? Well you're just what the doctor ordered. You'd be invaluable." And Hula reached out and touched Pui-Pui's lively hand gently.

"Would you really be able to go with me?" Rook asked P as he suddenly convulsed in a coughing attack.

"Well, I'd have to clear it with my boss; but I'm sure if you paid my fees, they'd be more than willing."

Rook turned to Hula. "Baby, what do you think?"

"Rook, you might call your rock star honies and ho's 'baby,' but don't call me that. Now that said, it's a good idea. It's why I wrote you in the first place. I didn't know how to tell you all this in the email, but I needed you to go after our daughter; I can't—S would kill both of us and bury me under a windmill if I left him—but you can. You must. I can't tell you how many nightmares I've had, how

I've turned this over in my head. I didn't know what to do. Then when you emailed me . . . ."

"I don't know," said Rook. "I don't know what I'm doing anymore." And as if to add insult to injury, another one of his songs came over the PA. Rook put his hands to his head as a Spanish, Penelope Cruz-looking girl gyrated to the beat on stage. *She's pretty hot,* thought Rook.

Suddenly, two customers in the corner, who seemed pretty hot themselves, stopped talking on their cell phones and began firing their multi-functional mobiles at the security. Everyone dove for cover. Back-up bouncers appeared and let out a round of heavy-fire rippity-rippity blast! until the phones fell to the ground, along with their subscribers, letting out a final beep and gasp.

"Everyone all right?" a voice from above demanded. It was Svidrigailov, standing at the top of the stairs. Everyone appeared alright, save for a bouncer with a bullet in his arm. After the smoke cleared, it was apparent that the two gunmen lay dead, their eyes staring up, looking at S. "Damn Yugos, *prishit,*" said S, storming downstairs. He pulled out a Magnum, and apparently aiming as everyone dove again, shot the gunmen's eyes out. "Clean up the mess. Call the police—tell them what happened. I apologize for the rude interruption, my friends. It appears one of my business rivals has tried again to take away my empire. Next time let him send the Carthaginians with elephants rather than Yugos with cell phones! Free drinks on the house! Enjoy yourselves!"

As S turned to go, he practically bumped into P, who somehow manifested herself upstairs. "Well, what are you doing here?" he asked.

"I jumped when all the shooting started," P replied.

"I'll say," said S, placing the warm gun against her cheek. "Like a cat. If you ever need a job in this cathouse, just let me know."

P purred. "I want you." And she took S's hand. Before they disappeared to some dark recess, P turned and winked at Rook and Hula.

"Sleeping with the enemy," said Hula, calculating something. "You've picked a clever girl for a bodyguard."

"I didn't pick her!" said Rook from underneath a blue velvet chair. "They just sent her to my room and things have been going mad ever since."

"I guess it depends on how you look at it," said Hula, dismissively, lighting up a smoke. "She may just be crazier than S, and that's probably what it'll take."

Rook gulped an eyeful of Hula's bosom, which just so happened to be spilling out at him from across an ocean of blue velvet upholstery. He rubbed his hand on the soft, luxurious fabric, and found himself back in high school, in the back seat of his car . . . .

"Hula, baby, I'm sorry . . . I've missed you."

Hula cast a weary look. "So has your daughter."

"Well, what the hell? Why didn't you let me know about her? You know I would have come in a heartbeat."

"Would you have? Weren't you caught up in your rock and roll quest?"

"Well, it looks like now I'm about to get caught up in a more important quest." Rook reached out for Hula's hand—she withdrew.

"I don't know, Rook. I was having so many issues back then. I was dealing with trying to find myself; I still am.

Also, I was having father issues. I had this whole issue with men and them abandoning their fathering responsibility, and I just couldn't deal with you as a father. It sounds messed up, but that's how it was. And then my mom helped get me into Oxford, where I studied economics."

Rook suddenly stood up and brushed himself off. He looked at the bouncers dragging out the bodies of the two dead and eyeless hit men. Evidently, they were from the former Yugoslavia. After the wars, many young men with military experience were suddenly out of work. Consequently, it was easy to hire them to kill someone like S. *Ubermensches* like S were hated by many—personally and professionally. *No wonder he had so many bodyguards,* thought Rook. He couldn't help but notice one of the deceased had a pair of curled Russian dress shoes on—just like a pair he had sitting in his closet in Beverly Hills. He thought of his home and his comfy coffin and was glad it wasn't quite time yet for pennies on his much sought-after baby-like eyes.

"Hula, how do you put up with this? How can you live in this madhouse?"

"What choice do I have?" she asked, rising. "What, go and get my doctorate and teach economics?"

"Why didn't you? Why didn't you continue with school, instead?"

"I had bills to pay and a daughter to raise. I didn't have that luxury. Supply and demand, baby, supply and demand."

"But that's what I can't get over! You knew I was loaded by the time you hooked up with $ for bucks. Didn't you?"

Hula nodded.

"Then why on earth didn't you just call? I don't understand."

"I guess I was tired of you. We had our thing, but it ran its course."

Rook looked at Hula as if she were one of those women he caught sight of over the years at concerts and mistook for her—*but it was her!*

"You're right. It's all over. It's been all over forever now. I guess I was holding out some little spark of hope— for a return to a magic time—but it doesn't matter. All that matters now is getting Boudicca back."

"Yes. Just don't do anything foolish."

Rook bent forward to kiss Hula on the lips; she turned her head and he caught her ear and the gold Byzantine hoop earring that hung from it and blew into it. She backed up, pushing Rook away as a bell began to ring.

"I have to go," said Hula. "Time for the frolick."

"What?"

"You'll see. Find her. Promise me. She's all I got."

"I'll try."

"You have to do more than that." She looked at Rook's shabby shoes with disappointment and doubt then disappeared.

Before Rook could take in what had just transpired, the DJ interrupted his feeble thoughts.

"Now, if you don't know the game, people, here it is," explained Franco from behind his turntable. "Our lovely ladies will be disguised as nymphs frolicking through the imaginary fields—a bush here, a bush there. If you decide you're in, throw in 100. You will be led by one of our escorts, blindfolded, to pick out one of the ladies-in-hiding. When you make your choice, if you find a girl that is, you'll be able to partake in a quick frolick upstairs. Any questions? Let's roll—!"

At first, just like the earlier contest, no one was eager. Then, a smattering of cajoling and peer pressure convinced several so-called men to enter into the hunt. Suddenly, as if raised by Adam Smith's invisible hand, Rook's arm shot up into the air. *If only to have some time with Hula,* he tried to explain to himself.

Rook tossed out 100 euro as the escorts came round. A Rubenesque one approached, smiling magnificently. Rook gave her an extra 100, whispering: "Lead me to Hula."

"I'll try," she said, kissing Rook on the cheek and pocketing the tip. She pulled out a black velvet blindfold and tied it round the rock star. "I'll bet you're used to this," she said.

"Not really," said Rook, feeling the cloth tighten around his head and catching an odd scent of shellac.

Some light, anachronistic piano music began—Glenn Gould—and suddenly an air of caprice fell upon the red-lit brothel.

"Let's go," said Rubenesque, pulling Rook by his aging hand.

Oh this is most strange. I'm in an Edgar Allan Poe story. Floating through a David Lynch movie, thought Rook. And unbeknownst to him, electric eyes gazed out from his pendants as he went through what felt like car-wash flaps––entering an antechamber—catching a scent of Hula.

***

Oh this is most strange. I'm in a poem by Catullus. Floating through some twisted Kurusawa film, thought P.

She sat tied up, hands behind her back, in a red metal chair, that she had to admit, matched the Bauhaus furniture. They were on a whole different level—actually, in the building next door. They had traversed a little Japanese garden bridge, and up a metal reverse-spiral staircase and into a sort of tea-ceremony room that opened as S put his hand to the reader and which then opened into a large white mod-pod.

There was artwork all about the loft. Some hung on the walls, but most was propped and in the process of being prepped with frames, waiting perhaps for a particular buyer. What looked like a Picasso caught Pui-Pui's eye.

"Is that real?" she asked S of the large, blue-period painting.

"Are you?" he retorted.

P pulled out her cell phone from her back pocket.

"You see this?" she asked, hopping around. "Would you say this is real?"

S peered at it nonchalantly, putting on his best gloves. "Looks it. Who you gonna' call? No reception here."

She pressed pound and fired a bullet above S's head. It went through the Picasso.

"Cubism has seen better days," said S, sighing, then studying P like he was going to paint her.

"If that Picasso were real, you would have probably be more upset now, yes?"

"You're right," laughed S. And he looked at her, really looked at her for the first time. "Who are you? What are you doing with that rock star idiot?"

"What are you doing with a roomful of fake master-pieces?"

"It's a good business. Do you realize how many fakes are in museums today? Some are known to be fakes, but the curators don't want to disclose because of obvious embarrassment. Many, they just don't know they're fakes or they're not sure. The best way to close the deal, however, is to sell off one fake in a package deal along with at least two genuine articles. It makes it more plausible."

"I'll give you something plausible," said Pui-Pui, stretching out her foot as far as the knots would allow. "Just come here and let's conduct some business."

"So, you're charging me after all?" laughed S, approaching. "A girl after my own heart. You really should come and work for me."

"I'm an independent contractor. I only work for my own conscience."

"I don't know what that is." And he ripped off her blouse.

"Pay me first," said Ming.

"The Picasso is yours."

"It's fake."

"So are you. Who are you?"

"I told you. A contractor. And after I find out where Boudicca is, I'm going to kill you."

S stood up from his crouch and laughed openly. "You tease!"

"I was a little girl once too. All alone. But I'm not little anymore."

"What? Who's paying you? Hula? She would never."

"The universe is paying me; I work for my conscience. All else is provided for."

"Sounds Buddhist."

"Shaolin. Now meet my invisible army."

And suddenly Ming was out of her ropes and had them around S's neck.

But then she felt a cut; she pushed him and backed away, looking at her bleeding thigh.

"Have you heard of female genital mutilation? It's a very sad practice; you see it still taking place in some of these third world, backwards-countries. I, however, believe that some of these old traditions are worth preserving."

And S sashayed closer with the knife, bending down upon his knees, aiming his gun towards her head. Ming studied his hands.

"Don't worry, my dear, while you may not feel any pleasure, I certainly will."

And S's blade traced the air with the cut he was about to make; P, of course, was not about to have any of this, and so before the delicatessen lesson, she sprung, kicking his potent hand and pretzling her legs around his neck, flipping him behind her. He landed with a thud on the concrete floor and groaned. She took the ropes she had been tied in and began to spider him up as he lunged feebly at her with another little knife he'd had hid in his shoe; she smacked his hand and the weapon flew toward the fake Picasso, sticking there with a panache and boldness that would have made Pablo proud.

"What are you doing?" asked S.

P smiled. "Making good on a promise to women everywhere."

She tied a Gordian knot around S's hands, legs, and mid-section; the more he struggled, the tighter it became. "Ow! This is unreasonable!" he shouted.

"Oh, I'm sorry," said P in mock apology. "I forgot something. Be right back." She scurried over to pick up the knife he had flaunted. As she was near the Picasso, she cut out the Cubist face of the old grandfather in the portrait, and brought it over to S. "You can wear this," she said, with apparent delight. "We'll make it a party! I love to party party. I love to party party," she sang, shaking her hips. She cut a thread off the rope and used it to tie the mask around S's face. "There, that's an improvement. Now, for the final touch. I'm going to do something to you that I bet a lot of women have wanted to for a long time." She ran the blade around his privates. "Oh, and by the way, thanks for giving me the idea! Your karma is served. The wheel of *dharma* has turned, and what else? Oh, do you have one you'd like to add?"

S gasped for breath. "What the hell have I done to deserve this?" he screamed.

"Plenty, I'm sure."

The knife gleamed sharply from the bright lights overhead. S quivered like a baby.

"Please don't," he said. "I have lots of money."

"And I have lots of anger," she said.

And with a swift, figure eight motion of the blade, P castrated S. Blood spurted out in a small geyser.

"Whoops, we can't have that now, can we?" stated P. "Apply pressure to the wound!"

"UGGGHHHHHHOWWWWWWWWWW!!!!!!!!!!!" yelled S, turning blue and red—a strange mix of Dali and

Pollock which would have fit quite well on S's modernist wall.

P ripped off the not-so dapper don's shirt and tied it around his mangled manhood to stop the bleeding. As she did so, she noticed a strange tattoo on his chest. She couldn't decipher it completely, but recognized it as a sign of having been in the Gulag. She held up his family jewels and looked at them, trying to get the light to reflect off them just so.

"No," she said, "I'm sorry, that just won't do. We can't have that on exhibit. That, my friends, is what we here in the trade call a sad sack."

P punctuated S's gonads behind her, hearing them splat, and walked away, ready for the next logical step in her quixotic mission. But somehow her wary eye caught something of worth—almost calling out to her for help. She looked towards the little voice ("I need rescuing too!"), and went to the middle of the room where it hung on the wall—a Van Gogh—a couple walking intimately through a garden setting.

"Now I've never seen this one before," said P. "But I feel it's real."

S coughed and tried to say something, but couldn't.

"What's that?" asked P. "Huh? You're not so tough after all, are you? S! What kind of pretentious name is that!"

"Please don't take that," he pleaded, straining, looking up from beneath the fake Picasso mask that had gone askew from all his writhing. Sitting ballless and bloddy, Indian-style, on the edge of lunacy, he reached out a macabre finger.

"It must be real then, huh?" asked P.

"It's been in my family; my mother, it's all that's left of her. And I'm saving it for someone special."

"At least you had a family," said P, buzzing open the not-so secure door and walking out, Van Gogh under her arm. "You better bandage up that boss of yours," said P to the bouncer who was pacing in the hallway. His double-chin dropped and so did he as she busted his chops.

***

That's her perfume, I know it, thought Rook.

"Stop. This is the one," Rook told Rubenesque.

"Are you sure?" she teased.

"Are you? Come on, for God's sake."

Rubenesque guided Rook's callused fingers towards the nymph. "Touch her. Feel her," said Rubenesque. "Make her sing!"

Rook went directly for her face, reading it, matching it to the sculpture in his memory; *yes this is definitely Hula's face. Surely this is sacrosanct.*

"This is Hula," said Rook, ripping off his blindfold.

And so it was! Hula smiled, took Rook by the hand, and together they began to frolick towards the upstairs. Rook caught that wild look in Hula's eye and felt glee, surprised that everything was going his way.

Then suddenly there was a pull in the other direction.

"P!" shouted Rook. "Let go! Can't you see we're busy?"

"We have to go!" urged P. "Now!"

The look on her face was such that Rook didn't question her. Hula turned pensive, yet still clutched onto Rook's hand.

"Find Boudicca," pleaded Hula, her veil of steel finally dropped. "Find our baby girl. She's all I have."

"Are you going to be okay?" asked Rook.

P awaited Hula's response. *How does she put up with S?* thought P.

What has she done? thought Hula.

"Of course," said Hula. "I'll be just fine. I'll keep S pre-occupied."

"Oh he's preoccupied, all right," said P. "He's going to need some nursing, if you know what I mean." And P smiled—something passed between the two women.

Hula smiled too and reached out and touched P.

"You two be careful," said Hula. "I'll be praying for you." And she leaned over to kiss Rook. Their lips met and they both closed their eyes, and for a moment, time stood still—or even went backwards towards high school. If you were an impartial observer that evening and happened to catch this kiss of this famous rock star with this high-class hooker, you might attest to the aura that seemed to surround them.

Hula and Rook exchanged one long look as he glanced back—he and P running wildly out the door. *I remember that look. I remember,* thought Hula. *I wonder if I'll ever see them again.*

Rook and P nodded confidently and pleasantly to the one brother bouncer smoking outside and strode towards the Rolls as calmly as possible.

"Excuse me?" said the other brother, just coming out. "What is that you are holding?"

"What, this old thing? Just a gift from your boss, that's all," said P.

Both brothers hesitated, pondering.

"Do you mind if we see it?" they asked, reaching out for the artwork.

"Not at all. It is beautiful, isn't it?"

And the bouncers held it up: the magical couple and the thick vibrant colors sparkled beneath the midnight moonlight.

"Quite a good fake if I do say so myself, huh?" said P.

"It's so nice of your boss to treat us like this. I get a lot of cool presents, but this one is definitely unique!" said Rook, putting on the charm times ten.

"It is good," the bouncers said, looking down at it, then back up at Rook and P. "You must have really gotten on his good side," they said. "S rarely passes out his artwork to people. He makes such a secret of his hobby. But he is talented, isn't he?"

"Why yes!" exclaimed P. "I will be showing this to some friends who are 'in-the-know'; I'm sure they'll appreciate his craft!"

"Hey, can I have your autograph?" asked one of the bouncers of Rook. "I've been a fan for years. My brother's not so big a fan though." And the other nodded.

"I just don't like it," he said. "It's not very soothing. I like to relax when I listen to the music, and this makes me not at all relaxed. I like to feel numb."

"Of course," said Rook, taking the menu and pen he was handed by the bouncer. He began scribbling his name next to the description of the veal cutlet. "I understand completely. I'm not relaxed at all, so why should my art be?"

And Aert pulled up with the Rolls.

P, taking advantage of this, quickly snuck behind the bouncer and nudged the Glock off the ledge with the aid of Vincent. She placed it in her pocket then put her arm around Rook.

"Good night," P said to the bouncers. "It's been a blast!"

"Good night!" said the bouncers in unison, smiling. The one looked at Rook's autograph, happened to also read the description of the "moist and delicate" cutlet—"from only the youngest, finest cuts of meat"—and suddenly was hungry.

"How'd it go?" asked Aert, looking in his rear-view as they eased away and reaching over to show them his baby pictures that he had so longed to show them.

"Hurry," said P. "But don't attract attention."

Suddenly the bouncers could be heard yelling after them. *"De ballen, bitch, de ballen,"* yelled the fan, the well-read one. The illiterate twin stood silent, searching for words that didn't come and throwing his fist in the air.

"Opgeilen!" said the erudite brute. And they began running in vain towards the speeding Rolls.

Aert squealed around the corner and sped off before the two brothers had a chance to fire.

Upstairs, S crawled about the floor naked, holding his once fine Swiss Eton dress shirt to his privates to stop the bleeding, and searching for his testicles. *"Godverdamme,"* he mumbled, spitting something disgusting.

"What is it, boss?" asked the recovering bouncer, stumbling towards S in a serpentine fashion. "What happened? I called downstairs for them to get her."

"Op z'n sodemieter geven!" shouted S. "First, help me find my balls. Then call my doctor. Then find that kung fu bitch and bring her to me alive. I'm going to enjoy cutting her up and eating her in a sushi roll." S stopped suddenly and sat upright, gently picking up one of his bleeding, mutilated genitalia. He brought his fat finger to his mouth, licking it clean. "Needs a little salt," he said, thoughtfully.

"Besodemieterd zijn," mumbled the bouncer, getting down to assist S with his strange quest. "He's out of his mind," he repeated, shaking his head.

Capri Club Documents[*]

* At the conclusion of this chapter a monogrammed envelope (with the Capri Club's logo—CC) containing assorted information regarding the establishment was inserted. Some of these records were trivial, such as the impressive wine list, some perhaps more important, such as tax records, and some possibly damning, such as tape recordings ordering mob hits, and documentation of other illegal activities, such as human trafficking, organ trading, drug dealing, money laundering, as well as art and internet fraud. These files were subpoenaed, and are under current multiple investigations by Dutch, Russian, Indian, and American authorities. Once again, it is unclear how the original author obtained these papers.

7

RECAPITULATION

Rain began to fall as Aert drove the Rolls down Prinsengracht—past the Anne Frank House. Rook turned his head and studied the old building.

"Are you going to tell me what the hell happened back there?" Rook asked P, picturing Hula and the chaos she was left to deal with.

"I just wanted to see what we were dealing with—with S. So I made a move. I discovered he's into forging art, though that seems to be real back there," she said, nodding at the Van Gogh. "He's sadistic."

"Van Gogh? I wouldn't—"

"No, Svidrigailov! He wanted to perform an FGM on me."

"What's that?" asked Rook.

"Female Genital Mutilation," responded Aert. Then, after a pause: "I read a lot while I'm sitting, waiting."

P began drawing with her supple finger upon the foggy window. "I got the best of him though and gave him the karmic boomerang."

"What?"

"I cut off his crown jewels."

Rook took a deep breath. "Tell me, do you think he's mutilated Hula? Or my daughter?"

"Who knows? It wouldn't surprise me. But he'll be out of our hair now."

"For how long? Goddammit! I hope you didn't make it worse."

"Sometimes you need to stir up the pot, break open the pool table so you can get a shot."

"And evidently you got one in. I just hope it wasn't the eight ball."

"No, it wasn't that big."

"Do me a favor," said Rook. "Arrange our tickets to Mumbai for the day after tomorrow. I need to do some thinking, and some walking. I need to—"

"No problem," said P. "But you mean tomorrow. It's already today."

"Yes, yes," said Rook, and he heard the church bells chime 3AM.

They drove back to the hotel—the rest in silence, save for the rain, which hypnotized. Rook watched the windshield wipers—shleep, shleep—then found himself alone in his expensive suite, listening to the pitter-patter and counting sheep, feeling the tears come as he thought about his colossal failure as a father. Ignorance is no excuse . . . .

He awoke, thinking he was in Beverly Hills. But the ceiling here was much higher and full of character. Why didn't I take P to bed? He put out his hand, imagining her there. *What am I thinking?* And he tried to force himself to think of Hula. Instead, he found himself picking up the phone and calling P's room.

"P?"

"Yes."

"Hop on over. I miss you."

"You're insane."

"Maybe. But life is short. Bring the Van Gogh."

P arrived with celerity, munching a celery stick and holding Van Gogh's garden lovers nonchalantly with her free hand.

"Do you think it's real?" asked Rook.

"Who know? It's fun not knowing. Anyhow, what is real?"

"That old question again." Rook smiled without contrivance. "I like you."

"I like you too. But we have a mission. Let us not forget that."

"I've never had a bodyguard like you."

"I've never had a bodyguard," said P. "Listen, I'm here to help you. I want to find your daughter too. We leave bright and early tomorrow." Pui placed the Van Gogh above the bed. "In the meantime, let's get comfortable."

"Yes," said Rook, playing with his pendants.

"What's those?"

"These? Oh, just some jewelry."

"Let's see." P handled them with curiosity, then opened one of the lockets. "What's this?" She held up the paper football with the numbers.

"Oh, just some thing—model number," said Rook.

"No, let me see the other." And P opened the other pendant. "Oh!"

4	9	2
3	5	7
8	1	6

"Who gave you these?"

"I don't know, who cares. Some girls."

"These are magic squares."

"What's that?"

"They've been around for thousands of years. This one here, I know: it's classic—Lo-Shu. There's an old story about a turtle carrying in the birth of the universe—order from chaos—with this strange pattern on its shell. It's also connected to *I-Ching*, Taoism, Buddhism, perhaps maybe the you know whatisit Feng Shui, astronomy, and even synchronicity, DNA, magic. Anyway, the numbers add up the same in any direction, see? Fifteen! It's supposed to bring good luck."

Rook looked with mild interest.

"I see. We could use it. But who cares? What's the point? It's nonsense."

"What makes you so sure? Why would someone put these in here?"

"I don't know."

"Unless they're trying to protect you or give you a message or something. These squares are sometimes used

as talismans and guides to figure out what to do. Maybe
we should cast yarrow stalks . . . ."

"Oh, come on, P," said Rook, yawning. "It's *your* job to
protect me and guide us to India." And they rolled around,
snuggling beneath the covers. Still, P wondered if she had
an *I Ching* handy. *No. But I should buy one,* she thought.

***

Across the sea, Aitchkiss took a break from his work
and paced about his office, wiping his brow, careful not to
open the boils. *What on earth? Magic squares? Goodness
gracious!*

***

At some point Rook awoke with a jolt and crawled out
of bed, sitting half-naked on the ledge of the window,
blinding his eyes against the sun.

"It's too bright," he managed, coughing.

"It's noon; you've overslept," said P, sitting in her
luxurious hotel bathrobe, hunched over the computer.

Rook stared at the Van Gogh. "Who knows," he said.
"Who knows?" And suddenly he got up, jumped up, and
spruced up. "I'm going for a walk. I'll be back later."

"That's what they all say," said P. "I'm looking up that
other square on the internet. It's from a famous engraving
by Dürer. It's called a Jupiter Magic Square—it corre-
sponds to that planet numerologically with the number 34.
It says a bunch of other stuff here . . . about Agrippa—the

square's been used for centuries, especially to protect artists from melancholy and increase joviality."

"Perfect, by Jove," said Rook. "But what does this have to do with finding my daughter?" And Rook stormed out angrily, not knowing why. Suddenly, he remembered speaking of Agrippa with Hula's grandfather, years ago in the old man's library, pulling down a tattered an old leather-bound volume entitled *The Occult Philosophy*. He flipped through its moldy pages—it smelled of the sea.

"What's this?" Rook asked Grandfather. Grandfather Kentucky peered through the cigar smoke he himself had created.

"Oh, that! Well, I suppose you could say it's a book searching for answers, attempting to unearth hidden knowledge," he answered, setting down the book on Einstein he was studying. "A very early version of the grand unified field theory, at least in Renaissance terms. But unless you want to go on an endless search, put it away! Can't you see we're fish swimming in the water and we can't be objective about anything? Goodness, your own name should tell you that!"

"Geez," said Rook to himself, venturing outside the hotel. *Just 'cause my last name's Heisenberg doesn't mean I know anything about the observer effect.*

P scrolled on her laptop, studying *Melencolia I*, trying to figure out what it all meant. *But where does the ladder go?*

Rook bought a cheap map and planned his route to the Van Gogh Museum. It took him forty-five minutes to walk there. He watched the river and canals flow by as he went and tried to let everything go like they did.

Waiting in a short line in front of the modern structure, he lowered his dark shades and inspected his reflection in the glass. *Am I that transparent?* Buying his ticket, entering the building, he was struck by the architecture, but didn't know how to articulate the effect. The creations of the different designers suggested a *Gesamtkunstwerk*, or synthesis of various ideas that entered into a dialectic. Rook wandered about the halls, marveling at Vincent's passion and intensity. The painting back at the hotel had that same intensity, it seemed to Rook. He looked into the eyes of the self-portraits, and wondered if his art would be remembered whatsoever in posterity. *It matters not.* And déjà vu took hold, and suddenly Rook was back in high school in the library in Iowa City, mirroring these same thoughts as he looked at a coffee table book of Van Gogh and carved his and Hula's initials into the old wooden table top.

He sat shaking outside in the Museumplein for a while, staring at the fine gravel, kicking absent-mindedly at it, watching the dust sail away. He felt a song coming on, and got up to allow it to ferment. Following his nose, and an ancient smell from the collective unconscious, he stopped by a *herringhuis* stall and ordered one of the little fishes that had been stewing in a jar of pretty pickles. Munching a little, creating a mess on his Ben Sherman shirt, trekking his way across town, following the canals, he felt like he was going in circles, so periodically perused his map, and stopped to buy a Cohiba, lit it up and puffed puffed away, then suddenly pretended to tie his shoes so not to be bothered by some fans who seemed to recognize him, and eventually he landed on the doorstep of old Rembrandt's House. He almost knocked on the imposing door, as if calling upon an old friend, but then blushed and crossed the threshold, wondering what Hula was doing right this instant (she was just waking up, drinking instant coffee, and thinking about Boudicca). Passing his hand over some of the old, do-not-touch articles, Rook was amazed at the feeling and accuracy of portrayal in the old master's works, and intrigued by his work studio. *Rembrandt had an uncanny ability to capture people's inner world so subtly. But what's with the armadillo?* And Rook reached over the rope to pick it up and feel it in the hope that some genius would rub off on him.

The song was still forming in Rook's hemispheres as he jaunted down the jeweled avenue of the diamond district. He stopped for cappuccino and a *broodje*, and asked the waitress for a pen and something to write upon. She frowned (she was very conservative and did not approve of Rook or his rock music and believed he would go straight to hell but she wanted a good tip from this rich man to help pay for her daughter's birthday present—a new piano), and procured for him a smooth-flowing pen that she had stolen from some hotel (in retribution for the bed bugs) and an order pad. Rook ordered up one song from his muse, but she was slow in coming and he wrote only two words ("Oh girl—") as he inadvertently knocked a tat of his frothy, cinnamon-topped shot upon the lined form by wobbling the wobbly tabletop and then he thought of Hula again. He gave up, gave a big tip (the waitress promoted him to purgatory) and walked towards the Anne Frank House. After touring the heartbreaking exhibition that was an all-too-present reminder of the suffering in the world—of man's inhumanity toward man—Rook plopped down outside on a bird-shit covered bench and looked up at the house and the gray, darkening sky. *Anne lived in that little attic with her loved ones as prisoners in hiding for some two years, pouring her heart and hopes out in her diary. What good have I ever done? What use am I? I need to save her; I need to save Boudicca.*

That evening, as Rook returned from his quixotic warm-up, he called room-service and ordered a Caesar Salad and a coffin. He paced back and forth, looking out the window at the lights of the city reflected off the Amstel River.

The hotel was use to filling the unusual requests of rich, eccentric clients, but Mr. Vruchtwater had to raise one superfluous eyebrow when he heard this. But this is why he was made manager in the first place: for discreetly, rapidly, reliably, and impeccably arranging for the most bizarre needs of the world-weary elite. And so he quickly called the man who had arranged his own mother's funeral three years ago. The mortician, a Mr. Jet Van der Wick, was a craftsman of utmost care, precision, and business savvy. He constructed coffins that appeared to be incredibly well-made and expensive, and indeed they were. He had learned a special technique of working with the best woods, oils, paints (and bodies), from his father, and his father's father, and so on.

When Jet had heard that the Genteel had a client who desired the very best coffin, not to repose in, but to recapitulate in in his penthouse suite, Jet shook his head. But business was business, it would be good celebrity magazine word-of-mouth—plus he would get the coffin back!

Jet lovingly carved his initials on the upper-right corner of the solid mahogany box, as he always did with his work, had his helpers pack it in bubbly styro poppers, and placed it in the back of the truck. His workers were surprised when he announced that he too wished to accompany them on this delivery.

So when the big diesel pulled up in the front of the old money Genteel Hotel around eleven that evening, and they started unloading the casket, Vruchtwater swiftly intercepted them.

"You can't bring this in this way!" he shouted, then with resumed tact: "Come, follow me." And he led the pallbearers with two flashlights, passing distinguished and confused stares, to the side of the hotel—the freight elevator.

"Vrucht, how are you?" asked Jet.

The two embraced as the lift closed and began rising.

"I'm fine. Thank you for fulfilling this, ah, unusual request. And so quickly!"

"My pleasure!" said Jet, with a bit too much enthusiasm. "Do you think this will do?"

"I don't know," said Vruchtwater. "I told you what he told me—but you know how these people can be."

Jet nodded. He had made so many alterations over the years—some even after the deceased had been buried— that not much surprised him any more in the desire for aesthetic abodes after the living had used up their space.

Suddenly all Vructhwater could think of was his mother. Any associated idea or object would often send him into reverie. But now seeing Jet, this flood of recollection poured all the more heavy. Vruchtwater pictured the last time he had seen his mommy, and how he had been uncharacteristically abrupt and rude, yelling at her even though it was his fault for missing the exit at the airport. Of course he apologized and told her he loved her, but he couldn't believe what an asshole he had been and he didn't even know why. She had always only been good to him and the whole family. He felt like jumping out the window right now just thinking about it as they wheeled the box out onto the top floor, but the window had bars on it.

They pushed it towards Rook's room, listening to it go squeak-squeak. Knocking on the door, with an odd feeling of delivering a living man—a living legend—his coffin— they waited.

"Hallo," said Rook, greeting them with open arms. "I see you have my request. Poopjean, you're indefatigable."

"I'm not sure if that's the right use of the word, but I'll take that as a compliment, sir." And he wondered how Rook knew his first name (which he himself avoided using).

"Where would you like it?" asked Jet.

"Right over there," said Rook, "next to the window."

"They wheeled it over, unpacked it, and dumped thousands of little styro pops on the floor. Rook jumped in the pops.

"I'll have someone clean those up momentarily," said Poopjean.

"Indeed! Indeed!" said Rook.

"Does this meet your demands, sir?" asked Jet, leaning forward for Rook's reply.

Rook inspected it closely. He decided to put on a show for them. He looked under the coffin, knocked on it, smelled it, checked the corresponding angle in relation to the river's flow, licked the wood, traced Jet's monogram, then finally laid down in it and shut the cover.

"You'll need to cut a few ventilation slits in it," said Rook. "But other than that, a piece of worthy craftsmanship."

Jet smiled.

"May I use that as an endorsement?"

"Well," said Rook, popping out of the box. "I've endorsed guitars, clothing, and sundry other items, but coffins are a new market. Why not?"

"We refer to them as caskets now in the trade. More gentle."

"But 'do not go gentle into that good night,'" said Rook, smiling.

"May I venture to ask, sir," said Poopjean, "what your use of this is?"

"Sure. I use it to recapitulate. To review my life. Not just cerebrally as at the psychiatrist's, although he does have me do that, but emotionally, with all my senses. My shrink said it would do wonders. At first, I thought *hell no,* but it actually helps me focus. It helps free me and clear myself of blockages that keep me from achieving all I want to do. Why wait till you are about to die to review your life? Should not one have a constant reminder of that final appointment, so that one might live one's life so they can be the person they always wanted to be and not just some half-hearted has-been? The next step would be to be buried in the earth, somewhere in the middle of nowhere, with a straw sticking up for air, and have a friend monitor me for 24 hours. But I'm scared."

Poopjean nodded: *he's truly mad,* he thought. Jet did too: *I hope more people take up this fad. More money and I'll retire early to Tahiti.*

"We're all scared, Mr. Rook," said Jet. "And that comes from someone in the business for years!"

"Now, if you'll leave me to my exercises," said Rook. And he ushered them out of the room.

Rook lied down in the box and began thinking about his life in terms of places he had lived. He began with his current mansion and worked his way back to how he got there. He allowed the memories to come. Suddenly he was reliving an experience in his hometown of Iowa City: it was his parent's place while he was in high school, and he was making love with Hula in the basement.

"Wait," said Rook, "I think someone's coming down."

They heard footsteps about, which stopped in the laundry room, shuffled about, turned on the dryer, and left.

"If a sock gets lost, I bet it comes out in a parallel universe," said Hula, smiling. Rook saw the sparklight in her eyes.

"We're each our own universe," he said. "Orbiting each other."

Rook forgot himself in Hula. Now and then he would open his orbs to see if she were forgetting too. Sometimes her eyes were open, sometimes closed, sometimes rolling back in her head.

Rook rolled his precious orbs at this memory. How could he have impregnated Hula and never have known about it? Why would she keep it a secret from him for fifteen years? What was the exact moment of conception? *My boys can swim . . . .*

He drifted off, instead of recapitulating, into thoughts of what his daughter looked like. *Where in Bombay is she? How on earth am I going to rescue her and get her away from the mafia? And what the hell is the deal with P?*

They would have to devise a plan. They couldn't just go down there without the faintest idea. Or perhaps they could follow the threads and stitch together a picture.

"I don't know," said Rook. "I don't know anything anymore."

He remembered a time when he was in kindergarten when he rode off on his shiny tricycle alone to get an ice cream cone. He enjoyed riding the bike, and didn't think anything of going off by himself. Of course his mother was horribly worried, and recruited a crew of neighbors to search for him. They found him sitting nonchalantly eating pistachio at a parlor about a mile away.

"Rook, I was so worried about you! Why did you do that?"

"Do what?"

"Go off by yourself."

"Ice cream!"

Ice cream! What a great idea!

And Rook shot out of the coffin like he was shot out of a metaphysical cannon, threw some latest fashion on, and strolled out of the hotel with styro pops in his ever-so precious hair.

"Mr. Grits," said Poopjean to Rook on his way out. "I trust that you found your coffin satisfactory?"

Rook smiled and nodded, flipped his mirrors down, and ignored the puzzled looks of the guilty bystanders.

"I'd like a motorcycle," Rook told the doorman.

"Wouldn't we all," the blue boy replied. "I'm sorry, but we don't have any available right now. I can work on it for you."

"See what you can do."

Meanwhile, Rook flagged the Rolls.

"To Dam Square," he told Arthur of the Tight Pants.

"Right away, sir. How has your stay been so far? Pleasant, I hope?"

"In a strange sort of way," said Rook. He lit up a cigarette and blew out his troubles to the wind which began to blow them every which way but loose.

Getting out at the Royal Palace, he told Aert he'd call for him. He walked past a group of people throwing bottles and rocks at the barred windows of the graying building.

"What's going on?" Rook asked a Dutch policeman who was standing at the ready.

"They're protesting a recent policy decision by the government regarding the housing shortage."

"Godverdomme, wat je me nou toch flikt!" swore a young man in a jeans jacket, throwing a little delft windmill which broke to pieces against the bars.

No one seemed to be responding. In fact, no one was even looking out the windows.

Another young lady threw a banana, which lodged itself between the bars. The policeman laughed.

"How come you're not doing anything?" Rook asked the policeman.

"Sometimes it's better to let people express themselves, rather than keep it all bottled up. As long as no one is as you say getting hurt. Besides, the funny thing is they're protesting against a government that's no longer there."

"What do you mean?"

"The Royal Palace hasn't been used as a city hall or a palace in a very long time. It's just a museum now."

And another person threw a red water balloon; it splashed and dribbled down a particularly magnificent architectural detail of the old stone building. Many years ago, a craftsman who had just lost most of his family to a strange disease, lovingly worked his magic and pain and desire into that granite lattice. But no one now knew this, or cared about the people in the dark, distant past.

Rook went off down the Damrak Street for a €1.50 ice cream cone.

Eating it, he wondered what he had accomplished since that little boy was eating that ice cream some 28 years ago.

"Hey, you're Rook!" said a young lady in purple coming out of an Internet cafe. "I was just listening to your song when I was tripping out on mushrooms yesterday."

"Lovely," said Rook. "Did you find the apyschedeline fungi helped you to make progress?"

"Uh . . . ."

"There are better ways to experience the wonders of life," said Rook. "Here, sit down on this bench with me and let's just watch some of the people walk by."

"Okay."

A bum in a brown bathrobe with an acoustic guitar was walking by, then stopped someone and mumbled incoherently in his face. He then broke into a song that went something like: "Fuck off, get a job, I know you want me to leave you alone, it's okay, I'm playin' my ukelele . . . ."

"See," said Rook. "What's that guy's story?"

"I don't know," said purple.

Meanwhile, a small crowd was gathering around a young man in a suit with a tie that was frozen. He too, was apparently frozen, with shades on and a smile on his face, briefcase in hand—running off to God knows where. People laughed and put money in his bowl.

"When does someone decide 'hey, I'm going to stand motionless for hours and people will like it and pay me'?"

"I don't know," said Purple. "When does someone decide to become a rock star?"

"Touché, touché."

Rook got up and disappeared towards the Red Light District, hoping he would run across Mandy again. He wandered the alleys and canals, until he finally remembered where her window was. The curtain was shut.

Rook went into a nearby bar, Popeye's, and ordered a Heineken.

"Oh God, what am I going to do?" he mumbled to the bartender.

"Are you trying to decide on a prostitute?" asked the bartender.

"Something like that," laughed Rook.

He polished his beer, then decided to head back to check on Mandy again. This time, she was there.

"Hi!" said Rook. "Remember me?"

"Of course," said Mandy, smiling. "Rook!"

And she ushered Rook in and closed the curtain.

"Listen," began Rook. "I'm more than happy to pay you, but I don't want sex right now."

"Okay," said Mindy. "What do you want?"

Rook lit up a cigarette and offered one to her. She shook her head no. In that innocent gesture, her hair moved gently—a single, sexy strand hanging down.

Rook cleared his throat. "I just want to talk. Find out your story. How did you come to work here?"

Mandy rolled her eyes and put on her kitschy cowboy hat.

"That's a long story," she said. "It's easier to make love." And she began taking off her top.

"No, really," said Rook. "Tell me your story."

Mandy looked into a distant memory. She hesitated, twisting uncomfortably, then began to speak.

"I was born in Portugal," she said. "I had a normal enough childhood. Catholic school, all-girls' school. By the age of sixteen, I had really developed into a lovely young woman. I had never had sex, but thought about it all the time. My school of course was repressive, my father overprotective, and my hormones raging out of control. I started getting hit on by some of the older boys—you know eighteen, good-looking. One night I was just riding my bicycle—it was a beautiful summer evening. This boy hit on me—he was from Barcelona—eighteen, very handsome. We went down to the beach and had sex. I cried; I felt like I was a bad girl. I made a promise to God not to have sex again or anything until I was married; and even then according to the principles of the Church. My vow lasted a while—I was really serious about it. Then one day I went to confession to get this weight of the loss of my virginity off my chest. The priest was helpful at first—and then went on to say for me not to be so hard on myself. That was helpful too—but then he went on to offer a little too much help—he slept with me, and all my good intentions and faith were crushed. I was lost in a sea of doubt and despair. I started having sex with all sorts of boys— girls too—though I prefer boys—trying to lose myself in the act. I found that if I really got into it—I actually did forget myself and my sadness. My sadness draped over me like a rain that went on and on. The only time the rain stopped was when I was doing it. I escaped to another place where I liked living. I've heard that sometimes actors become actors because they don't like themselves—they escape into the character and become someone else for a time. That's how it is with me with sex. As soon as I turned eighteen, I ran away from home and came to Amsterdam. I decided I would make a living doing the only thing that would help me get through the day. I've been here three years now. But I don't know how much longer I can do it. Realistically speaking, it's not a career move."

And they looked at the garbage can full of used paper towels and condoms.

"I'm sorry," Rook told Mandy. He thought of placing his hand on her shoulder, but didn't.

"It's okay," she said. And she cried a little.

Rook looked at her and couldn't believe that he had slept with her just the other day. She was sitting topless on the edge of the bed, staring at the floor. He started to reach out, then stopped. He stood up and paced about the small little steamy room. He wondered if anyone else had ever paced anxiously about like this in this odd and desperate space.

"What's wrong?" Mandy asked.

"I just found out I have a daughter who was trafficked off to India and might be being held as a sex slave. And I feel so guilty for having slept with you!"

"Oh. I don't know what to tell you," she said. "I'm sorry. Are you going to help her?" Mandy reached out and massaged Rook's shoulder.

"I'm going to try."

"It's your job as a father. Be kind to her when you find her."

"I will," said Rook, extinguishing his smoke and getting out his billfold. "Listen, I like you Mandy. I really do."

"I like you too."

And she placed his hand on her knee.

"So what are you going to do?" Rook asked.

"I don't know. Become a doctor someday."

And then she leaned over and kissed Rook on the cheek.

"You're a good person," said Mandy. "Find her. Then come back and see me sometime." She smiled.

"I have to go," said Rook, giving Mandy three hundred euro. "I feel guilty enough as it is."

"Get over it," she said. "A little guilt goes a long way," she said. And they hugged goodbye. She watched his motorcycle boots trudge out the door. *I'll never see him again,* she thought. She sighed and began fixing her make-up in the mirror. She adjusted her white cowboy hat with a tilt, opened the red velvet curtains, and stood back in the window, leaning suggestively on the frame, facing the endless stream of passersby.

Rook walked down the canals and alleys and past the old church near SexyLand. It and he felt different; it felt seedy and he felt like his feet were sticking to the pavers. He stopped to use a green outdoor spiral urinal, being careful of the eternal puddle of piss.

Suddenly, his cell rang.

He did his best to answer. "Yeah."

"It's P."

"Yeah." Rook heard feet and voices behind him, waiting.

"We're all set to leave early tomorrow morning for Mumbai," said P. "But I need you to do something."

"Yeah."

"I need you to go and see Hula at the Capri. I'd do it myself, but for obvious reasons, I can't. I need you to get as much information as you can about your daughter—pictures—whatever. But be careful."

"Easy for you to say."

"Hey, I've been hiding out very carefully. My training has prepared me for this kind of sousveillance. But don't worry—they're after me, not you."

"Yeah."

"Meet me at the airport at 7 A.M. Be discreet."

"Yeah."

The phone went dead. Rook stared numbly at it and tucked it and another precious item away. Across town, P stared numbly at the self-portrait she had created of herself. It was her, but as a child. *I need to save her, she thought,* thinking of her inner child. *And I need to save Boudicca.*

Rook walked around a bridge three times pacing. He walked past Popeye's Bar, and came across a Harley-Davidson with a Hells Angel insignia. He walked into the kewl joint and strode confidently up to the front, standing upon a stool.

"Hey, who's the owner of that Harley?" Rook yelled.

The bar went dead, the digital jukebox went hush, and everyone looked at Rook in silence. A big fella with a Hells Angel tattoo stepped forward.

"What do you want?"

"I need a bike. I'll pay you a good price for it."

The biker stepped forward.

"You're Rook, aren't you? Hell, I listen to your tunes all the time. I'd be happy to help you out."

Rook and the biker worked out a deal; each thought they had got a steal.

Rook rode off on his new Harley with a smile on his face. He roared the throttle, and made his way down the road.

He rode straight to the Capri Club; rain started to fall again.

"I'm here to see Hula," Rook told the doorman, who pushed aside the bouncer standing next to him.

"Yes, Mr. Heisenberg," said the doorman most politely and cheerfully. He was impeccably dressed—Armani head to toe, and a real gold Rolex. "Please come in. Take a seat at the bar and make yourself comfortable. I'll see if she's available."

Rook took a seat and ordered a bourbon. Before he could even drink it, Hula was walking down the stairs wearing a sexy black negligee.

"I need some pictures of our daughter," said Rook. "I'm going off to find her soon."

Hula kissed him.

"You have another woman's lipstick on your cheek."

"And you have another man's business in your hair. Come on, Hula. I also will need as much information as you can get on exactly where our daughter is now."

"I'll do what I can," said Hula, quietly, pretending to smile, knowing she was being watched. "When do you need it by?"

"ASAP. I'm leaving for Mumbai at 7 in the morning."

"It's going to be a long night," sighed Hula. "Don't worry, though. I'll drop it off at the airport by sunrise." And she kissed Rook on the other cheek, giving him her best *Casablanca*.

Rook gave his best Marlon Brando and slipped out of the place, roaring off on his Rocinante.

From upstairs in one of his many secret rooms, S watched out the window as Rook's red taillights disappeared.

"Follow him," S ordered one of his bouncers. "And see if he leads you to that knife-happy bitch." *If only I could get someone with her skills to work for me,* thought S.

The bouncer nodded his head and left silently, leaving S alone to cup his phantom privates and wonder about the chances of the reconstructive surgery, which was scheduled for tomorrow—promptly at 7 A.M.

Many doctors had been consulted, much money had been offered, but only one physician agreed to accept the job (for some it was not their specialty, other specialists considered it too mangled to attempt and believed it to be dangerous to their own health if they made the situation more "complicated"). The urologist who was to perform the operation, a Dr. Van Halen (no relation to the guitarist), at this very moment sat across town at the hospital and removed S's testicles from the refrigerator. They were kept in the meat section in a mason jar, at just above freezing (next to black Russian beluga caviar), and labeled Svidrigailov in a fancy calligraphy that, Van Halen deduced, must have been written by that pretty new nurse who was always doodling sketches like Da Vinci in a notebook she kept next to her phone. *I wonder if she's single,* thought the doctor. Van Halen, a middle-aged widower, chided himself for taking a fancy in a woman who was probably just a little older than his college-aged daughter. *But I'm so goddamn lonely.* He held Svidrigailov's jewels up, squinted, and put them beneath a large magnifying lense. "Let's shed a little light on the subject, shall we?" the good doctor said to himself.

And if Svidrigailov could have seen the pained look on Dr. Van Halen's face at that moment, he probably would have cancelled the operation and resigned himself to going through life as a eunuch.

***

In Beverly Hills, Aitchkiss read article after article about Lo-Shu and the *I Ching* and Dürer, and finally set down his glasses, lost in deep thought. One of his boils began to run and he dabbed at it with tissue paper. The flimsy paper stuck in bits and pieces all over his sallow face.

"Gladys?" he said, paging his secretary. "I need you to arrange some plane tickets for me. To Mumbai. Tell everyone I'm going on vacation. There should be no record of my travels—I don't want the paper to get in trouble. And see if you can get Monique and Meriweather on the phone."

"Okay, okay, what's the rush?" she asked, coming to the door.

"I'm working, can't you see that? I'm working on something big! Something nobody else knows about! I'll also need you to ring in a favor at one of the studios. I'll need a disguise and a fake passport, medical license. I'm going to be a psychiatrist," said Aitchkiss, looking at himself in the mirror and frowning. Even he didn't believe it.

"Who on earth would go see you for advice?" asked Gladys, adjusting her old pearl necklace.

"It's not me. It's Dr. Cartwright." And he winked at himself. "I'm going to need a very good disguise, indeed."

File on Ted Southhampton[*]

---

[*] At the end of this chapter was an extensive file on Rook's manager. As the reader might guess, I am unable to reproduce the scandalous details here due to the threat of numerous lawsuits. In addition, the Los Angeles Superior Court has subpoenaed the documents and has issued a gag order as the LAPD and other agencies continue their ongoing investigations.

8

BOUDICCA IN BOMBAY

"A motorcycle?" asked a thirty-something and very fashionable attendant from behind the counter at KLM. She gawked at Rook, then fixed her delicate blues on the bright lights of the ceiling, allowing the rock star ample time to take in her splendidly tapered Viktor and Rolk le smoking outfit. She floated out there somewhere with the photons, her fingers no longer properly positioned on the keyboard but revving an imaginary throttle; she pulled at her bleached blonde locks—already windswept by a *Wild One* cruise through Waterland. "Vroom, vroom!"

"It's not just a motorcycle," frowned Rook, tapping a euro on the counter and swaggering calmly. "It's a Harley Davidson and her name is Rocinante."

"Double vroom-vroom! Listen," she stammered, finally returning to earth and looking into the real eyes of the rock star she had stared at in magazines for so many years, "are you supposed to be someone? For if you are, your ego should arrange these things in advance. I like dancing and movies by the way and my favorite of yours is *Free Fall!*" She smiled, then pursed her lips and pulled again at her hair. It had a tendency to rise, subjected to a constant internal electrical charge.

"Is there a problem here?" asked an officer with a guarded accent.

"Not really," said the Dutch Dulcinea. "I'm just starbucks."

"Me too!" said the officer, doing a double-take. "Bring me a latte! Hey, do you remember me?" he asked Rook, smiling and patting his Glock. "My friends just couldn't believe I met you!"

"Of course," said Rook. "You're one of the best. Maybe not *the* best, but one of the best." And Rook gave his best magazine-cover smile.

"Super!" said the politieagent, smiling greatly and reaching out to shake Rook's hand. He shook it vigorously, while Rook felt like taking his Glock and shooting him.

"Vroom!" said Dulcinea, swaying back and forth and staring at something else. She pulled at her collar as if it were about to inflate and carry her away.

"Listen, lady," said Rook, "Are you for real? Cause you're making me mad. I don't mean to be mean, but I need your help. My daughter's in trouble and my bodyguard and I need to get on this plane to India as inconspicuously as possible. Is that possible?"

Their faces froze—actors in a movie caught with unscripted lines.

"Sure," said the officer. "I didn't know you had a daughter. Wait till I blog this! What a story!"

"No, please," begged Rook. "Don't say anything to anybody."

"Okay," said the officer, a little sadly. "Okay. I apologize for acting unprofessionally, but it's not everyday that we meet a superstar."

Suddenly Dulcinea began tapping madly, her fingers positioned correctly on the keys—all business. "I've never been to India," she mumbled. "I never go anywhere."

Rook looked over at P, waiting with her shades on by the ladies' room like an Abercrombie girl on a fashion shoot, and put his hands to his head.

"I'm sorry," Rook said. "I appreciate all your help. God knows I need it."

Dulcinea popped her gum, causing the officer to flinch and place his hand on his gun. "We're here whenever you need us," they reassured the rocker.

Ten minutes later, the Harley was wheeled onto the plane. They also arranged for Rook and Pui to wait in a secret lounge, reserved for celebrities and politicians and people with old money or at least the air of aristocracy.

"So," said P, as they sat alone in the little lair, equipped with a mini-bar and two-way mirror. "Let's see what you've got."

Rook whipped out the white glossy folder Hula had sent over a few hours ago, a Versace-embossed dossier sandwiched in between a copy of *The Interloper*. He opened it carefully and handed P the contents.

"Hmmm," mumbled P.

"What do you mean, 'hmmm'?"

"Isn't that a photo of you?"

"Where?"

Sure enough, at the bottom of the scandalous rag, Rook was walking about the Red Light with the caption: **Rook— "you don't have to put on the Red Light!"**

"It never stops. Okay, what we got?"

"It's an interesting profile. Boudicca—she's pretty," said P, studying the three photos. All had been professionally taken about a year ago, so dictated the date stamped on the back. Rook had studied the pictures earlier that morning, staring at them, wondering what his daughter would say when they met. "Papa! Daddy! Asshole!" She had auburn hair, the color of leaves in the fall, and a mischievous streak in her dark brown eyes. She dressed very Euro with high-style—Hermes purse, Gucci shoes, Versace couture-jeans, colorful Armani outfits—displaying a different color in each picture: blue—a tranquil pose by a fountain (perhaps in the Blue Grotto?); purple—a royal display upon a golden throne; and bright red—a twirling dervish in front of a fireplace. This is the one that disturbed him.

I hope she isn't growing up too fast, thought Rook. *But what am I thinking? I just hope I find her!*

"The only contact here is a Purushottam Petro, Kali Club, Rajahranee Hotel, Mumbai," said P.

"Then let's go there."

P got out her cell phone and called someone. She began speaking in a whirlwind of Cantonese.

Who is this strange woman? wondered Rook. *I've only known her a couple days, but I have such trust in her. Should I?* Rook watched P's body posture. She sat up straight and poised, as if ready to spring into action or explode at a moment's notice. Petite, she had a very firm and toned build, though one would never suspect her to be a lethal weapon. Rook found himself staring at her black leather skirt, and found it hard to believe what transpired the other night. She had the strongest pelvic muscles he had ever experienced. He looked away wistfully through the two-way mirror at the people walking by, some absently, some hurriedly, some lost.

P hung up the phone. "I got us a deal at the Rajahranee; it's an old hotel by the Gateway of India in Mumbai. You probably heard about it in the news a while back—there were terrorist attacks nearby. Anyway, they've fixed it up and it's open for business again. Hopefully, we can find and mingle with the Mumbai Mafiya there."

"I don't want to do any mingling," said Rook. "I just want to find Boudicca and get her out of Bombay as quickly as possible."

P looked at him a long moment, then sat close and put her head softly against his. After a long while, she murmured, "Let's make sure we work together and stay focused. In this business, you screw up one time, and you're dead. It's not as simple as your sport football!"

"What?" said Rook. And he felt like a character in a bad movie by his friend Anatoli Anti.

"Your plane is about to board, Mr. Rook," said the officer. "Come on, I'll take you a special way."

The smartly-pressed uniformed man led them very officially out a doorway, down the tarmac, and drove them on a little golf-cart to the plane. The officer said nothing, but inside he was feeling very special and somewhat important. He tried his best not to smile and thought of yesteryear, when he and his ex danced to The Little Bang.

"I just want to thank you for everything," said Rook as they were led up the stairs to the jet.

"No problem. I am always happy to help some lovebirds."

"We're not 'lovebirds.' Anyway, do me one more favor," said Rook, earnestly. "If some mafia-types come looking for us, just lead them astray."

The officer hemmed, and tried to haw.

"What's going on?" he asked.

"Have you heard of Svidrigailov?" asked Rook.

"Of course!" he said. "Everyone in law enforcement has been trying to get that guy for years. But it's big problem. He's well-connected."

"Yes, well, he's after P here and something she took from him."

"Two things," corrected P.

"Oh yeah," laughed Rook. "Anyway, he has something of mine, which I plan to reclaim. So if he and his thugs come, just tell them we went to Australia or something."

"Well, if I can." The officer looked down at a grate in the pavement, wondering what was down there and where it went.

"Listen, you have access to the flight data?" asked P. "Put Sydney."

"I can try to arrange that," said the officer, looking at P and wondering where she went. He saw pain and sadness there and wondered if she were abandoned as a child too—his parents killed by a malevolent meteorite as they slept. He always thought they should have known better and taken precautions—both being science teachers. But all he could say was, "Sydney. I'll try to help."

"I'll send you some concert tickets," said Rook.

"That'd be great!" And the politieagent regained his boyish smile. *I will take starbucks girl*, he thought, unable to recall the fashionable attendant's name. *But she will expect me to dress sharp. That won't be problem; I'll ask Rook for some of his clothes. It's the least he can do. I'll look like a rock star! But I can't wait forever! I'll talk to him. He'll give us a concert when he gets back. I know he will—that's just the kind of guy he is. Yes, I think she's the one. And to think—Rook brought us together!*

"My God," said P as they were taking their seats and people noticed Rook and started snapping pictures and asking for autographs. "When does the act ever stop with you?"

"Never," replied Rook, matter-of-factly. "Celebrity is a 24-hour business."

"Hmmm," said Pui. "Maybe we can use your fame to our benefit. I don't know how yet, but we'll see. Perhaps your celebrity will help us gain access to places we would not normally have."

"Whatever helps," said Rook. "Whatever helps me find my daughter." And as they hid themselves behind sunglasses and blankets and pillows and magazines and newspapers in the big first class section of the 777, Rook wondered what Boudicca was doing right now. He tried to send her a telepathic message: *Don't worry. Daddy's coming to save you!* And as he did, he couldn't help but notice P inspecting the picture of him strolling through the Rossebuurt, hands in pockets, gawking like a teenager at some lovely bird.

And suddenly it dawned on P that they were sitting in Row 15. *It's nothing,* she told herself. And she went back to reading the paper, wondering if she too would soon be blazoned across the page.

***

Meanwhile, on Falkland Road in Kamathipura in Mumbai, Boudicca sat in a "cage"—staring out at the legs of the passersby. It had just rained heavily—the monsoons were in full swing—and most of the men window shopping splashed mud about, getting their nice clothes soiled. Boudicca wondered what the madam would give her for food today, and wondered if she would get sick again from it. *What day is it? I don't know.* She had lost track many weeks ago, when they started giving her opium to calm her down. Since then, she had been in a state of delirium, and the summer humidity only made it worse.

Across the street, a big black rat scurried by. *Come here, supper! Come here!* During her first month in her little cubicle, the rats scared her. She tried to scare them, banging her water bottle, but after a while she would tire, and they would return, sniffing about and occasionally nipping at her, when she would come alive again and go mad. She managed to kill two and felt bad afterwards, wondering if they had a family somewhere. She was examining a dead one one day, remembering biology class, when a potential and eager customer approached, rapping on her dilapidated and locked door. She turned to look at him with her disheveled hair, and he saw Kali—and he went—fleeing screaming as she bit into the raw meat of the rodent, blood dripping from her purple tongue.

She still had her fears though. Snakes sometimes would slither through the bars, looking for dinner. Once she awoke to something crawling on her leg. She was about to scratch at it, then became cognizant of the clammy skin against hers. She carefully looked up and was eye to eye with a cobra. She remained very still, slowly imitating its head gestures. She had heard somewhere that people subconsciously like you if you subtly mirror them. *Maybe it'll work on this species too.*

Luckily, it did. After a minute, the big monster serpentined out of the cage, continuing its endless crawl.

Boudicca also feared her fate. *What's going to happen to me?* She almost didn't want to imagine—fearing her mind would play tricks on her and make the worst of it. So far, much to her surprise and relief, she had not had sex with any customers. She was "being kept" and would be on display, as she understood it, until she was called back home to Amsterdam. If that didn't work out, she would become available to the men of Mumbai: a rare, Caucasian virgin, for sale to the highest bidder. Every time she was "shown," her pimp or keeper, Abhishek, would whisper confidentially in Hindi to the prospective client about his precious commodity. They would then lean over and peer down into the cage, mumbling *"Acha, acha"*—heads rhythmically swaying back and forth, and the customer would walk away. Boudicca thought she was beginning to understand her mother a bit better.

Two days ago, however, after a particularly violent storm, Abhishek approached awkwardly and dithering, speaking in broken English. Boudicca sat up and saw a Western man soon appear, speaking softly to Abhishek in a British accent about the tempestuous Mumbai weather. He was dressed in an immaculately white suit and a Montecristi Panama hat. Boudicca ran her eyes up to meet this angel, but when he knelt down to peep into the cage and pulled back the brim of his finely-woven hat, she gasped— he was missing an eye and in lieu of it had some strange, gaudy piercing protruding out of the socket.

"Hello, love," he said. "I am a friend of Svidrigailov. You know the man, I take it? He sent me." He now took off his hat completely—inspecting it, turning it, as he waited for Boudicca's response.

"Sure," she said, her voice raspy from disuse.

He laughed and Abhishek echoed him. He stopped turning his hat and glanced at Abhishek, who stopped twittering. He turned back to Boudicca, then said in a most soothing voice, "I'm just checking up on you. And I see you're checking my eye, or should I say, my missing one. Well, let's get over it; just call me Old One-Eye. Everyone else does. Let me ask you something: what are you doing in that cage, dearie?"

"What are all these girls doing in these cages?" she managed, surprised at the strength of her own voice and conviction.

"That's a good question. Unfortunately, we British had something to do with that. Long ago, as we were coloniz- ing here, we set a bad example with our, how shall I put it, our Western propensity for sex à la prostitution. At first, the locals were somewhat taken aback, but now you can see that they've picked up our bad habit, along with many of our others. But that's neither here nor there. My God, have you had a shower?" he asked as a wind swept by, fully revealing the cage's putrefaction.

"They hose me down once a week," said Boudicca.

Old One-Eye stood back up, with some difficulty, and slapped Abhishek.

"What's the meaning of this?" he shouted. "When S gave you her for safekeeping, he meant in accordance with Western standards. This is unfit for a rat." And as if to emphasize this, he kicked a dead one that littered the outside of her cage. "Get her out of there, get her cleaned up, and keep her in a proper room. If you don't, you will be dealt with severely."

"But she is big problem to handle," insisted Abhishek. "You must believe me, yes? When we first got her, we did keep her in a room! But she always tried to escape and would bite us and give us such a time—impossible! Believe me! I am not in the making-up business, I am not the Big B, I am not an actor!"

"Jesus Christ, are you professionals or not? Just take care of it. I will be back soon. At that time, I will decide if you live or die."

Before leaving, Old One-Eye bent down and gazed lazily into the cage with his good eye, very careful not to strain it.

"Get yourself together," he encouraged Boudicca. "S and your mommy can't afford to lose you."

Boudicca nodded rapidly. "Where is mommy? Can I see her soon?"

"Let us hope so," said the man, putting his hat back on and walking away as suddenly as he had appeared.

This was two days ago, and still Abhishek had not moved her. After the incident, Abhishek confided to her that she would be relocated soon, and that although he might seem like a villain to her, he was really just acting. "You see, I have to play this part. I don't like it, but I have a family. And I would like to be an actor for real someday up there with the Big B! My name will be in the lights and you will see me the singing too! This I promise you! *Acha!*"

But aspiring actors make many promises, and often don't deliver. Boudicca wondered if he were still alive. She went to pee in her green plastic bucket, which at one time apparently contained Cartier jewels and watches, or fake Cartier products. She imagined the elegant items that use to occupy the container, when suddenly the door of her cage was being unlocked by mysterious and agile hands. Quickly finishing—she moved so fast that the bucket fell over and spilled on her makeshift bed.

"Let's go, let's go," said Abhishek, who was with a man she had never seen before. He was a good six inches taller than Abhishek and avoided eye contact, even with his Guess glasses on.

"Where are we going?" cried Boudicca, wiping her hands on her grimy clothes.

"New place. Don't worry. It's much better," said Abhishek, furtively scanning the vicinity. "Malabar Hill."

"Malabar Hill," mumbled Boudicca, trying to remember.

"Malabar Hill, yes! I told you I would get you places!" said Abhishek, smiling. His teeth, or the ones he had left, were brown and rotting. *He's definitely typecast as the villain,* thought Boudicca. *So why do I feel sorry for him?*

"I can assure you, you won't believe your eyes," said the other man in a Gujarati accent, smiling as he shoved her into the back of a white Mercedes. He actually had all his teeth, and was rather handsome.

Now he could be a movie star, she thought, admiring his tan against his crisp white Prada shirt as he handled the wheel. *And he's got style. Maybe he can hook me up with some duds—I definitely need some new outfits! I wonder what's in this summer?!!!*

The sedan sped out of the Red Light, and as it did so, Boudicca for the first time got a clear view, in broad daylight, of the hell she had been living in. Eyes pleaded out to her, reaching out for release. But what could she do? A chicken flapped its wings to avoid the speeding car, which was about to turn the last corner before clearing Kamathipura. It tried to land on its coop, in a busy and shady little alley, but it couldn't—for it was occupied by a young hijra, pleasing his client beneath a blanket atop the bird's home.

Fly away, prayed Boudicca, *learn to fly again!*

***

Meanwhile, high in the air somewhere above the Netherlands, Rook held P's hand and peered out the window of the plane at the pretty, orderly, and colorful fields, wondering when he would return to Hula with their daughter.

I still can't believe I have a daughter, he thought. *It really is like something out of some movie.* And he pictured how he would very much enjoy treating Boudicca and Hula to a cup of ice cream back in Los Angeles, on the Santa Monica

Pier. *That would be like a dream come true. But I would want vanilla. On top of some blueberry pie!*

He imagined how it would be there on the pier as the sun set over the ocean, with that homeless guy blowing the universes of bubbles, and the breakdancers, and the guy who swallowed his lit cigarette and then made it reappear, and all the other surreal characters performing their acts and selling their wares, one giant phantasmagoria, as families walked hand in hand amidst the calls of seagulls. And Rook looked over at P, sleeping, and carefully slid his hand out from hers so as not to wake her. He turned toward the window again to contemplate the fluffy white clouds, put on an iPod to review the Little Bang's last concert at the Hollywood Bowl, and wondered why these strangers on the recording were cheering for them.

9

CULTURE SHOCK

As the plane touched down in Mumbai, the sun came up. Rook peered out the window as if struggling with a periscope, smearing his famous face against the pane and wondering about the next passenger to rest nonchalantly against it—sadly oblivious of his greatness just here. The little dots moving below paraboled his attention. *Is she there? Or there? Where is my Boudicca!* He watched the chaos of motion and forms slowly come into focus as the "Macarena" bopped over the plane's speakers. *I don't believe it. I go to the other side of the world and I still can't escape Western commercialism!* He started the dance—ever so slightly.

"Snap out of your childishness," commanded P, slapping Rook on the hand. "You can't just stare out the window and act like some geeky tourist, ugly American. It's time you get your act together. We have a job to do."

Rook looked away, back out the window. He catapulted himself again into the drama unfolding below, observing the sprawling mass of the metropolis coming to life like some creature arising from a bowl of soup. *I just need some crackers.*

Spilling out of the plane, Rook made a spectacle of himself, laboriously taking out his can of OFF with DEET (evergreen scent) and spraying himself from head to foot.

"I think you're being just a little too paranoid about malaria," said P. "Why don't you leave that song for the Ozzy."

"For your information, it's not 'the Ozzy.' It's just Ozzy. Secondly, I'm not being paranoid at all. My doctor recommended this following state department guidelines. I even brought some malaria pills. Whenever I travel, I try and get all the shots, but this time I'm just going to have to use my medicinal bag. I have a ton of stuff I carry with me when I tour. And hopefully my typhoid and hepatitis shots are still good."

Pui sprayed some OFF on herself. They went through customs, showing their visas that they had expedited in Amsterdam. The officer looked at their passport photos, holding them up to the light, then back up at them.

"What is the nature of your visit?" he asked. He wore a khaki green army uniform. A rifle was slung across his shoulder and back.

"Umm," was all Rook could say.

"Business," replied Pui, faxlike. "All business."

The officer nodded as he gave them the twice-over. "What is that smell?" He spoke English with a decidedly British accent.

"Oh that?" asked Rook. "That's just my mosquito spray." Rook got it out and held it up to show him. The officer peered at the label, and pointed at the symbol of the green evergreen tree.

"I like this," said the officer emphatically, whiffing in the foresty aroma. *It reminds me of the time my father took me to the North. That was before. Before the accident. Oh, I wish to go back to that forest!* thought the officer.

Rook looked at P and shrugged his shoulders.

"Yes, it has a very nice scent, doesn't it?" he said.

"I want this," said the officer. And he proceeded to take out his wallet, stuffed with crisp rupee notes.

"No, that's okay," said Rook. "I need it."

"I will pay you," said the officer. "How much?"

Rook started shaking his head, but he couldn't take his eyes off the officer's rifle, which had now slung forward a little.

"Uh, you know what?" said Rook. "Just have it. It's a gift. And it protects you from mosquitoes and malaria as well as smelling nice."

"Really?" asked the officer, smiling yellow-toothed. He sprayed a little of his new-found cologne on, then stamped Rook and P's passports. "Enjoy your stay," he said. "Namaste."

Rook nodded. P grabbed him by the coat sleeve and began tugging him toward the baggage carousel. They arranged to have their motorcycle delivered to their hotel, wanting to get their bearings first before braving the strange streets.

"Don't act like such a stupid, rich, ugly American bastard," said P, checking her make-up in her compact.

"Okay, okay," said Rook. "What do you want me to do?"

"Try and blend in. Don't throw your money and gifts around. And for God's sakes, wear a normal shirt—not something so loud!"

Rook perused his mad Hawaiian rayon—blazoning like a red sun reflecting off the ocean with a hovering helicopter rippling 'round.

"But I am blending in," said Rook. "Look at all the colors!"

And he was right. As they exited and went to hail a taxi, a vibrant array danced in front of their eyes: gules, vert, sable, azure, and purpure heralded their arrival. Red fashions swam by, green advertisements, and an elephant taxi with a bright yellow turban draped about its body.

"Shall we take that vehicular?" asked Rook, pointing at the pachyderm.

"Too slow. We don't have time to be tourists," said Pui. And she hailed a black, British Ambassador. "Rajahranee Hotel," she said. The driver nodded, and they were off.

Traffic was busy, non-stop honking—driving was war. They meandered through the maze of Mumbai, accosted by beggars when they idled. The driver shooed them away; Rook tried not to look so as not to cry. One supplicant was a blind man—the eyes in his sockets long truant—withered, puckering vacuousness called out. He was led by another beggar, who guided his outstretched and branch-like hand. Other homeless were small children, some who made motions that they were thirsty or hungry. Rook shrugged—he had no rupees, and even if he did, was he supposed to give to everyone? Instead, he placed his hand on P's knee and stared at the odd assortment of debris on the cab's floor.

An hour later, they arrived at a palace of a hotel—the Rajahranee. Situated next to the Gateway of India, overlooking the harbor, they were ushered in by royally dressed Sikh doormen towards private check-in.

They had the Kingqueen Suite in the old wing, Room #15, on the 15th floor, with a view of the twinkling water and the ships coming in. It had a slight musty smell, after all it was 100 years old, but the decor made up for it. Exquisite Rajasthan woodwork, plush golden carpet with burgundy accents and throws, alabaster inlays and marble abounding, they stood together on their private patio and Rook whispered in P's ear: "I call first shower!"

"This is too much," said P, rummaging through her frumpy bag, looking for the new copy of the *I Ching* she had bought.

"What? Did I say something wrong?"

"It can't be coincidence."

"What, that we both need to take a shower? I won't be offended if we take one together."

"No, you *Bak Chee Tsee*! 15! That number keeps coming up! It's synchronicity! I'm trying to find what hexagram #15 says . . . " and she shuffled through the pages with her delicate yet deadly fingers. "It's about humility . . . it's very important for you to be humble in your quest, hallo? Does this sound like it's for you, Mr. Celebrity? Okay, and just like the sun at its zenith has to fall . . . it will eventually have a new dawn. It's a bit unclear, but I think it means that we must be humble in our dangerous journey and persevere, and eventually we will succeed . . . you can help shape your fate, but you must follow the Tao, and act quickly and simply, but we have to see it all through . . . at least that's my humble interpretation," said P, trailing off.

Rook stared at her a long time. Then said, "Do I pay extra for your reading? Or is that part of your overall package?"

"Come on now! I'm just trying to help. Take it or leave it."

She reached out and caressed and tried to tame Rook's wild hair. Rook said nothing; he just stared at her Manolo Blahnik leopard-print boots.

He thought of Bob Dylan, then kissed her head, feeling her black silken hair against his lips. He pulled himself away and trudged to the marble bathroom.

He tried to wash the mugginess off his body. Outside, it had looked like it might downpour any second, and as Rook was thinking this, a sympathetic monsoon began. He drip-dried on the carpet, watching the rain, and stared out at the ships hovering on the vast Arabian Sea in the distance and the people scrambling for cover below.

"Where are you, Boudicca?" he whispered, tracing a half-hearted heart on the glass. "Where are you?"

P suddenly entered from the adjoining room, half-naked. Her body taut, her pupendo pierced with an Egyptian bangle, she looked like she were about to fly off like a genie popped out of an ancient bottle.

"All done?" she asked. "That was quick."

"We have my daughter to find. That is my wish."

"What are your other two?"

"I dunno," said Rook. "I'll have to think about that."

Rook sat down on the edge of the king-sized bed, stared at the blank TV screen, and imagined who would play him in the movie of his life that was bound to be made someday soon. He watched P's reflection disappear.

When she reappeared, she was stunning. Glowing. Dressed in a conservative, business beige suit, it soon became apparent that it was almost transparent, and allowed one's imagination and eyes to strain to the utmost. Her make-up had a hint of gold to it—glittering even without the sun.

"Are you trying to distract me from my purpose?" asked Rook, wiping his eyes and forgetting the actors he had cast.

"Of course not, darling. I love for you to have a purpose. We're just trying to distract others from theirs. As we're gathering information, I want the men, and women for that matter, we interview to be so taken by my beauty that they forget what they're babbling on about. And judging from your reaction, I see we're going to hear lots of babbling."

"Oh, I'm glad you're on my side," said Rook. "The wiles of women!"

"The weakness of men! Come on; let's go down to the buffet and scope out the joint. Then we'll see if we can find this Purushottam Petro in the Kali Club."

As they were heading downstairs to brunch, Rook noticed a sign in gold with black Apple Chancery script for *The Kali Club*, and a private elevator that led up to it.

"Look!" said Rook.

P nodded. "I'm not blind," said she. "But it's members only. We can't just go storming up. We'll, or I'll, have to finagle my way."

They followed their noses and were ushered into a large dining room with a spectacular spread of food. As they ate this moveable feast, going back for seconds and thirds, and enjoying a complimentary bottle of champagne, Rook felt and then verified the stares of many around them. Some were looking at him. But then their eyes wandered to P, and stayed there. *Okay, perhaps I'm the famous one, but she's definitely the beauty.*

One rather portly Marathi man approached. It was unclear if he were about to speak to Rook or P—his eyes darted back and forth between them. Finally, he addressed Rook.

"My dear sir," he said, bending over a little too much for a man of his age and girth, "you are the famous, Rook, are you not? I don't mean to disturb you and your, uh, beautiful companion," and here he turned and bowed at P, "but I would like to introduce myself. I am Patchy Putabi, fashion designer. I have heard through the willows that you have a new fashion line coming out."

"Why, yes. But I can't believe how fast this news travels. My manager's developing it with a few people. I'm just lending my endorsement to the product. It's barely off the ground. Really just launching."

"But you are, sir. You are definitely 'off the ground!' And your idea is a time whose come. There is a fashion show very soon now. Your line should make its debut here now. It's bound to do well—your name is so beloved. It would be electric! A big bang! Young Indian men are now spending more money on things like clothing and cosmetics. Your beautiful face will go far here!"

"Not far enough," chuckled Rook.

Patchy patted Rook on the back and grumbled confidentially, as if he were privy to vital information.

"I want you to know I will be at this show, and happy to help out in any way to promote your line. Not only am I designer, I have many contacts in the industry and throughout all of India. Yes. And I must say, dear lady," addressing P and burping, "that it would most pleasing all of us if you would please model Rook's lingerie. It would be the best, the best!"

"Perhaps," said P, cooly. "But I always believed in the birthday line, myself."

"This is Ming Dynasty," said Rook, introducing her to Patchy.

"Well, no wonder the vases are so priceless!" replied Patchy, producing a tactile, plaid 3D-business card and giving one to each of them. He bowed and said, "I will leave you to your meals. Bon appetite! Birthday line! If only all of us were so blessed!"

"Namaste," said Rook. And he chugged his champagne, letting it go to his head. "I didn't know I was in the lingerie business."

"Aren't all rock stars? Did you know you were so popular here?" asked P, canvassing the room.

"No," said Rook. "We've never toured India. I've wanted to, just my agent Ted never lined that up. Maybe we should next time."

"Yeah, along with Russia. Get Svidrigailov to help you out, huh?"

"Come on, I've just been playing the game! I've just been trying to play the game! Just like you. You know what it's like."

"Yes, but you don't stay focused to win. You need to sharpen—keep your mind on the objective. The purpose."

A waiter approached and Rook flagged him down.

"Excuse me," he said. "Do you know a good music or dance club in town?"

"There's a very lively one at the Marriott, sir. I think you would like it."

Before the man in white left, P grabbed onto his sleeve.

"Excuse me," said P, "but do you know Purushottam Petro?"

"Why yes," said the waiter. "Why?" His face went plastic and he bit his lip.

"I would like to meet him. I heard he's a very powerful businessman."

"Sure. Everybody knows this information. This is easily available information, to anyone on the network. Please, you just surf the network and find this news, but it's not so easy to meet him. Powerful men have the powerful enemies, so he's very careful. You must too be very careful!"

P whispered into his ear:

The waiter bolted upright and almost dropped his tray.

"Yes, that is most lovely. Nice!" He looked about the room. "Unfortunately, the gentleman in question hasn't been in in a while, but that man over there is a friend of his. Perhaps I could do a meetings?"

The waiter had nodded over at a very thin, tall, balding Gujarati gentleman in a very elegant and expertly tapered coat—a sherwani, who was stirring his chai very slowly counter-clockwise, deeply contemplating something. To his right sat a white man—perhaps British, blind in one eye, with a strange ornament hanging from where his orb had once been.

"Why are so many people missing eyes in this country? Send a drink over to him, compliments of me," said P. "But wait for my friend Rook here to leave."

"I get the hint," said Rook, finishing off his champagne. "I'm gonna go out and take a walk. I'll leave you to your business."

"We'll meet back upstairs in a few hours," said P.

And Rook cast off from the table, giving the cast of characters a last look and automatically performing a semi-bow as he left the stage.

He wandered outside into the courtyard, where a gorgeous pool, glamorous garden, and fantastic fountain just cried out for a celebrity to sit down, so Rook did. He asked a passing waiter in white to bring him a box of Marlboro Reds, then looked about to see if anyone was noticing him. No one was, although some aristocrat was being interviewed off in a nearby alcove.

How depressing, thought Rook. *And I thought I was so adored here.*

When the waiter returned with the cigarettes, Rook paid for them and gave him a large tip—more than the pack itself cost. He lit a fire, breathed in, watched the ripples on the surface of the pool, caused by the gentle breeze, and blew out smoke rings in a prayer towards the heavens. *I can't just sit here; I'll go crazy!*

He got up and reentered the Rajahranee, meandering his way through the cultivated and cultured foyer, back through the bazaar of jewelry, antiques, carpet, designer clothing, book and magazine shops—pausing to read the latest gossip about himself, and out into a back street, almost an alley, with speeding rickshaws and cows and beggars with grinders and monkeys and honking honking honking instead of braking. He dodged the traffic war and went off to find his daughter, the taste of champagne and crème brûlée still in his mouth. He stumbled, having no idea of where to go, and approached a taxi.

"Excuse me, do you speak English?"

"Yes, yes," replied the driver. "Where to?"

"Where do they keep the girls?"

"Red Light? You want sari girl? I take you there! No problem!"

"Maybe. I don't know. All I know is that I'm looking for a girl who is being held here. Boudicca."

"Yes, yes, come on, Red Light, Falkland Road," said the driver, tapping his eight fingers and one thumb upon the wheel. "We will find this Bud—Buddha!"

"Okay," said Rook. "Okay. Lead me to the Buddha."

"Don't I know you?" asked the driver. "Aren't you that famous singer? You must be! That face!"

"No," said Rook, smiling. "You're confusing me with someone else. I'm just, just a father looking for his daughter. That's all."

"Yes, there are so many celebrities and many fathers and daughters coming and going from here. Coming and going. Did you know John Lennon and Yoko stayed there once?"

"I did not."

"Many others. Many others. And sadly we just had that tragic incident. With the horrible attack. Most horrible! So many died, and what for? Senseless violence. But then all violence is senseless. But that is behind us now, God willing, and the dharma will serve the justice. Who are you so I might say?"

"I'm just one of the many others," said Rook. "One of the many others."

As they pulled into the mad stream of movement, Rook shrugged and put all his trust or lack of it into the stranger behind the wheel. He watched a Rolls Royce go past, its occupants going in the back door of the hotel from which he had just come. They appeared to be some sort of royalty, as they had a retinue of bodyguards and several bullet-proofed Mercedes with tinted, menacing windows.

A hint of gold sparkled as it caught the sunlight from off the diadem of some princess or movie star or both and then Rook turned around because his head hurt and he braced for the huge pothole coming up. He lit a Marlboro and blew the smoke towards the sheltering sky. He had read somewhere that breathing the air in Mumbai was the equivalent of smoking four packs a day; he hoped to counteract the effects, but immediately felt dizzy and short of breath in the ungodly heat. But then he had a vision—or maybe a mirage—of his daughter with her hand out— ready to be saved.

It's too early to celebrate. That can wait. That can wait. And he shook his head and found himself staring into the forlorn eyes of a frail, young, frazzled Punjabi girl—her hand outstretched. He went to wave, but then stopped himself, deeming it inappropriate.

"I take you to pretty girl," said the cabbie. "Sari girl, very beautiful, yes? You will like her! Her name is America!"

Idling at a stop, Rook doled out some rupees for a Limca cola to parch his thirst. As he gulped it down, and rolled the cool glass bottle against his perspiring forehead, he managed a smile at the street vendor who said, "Hello!" Rook couldn't help but notice the ad for Hello! cigarettes, with a red, white, and blue flag, behind him, prominently displayed at his stand.

"Limca!" said the driver. "Very good! 'It's very very Lime and Lemony!'"

Rook finished off the refreshing beverage, inspected his burning smoke, and wondered what kind of printing press typed the word "Marlboro" upon it in such an addictive and delicate font. Across this country of over a billion people, smoke of various sorts rose up to join with Rook's offering—smoke from other cigarettes, from fires, auto rickshaws, Ambassador cars, from the cooking of delicious meals, to the belching of hideous factories, to the burning of petrified leaves, to the burning of tired, expired, and vacated bodies, to the energetic burning of cleansing sandalwood incense. It all blended together, waiting for something big, or little, or nothing at all to explode.

10

INTO THE VOID

"This is Red Light," said the driver to Rook, swirling his finger. "This whole streets, Falkland Road, Grand Road. All around around. Thousands girls."

"Yes," said Rook, "thank you." And he gave him 500 rupees.

"You want me wait?" asked the driver, scratching his stubbled neck. "You want America?"

"No, that's okay," said Rook, stepping out into the circus of the neighborhood. He dropped his cigarette into his empty Limca bottle.

"Careful, candy cowboy," said the driver. "There is many weirdos! I will take bottle for deposit most please!"

"Yes," said Rook. "Yes." He handed it to the driver and tried to avoid looking at a funeral procession that was passing by on foot. Instead, he looked overhead, where he noticed vultures circling; he decided to follow them, ignoring a tug at his shoulder until it became too much.

"What?" snapped Rook. A poor girl, who could not have been much older than fifteen, took Rook's hand and placed it on her breast. He pulled it away like he had just touched the fires of hell, shouting, "Jesus, no!"

The girl, taken aback and stepping back, looked like she were about to cry. Rook took some money from his pocket and gave it to her. Suddenly, a pimp approached.

"You want sex with her Mister? I will show you where. Prime real estate!"

"No, I don't want sex! I just want to help her."

"No sex? What is problem?" The pimp raised a wavy eyebrow that kept undulating.

"No problem. I just want to help her. Please, for you," he said, motioning to the girl, holding up his hands, palms open.

Rook walked away but felt compelled to look back. He saw the pimp take the money he had just handed the girl, slap her, and go sit back on his roadside bench. The girl, meanwhile, continued to be on the lookout for new customers.

I should go and do something. But what? I have my own mission . . . .

Rook began wandering the bazaar. Realizing the odds of just happening to find Boudicca were not in his favor, he sighed, but continued to ambulate and triangulate the area. He pulled his sweaty, yet stylish Dolce and Gabbana T-shirt away from his over-lotioned skin, and sat down on a rock to rest and contemplate his next move on this new chessboard. Suddenly, he became aware of a strange odor, similar to marijuana. A druggy smoke pervaded the air. Rook shifted and noticed a group of three men sitting behind him, puffing from a hookah. *Perhaps it's opium,* thought Rook. The men were naked and painted blue with strange symbols scattered like constellations upon their bodies. Rook nodded at them. One, with piercing, bright eyes, nodded back.

"Would you like to join us?" Bright Eyes asked in surprisingly good English.

"Uh, that's okay," said Rook. "What is it your smoking, anyway? Opium?"

The man laughed. "No. No, nothing so profane. Amanita Soma."

Rook nodded and looked about cluelessly. "Sounds good."

"What are you looking for?" asked Bright Eyes. The other men asked him something in Marathi; he translated quickly. They nodded and stared piercingly at Rook; the rock star looked away, guiltily.

"What are you looking for?" repeated Bright Eyes. "Perhaps we can help you find it. We are ascetics in search of absolute freedom. Samadhi. We worship Kali. We follow the left-hand path. Aghora."

"I wish I could say my search is as high as yours," said Rook. "My search is much more human. I am a father. I am a father in search of my daughter. My daughter whom I have never met. I was told she is somewhere in the area— trafficked illegally from Amsterdam, being kept prisoner or something, somewhere around here, I assume. Her name is Boudicca."

Bright Eyes nodded slowly. He said something in Marathi to his two friends, both who started swaying their heads in thought. For a long suspended moment, they swam in contemplation, mumbling, "Buddha, Buddha, Buddha . . . ." Then one of them said something animatedly. Bright Eyes translated.

"My friend here says that he remembers seeing a Caucasian girl about a week ago—down the street there. She is of the cages."

The friend mumbled again. Bright Eyes nodded and held up his hand, saying, "We will lead you there, and help you find the Buddha, but first you must do us the honor and smoke with us. Please." He held forward the hookah for Rook. Rook hesitated, then grabbed the casket jar and took a deep breath.

What the hell am I doing? thought Rook.

"May your eyes be opened," said Bright Eyes.

Rook inhaled and almost coughed. It was a strong smoke, and he felt his face turning as blue as the men he was now sitting with. He passed the pipe back to the ascetics, and it made its round several times. Rook pretended to smile, looking up at the people milling about, pointing at him. He slowly started spinning. He got up to go outside and get some air, but then realized he was already outside.

He sat down with some difficulty as Bright Eyes lent him a hand. Rook was swimming now, but in an unknown river.

"Let me help you," said Bright. "We will guide you."

"My daughter."

"Yes, Kali will help us."

And the three naked, blue-painted ascetics, and the blue American rock star, trudged slowly down the muddy mess of Falkland Road. Faces groped out at them and eyes like molasses stuck to Rook's heart as he was paraded through the strange grocery store.

"This is where he saw her," Bright Eyes told Rook, pointing to an empty cubicle of a cage.

"Are you sure?" asked Rook, staring fixatedly at the empty space.

Bright Eyes asked the austere witness, *"Hey uttar aahe ka?"*

The earnest man replied: *"Ho, ka nahi."*

"Yes, he's sure," said Bright Eyes.

And Rook collapsed to the ground, everything carouseling around him, and the black enveloped him and sealed him.

"Tu kasa aahe? Tu kasa zoplas? Majhya hatat kiti safarchand aahe? Tu box uchlu shakto ka? Me magcha athaudyat film pahile."

Rook surfaced to a blurry blue face mumbling and hovering against the backdrop of the sky, as the sky-clothed ascetics helped him to his feet.

"Where did she go?" asked Rook, looking at the nothingness.

"Where do any of us go?" pondered Bright Eyes.

Rook gripped the steel bars for support.

"Well, would you like to return to our circle?" asked Bright Eyes. Rook groggily gazed at the Kali around his neck. "Do you like my worship? *Panchash Munda Malini.* It has to do with Kali wearing a garland of fifty skulls; it represents creation and dissolution."

"No, I think I want to break free. I will stay here a while, just until she comes back. She has to!"

"Very well. Namaste. But before we part, let me give you this astrological bangle. I see you already have some. You do need really to be humble. You are climbing an endless ladder with no gateway in sight. This too will protect you from certain karma approaching."

Rook took the silver bracelet, stared at the Sanskrit, and said, "Thank you. But what does it say?"

KRIM KRIM KRIM HRIM HRIM HRIM HUM HUM DAKSHINE KALIKE KRIM KRIM KLIM HRIM HRIM HRIM HUM HUM PHAT SWAHA.

"It is the cryptic mantra. Chant it with devotion to Kali and She will quickly make things right."

Rook slipped it onto his left wrist, where his watch normally was, and he then realized that his watch had disappeared. *Lost? Forgotten? Stolen? Dematerialized?* He lost track of time. He looked up but the blue men were gone and the blue sky was turning gray with oncoming rain. *Were they just a hallucination?* His lower lip stung; he reached his hand and touched it. Blood. *I must have hit my mouth when I fell. My teeth hurt too, I wonder if they are now crooked. More veneers back in Beverly Hills.*

He looked at the empty cage and felt a compulsion to climb in. *I need to find her! Boudicca, where are you? It's okay, Daddy is coming to help . . . it's okay.*

He dragged his body in the dirt, over the frame, and into the squalid cage that reeked of shit and sweat and something else indefinable. No-thought took over: everything simply was—as the bamboo of the cage displayed its bambooness, and the feet of people passing by were right out of a Technicolor® cartoon. Rook reached for his daughter, but she was not there, and he spun into oblivion clutching the empty air. Falling, falling, falling, Möbius stripping, gasping for air, the drug overwhelmed him. *What the hell did I smoke?*

Uh-oh, and he saw an animal spirit approaching—a deer—and followed its sprint to some unknown world where creation dissolved into the void.

As he dreamt, he felt some monster chasing him and pressing down upon his chest; he looked for his guide the deer, but couldn't see it. He looked down and around him, but it was most difficult. Finally, he was able to see his hands, and noticed they were acting as wings and he was flying. He gained speed and outflew the monster. Then suddenly, there was the deer again, at the clearing to the forest, and he made his way toward it and the breaking light. He cleared the trees and was on a vast plain, overlooking white sands too bright to view. A motherly voice whispered, "It's okay, it's okay!" Suddenly, he awoke.

He smelled a rat. Was it part of the dream? No. It was nibbling on his foot. He shook it off and scurried towards a mango that was rotting just outside the cage. As he brushed the bugs off and bit in, he watched detached as cars appeared and day started to break. *Where do I go? I need to stay here and find clues.*

He looked about him and found one left-behind Birkenstock sandal. He picked it up. *It probably is Boudicca's! What is it like to walk a mile in her shoes? Where did her shoes go? This is not helping!*

He peered out to see if it was safe. Somebody noticed him, a client, and approached.

"Tu mala prem karto ka? How much?"

"What?"

"Money?"

"Fuck off," said Rook.

The man ran away and Rook felt a heaviness cloud over him. He played with his bangle, orbiting it about his wrist, and once again could not ascertain the time. Everything was crumbling apart. Touching his lower lip, he winced. Overwhelmed by thirst, he scrambled out of the cage like a wounded animal, and emerged into the fresh daylight. As he stood, he swayed, dizzily, but was able to maintain his balance by leaning upon the steel bars. He looked up and down the puzzling, jigsawed street, and noticed a few lollygaggers giving him the wavy head and eye. He put down his daughter's shoe for a moment, trying to determine which direction it would like to take. A gust of wind urged him leftwards and he headed into the sun.

Walking past the other cages and windows, he hobbled—his right leg and foot had been chewed on during the night, and there was caked blood all over. He had a hard time believing it was real, however. He also had a hard time believing that the people on the street were real, or that he was.

"Ted!" shouted Rook. "Ted Southhampton!" This is a time where I could really use him, the good for nothing. People looked at him as if he were crazy—a grown man all disheveled and barbarous and carrying a girl's shoe—hobbling and yelling. He heard whispers in transliterated Hindi: *I think he's insane. Look at that guy. Stay clear!*

Finally, he found some water coming out of a pump on the corner of the street. He put his lips to the spout and began to slurp happily. He drank and drank, and felt refreshed. He went to try and buy some fruit from one of the street vendors.

"Banana, please," mumbled Rook as if he were at Albertsons. The merchant nodded and handed Rook the fruit. The rocker pulled out some rupees and gave the man entirely too many; the merchant nodded and eagerly took them.

"You gave the man too much," someone next to Rook said. It was a rickshaw driver. "You gave him much much."

"Who cares?" said Rook. "Who's to say the true value of a banana?" And Rook peeled it and ate it like he was a chimp in the zoo.

"Do you need ride?" asked the driver. "Who's to say the value of nice rickshaw ride?"

"Who indeed? Take me to my daughter!"

"If you could just tell me where?"

Rook handed the driver the banana peel.

"I'm sorry, I don't understand."

"Oh, silly me." And he handed him the shoe. The driver stared at it.

"Uh, if you could give me a clue . . . ."

"They took her away, don't you see? She was down there in the cage and they took my girl. Don't you see? And I've never even seen her before! And they took her!!!" And Rook began sobbing deliriously.

The cab driver, whose name was Pompeii, after his parents visited the volcano when he was in the womb, looked down sadly at the tattered slipper.

This man is definitely on drugs, or out of his mind, or both. But I will do what I can to help . . . .

"Listen," said Pompeii. "Do you have any idea where she might be? What is her name?"

"Bo, Bo, Boudicca."

"Boudicca, good," said Pompeii. "We will try the beach then, what do you say?"

"I don't know, maybe. She always liked the beach," said Rook, shading himself from the hungry sun. "Okay, let's go."

"Juhu Beach it is then," said Pompeii. And they climbed in his rickshaw and carted off. *This is hopeless. But what else am I to do? Where am I to go? I can only follow my instinct,* thought Pompeii.

This was only partially true. Sometimes Pompeii's instinct led him down unerringly on the right path. He tended to remember only these times. Other times, he was just wrong, mistaking misguided desires for instinct or intuition; this would catapult him towards disaster.

Pompeii managed to meander the rickshaw across the bumpy streets of Mumbai without too many bumps. Still, Rook in the backseat felt like he was getting sick, like he was about to throw up. The rising heat added to this feeling, and finally Rook had to tell Pompeii to pull over; he threw up and up and up, although the vomit actually projected down down down onto an old hubcap. It spattered as Rook happened to get a glance of his face in the tarnished reflection.

Is that really me? I've let myself go!

He got out of the cart and decided to do something about it immediately. He found some water in a merchant's bin, splashed it on his ruddy face, poured the rest of it upon the ground, making a mud mixture. He paid the merchant twenty rupees, asked for a mirror, and administered the mud treatment. The merchant started to laugh and point at Rook, so Rook pointed and laughed at him. *What else can I do? I have to stay young, even if they laugh!*

"I'm not vain, I'm just practical!" Rook shouted to the people gawking.

But little did Rook know, because his senses had been so altered by the hallucinogenic smoke, that he was putting on a mixture of mud and cowshit and it smelled like hell, and made Rook look like hades. As far as the medicinal benefits of this mud bath, Rook had no idea about the history and worth. If he had done a little research, instead of just listening to what his trainer had told him, he would have discovered that the main benefits were thermal, resulting in increased circulation and cleaner skin.

Rook smiled and his white teeth appeared unusually bright in contrast to the dark shit on his face. He then noticed an old car axle with the wheels in cement just lying on the side of the road and he lifted it and began doing clean jerks like an Olympic athlete. A small crowd began to gather as Rook made it to twenty reps. When he put it down, they all clapped and cheered.

"Are you from America?" one young teenage boy wished to know.

"Last time I checked," said Rook.

"One rupee, one rupee," yelled some kids.

"One rupee, one rupee!" sang Rook. And in a bizarre, carnivalesque, Fellini-like moment, they all held hands and began to dance around in a circle, singing: "One rupee, one rupee!"

"Are we going to Juhu Beach or not?" interrupted the cab driver.

"Of course!" said Rook. "I am sorry. I am feeling much better now."

And there was a smattering of giggles and laughter as Rook took some of the crap that was running down his face, smelt it, and turned up his nose in disgust.

"For God's sake, sir," said Pompeii, who was about to blow a spark plug. "Wipe that shit off your face! Do you realize what you're doing?"

"Of course!" said Rook. "I am from the left-hand path and Kali will help me find her!"

The driver shuddered, remembering his kundalini experience. It had frightened him out of his wits spiritually, causing him to stop practicing his kriya. And it dawned upon him that Rook must have encountered the blue ascetics and shared their smoke. He remembered his Vedas:

> Heaven above does not equal half of me.
> Have I been drinking soma?
> In glory I have passed beyond earth and sky.
> Have I been drinking soma?
> I will pick up this earth and place it here or there.
> Have I been drinking soma?

Rig-Veda X: U9, 7-9

Pompeii watched Rook pick himself up from the earth and submerge his head into a cloudy bucket of water next to a cow trough.

Dripping with liquid shit, Rook wiped his face with the back of his hand and heard a symphony in his head. He believed it to be something by Beethoven. *Duh-duh-duh-dum!*

Rook for a moment thought he was back backstage at the Hollywood Bowl and took a towel handed to him by a fawning Indian girl dressed in a purple sari and wiped his mug clean. He stared at the rag when he was done, and saw his beautiful, rugged face outlined with shit.

"What am I doing here?" asked Rook to a nearby cow.

It gave him a wide berth and a cautious, lazy eye that wandered uncontrollably.

"We're going to Juhu Beach," said Pompeii, finally taking control.

"And who are you?"

"Pompeii, your driver!"

"Like the volcano, make me want to go boom!"

"Sir, I must protest this exasperation."

"I know I'm dyinnnnnng, we're all dying."

"Can I have your autography mister?" asked some kid with a backwards hat who admired Rook because he was a crazy American who had lifted a barbell of tremendous weight while under the influence of soma like an ancient Viking who had gotten superhuman strength before a battle and not because he knew him as Rook the rock star. This boy didn't even listen to rock; he listened to hip hop from Detroit Rock City and this boy did not look pretty; there was green pus discharging from one of his eyes.

"Sure," said Rook, motioning for a pen. The boy handed him a crayon that was the only color that his goat had not eaten—gold. "Go for the gold," said Rook, signing his name as Piliper Grits. And then Rook did a double-take, for he thought himself walking out of the corner of his eye—but then, whoever it was who resembled him (wearing a red bandana), turned half-way and smiled and then turned the corner and disappeared. "What do you know? My alter ego. My doppelgänger. They should make a movie."

"Wouldn't it be nice if we could all be actors!" shouted Pompeii, and he pulled Rook into the taxi; finally, they resumed their journey to the beach.

"Why did we stop there?" asked Rook. "Don't you know I have to find my daughter if I don't my wife—"

"You got sick, sir."

"Oh. But how do we know where to go?"

"Intuition. Have you never trusted your intuition?"

"You've got something there. You've definitely got something there. I remember . . . ." and then Rook forgot what he was going to say. He stared out at the colors washing by like a Vermeer painting he had seen on the wall at S's club.

They blended together and Rook lost his perspective. He was sinking, losing his grip—everything was out of order, the driving was a war, and he fell into the void again, returning to his childhood and the river in Iowa.

Pompeii had had enough. He had had crazy rich asshole American customers before, but he had lost his patience with this one. *He's acting like the goddamn prime donna! And I don't even know that word!* He found the smelling salts in his little travel kit, and applied them under Rook's nose. Rook came to from the deep end of the pool, leaving his summer lessons early.

"Mom?" asked Rook. "Where's the tennis ball?"

"Sir, I'm Pompeii. Wake up. Wake up and smell the coffee!"

"Coffee, yes, that'd be good."

Pompeii motioned and yelled to a nearby vendor.

"Where's Boudicca?" asked Rook, fading.

"Well sir, we're here to look for her. This is the best I can do. Lots of girls, if they run away from the brothels, come here to Juhu. They like to see the view; it makes them feel clean and free." And Pompeii stared a moment too long out at the Arabian Sea.

"How do you know this?" asked Rook, gasping for breath.

"Oh, a friend of mine . . . ." Pompeii was not about to go into his history of being a transvestite prostitute for four years as a young boy to pay for his passage from Nepal. That was something, now that he was out of that racket, which he wished to forget.

The coffee came and Rook drank it and it tasted good. It smelled of hickory, and Rook recalled camping out in the woods of Michigan as a child.

"Oh my gods," said Pompeii, staring into Rook's eyes.

"What? What is it?" asked Rook, sipping the drink.

"Your eyes. Your pupils. They're huge!"

"What are you saying?"

"You must have really taken something."

"That's what I've been trying to tell you, man. I'm tripping out. Those blue guys, I was smoking with them, and

I'm trying to help and they were trying to help and now I'm just flying and that was yesterday. I need to rest, and I need to look for my daughter."

"Kali and soma! What a combination! Maybe," said Pompeii, pensively looking at a yellow kite against the sky, and remembering his childhood in Nepal with yellow kites and meditation in the snow, "maybe the men of the blue, clad in the sky, have already found God—maintaining nirvana in the midst of chaos—like Vishnu controlling the universes calmly as everything flies by like madly."

"That was good coffee," said Rook, smashing the cup on the ground. "I'm ready." And he got out of the taxi and started walking towards the Arabian Sea.

"Sir, you need to pay."

"Oh, right," said Rook, and he got out his neck wallet which he was amazed was still on him and paid Pompeii and then threw a tip down for the broken cup and then forgot what he was doing.

"What?" asked Pompeii.

"I forgot what I, where I, who I . . . ."

"Your daughter."

"Yes," said Rook. "But where do I look?"

"Just sit and watch the people walk by. Hopefully you will recognize her . . . hopefully you will recognize that all people are your daughters and sons and sisters and brothers and mothers and fathers and you and God are one."

Rook watched Pompeii walk away and wanted to wave but his hand was lead.

Pompeii got into his taxi and watched the strange American looking at him. *I hate to leave him here, but what am I supposed to do? How am I supposed to help? He's out of his* mind. *I don't even know if he has a daughter. It's insane, why would his daughter be here? It is in God's hands . . .* and he drove off, rejoining the maddening honking battle. *I want to see my daughter's face.* And he headed for home.

Rook walked off the pavement and onto the burning sands of the beach. He removed his shoes because it felt good and he didn't mind the heat. But then it got worse as he walked towards the steady sun and he thought *am I related to you sun? Am I a god? I am a rock god. I command you to worship me, brother sun.*

He walked until he felt an unusual sensation—he looked down and noticed someone had painted a very nice color coming out of his foot and look at it slowly go and turn the whitish sands crimson. *I better sit down.*

And he plopped down just out of reach of the waves and stared at them coming in and people going by and he wondered who they all were and decided they were all his relatives that his friend Pompeii the Volcano had erupted.

Gripped by a strange compulsion, he got up, and began handing money out to passersby, and then a crowd gathered, eager for a lakh or two, and when he ran out of money, he passed out his credit cards, saying, "Wouldn't a father give a credit card to his kids?"

They all laughed as if they knew what he was saying and smilingly took the goodies except for one who looked on cautiously, thinking this person is insane or rich or both or maybe a cop, or maybe he's just wasted out of his mind. This man, Shanti, just continued watching the spectacle from a safe distance, and wanted no money because he believed it would bring bad karma to him, which, when he consulted his astrologist a week later, assured him it would have and he did the right thing though he should have helped the stranger. "But what could I have done?" asked Shanti. "Stop the man from giving to the poor? Walk him to the hospital?"

"Are you not your brother's keeper?" asked the holy astrologer, wearing an elastic bangle around his head to protect him from an upcoming inauspicious event relating to meningoencephalitis that he saw in his charts.

"Yes, but then that would make this crazy American not so crazy!"

"A crazy fool! Are not all saints sometimes considered by the sane to be crazy?"

And Shanti looked back at what he could have done, and was stuck. *All I can do is change the present. All I can do is change the present. All I can do is change the present.*

Rook too had lost all sense of time and when he ran out of credit, he started giving away his identity—CA driver's license, US passport—and this passport was treated more valuably than anything else—like it was a brick of gold—and a little scuffle broke out over it and now that Rook had gotten rid of all his belongings except for the pendants and bangle (no one would take them—they thought it was bad luck) and even his name there remained but for one thing for him to do and that was to get rid of his clothing and run naked into the sea and cleanse himself of his sins. *Now I see why the blue men do it! It is so freeing! But I should be in the Ganges! Oh well!*

As Rook ran and hopped out of his clothing, he flung it with reckless abandon into the air but nobody wanted it until the next day when a strange little orphan boy who was short on nice clothes scooped them up even though they were entirely too big and draped them about his body and when his mother asked where he had gotten them he said he found them on the beach and she slapped him and said don't lie nobody would throw away such good, expensive, American clothing and from that day on the boy had a weird phobia about dressing and wearing the plainest clothing possible and never telling the truth because nobody believed you anyway—a plain-dressing, compulsive liar.

Rook waded out free and easy into the water, which upon closer inspection (Rook put his head under), was quite dirty. *But I don't care. I just want to fit in. I'm tired of living in my mansion on the hill. I'm tired of all this baggage! I loved giving it away! But my daughter! Where is she?* And he looked back at the crowd of people staring at him like some mad ascetic who had come down from the Himalayas and he walked towards them and began yelling: "Has anyone seen my daughter? Boudicca?" People just shook their heads and he panned from face to face and ran to get the one thing back that he wanted—the photograph of his daughter which he had given to one of them. "Who has the picture? The picture of the little girl?"

"Picture?" replied one boy who must have been about nineteen. He wore a magic Ganesh amulet about his neck that he rubbed constantly hoping that his mother would recover from her recent breast cancer surgery. "You mean make photo?" And he held up the picture of Boudicca that Rook had thrown at him in delirium a few minutes ago.

"Yes!" shouted Rook. "I need it! It's all I want!"

And as Rook grabbed it, he fell to the ground.

"Let us make a photo then," said the boy, getting out his camera. " A photo to replace that one you gave me."

"Okay," said Rook. And the people who were left (about twenty of them) and not scared off by a naked white guy all grouped together to make a photo.

Later that night, the nineteen year old, as he was look-ing at the Polaroid, wondered how strangely familiar this birthday suit looked, and turned over and over where he had seen him before. And the boy went to sleep, rubbing his amulet and praying that he would find a job soon to help pay for his aging mother's operation. A few days later, when it finally dawned on him who this Americano might be, with the help of an IT friend, he posted the bizarre group photo on his Facebook page (with Rook's privates censored out), with the caption: **Rock Star Rook?** It took many months until people really noticed it, and it started to circulate, with accompanying conjecture.

Rook, meanwhile, had wandered down the beach a lit-tle and buried himself in the sand up to his belly button. And he watched the people come and go and the traffic honk by and disappear and the smell of delicious food and he supplicated for water with his hands out and got some from a Caucasian who stared at him a long time (and actually did recognize him but was so shocked that she would see this American rock icon naked in the sand that she just gave him her whole bottle of Bailey's Water and left wondering what the hell had she just seen and how could she make money off it and then she forgot about it when she got sick later despite rinsing her toothbrush with bottled water and had the shits all night and down into the deep dark hole that was the toilet in the hostel she was staying at and that ruined her plans for going to the disco later that night—she heard there were a couple of lively clubs that would be a blast but now her blast came from her ass with such force it would have killed any cockroaches or rats that were lurking about the WC. "Are you sure you don't want to come?" her friends asked, putting on their make-up in the little foggy mirror.

"I can't," she said. "I'm dying in here."

"We're all dying, albeit, slowly," said one boy from the Czech Republic who liked to be a smart ass and now he thought how funny it was that he was being a smart ass when this American chick's ass was smarting from wiping it so much but where to flush the toilet paper even if you got some?

After Rook drink, drank, drunk the water that passing kind stranger (*American, I think,* he thought) had so graciously given him like that girl in that Fellini film, he tried to meditate like he was back at home in Beverly Hills in his coffin. And for a short time he felt like he was making some progress, *maybe I will see the third eye,* but then the sun was hot and he wanted to move but couldn't and felt like he was dying and knew he had to someday *but not yet cause I'll feel like I have failed* and then he made a struggle to get up but his throat was parched again and he couldn't budge he could barely breathe and then he made a gasp for air and then blacked out and felt like he was falling off a cliff and imagined people ringing up his credit and his FICO plummeting. He fell into a deep sleep, and dreamt of finding Boudicca. And he envisioned that in his efforts he did find her but that he died of heat exhaustion and then he remembered that saying that if you die in your dreams you really die and then he tried to see his hands in his dream because he remembered something about seeing them would help you wake up and gain control and then he felt like he couldn't see them try as he might and then he felt like he really was dying of heat exhaustion and heart trouble and in reality he almost did, and could have, perhaps, if his health had not been somewhat sound (in part due to Dr. Vilhelm's extravagant, if inconsistent efforts) and his mind not strong and positive and motivated to find his daughter and to help Hula and to play his music much much better and so instead of dying in his dream and also really dying on that beach and the story ending very sadly here, which sometimes in life it does, especially for rock stars, after an interminably chilly and starless dark monsoonal night of the soul the sun rose again the next morning with the dawn, and miraculously, so did Rook.

Photos*

---

* Inserted at this point was a copy of the photograph of Boudicca that Rook was carrying, along with a photo of the rock star himself, half-buried in the Juhu Beach sands in the intense sun, asleep with apparent second-degree burns. In the photo, Rook is indeed clothed in only the two pendants around his neck, with the bangle about his wrist, clutching the photo—his only link to his missing daughter. Who took this photo of Rook and made this copy is unclear, although the reader may speculate. Unfortunately, once again this poor editor has been threatened with additional lawsuits over the reproduction of said documents. However, there is talk that perhaps one day, when enough time has passed, that *The Interloper* may publish these heartbreaking yet notable pictures.

11

FREE FALL

So on the third day of Rook's unwitting excursion from the air-conditioned confines of luxury at the Rajahranee Hotel, he rose naked and in sync with the sun, and his smog gradually started clearing. However, when it cleared, he found that he was still in free fall, not knowing where the bottom was—no parachute.

Meanwhile, on the other side of the world, in Beverly Hills, Ted Southhampton was poring over more fashion shoots for Rook's new clothing line, which had just had its launch, thinking how they would make a gold mine off the rock star dressed very unlike a rock star. Ted placed his periwinkle glasses strategically beside a cappuccino and gelato upon a pristine white powder acrylic designer table (just in case someone should happen to walk in) and wondered where his cash cow now was.

"Where am I?" Rook said aloud. He looked about but couldn't really see. Everything was exploding and burning within his field of vision. "OW! Goddamn it!" He put his hands to his eyes and afraid to touch them, felt them ever so gently. "Ouch!" he whispered and winced. "Hell!"

Sunburnt and puffy, he took some deep breaths and tried to calm himself. From what he could see from the dawn awakening upon him, his upper, naked body, was burned to a crisp! *What the hell happened to me?*

A crab scurried across the beach and Rook called out to it. "Hey, hey!" *The crab crawls sideways, but still arrives—who said that? I could be in Malibu for all I know, Christ, where, ah India!* And his mission and almost blunted purpose all came back to him in a flood and so did the albatross.

"Shit! Help!"

But there was no one there to help cater to him and pamper him. Off in the distance, he thought he saw people walking around, but he couldn't be sure; he couldn't be sure of anything. *Was it all my imagination? Okay, I've just got to calm down, take it easy.* He started to hyperventilate and tried to massage his beautiful eyes again. "Ow!" He caressed his head and rubbed his long locks. And as he came back into acute consciousness, he was gripped by a tight burning sensation about his torso, and noticed with clarity the severity of his frying—akin to a baked lobster. He felt his skin—and ran his hand akimbo across all the blisters that had formed and would soon pop. "I need to get some help," he mumbled.

With great effort, he managed to extricate himself from his self-dug hole and stood up. He stretched and cracked his back. "Ow!" He examined himself as objectively as possible. There were sharp pains in his feet; "Owwwwwwwwww!" He sat down and carefully removed the shards of glass, but couldn't see well enough to get them all out. *Damn, it looks infected!* thought Rook. His feet and legs were caked and blotted with blood that had taken on a culinary appearance with the addition of the golden sand. There was major swelling in both feet. However, he could not focus his care on them for too long, for suddenly he felt like he was going to explode. "Shit!" He hopped out to the sea and let out a stream of diarrhea that just kept coming and coming and when he thought he was done he had to go some more. Finally, the barrage was over; and not knowing what else to do, he cooled and washed his ass as the water stung like hell.

"Oh my God," Rook mumbled, shaking his head. "What the fuck? What the fuck am I doing here? Goddamn it!" He started hobbling like a wildman towards civilization, naked as a jaybird, burnt like a lobster, blind as a bat, as swollen as a jellyfish, covered with sand like a starfish, smelling like dead and pruned skin, he realized he had to put on some clothing—fashionable or otherwise. He felt people gawking at him as he neared the street, and heard laughter. *It'd be better to be tarred and feathered.* He sat down on a cement building block and tried to get his bearings. *I'm so goddamn thirsty. Okay, I need to think straight. Water. Then something to wear.*

He took a deep breath and looked about. There were some young kids pointing to him and jumping about. Little did Rook know, but they were some of the street kids that yesterday Rook had given his money and identity to. "What?" Rook shouted. "What's so funny?"

They didn't speak English, but they did understand that the American was angry. Feeling guilty and suddenly like they had to do something, they approached Rook and took his hand.

"Kyaa tum bhookhe ho?" one asked with a wide-eyed expression.

"I don't understand," said Rook, the words coming out dry and haltingly.

The other boy made a hand to mouth motion.

"Hungry? Yes, but first water, water," and Rook made a drinking signal. The boys nodded and one held up a finger to signal one moment and ran away. Rook felt dizzy—he lied down—the remaining boy helped him. "Clothes?" Rook asked, pointing to his battered body and pulling on the boy's T-shirt. The boy nodded and ran off to search for something decent for this lost white lobster of a man to wear.

As Rook was lying there, waiting, he happened to look up and witnessed the application of a billboard. It was an ad for his new clothing line—Rookster!®—with Rook pointing a savvy finger, winking, and singing to an imaginary crowd as he sported retro 70s duds. The man wallpapering the sign felt Rook staring at him. He cast a weary look down at the naked lunatic, then back up at his work, shaking his head as he continued applying the messy glue. Rook remembered posing for that ad several months ago, thinking *what a joke! Now I'm the joke.* He observed his handsome face being plastered. *I've really let myself go.* He felt the pendants about his neck, and squeezed them tightly, as if they gave him some link back to reality. He searched on his wrist for the bangle that the blue men had given him, but it was not there. *Was it ever there? Did I really meet those guys?*

Suddenly the one boy returned with some water in an old coffee can—Rook eagerly drank it and it tasted so good as it refreshed his throat and when he finished he asked for more and the little boy laughed and put his hands in his pockets and felt the money that Rook had given him yesterday and tried to reassure himself that it and he were real.

The other boy had scoured the area for some clothing for the strange white man to wear, but had no luck. He settled on grabbing some fronds that had fallen from a palm tree. He brought this back to Rook, sheepishly, and shrugged.

"Better than nothing, huh?" said Rook, accepting this latest fashion trend. "Now if you found me a sock, they'd just say I was copying Red Hot Chili Peppers."

"Kyaa tumhein tatti karni hai?" said the boy, not understanding. Rook laughed and so did the kids. The boy squatted as if shitting.

"No thanks, I want breakfast?" said Rook, motioning to his mouth and smiling though it hurt. The boys nodded and together the three of them walked towards the main strip of Juhu, where the vendors were just coming to life. Rook began stumbling as pain rifled through his feet and his palm leaves were falling; he tried to tie it tighter. As they walked, the boys guided him as he could not see the broken glass and other dangers so very well. A cow stood in their way. Rook hoped it would move, but it charged slightly, so he gave it a wide berth.

When they approached one vendor, Rook heard the most guffawing laugh. *"Ah, tek, tell, tahalowli?"* asked the man. The boys nodded and explained in Hindi that this crazy American yesterday had given them money and now he was naked and lost and poor, just like them. The vendor laughed again. The boys produced some of the currency Rook had given them yesterday—which they had yet to exchange for rupees. They held up a twenty—Rook saw it and shook his head.

"No, no," Rook said. "Give him something smaller. That's too much."

But Rook had not given them anything smaller yesterday, and so the boys gave the man a twenty, to which he just shook his head and said he could not change it, but the boys could eat here for a month for that.

They ate up—coffee, oatmeal, Indian breakfast, sweets, and Thums-up! cola.

"Thank you," said Rook to them all. "Thank you very much. But I have to go now. I have something to do."

And they looked at him as if he had fallen from outer space.

"Could you tell me how to get to, to the Rajahranee?"

"Taj?" said the vendor. "Yes, in Agra."

"No," said Rook, "Rajahranee Hotel."

"Ah yes," said the vendor, lighting up a cigarette. "Gateway of India."

"Yes, near there."

"Taxi?"

"Yes, but . . . ." and Rook made a gesture indicating he had no pockets, let alone deep pockets, and therefore he had no money.

The vendor had a short conversation with the boys, and told them to go fetch a driver who would take pity and drive Rook to the hotel.

But before this could be done, a taxi pulled up; it was Pompeii, who could not sleep all night, feeling guilty at abandoning this poor fellow.

"Come," said Pompeii. "I'll help you." And he explained in Hindi to the vendor that he had driven Rook yesterday. The vendor tossed Pompeii a pack of Hello! cigarettes with a US flag on it.

"He needs help," said the vendor in Hindi. "Much help. Crazy naked American. Rajahranee Hotel."

"Acha," said Pompeii, and let Rook in his little bumpity bumper and together they started off for the other side of Mumbai and Rook waved goodbye to his new-found friends and they and he were smiling and Rook wondered how they and he could be so happy when none of them really had anything. And he wondered how he could help someone besides just his daughter. He adjusted his palm fronds so they wouldn't hurt so much; one, however, slit across a blister on his back.

"Damn't!" said Rook. It had lanced it.

"You okay?" asked Pompeii in English. "You remember me, Pompeii? I tried to help you the other day, but you were in a bad way. So maybe today is better?"

"Maybe," said Rook. "Just maybe." He took a deep breath and tried to ignore the big trucks that came close to smashing them. The honking and business of the morning contributed to Rook's already severe pain; he put his hands to his head and tried to drown out all the noise. *Okay, I've got to get myself together.*

After an hour, they finally reached the hotel. Pompeii pulled Rook's hand and guided him out. Rook looked out at the Gateway of India and the harbor, and turned and remembered the Rajahranee and looked up at it and the impressive architecture and then down and ahead at the Sikh guards royally-dressed and guarding the doors.

"Thank you," Rook said to Pompeii, putting up his empty hands to show he had no money. "Please come by later. I could use a friend like you." And Rook approached the hotel with determination, and as he did, the guards formed a wall together so as not to let him pass.

"I'm staying here," said Rook, his eyes puffed out severely.

"Not like that, you're not," said one of the guards.

"But I'm paying for the royal suite!"

They laughed. "Get lost, mister. Go back to your bottle and your hashish. Just who do you think you are?"

Rook shrunk away, noticing his appearance in the window, framed by the hotel's golden sheen, and he too realized that he had become an untouchable.

My God! I look like a monster! And he walked away and sat down across the way, near where all the tourists gathered by the Gateway, and watched an organ grinder and a monkey in a handsome red cap wait for customers to put on a show. When they saw Rook, they ignored him and his plight. Then the monkey stuck his hand up in the air to shoo the naked rock star away. Rook began to sing: "Monkey, I used to be like you—" Monkey hissed and Rook jumped back. *I am lower than a monkey,* thought Rook.

"It's okay," said Pompeii, laughing a little. He had been watching over Rook the whole time. "Togethers we wills humbly figure out this algebra!"

"Yes, together we humbly will," smiled Rook, remember P's *I Ching* reading. "Thank you, Pompeii. P! P can help me!" he shouted suddenly, getting up and heading back towards the Rajahranee's doors. Pompeii followed close behind, happy to have a new, perhaps important friend.

But as they shuffled across the street, two lost men trying to find their places in the world, and provide for their daughters, they had no idea that P too, was lost and in much more dire trouble.

Across town, in Malabar Hill, Mumbai's version of Beverly Hills, P hung suspended from the ceiling, her silhouette twirling behind her. Old One-Eye took her foot, which sparkled orangey from a recent pedicure, and spun her again.

"You know, it was just too easy," said the Brit. "Svidrigailov has a hunch that you and Rookie are down here, sends me your photo, and you walk right up to me at the Raj. Could it get any easier? It practically takes all the fun out of being a bad guy."

P twirled, chained and locked up. The circulation had left sometime yesterday. Oh my head! She took deep breaths and tried to snap awake. The last thing she remembered was being at the hotel and having a lovely lunch. Someone must have drugged me. "Who are you?" she asked One-Eye.

"His name is immaterial," P heard a familiar voice say over a speaker phone. "My name, you cunt, is Svidrigailov. And you will remember that! No one, no one I tell you does to me what you did to me."

"Your voice is still a little high," said P. "I imagine the operation didn't give you back your manhood after all, huh?"

Dr. Van Halen, after considerable sweat, effort, and worry, was able to reattach S's sac, but it was unclear as yet whether they would ever "work" again. It truly was a sad sack. And S was more aware of this than anyone.

"I am going to chop you up into little bits and eat you with wasabi," said S, his voice actually rising in pitch slightly higher. He waited for a response. P said nothing.

"One Eye!" shouted S, breathing heavily now.

"Yes?"

"Pack her up in a box and ship her to me. But make sure she's alive when she gets here. Poke some holes in the cage or something . . . ." coughed and laughed S. "I want to enjoy her. In fact, I'll make her the cuisine and charge money for it! I love making money off the sickness of others! Now, Pui, and yes, I've found out who you are, you are dead. There is no getting around that. But if you want to see that little girl, Boudicca, you will tell me where the Van Gogh is."

"Yes," smiled One-Eye. "Why not save Boudicca's life?"

The phone hung up and P listened to the dead tone.

Old One Eye took out his orbital piercing and new glass eye and placed them next to P's lips like some marble and jacks he had found on the playground. The glass jewel sparkled as the light from the lone lamp passed through it. "Now will you play nice and tell me where you put the painting or do you want me to kill Boudicca in front of you?"

P stared into his good eye. Van Gogh would have a field day with his portrait. Especially with this lighting. "Did anyone ever tell you that with the proper facial regimen you'd be quite a handsome customer?" she asked.

One-Eye circled around her, pacing.

"You are not helping yourself or anyone else for that matter," he said.

"What do you want? I'm not scared of you. You should be scared of me."

"Really? Listen, just give me that damn painting!" He stabbed her in the thigh, blood spurting madly.

"Grrrrrrrr!" screamed P. "Fine, I'll help you find that Van Gogh. Just don't take an eye for an eye." She tried to focus, taking deep breaths.

"You don't have to worry. That honor is saved for Mr. S."

"Why do you care about him?" asked P. "You're British."

"I don't. But currently he pays the most for my consulting services."

"And so what you're saying is that you go to the highest bidder?"

"You could say that," said One-Eye, applying a tourniquet to her leg.

"Then how about I just give you the VanGogh and you give me Boudicca and let us go?" She fought the dizziness and the fainting.

One-Eye stopped, removed his Panama hat, and gave P a good long gander.

"You're a tall drink of water, aren't you?" He played with her ear. "I like this. I like it a lot. How about we have a deal if you give me your ear as well?"

"Now why would you want it?" The fainting went away as she breathed deeply.

"Something to remember you by," he whispered close to her.

P looked at him, discerning. *He's as whacko as I am.* "Okay," said P. "It's back in Amsterdam. I have it safely hidden. I'll tell you where it is. Just let Boudicca go. Then you can have my ear, you crippled man, you."

"It doesn't work that way. You tell me where it is, we'll send someone to retrieve it, then you can see Boudicca. If it's real, you can both go. If not, you will both die. Either way, I will enjoy your lobe. You see, ever since I lost my eye, I've turned to collecting body appendages. It may be a bit old-fashioned, medieval even, but that's just me!" And he looked at his lost eye, floating in formaldehyde in an old Mason jar upon a frequently-dusted shelf.

P tried to squirm out of her restraints, but they were expertly tied.

"Don't waste your effort," said One-Eye. "I've been in this business long enough to know how to secure someone." He gave P a spin, turned off the interrogation lamp, and left the room, deadbolting it behind him.

What is this hell? thought P. *Stay calm. Stay calm. I'll figure something out.*

On the uppermost floor of the mansion, Boudicca looked out the window at her strange new world. *I don't understand any of this. But I like this pad. It's hip!*

"Boudicca?" called Arjun, the actor who had driven her away in his white Mercedes and who had been watching her the past few days and whose house this was. "Would you care for a cup of tea? Earl Grey?"

Boudicca turned from her spot by the window and got up. Abhishek approached her. He smiled crookedly, showing his yellow teeth. His face was sagging and hollow, and he looked hungry.

"Boudicca, please come," said Abhishek, murmuring something under his breath. "I made tolds you I would help you and now you see how beautiful this city and its people can be. Look at this view!" He ushered her eyes out to the garden and to the sea, then led her towards the kitchen, where Arjun was pouring the chai in Zen-like fashion. Abhishek bowed and then disappeared along with the steam from the whistling kettle.

"You are the man who saved me," she said to Arjun.

"Oh, that makes me happy. That makes me so happy that you would even care to say that. No one cares about me. Not anymore."

Boudicca studied him.

"Why not?"

"My name is Arjun Alexander and I am dying."

"Oh," said Boudicca. She thought of running. *But where would I go?*

Arjun walked to the window Boudicca had been staring out of and rubbed her head. "Here is your tea, my dear. My fame, movies, and being related to Alexander the Great is not enough to cure me. But I want you to know, I never forget a friend, or an enemy," he said, quite too dramatically.

Boudicca laughed. "You are a riot!"

"What? What do you mean?" asked Arjun, searching for a face.

"It's just that you're funny. You remind me of the main character in *The Great Gatsby*. I read it last year in school and I wrote this great essay. You should read it! It's a really good essay! My mom always said I had her mom's gift."

"Yes, well, I guess you could say I'm a fading, hopeless character, like Gatsby. But what can I do? I must live, I must act!"

"Are you really a famous actor then? How famous? How come I've never heard of you? Can you take me shopping? It's been months since I've had anything decent to wear! Can we get some nice clothes and some jewelry? I'm just dying for something presentable!"

"Sure, we can go to the shopping," said Arjun. "Perhaps then you will see how so many have forgotten me. It isn't easy, I'll have you know. To go from the peaks to . . . to tabloid obscurity." Arjun turned back to the window. "Of course, some kind fans still remember my films. Back in the day when Bollywood movies had something to write home about."

"Why don't I know this famous name, Arjun Alexander? I watch a lot of movies!"

Arjun lit up as if he were about to go into a dance number, and actually did shuffle a step or two.

"Do you know *The Magic Carpet?*" he asked her.

"I can't say that I do."

"Indian films are just not as popular overseas. And soon I will be completely forgotten, even here." And Arjun sipped his tea with great care, then stopped; it was too hot.

"Why?" Boudicca asked, drinking her tea quickly.

"Why does the world spin? Why do some people succeed, and others eke out the most meager existence? Why do some have it easy in love, and others not so easy? Why are some people bisexual? Who knows? That's Kali's way, the Divine Mother! Nature's way. Ahh, however you roll the dice, have you ever heard of true love being easy?"

"No. No, I haven't." Boudicca looked with pity at this actor standing by the window, doing entirely too much acting.

"It's all a mystery. That's how She rolls. Hey, I wrote a poem called 'Actor's Last Stand.' Would you like to hear it?"

"I'd love to! I write poetry too, you know! I'm quite talented!"

"Yes, you have your grandmother's 'gift.' I've read all her books!" Arjun searched his pockets and came up empty. "I'll have to find it and commit it to memory. I promise to read it to you soon."

"Mr. Arjun," began Boudicca. "Could you help me get out of here?"

"Don't you like it here? Is it not preferable to your prior accommodations?"

"Yes, thank you. That cage was the pits. But I miss my mommy."

"Don't we all," said Arjun, looking far off. "Listen, my dear, I will help you get back to your mommy, but first you have to help me with something."

"What?"

"You have to take a little trip with me. Help me find something."

"What?"

"My innocence. My health. My God."

"But how can I help?"

"Sometimes it takes someone innocent to help one find one's innocence."

"It's a good theory, but you know I'm not that innocent."

"What do you mean?"

"You know, although I love my mother, she sleeps with men for money."

"So. Some do it and call it marriage. Some do it and call it business."

"So I'm just saying perhaps I'm not the best one to help you."

"But darling," said Arjun, "isn't it worth a try? I've tried everything else, and so before," and he began to cough and cough and bent over, "before I die, I've got to give it a shot."

"Okay, so do we get out of here now or what?"

"Boudicca, you said you're mommy is a prostitute, and well, you've been exposed to seeing a lot of sin. But still, you haven't sinned, have you?"

"What do you mean? Had sex like her? Not yet, no. We've talked a lot about it, and she said I should save myself until I find someone I truly love; I haven't found that person yet, but then again I'm still young! Plenty of time!"

"Yes, indeed, plenty of time. Oh, I envy you, young Boudicca, to be young and still have love and life ahead of you! But perhaps you can help me get back on the right track, huh? Like I said, I'm at my wit's end. I don't know, maybe I'm out of my mind. The critics have been saying that for years."

"I'm sorry," whispered Boudicca, taking a sip of tea, and then beginning to wheeze. "Just don't read the bad reviews. Hey, I need to use your potty. I'll send a message to those critics!"

Arjun laughed and rang a bell. Abhishek came to escort Boudicca.

"When you return," said Arjun, "I will perform the Buddhist Tea Ceremony for you. It is quite soothing. And orderly."

"That would be nice," said Boudicca, seeming suddenly to regain her strength upon noticing a bird flying by outside towards the mist of the sea.

Arjun suddenly broke out dancing across the room, dragging his feet a little, however. "Dance with me, Boudicca!" He took Boudicca's hand and together they did a Bollywood dance with sharp classical hand gestures. Boudicca started laughing, then so did Arjun and Abhishek.

Boudicca bounded towards the bathroom. Abhishek stood sentry outside the door, gyrating and snapping his fingers to the music from the movie *Chandni Bar,* playing somewhere in the distance.

Old One Eye suddenly popped in.

"Well? Do we have a deal?" he asked, frowning at the spontaneous dancing.

Arjun boogied over to his desk and got out his check-book and wrote one to:

Purushottam Petro
5,000,000 rupees*
Memo: Virgin

"Arjun, aren't you being a bit melodramatic?" asked One-Eye, wondering if this double-dealing would get him killed before he and Petro killed S and consolidated his holdings.

"You forget, that's my business," said Arjun. "Now I'll also need a nice SUV or something."

"No problem, although that's a separate purchase. Where do you want to go?"

"My ancestral estate in the foothills of the Himalayas. Rishikesh."

"Classic. I do have one request, however," said One-Eye. "Just try and make one more movie before you go. I like your overacting. And the laughs."

Arjun paused. "My friend, I hope to make many more movies after this virgin cures me of AIDS!" But then his look towards the window and frown at the sudden muggy downpour indicated his uncertainity of this treatment. So he lit up a menthol Tiparillo and blew a smoke ring, coughing, then suddenly broke out in his trademark guffaw. This laugh, however, now had a tint of lunacy.

---

* This is an editorial assumption; the amount was smeared in the manuscript, but perhaps written as 5mr.

***

As Rook approached the doors of the Rajahranee Hotel again, he held up his makeshift palm skirt and a not-so savvy finger. Pompeii stood nearby, ready to run.

"Listen, I realize I look like some homeless hippie who's been hanging out here for thirty years, but really, I'm staying here. I'm a famous rock star on holiday. My name is Rook! Haven't you heard of me and the Little Bang?"

The doormen shook their heads despairingly and started pushing him away.

"Listen, if you don't believe me, call up to the Royal Suite and ask for Ming Dynasty. Or Pui! She's my partner! I'm begging you!"

One of the guards took pity.

"Okay, but which one is it? Ming or Pui?"

"Either one! Either one!"

"Please sit down and try and blend in with the flora and fauna," said the guard. "And I will make the effort." A minute later, he was back.

"There's nobody there, sir," said the guard. "I'm sorry." The guard took out a red handkerchief and wiped his brow.

"Well, keep trying! Ask the manager! Do something! I'll have both your asses fired if you don't let me in! Can't you see I'm famous! Can't you see I've been burnt at the stake here and I need some treatment?"

"Yes, you need treatment all right," said an innocent bystander who had been eavesdropping for the past minute or two.

"Who the fuck are you?" asked Rook to the Russian-looking guy, who inspected him from behind his sunglasses. Rook squinted from behind his puffy, blistered eyes and shitfaced caked face (literally—Rook wondered how his bandmate put up with his Dionysian trope).

"Who on earth are you supposed to be?" asked the man, lighting up a Cohiba and still peering at the half-naked lunatic.

"Who am I? Who am I indeed! I'm Rook! You know! The musician! The one everybody loves."

"Sure you are. That's what they all say," said the man. "Prove it. They make musicians prove they're really musicians at the US Embassy, applying for passports from India. Prove that you are who you are."

"Could I have some water first?" begged Rook.

A crowd had started to gather to see what all the commotion was about. One aging lady with a canteen of water squirted some into Rook's mouth as sanitarily as she could, *after all, who knew what diseases this strange white homeless person had?* Pompeii started jumping up and down.

As Rook swallowed, and tried to limber up his throat, he noticed another billboard being put up across the street, with his image on it. *Rookster®!*

"I'm that guy!" exclaimed Rook, earnestly. The people turned to look. "I'm the Rookster®!"

"Is that something to be proud of?" somebody inquired. "I can do better than that jokester. Sing their only good song—'Free Fall.'"

"Okay," said Rook, feeling strange because he hadn't auditioned in so long, let alone an audition naked to prove his identity. "Travelling from planet to planet, coast to coast, I realize I am lost in space, and lost, without you, I am nothing at all, I'm in Free Fall . . . ."

There was an awkward moment of silence. Rook thought—*I sang that pretty well for someone who's all beat up.* But then he farted and even he could smell it was like sulfur.

The little crowd clapped, until the smell got to them, then they made faces and some walked away. One slapped Rook on his sunburnt back.

"So much for the Little Bang!" joked one.

"Do you want my autograph?" asked another.

The two guards began talking amongst themselves amusedly in Hindi.

"Leave the man alone," said the Russian. "Can't you see he's in poor health?" And the nicely-smelling man removed his sunglasses and took Rook aside. "It really is you, isn't it? Boy, you look like hell! What happened?"

Rook squinted, then almost started to cry.

"Anatoli?"

"The one and the only!"

And for the first time Rook was very happy that he had made such a horrific movie with the infamous director.

"What are you doing here?" And Rook's tears flowed. He smiled, but he had to stop—it hurt too much. Pompeii too started crying and smiling. And though he was not in pain, he stopped smiling when Rook did.

"I'm here for a Bollywood Festival! It's great fun! I'm going to try to make a Bollywood movie. Film City! Want a cameo? Yes, that'd be great! But first we have to get you fixed up! You look like shit! What happened to your pretty face?"

"I am shit," said Rook, looking at the dwindling crowd pointing and laughing at him.

"Aggh! That's the movie business!" said Anatoli, comforting Rook, delicately placing his arm around the rock star's burned shoulder. "You can always redeem yourself!"

And Anatoli began to march with Rook through the front doors of the golden Rajahranee.*

"Guards, let us through! We have work to do!"

"Wait," said Rook, turning back for Pompeii. "Let him come too."

And the guards looked at one another and shrugged, parting the way for this man in a Zeggidelli suit, this man in a palm frond, and this lowly taxi driver running to catch up, smiling like a schoolboy who's just become popular.

An older couple from Australia on their way to the jewelry store in the back for some diamonds noticed Rook walking across the lobby, fronds falling, and murmured: "What is this place coming to? It's going to the dogs!"

Meanwhile, back in Beverly Hills, Rook's Labrador, Black Dog, sat in the backyard and looked out at nothing in particular, panting, smiling, wondering when that guy whom loved him would be coming home. *I love that guy!*

And he followed a scent of shit off into the garden.

---

* There were some puzzling marks here in the margins: CXA, BIG FAV, RJR B. Perhaps cross-check with Anatoli? (KG tried unsuccessfully to call the number listed; it is now unlisted.) Perhaps Big Favor (from Anatoli)? Perhaps Rajahranee background? The author never went into depth about the history of the Rajahranee Hotel or the recent tragedies in the Gateway of India area. Of course, it is not at all clear if this is what these notations mean.

Also back in Beverly Hills, Aitchkiss Killawathy had finally tracked down the renowned psychic whom Monique and Meriweather consulted. After ringing the bell and waiting forever to be let in, and explaining as delicately as he could the nature of his project, and inquiring as to what possible meaning Lo Shu and Dürer could have in relation to this far-out rock star, the old Romanian woman said, "I cannot divulge the details of their readings. That would, to me, be akin to breaking the law of confidentiality. But I can give you your own reading, if you would like, and perhaps that may be of use to you. I say 'perhaps,' because sometimes people do not like what they hear. Payment now."

Aitchkiss frowned, momentarily, most seriously displeased. But then, after wiping a crusty boil* (which made even the seasoned psychic recoil), he managed: "I would very much appreciate that." He wandered in, his eyes still adjusting to the darkness of the 1920s-house, and wondered at the peculiar smell hovering about.

"Method?" she asked, wiping her hands with sanitizer.

"Uh, let's stick with the *I Ching*."

"Tried and true." She swiped his credit card, then got out the yarrow stalks and led Aitchkiss to a round table covered in black velvet cloth. "What's your question?"

Aitchkiss smiled shyly, a little embarrassed. "What should I do?"

She cast the stalks with a restrained sort of pleasure, then squinted at their arrangement.

---

* A cartoon bubble appeared here, perhaps as the author's note to self: Tell the ugly truth?

"Ah, Hexagram 25," she whispered, the keratoses on her forehead now clearly visible as she neared the glow of the candle. "The Unexpected! You may expect progress and success, if you are true and correct. If your action is untrue, you will fall into errors, and it would not be wise for you to move in any direction. You see, if you are free from all insincerity, you will be accompanied with good fortune. But the situation is also changing, and Yin is gaining ground. Be on guard, because the future is in Po, or Splitting Apart; you see, in this case, it would not be wise to move in any direction until you have resolved your inner issues."

Aitchkiss's boils began to fester like never before. "But what on earth are you telling me? What is this?"

"It's a tad obscure," answered the old woman tiredly, as if she had said this line many times over the years. "But my advice would be to be sincere as possible. And I say that most sincerely."

"But that's impossible!" stammered Aitchkiss, standing up quickly causing his chair to fall back. "The very nature of my job requires stealth and duplicity!" And he stormed out of the dim, musty house, happy to be breathing the unclean air of the City of the Angels.

Just above him, a feather was slowly drifting, free falling to the hard ground. But he did not notice it as it landed lightly and stuck upon his shoulder blade.

The psychic, watching from behind a veiled lace curtain within her cozy house, shook her head. "Some people don't want to be helped," she said, climbing up a ladder to retrieve an old book and petting her favorite cat, Gabriel.

12

MONEY, MONEY, MONEY

Rook withered on his king-sized hotel bed like a big baby, naked, curled up, a little bloody (all that was missing was the umbilical cord). The hotel doctor had removed the remaining shards of glass from his feet, bandaged them up, covered the rest of his ragged body in aloe vera, placed sliced cucumbers over his eyes, gave him some antibiotics, painkillers, and pills for dysentery (that were explicitly labeled to have not yet been approved and had been found to cause cancer in laboratory rats), and ordered him to get some rest. As he rested, Rook tried to focus upon his blunted purpose. However, every time he moved the slightest inch, not-so blunt pains shot throughout his torso.

I need to find Boudicca. But I'm in worse shape than when I left and where is P? I've got to organize some sort of rescue party. But that takes money . . . .

Distracted by how he would get any cash now that he had given it and his passport and wallet away, he made a call to Ted Southhampton, but only got a curt voice mail. He left an out-of-breath message: "It's me, you moron. If I've ever needed your help, it's now . . . ." He went on, mumbling, still somewhat hallucinatory and shaking. He pictured someone racking up huge bills and going to the US, trying to get in on his identity and perform a show. And Boudicca disappearing off the face of the earth.

But those kids in the streets, thought Rook. *They were poor, but so happy! I don't understand it. Money is only a tool—it helps you accomplish certain things, get to certain places, but does it really buy freedom? Have I ever in my life been as free as I was the past day or two? Without a goddamn thing to my name? Still, I couldn't live like that. I couldn't survive out in the streets. I don't know how they do it.*

He stared up at the Casablanca fan whirling quietly and enjoyed the breeze that came in through the open windows from the sea.

"What am I doing with my life? Boudicca! Hula! P! Where are you?" And Rook tried to sit up and tried to stop the trembling. But his pampered life had not prepared him for the rough and tumble, and so he kept on shivering. Despite the ungodly heat and humidity, Rook felt as cold as he did when he was a kid making snow angels by the Iowa River with his brother, who was now long gone.

Boudicca was out shopping in Malabar Hill with Arjun and Abhishek.

They were buying pretty, frilly outfits for their upcoming pilgrimage to Rishikesh. When they noticed a sale, they jumped up and down.

"Oh Arjun, I love this outfit!" said Boudicca, holding up a black and gold Fendi coordinated blouse, slacks, purse, heels, and fur.

"It's yours," said Arjun. "But really, you must bargain for it! Now please put it down. You're blocking the view of those paparazzi." And Arjun pulled down his shades for the cameras and handed his credit card to Boudicca.

***

Hula was just going to sleep, what with the time difference and all. It had been a long night of entertaining wealthy Russian businessmen, and she could barely keep her eyes open. Still, she thought of calling her mother in Iowa.

"Mum? It's me. How are you?" There was a long silence.

"Hula honey? What's wrong? I can sense it in your voice."

"Mum. Boudicca's in trouble. I, I wanted to call you earlier, but I didn't know what to say or do. It's complicated."

"It always is. Honey, don't you worry about a thing. I'll be over there tomorrow. I may not be able to save my career, but I'm sure as heck going to save my daughter and granddaughter!"

"Rook's here, Mommy."

"Well it's about time."

"Don't blame him. He just found out."

"You should have told him sooner, honey. But it doesn't matter. I'm coming. I'll see you tomorrow. I love you, honey. Keep your head up."

"I love you, Mum."

Hula stared out at the red neon light of the bar across the street flashing.

Suddenly, the door to her room flung open. S was standing there, smoking a Pall Mall in a majestic red velvet jacket.

"Honey," said S. "I appreciate you meeting my friends. They liked you. Business is good. You helped smooth out the wrinkles in a deal worth millions." He sauntered up to her bed, sat down, and kissed her on the cheek from which she had just removed her make-up.

"I'm tired, honey," said Hula. "I can't keep doing this forever. I know we keep playing this game for money, and it's hard to get out of it now. But I'm so tired."

"I know. That's why I've been thinking. Why don't we get married? And be a real family."

"Really?" Hula took a deep breath and clicked her tongue.

"Yes. This old flame of yours coming back got me to thinking. I can't live without you. I, I think I love you."

"'Think?' You don't know by now?"

"I am not use to expressing these emotions. All I know is extortion and killing and business. I don't think I ever loved anyone. Only my, my sainted mother. And that other woman . . . but that was a long time ago."

Hula hugged him delicately.

"Bring Boudicca back. Please," she said, taking a drag off S's cigarette.

"I will," said S, looking into Hula's eyes. "I will. I always was going to. I'm sorry. But you can make things so difficult." They both sighed and stared at each other a long time in silence. "First thing in the morning, I'll call and have her returned."

"She's missed so much school."

"That can be made up. Everything can be made up. We can even try and have kids. I know I'm pushing 60, but that would be so great, don't you think? I would be a very good father, don't you think? I just hope this little surgery has made me up. Can we try it out?"

"The doctor said wait a week, honey."

"I can't." S rested his head against Hula's neckline and the Tiffany diamonds he had given her. He thought of the blue box they came in.

"Well let's be gentle, then," said Hula. And she and S made love with the care and grace of porcupines.

"I really do love you," whispered S.

And Hula wondered if he really meant it, or if the operation had somehow changed him.

"And I really love Boudicca," said Hula.

P was still hanging out in Malabar Hill, literally, in the dark basement of the ancestral mansion owned by Arjun. Attempting to wiggle out of her restraints, she stopped as the door opened and One-Eye walked in, tripping over a stool that was out of his line of sight. He got up quickly.

"Here's what's happening," he said, speaking very quickly and polishing a crystal eye which he had taken out of a little drawer with the label: **Odds and Ends.** "I have what you might call an expert acquaintance in Amsterdam who will make arrangements to go to the location you disclose to me. He will examine the Van Gogh, and if it turns out to be the real thing, I will let you and Boudicca go, providing you leave me with the gift of your ear. I'll leave it up to you which ear—which Vincent—it doesn't really matter to me, although I already have a right earlobe in my study, so a leftward specimen would be preferable. As far as the value of this particular painting, if it truly is

Lovers: The Poet's Garden IV, it will fetch quite a handsome price. You see, dear P, I live for chasing the priceless. Even more than your beloved Mr. S."

"Fine," said P, tired. "But my hands are dead. Can't you untie me?"

One-Eye circled her, rolling his crystal about in his palm.

"How about you tell me where it is, I cut your ear, then I untie you?"

"Fine. I just can't take this anymore. It's a zero-sum game. You'll find the painting in the main safe behind the desk at the Genteel Hotel. It's stored under my name, rolled up in the sleeve of a mink coat that is kept inside a garment bag. It really does protect it from moths."

"But not from the mafia," said One-Eye, putting his crystal in his pocket and taking out a serrated knife. "Now, would you like a drink before I cut?"

"No," said P. "I want to feel the pain."

"Really? Well, I'll have some alcohol ready and a rag and a stick. I am British you know, and a gentleman." He went over to the corner and under the bright heat of the interrogation lamp prepared the torture toolkit. He opened some Jaegermeister, poured it on a rag, and brought it over, along with a hunting knife. "Here you go," he said, draping the drenched cloth around her neck like a fur and allowing her to bite down on the stick. "Now hold still, you don't want me to slit your neck, do you?"

He examined her delicate ear, and wondered which antique mason jar he would keep it in. He rubbed his fingers along the delicate, smooth cartilage.

"You might say that ever since I've lost my eye, I've become a connoisseur of body parts. Strange, I realize, but everyone has to have a hobby! I'm sure my ex-wife would have preferred me taking up philately, coins, or baseball cards, but then she's not around anymore, unfortunately. Opened a letter-bomb that was meant for me. Turned me off of stamp-collecting completely."

"And yet you play with glass eyes like they were marbles. How did you lose your eye anyway?" asked P, feeling the faintness coming over her.

"A drug deal gone bad. It was back when I was first starting. I got into a rough scene in London with some Russians. They scooped out my eye with a sterling silver tipped mother of pearl caviar spoon—I remember it flashing in the sunlight before they dug in—last thing that eye saw . . . they began playing marbles with it, betting all sorts of crazy shit. They were wagering for my heart when S got there. He saved me. But it could have gone either way. For a while, it looked like he actually might join in the game. But he sized me up, figured I'd be more use to him alive than dead, and forgave my debt. But I had to kill my boss, the one who was trying to pull a quick one on him. I had to go that night and kill him in front of his wife. I could barely see, or focus my perspective—I had only been one-eyed for a few hours. But I did it! I killed him with a piece of string! Am I creative or what?"

"Let's get out of here," said P.

"Yeah, I'm sick of livin' in this dump too, lovebird. They promised me a nice place and gave me the cellar. Oh, sometimes crime pays, and sometimes it doesn't." And suddenly One made a quick and decisive slice and off came P's left ear (and she thought of the last time she was at the old deli in Amsterdam near the Van Gogh Museum and she ordered baloney and they sliced it thin)—blood began spurting and she screamed—just once. One put the Jaegermeister-soaked cloth to her head and did his best to stop the bleeding. "That might need a few stitches," he mumbled, not looking at her but at his new trophy, which he placed in a jar with a porcelain lid and formaldehyde and labeled it PPP/MING DYNASTY. "Okay," he said, very methodically. "Let us go and see the little girl."

He brought the bleeding P down, her hands still chained behind her back, and led her, very slowly, past the reinforced steel door and up the spiral stairs.

"I'm sorry, my dear, are you still bleeding? We'll attend to that in a minute. Be careful not to get any blood on the floor. Arjun gets very particular about the cleanliness of his house. He might kill you if you make a mess. Ha-ha!"

And One-Eye laughed insanely, adjusting his glass eye in its socket so that it was slightly off-kilter. "Ha-ha-ha! Never keep a good man down! Ha-ha!"

P looked at the blood on her hand as if it were not hers. *Okay, that can be reattached, or fitted with a prosthetic. Not a big deal. What else could I have done? Is this how Vincent felt?*

But before she could indulge herself in self-pity, One-Eye had led her to the uppermost floor, where she heard Boudicca talking of Versace behind a green door.

"I will introduce you as my business partner," said One. "Don't make a scene, just say your hellos, see for yourself that the girl is fine, and then you'll have a nice wait in the basement until I pick up my Van Gogh."

One-Eye gave three quick knocks, followed by his fingers tapping upon the forest-colored entrance. After a moment, someone pressed a working eye to the peephole, and the door slowly opened.

"We were just about to leave," said One-Eye. "Wanted to say cheerio and goodbye before we left."

Arjun sat back down in his oversized chair. "And we just got back from shopping! We had a lovely time at the mall! Found some sale items! "

"Hey One-Eye," said Boudicca, coolly. "Who's the dame?"

"Oh, I'm sorry," said Arjun, clearing his throat, "pardon my manners! Allow me to introduce . . . ."

"Your business partners Old One-Eye and Ming Dynasty," said One.

Pui/Ming nodded, still holding the bloody rag to where her ear used to be.

"Nice to meet you," said P, reaching out to shake Boudicca's hand.

"What happened to you?" asked Boudicca, aghast at P's condition while appreciating her smart beige business suit. "Hey, is that Dell'Acqua?"

"Why yes, you're very observant," said P. "I hurt my ear, I'm a martial artist, but a bit clumsy!" she said, telling a half-truth. She always found it helped to make a story convincing if you at least began with the truth. "I was demonstrating a move to my partner here, when I accidentally fell upon a bottle of Cristal. What a waste, huh?" They all laughed, awkwardly. "I'll be okay. How are you?"

"Me?" asked Boudicca, surprised and happy that someone was inquiring about her well-being. "I'll be fine soon. This nice man here is going to help me get back home to my mother."

P raised her eyebrows and tried to hide her concern. "Oh, really?"

"Really," said Arjun in his best movie voice. "Like yesterday!"

"Well, we must be going," said One-Eye. "We have to tend to Ming's injury here, and then take care of some business. Money, money, money—I tell you, the world revolves around money!"

"Yes," said Arjun. "Very nice. Just do it nicely. Nicely."

"Yes," said One, "I will do my best to do it nicely."

As they left the room and the door shut behind them, Boudicca tugged at Arjun's hand. "So when do we get out of here? I can't wait to get going!"

"Soon, honey. Probably tomorrow," said Arjun. "Abhishek? When is that SUV getting here?"

Abhishek answered from the other room. "Tomorrow morning. We will be getting lickity splits then! Rishikesh! I will bring an offering to my guru! I must be gets flowers—he likes the white roses the best!"

"Isn't that exciting?" asked Arjun, looking at Boudicca. "This is all so terribly exciting! I love trips! All the games in the car! Ah, life! Ah, how I love the fantastic trippings!"

Boudicca, however, was now browsing through Arjun's small library and came across the first Harry Potter book. She wanted to finish reading the series and she hoped to do so when she returned to Amsterdam. *That is, I'll read some and have Mom read some to me,* she thought.

Arjun sighed, noticing Boudicca wasn't paying attention to his celebrity, went to do something, but then forgot what he was about to do. *I'm washed up as an actor. Even if I'm cured, who will hire me now? Maybe there is someone, I just need to convince Puroshottam to carry the next film, and that we will make much dollars on it. Much money, I just need to talk to him about my idea!* He stared out the front window and forlornly at the kids skating down the street. *Everything used to be so easy. Now I forget . . . .*

Arjun shrugged, went to the bar and made himself a mojito. He noticed a tumbler glass with a wad of curled-up bills. *How'd this get here?* He counted it: $9820 American. *Hmmm.* He put it in his pocket. *I will bring this to the next game of poker at the Kali Club.* And he savored the liquor, letting it swirl about his mouth. Suddenly, he experienced déjà vu, remembering back, way back . . . his fake marriage and accompanying honeymoon at the ancestral estate in Rishikesh and how he got drunk out of his mind on mojitos, smoking so many fine Partagas Reserva cigars that they were no longer fine and they gave him a headache. The next morning he was unfortunately awoken by his butler, who was stirring the cream and sugar into the Kopi Luwak coffee too loudly with a slightly tarnished silver spoon, and feeling like a stunned sturgeon, Arjun took out an old pistol, which was given to him by his father who had worked for the Indian government for years, fighting drug smugglers, and blew a hole through the young man's freshly-pressed white ruffled shirt and gentle heart. As he collapsed, the butler mumbled, "Help is on the way," in Hindi, dropping the serving tray, spilling hot java all over the plush champagne carpeting. Arjun rolled back to sleep, wrapping himself in his expensive down comforter arrayed with pictures of famous Hollywood stars. When he awoke, he called his agent, who arranged to have the body of the innocent butler disposed of in the Ganges without a hitch . . . .

Across town, at the Rajahranee, Rook looked into the mirror at his burnt face and swollen eyes. *I'm a wreck!* He rang up the desk and asked for a doctor to come up and help him out. "Just add it to my bill."

Oh the endless bills! Hotels, the tour caravanserai, the estates, the parties. I need to make more money! He took a deep breath and looked at the picture of Boudicca. *I need to support her! How can I make up for all those years?* Then he tried to remember exactly how Hula looked the last time he had seen her. *She's changed. But then, so have I. I want to be a good husband and father. I want to do something worthwhile. I know that this life is all some sort of cosmic- joke, I just don't get it!*

The phone rang.

"Rook? This is Ted. I got your message; what the hell happened? I know I should have sent someone with you! Do you realize how you're endangering not just your well-being, but the well-being of all who depend upon you? I can't believe it! You're in India—lost and broke. Are you out of your mind?"

"No, actually, I'm coming to my senses. I know it sounds a bit melodramatic, but I'm trying to track down my long lost daughter . . . it's not as easy as it sounds. It's getting more and more complicated."

There was a long pause.

"Are you sure she's yours? Let's run a paternity test."

"Damn't, Ted, yes, of course she's mine. Now send me some goddamn money! I can't do anything without some dough! Help me get my life back!"

"Okay, okay. But wait. I'm coming there. I'll be there very soon now. You're going to need some help getting all this on track. This is what I do best, so please let me help you. You know this is what I do." And he thought of how Rook was acting just like his teenage son, whom he had to bail out of the shithole of irresponsibility many a time.

"Okay," said Rook. "I appreciate it. Please. Get the money fast. I'm up the creek. I'm all alone right now, my bodyguard is missing, and I could use a little help."

"What am I paying these people for? Damn't, how hard can it be? Do I have to do everything myself? Isn't there anyone who can help out until I arrive?"

"Anatoli. I ran into him while I was standing outside in a very unfashionable palm skirt. He helped get me back in here and get my name back. And this driver named Pompeii. I think he's named after that volcano."

"I don't care about that, damn't! Okay, okay. Let's take this easy. Anatoli is an old friend. He should be good."

"Of course he will. But you know how it works; he wants me to make an appearance in the movie he's filming here."

"Why not? It's a good business move!"

"Jesus Christ, Ted! My daughter is missing!"

"I know, I know. We'll find her. Listen, I'm going to get some things together and I'll get on a plane. In the meantime, stay calm, and relax. You need to take better care of your appearance, especially if we're going to make some money off your face for the new clothing line!"

"It doesn't even look like me," Rook said. "I don't know who that person on the billboard is."

And they both enjoyed an awkward laugh from opposite sides of the world over this strange invention the telephone that was miraculous, but taken for granted because although it was common, it was not really understood by the common man.

Rook hung up the phone and looked out the window at the Arabian Sea.

A monsoon rain was beginning to fall; he pressed his face against the frequently-cleaned glass to watch. People scattered like ants below, trying to find shelter. One man held up a broken umbrella. One lady hid beneath a covered bicycle built for two. And one child danced, tilting his head back, holding out his arms to his sides, sticking out his tongue and letting the rain fall upon him, absorbing it like a Bounty paper towel with nice flowery designs, as his red shirt with nice flowery designs got a much-needed laundering.

The window fogged up, and so were his recollections of Hula and Boudicca. *Why are they so foggy?* he thought, and then he whisked himself to the bathroom—barely jettisoning his cargo upon the porcelain tarmac into the hole that went through a maze of discombobulated pipes to God knows where.

"Uggh," moaned Rook. "I need to see a doctor." And he shat and splat and the past tense of that. If Hula or Boudicca could have seen him sitting there on the bodet, or if his fans could have, they would have been struck by a certain twinge upon his rugged, not quite Hollywood-handsome face, a twinge that said *I used to have it together but now it's coming undone.*

And as he waited for his money he thought of all the money he had pissed away in his life and how he wished he had it back now and could make good and proper use of it, helping some of these Indian street kids.

He went to the window again, wiping away the fog. "I'm coming, Boudicca. Believe me, I'll be there just as soon as I can. I'll find you and then we'll find mommy. Then we'll go back to Los Angeles, wouldn't that be nice? We'll have a good life together; like a normal family. A normal family. What is normal?" It had been so long, Rook had forgotten.

Someone cleared his voice. Rook turned. It was the butler.

"Sir, you rang?" he said in English with a slight British accent.

"Yes," said Rook, walking unabashedly towards the two outfits hanging up in the closet. "You're not a doctor. Never mind. Look," he said, shaking his head. "I was in a rush and packed some real shitty outfits. I can't wear this," he said, holding up a bright yellow cotton. "Sunshiny? I look like a traffic light, in between ... go to the store around here that sells the new Rookster® brand of clothing; get me all you can. There should be a wire of money coming into the front desk. Bring me the remainder and carry the seven."

"Pardon me, sir?"

"Just a bad joke. See if you can set me up with a doctor. A real doctor! Before I can hit the road, I need to be in top tip shape."

"Very well, sir," said the silver-haired butler, twirling the tips of his moustache as he left. And he wondered, thinking in Bengali, how a man who had no clothes at all when he walked into the hotel a few hours ago could be so picky. And he wondered where this rock star's companion Ming Dynasty was. And he remembered years ago waiting on John and Yoko in this very same suite. And he wondered why that in Ming's room there was now a taxi driver resting in the bed and giddily kicking his bare feet upon the satin spread. And he wondered why he was still working as a butler after all these years, when he had had dreams of becoming a concert violinist when young. But those were the dreams of youth and they had flittered away like an elusive rainbow butterfly. A tear rolled down the butler's wrinkled face ever so slowly as he took the elevator down.

Rook returned to the fetal position upon the bed, rubbing a little more lotion on his skin and reaching over to take an ice-pack out of the mini-bar. He placed the compress over his eyes and tried to feel no pain. He got up and took some more painkillers and waited for his money to come. *Most of our lives we spend waiting for money to come,* thought Rook. *Waiting, waiting, waiting. And when the money does come, we want more. And all these kids on the street and all these horns honking, chasing the buck and fighting time that does not stop.*

And Rook dozed off, covered in green aloe vera with green cucumbers askew and dreaming of piles of green money money money being loaded upon the downy bed—

so much money that it would solve all of the world's problems.

And Ted had his young female secretary arrange a meeting with some of the most fashionable fashion designers in India, such as Patchy Putabi, so he could take care of two birds with one stone. And then he thought: *things might get ugly.* And so he pulled out one of his fake passports, where he admired how fine he looked with his windswept hair and periwinkle glasses and his fake tan and his pseudonym (Garrett Sand), and called his secretary in again.

"Rianna," said Ted. "I need you to go over these shoots with me," he confided, spreading the photos of a precious looking Rook upon the pristine white powder acrylic designer table. "Let's make some money!"

"Let me first turn up the AC and get us some cappuccinos," said Rianna, massaging Ted's neck. "You work so hard."

"I have to!" said Ted. "You wouldn't believe how much my ex-wife gets every month! Oh, and pack an emergency kit. I have the feeling that this is going to be a bad mess to clean up."

"No wonder they pay you the big bucks," said Rianna, who had actually earned her masseuse license but only practiced for a short while—until she lost three of her fingers in a boating accident. "Do you want the Taser?"

"Definitely. Also, put in my grandpa's old trench knife. His chute too. Just in case."

"That old Mark I? But why?"

"Don't ask 'why.' Just do it."

And Southhampton remembered as clear as day one Christmas, some forty years ago back East, his grandfather holding him protectively, telling him all the old para-trooper stories from WW II, as snow gently fell from the Boston sky.

Rookster® Clothing Line: Fashion Shoots*

---

* An extensive dossier of the Rookster® clothing line was paper-clipped here in a handsome, glossy folder. There is not room for the lengthy addition presently, but the curious reader may find the documents on file at the invaluable Library of Congress. Many of these photos have also been widely circulated, as part of the well-known advertising campaign. As a matter of fact, according to the most recent financial reports, Rook's clothing line is currently producing more profit than his music (until his next album and tour, most likely). The 20-35 year-old male Indian market proved to be a wise business move on Southhampton's part, as that niche is showing signs of significant growth in general. Finally, Billy Todd, the unsuccessful Los Angeles mayoral candidate whom Rook met in Amsterdam, has apparently found success, having just recently been featured in the trades as the new manager of the West Coast office of the Rookster® line. The gossip is that Todd is contemplating running for office again. I suppose the old adage is true: "the clothes make the man." (Even for a naked rock star.)

13

THE KALI CLUB

What's my life come to? thought P, coming to. *I'm living in a damn hole! I'm a baby all over again!*

She rolled over on a strange, child-like blanky in the basement of Arjun's mansion. She noticed figures of Marilyn Monroe and other Hollywood icons adorning the cotton down with Warholian sequaciousness. Placing her hand to her aching wound, she allowed herself to enjoy deliberating on how she was going to decimate One-Eye when the opportunity presented itself; *I'll teach him a math lesson in division, and no remainders.*

But she pushed these thoughts out and focused on the task at hand: *escape, help get Boudicca; bring back Rook; and then what?*

This is not happening. It's like some sort of bad movie.

But it was happening. She noticed a cockroach scurry across the shadowy dank wall. And try as she might, she decided she would just do one thing at a time, and then find a way to retire and get out of this crazy business.

She felt where her ear used to be. She recalled how soft that earlobe had felt, with nice lotion, and how she would caress it and boyfriends would blow into it and give her pretty diamond earrings to hang from it. If she took her hand away, it almost seemed as it were still there—a phantom ear. She cocked her head and tried to hear out of it, covering her good one and snapping her fingers. She caught some muffled sounds, but it was as if she were under water. She put her hand up to it again—it smarted, and seemed to be crusted over in dry blood. But then she felt something mushy. "Uggh!" *I'll have to see a doctor. Now how do I get out of here? I guess I'll have to play it by ear. Damn't Rook, where are you?* And she gulped some water and overcome with fatigue, fell into a deep sleep again.

"Are you okay?" Anatoli Anti was asking Rook as they supped together in the restaurant of the Rajahranee that glowed like a big orange.

"I'm getting there," said Rook, watching warily as a band of musicians in sombreros approached

"Where are you from?" one of them asked.

"California," said Rook.

"Oh, California! We will play 'Hotel California' for you!" And they began.

Rook smiled, yet wondered when he would ever leave the Rajahranee to finally find Boudicca.

"Anatoli, I need a favor."

"You name it, my friend." Anatoli tore off a shrimp's tail and put it in a little pile he had been making.

"I need to find my daughter. And in order to do so, I need to meet this person in the Kali Club.* I've tried, but I can't get in there. Do you have any connections?"

Anatoli looked at Rook seriously, for the first time ever.

---

* Author's note in margin: verify, really an exclusive club, or bs?

"And what does your daughter have to do with this man?"

"I don't know really. All I know is that my old girl-friend got involved with this guy named Svidrigailov in Amsterdam. In order to keep her, he took our daughter and sent her to India for 'safekeeping.' The only contact name I was able to get was this Puroshottam Petro. I had a partner, P, who was working on getting in there, but she's disappeared. Last time I saw her was four days ago, just before I went off the deep end."

Anatoli looked at Rook a long time, as if judging whether or not to get involved. He shook his head ever so slightly, and ate another shrimp. He organized his little pile of tails like they were poker chips.

"Hmm . . . I'll tell you what—you make an appearance in my film here and I'll get you into the club. Believe it or not, I know Svidrigailov. When you're in the film business, you meet all types, mafia included. In fact, here in Bolly-wood, they practically run the show!"

"That's right! I remember S saying he knew you!"

"Really?" Anatoli looked worried. "Never mind. As far as this gentleman you mention, I don't know him, but I've heard his name. I believe he is Mumbai mafia. You know," and here he lowered his voice, "ever since the collapse of the Soviet Union, there seems to have been an increase in Russian mafia dealings with other countries. I'm not talking just drugs here, but a network that's all linked—stolen art, which sometimes is used as collateral, credit cards, identity theft, old submarines, even nuclear mate-rial—red mercury . . . S deals in sex—it sells—everyone knows that—that's his cover in Amsterdam—that's why he went to Amsterdam—prostitution is legal there. Also—marijuana—he grows his own, and runs a coffee shop too, but he smuggles a great deal out of the country. People sort of know about that too. What most don't know about is his other love—art—and of course Amsterdam is the home of many famous artists—Van Gogh, Rembrandt, some Vermeer, some Hals. So S is also in the business of art forgery, theft, and his drug business works hand in hand with his art business. Lately, how, you say, well he's going deep under water; he's maybe been getting into smuggling nuclear stuff—in the form of tiny canisters of red mercury, which now is code name for Lithium-6, out of Russia, through Amsterdam, and to the highest bidder—which is usually a foreign mafia or terrorist group. Bad news."

Anatoli cleared his throat, finished his plate of shrimp, and tidied up his pile. Rook looked at the missing creatures and then at this aging Russian turned Hollywooed director, who frantically began writing sudden ideas down for a classical movie soundtrack for his film scheduled three years from now, tentatively titled *The Melancholy Artist.*

"I don't want to save the world. I just want to find my daughter," said Rook. "Find her and get Hula and take them back to L.A. That's all. Will you help?"

Anatoli put his pen down and slapped Rook's sunburnt arm. "I'd be glad to," he laughed, then went back to his inspiration.

Rook winced, thought of composing too, but felt too melancholic; he gazed at the shrimp tails. *We've swum a long way*, he thought.

Anatoli, evidently done scribbling, stuffed the napkin in his pocket and got up suddenly.

"I need to call a few people," said Anatoli. "I'll call you when I know what's going on. We'll see if we can meet this guy and find your kid. And save the world through our art," he said, smiling.

"Thanks," said Rook. And the rock star hobbled up to his room, a shell of his former self, and sat gawking out the window, past the Gateway of India and into the Arabian Sea.

Lights from ships reflected and he wondered where they were going and what they were doing. He wondered if his daughter was on any one of them.

Rook paced about, and suddenly found his guitar in his hands. He started playing and singing—improvising, for he knew not what else to do.

He scribbled down an idea for a song that flowed from who knows where the wind comes from:

Em pluck   Asus pluck
See what's become of me
As I stare out at the sea
Monsoon's stopped but you're still not here
And silently runs a tear
Put out my hand but they think I'm waving
They don't know that I'm really drowning
They don't know nothing
And neither do I
The ship passes by
See what's become of me
Floating in the Arabian Sea
Lost my mind looking for you

Lost everything
Still haven't a clue
I'm falling to the bottom 2x
And it's all caving in   Sink or swim . . . .

Rook stopped and put down his guitar as thoughts of a concept album went through his aging brain. *I've given up. I've really given up, haven't I? If she wasn't my daughter, I'd say it's hopeless. She's already dead. Face the facts. Face reality. But I can't. I've got to keep trying. I've got to—I couldn't live with myself . . . I've got to find her.*

Rook stretched out upon the bed and stared up at the ceiling. He felt like he was swimming again in that pool as a kid. Rolling over and looking at the photo of Boudicca, for the first time, he noticed there was a sleeve to it, and something was taped inside. He undid it and looked at another photo inside—of Hula, S, and Boudicca. He sighed, then also discovered a note, evidently written by Boudicca to a boy named Cameron. It went:

Cameron [and Cameron was shaded], *1/25/09 (w/a hug!)*

Hey stud what up? Well N2M here but taking a break from the homework & decided I would write you since I never did when I said I would. LOL. Anyway, hows school been for ya? Good grades to keep your parent's proud? Mine are aiight u know the regular. Well how are the ladies? Any one in particular? Im sure you have plenty w/the stud you are :) seriously. So basketball is fun? Is your team good? How many wins do you have, or maybe; I mean what place are you in? LOL. IOK.

Anyway can't wait til summer, you excited? I am. No more work, drama, im free! :) Do you have any plans or vacations? I might go to the beach a lot LOL and chill w/friends that about it. Do you still skateboard? How is it? U pro yet or what? J/K. Well Im excited for sophomore year, we wont be scrubs anymore and were up in the food chain LOL. Finally. U gonna play NE other sports next yr? Idk if I am but oh well. Well I am sure [and this part was in the right-hand margin] *glad I am writing you, but now you have to write me back LOL. HAHA. Tell me all the interesting things about your life. Hows the family etc. Well out of room. LOV YA!* [and here the drawing of a heart] *Always, Boudicca* [and this part was jammed into the left-hand margin] *P.S. I couldn't find my markers but nxt time it will b pretty!*

Rook let the letter fall. *I don't even know this person.* He chuckled at his disbelief. "Oh Boudicca . . . ."

He laid back on the bed and fell into a deep sleep, dreaming of high school and a note he once passed to Hula; he tried to remember what he wrote . . . .

The phone woke him up.

"Yeah?" said Rook, recalling one line vividly from the note to Hula: *I'll always be here for you. Really.*

"I'm waiting for you. Where are you?"

"Anatoli?"

"No, it's the ice cream man. This isn't a movie. Stop the interstitial dialogue and get down here so we can go up."

Rook splashed on some Aqua-Velva, something he had always done since his daddy showed him how at the health club, the same club where he saw a large toenail lying on the tiled floor and he wondered how it got there and he wondered how he got there and he wondered how everything got to where it was and *what was stopping it from disappearing?*

He stood staring at himself in the mirror. For a moment, he thought he saw a double of himself. He rubbed his eyes and it was gone. His face and body were slowly healing. He was coming out of the void. But he still felt himself receding. *Where am I? Grasping for balance in the universe. What's to hold on to? Or do I let go?*

He felt himself losing focus and had to shake his head to snap out of it. "What am I waiting for? Let's go!"

"Yes, let us be going!" echoed Pompeii, popping in from next door, holding a plush pillow. "I hopes you have had the pleasure of the sleeps! I am loving the bed. It is so loveable and huggable! After great rests, I am readies!" And Pompeii squeezed the big ol' fluffy pillow.

"Okay," said Rook. "I'm counting on you though."

"You're lucky you're a friend of mine," said Anatoli as Rook and Pompeii approached. "I don't lay my neck on the line for just anybody."

"What are you talking about?" asked Rook, approaching as dapper as the new duds he was wearing. "You have a fabulous neckline."

"I don't think you understand how difficult it is to bring a stranger in there—even a celebrity. When John and Yoko stayed here, they didn't even go up."

Rook shrugged and rubbed his eyes—they were really itching now. "Everything's converging."

"What? What the hell are you talking about? You sound like one of my bad actors. Who the fuck is this ragamuffin with you? A taxi driver?" asked Anatoli, as if he didn't remember Pompeii from a few hours ago.

"Why, yes," said Rook. "He helped me out earlier so I thought I'd return the favor. He can translate for us."

"Actually, that's not a bad idea," said Anatoli, framing the driver in the camera lens of his mind. "Okay." And Anatoli pulled Rook by his Rookster® shirt sleeve and together they headed towards the golden elevator, Pompeii puffing behind. Rook remembered a book from his childhood: *Charlie and the Great Glass Elevator* and wondered if he were entering some bizarre otherworld.

Why is he not remember me? thought Pompeii.

Anatoli inserted a magic key and the door opened with a WHOOSH!

The interjection excited Rook—he took a deep breath and they crossed into the strange world of billionaires and golden elevators and golden toilet bowls and golden teeth and golden everything and that precious metal that is forming in running streams and caused the westward migration to California and the eventual real estate boom and eventual bust of the early 2000s was that same gold that was lying at the bottom of oceans in lost Spanish doubloons and in various banks and bars in Dublin, Ireland and environs.*

And then Rook snapped out of it and noticed (in this strange state he was in—an aftereffect of the soma?) as clear as day everything—almost as if a sixth sense had

---

* Author's note at top of page with line drawn: FIX. More tabloid journalism, less Joyce. Ref Nietzsche's eternal recurrence of the same?

become acute and he was fully aware of his eminent and imminent death and he saw everything crystal clearly and noticed that Anatoli, usually calm as a cucumber on the set, was now sweating and not calm and perhaps claustrophobic?

As they got to the top and a bell rang and maybe an angel got its wings they strolled out as if they were in a hip-hop video but anachronistically.

"Yes?" inquired a man at another golden door.

"Anatoli Anti, They're expecting us."

"Yes." And the man looked at them seriously and dialed a number.

"Yes?" he asked into the receiver, looking up at the video camera. "Yes."

And he hung up the phone and looked at them. "Yes," and he showed them up to the next level.

As the door opened, they were greeted by a beautiful hostess in a very business-like sari—burgundy in color. "Follow me," she said, smiling, her lips pursed.

"Gladly," mumbled Rook, almost drooling, "I'll follow you off the edge of the earth." And if any impartial observer were watching, they would wonder why Rook's lips were full of blisters and they would think STDs but be wrong and maybe only afterwards consider the unforgiving sun.

The fashionable woman deposited them in a room with a view with a group of men in baggy designer suits with their backs to them and a wade of cigar smoke drifting languidly through the air.

"You may wonder what we are doing here," said a gruff voice with a Hindi/British accent. "Why don't you know, we plan and scheme here to take over the world, and of course play poker and gamble like madman. All the world's a gamble—a flying fuck, isn't it?" And the man turned and laughed and started coughing and waved through the cloud of smoke he had just created and began coming towards Rook and Anatoli like a crocodile on the Discovery Channel.

(Here is where the author would describe the face of this rogue—the deep lines of time that resembled fossils in the bedrock at Death Valley—the eyes that were bloodshot from lack of sleep and scheming demons of greed—the rubber tire around the waste that he was no Goodyear at—and the decaying yellow teeth and gold and gold-rimmed glasses and gold Rolex and gold lame belt that accented his otherwise drab beige camouflage khaki demeanor. But the author will not bore you with tired and tried literary intrusions and crap and dispense with the rhetorical strategies and stick with the gossip journalism that sells! Photo please! Scandalous, far-fetched caption!*)

"Puroshottam Petro, should have shunt ya," and the smoking man appeared to be smoldering, extending his four-digit hand to them. "Anatoli, I think I met you, many years ago. How's the Hollywood cages? And Rook, I've heard the name, but you'll have to sing for me."

Rook smiled as he shook his hand but then his face turned blue as the man increased his squeeze and would not let go no matter how Rook tried to squirm out.

"What?" asked Rook.

---

* Author's mark of a star and then heavily underlined: PLEASE! DELETE! Settle libel suits later. Always worry about lawsuits later. After laundry. (As the reader can see, this editor has not deleted this and other passages as the author may have wished; hopefully, retaining them adds insight into the somewhat haphazard, recursive writing process of Anonymous.)

"Sing! Prove you can do it—prove you're a talent—or I swear I'll shoot you where sleeping dogs lie goddamnit!" And the Petro had the gumption to pull a pistol and cock it with unction. "I have friends who are dying and in desperate need of your vital organs."

And the men by the window in leisurely leather chairs waved through the Havana smoke and nodded from behind Thums-up bottle glasses that this indeed was the case.

"Come on, chessboy," said Petro. "Prove that you deserve your life more than they do!"

Rook looked to Anatoli for guidance, but Anatoli subtly shrugged, took one step back, got out his small camcorder, and surreptitiously began filming.

"What do you want me to sing?" asked Rook.

"Sing a song that makes me emotional," said Petro, putting the gun to Rook's temple. It felt cold. There was the clearing of throats from the others in the room, or maybe they were just oversmoking. Rook averted his eyes from Petro's and fought the urge to smile.

"Do you mind if I face the sea?" asked Rook, thinking of the song he had sung just a little while ago in his room, looking out at the Arabian. "It helps me get into the mood."

"Fine," said the floating tire of the Petro, a little haltingly, "But I'm tired of delays. Break his fingers! Do it!"

"What?"

But Petro's men had already gone into motion. One of them picked up an old heavy tablet. Another grabbed Rook's right hand, and before Rook could protest again, they had smashed his fingers.

"What the fuck?" said Rook, holding his right hand with his left hand. "Why did you do that?"

"I mean business. When I say something, it gets done right away, so you better make sure that you just go!"

"Okay, it starts off slowly," said Rook, "with just a guitar, and then the haunting melody, Em, Asus . . . ." And Rook took a breath, tried his best to ignore the throbbing pain in his fingers, then looked at the night waves and moonlight, and began singing, as calmly as he could, thinking: *if I die here, my life will have been incomplete, I need to sing to please this crazy man, but I also have to please myself—an artist's aesthetic down to the very end—you can't teach creativity . . . stop thinking so much and just be . . . .*

"See what's become of me
As I stare out at the sea
Monsoon's stopped but you're still not here
And silently runs a tear
Put out my hand I think I'm sinking
They don't know that I'm really drowning
They don't know nothing
And neither do I
The ship passes by . . . ."

Meanwhile, Anatoli Anti, who was waging fifty/fifty odds that Petro would shoot Rook and dispose of his body at the local hospital which he owned (and was named Day and Night Petro Hospital), and who looked over to observe and film the other men laying a wager on something— perhaps the same sentiments, suddenly, if he were in on the game, would give it to letting Rook live when he heard the pure emotion coming from the aging rock star with no pretense or contrivance or jockeying for his niche or position and Anatoli thought how he could use this scene and song in his movie—played by Rook himself—fictionalized of course. Perhaps he could get Petro to take part, but that was asking for too much trouble . . . unless he appealed to his megalomaniacal ego.

Rook continued, trying to melt into the waves and the monsoonal rains that began to fall:

"See what's become of me
Floating in the Arabian Sea
Lost my mind looking for you
Lost everything
Still haven't a clue
I'm falling to the bottom 2x
And it's all caving in   Sink or swim . . . ."

Rook finished and turned around, surprised he was still breathing. To further his astonishment, Petro was crying, and feigning putting up the gun to his own head.

"My son, you have touched my heart with pure emotion, thank you, thank you for reminding me." And Petro stared off into some distant memory.

"Mother? Where are you Mamaji?" asked Petro.

Rook stared down at the white cashmere carpet, not sure what he was expected to do next. So he pulled out a cigarette, lit it with difficulty as his hands trembled, and began smoking.

Petro promptly snatched it away.

"My dear boy, a voice such as yours needs to be preserved. Come, get some ice for this man's fingers! No wonder you're a star! It's all about emotion. It's all about emotion!" And he put his arm around Rook. The men at the table quickly exchanged bets. Petro led Rook over to the table and offered him and Anatoli a chair. "Do you know how many people in India would kill to get a seat at this table?"

Rook shook his head. "I don't know, sir. I don't know anything anymore."

Petro looked at Rook for the first time.

"What is it? How can I help you? I will try."

"I'm just trying to find my daughter, that's all."

"Ah, ah, yes, children—that's a whole 'nother story. But India is full of wandering children. How can I help?"

"Svidrigailov," said Anatoli.

"Ah," said Petro, nodding. "I think I understand."

"Your name was the only contact I had," said Rook. "I came from Amsterdam, having met my ex there, working for Mr. S. I found out he's keeping her there by hanging on to our daughter. And all I know is my daughter has been kept here—I just missed seeing her in her cage on Kamathapuri."

Petro turned and looked out at the city profoundly. "Oh, just to be an old Mahori fisherman," mumbled Petro. Then, turning back to Rook: "I will do what I can—make some enquiries. In the meantime, join us in a game of poker and drinks?"

"Sure," said Rook, sitting down. Petro motioned into the camera for someone to go and do something. Rook looked at the hand he was dealt, and determined it was all on how you played it.

"What shall we play for?" asked Petro, rubbing his palms together.

"Artwork," said Rook, not sure why, going on intuition. "Because art matters."

There was a short silence.

"Why not?" said Petro. "Allow me to introduce you to my friends at the table," he said. "On my left, Abrasive, in trucking, on my right, my right-hand man, Thorton, on both sides of you, Mahesh and Mukesh—the best in the IT business, and of course, I am Petro, I own everything, from cars to textiles to coffee to weapons, and yes, even some art! Let's play!"

Rook was embarrassed by his hand, yet he bet large anyway, bluffing his way through, just like he had always done in life. *There's nothing else I can do right now, so I won't worry, I'll just let it go and play along.*

His gaze happened upon some paintings lining the wall. *Was that a Vermeer? And that a Van Gogh? No, well, maybe. A Rembrandt? The Dutch Connection? Svidrigailov? And where have I heard that name before? I should call Hula. And Pui. Where the heck has she gone? But she's a big girl; she can handle herself. I hope.*

"I fold," said Rook, getting up. "Where's the bathroom?"

"Don't you want to keep playing?" asked Petro. "The prize is that rare Vermeer over there. You don't get the chance at one of those pretty ladies every day! Her beauty lasts forever!"

"I'll be back, thank you," said Rook.

In the gold-plated bathroom, Rook adjusted his pendants, took out his lucky back-up phone (he had lost his other on the beach), and called Hula. It rang and rang—no answer, no voice-mail even. He then tried P and got her recording; it was a pleasure just to hear her voice. He left her a message: "Hi P, I'm still down here, looking for a lead to Boudicca. It's been rough, but I think we're making progress. Hope you're okay. I'll see, we'll see you soon. Love you?"

He couldn't believe he had said those last two words. Perhaps they were true, perhaps not. *Do I still love Hula? What am I doing?* He quickly deleted the message.

Rook made his way back to the card table and sat down, saying as kindly as possible: "Gentlemen, I don't know what I was talking about. I thought we would play for some nice art, you know a couple thousand dollars' worth. But I don't have anything to gamble that's comparable to these masterpieces on the wall."

"What about your daughter?" asked Thorton, without missing a beat. "Why not gamble that little piece of treasure? I could use a lung of hers," he wheezed, coughing up some phlegm.

Rook's first impulse was to kill him by casting off his petrified head with the still-sharp blade of an ancient chakram that hung on the wall. But then, that would get him nowhere, except chopped up into little pieces and into some mobster's body.

"I'm sorry," said Rook. "I'm trying to find her, not lose her again."

"Thorton is just trying to, how do you say, 'get your goat,'" said Petro, adjusting his earpiece. "Don't you worry, Rook Heisenberg. You'll be happy to know that my associates from the netherworld have just informed me that your daughter is still alive and well. She is currently being transported, as we speak, to Rishikesh. She has been sold as a great *randi*, or highly-valued prostitute, against Svidrigailov's wishes, and unbeknownst to him, to a famous actor. She was sold according to my and my associate's wishes—but this is before I know you! Now this actor is a bit crazy—and not even a very good actor anymore (if you ask me). God only knows what he has in mind. I would suggest you hurry to get her. I will give you a car if need be. I like you. I want to help you. In return, you maybe do me a favor someday. I trust you will comply. Please comply. Don't make me look bad. I'm old."

Rook didn't know what to say. Instead, Anatoli spoke. "Is it Arjun Alexander?"

Petro nodded. "He used to play poker with us. In fact, he sat right where you're sitting, Rook. Always played the Joker. I should use him for organ donation. But he's sick."

"Everybody knows he's sick," said Anatoli. "I know him. He was in a movie of mine once. He's washed up now, though. He's insane—crazy method actor, Don Juan wanna-be. You should go armed."

And Anatoli thought: *what a neat movie it would make if I went along and filmed, but that would be big trouble! Bad news!*

"You think so," said Rook, getting up, seriously. "I'm not very good with weapons. But I have a bodyguard."

"Indeed," said Petro, cautiously, "indeed? Where is she? Have your driver, Pompeii, drive you in one of my SL600s. There are many weapons in that car at your disposal, Mr. Rook. But you should practice. Be ready."

Pompeii, who had been standing by the door this whole time at attention almost erupted. He was amazed that Petro was commissioning him to drive Mr. Rook in a souped-up Mercedes. And he was curious as to how Mr. Petro knew his name. And then he was nervous that he might get involved in this underworld and wind up at Petro's hospital—making an unexpected and early donation to science. He held himself back from complaining, knowing that Petro had taken a strange sudden liking to this American rock star who only a few hours ago was naked and nameless at the beach. Pompeii didn't want to make Mr. Petro upset; he had heard that the mobster had killed for much less—in fact, his first killing was for breakfast when he was twelve. And this was Petro's philosophy: you don't get rich without breaking a few eggs.

"Thank you, Mr. Petro," said Rook. "I am indebted to you, and if I can ever return the favor, I'd be happy to." Petro got up and hugged Rook, as if he were a long lost son. And images of mafia movies came to Rook's mind, but what else could he do? He had to find Boudicca. *Why do all these mafia guys like singing?*

"This is not a problem, for you are reminding me of one of my sons—whom I lost, long, long ago . . . ." said Petro, staring out at the sea. "But time is of the essence—go, go. They are way ahead of you—they're probably getting close to Rishikesh, and will be probably the staying at Arjun's old mansion. But go, go, and Krishna be with you. You've got a lovely voice!"

As Rook, Anatoli, and Pompeii left, Rook took a look at the Rembrandt and Van Gogh self-portraits on the wall;

their eyes followed him as he departed, and he tried to figure out what departing advice they were whispering to him.

"After you find her I'll help you remake your movie career!" said Anatoli, huckstering down the elegant and elongated hallway, tapping his feet to the music of *West Side Story* that was playing in his graying head and thinking of the Bollywood meeting he had in an hour.

Rook nodded. *I'm already in a movie. I'm already in a crazy fucking movie. I just have to learn how to be a better actor.*

Rook took out his phone and called P: "P, it's Rook. If you get this, come on Rocinante and meet us up at Rishikesh. We know where they're taking Boudicca."

And Pompeii looked at Rook's shiny cell and thought of calling his own wife and daughter but was now too shy to ask this most and famous and strange man. *How is it that so many spend their whole lives half-naked and with nothing, and this man in a matter of minutes—by singing—can turn his whole life around? I should be taking up the singing! No more taxis!* And he opened his mouth to sing, but nothing came out except: "Hmmmm." And very lowly at that.

"What are you 'hmmmming' about?" asked Rook.

"Nothing," said Pompeii. "There is nothing wrong."

"There is a lot wrong," said Rook. "But we're going to fix that. It's time for a change."

As they took the private elevator back down, a ghastly painting of Kali stared out at them with her red eyes and mad hair, beckoning mysteriously with her four arms as they descended.

14

MING'S MISSING EAR & THE MISSING VAN GOGH

Pui Pui Poon, aka Ming Dynasty, awoke with a jolt to the sound of her whistling *Kill Bill* ringtone and mumbled, "It's not too late to have babies!" It slowly dawned on her that she was free—and she was no longer tied up. She tried to remember what name she was going by. Her limbs were slow at first, near-dead then tingling, but she stretched out all four to reach the beats of her phone.

"Huh," she managed to the rhythm.

"Aye, I see you are up and about. Good. Listen, dearie, your Van Gogh seems to have checked out, and so, I have checked you out. I am a man of my word. You are free to go. But please, don't try and track me down. It is not worth your time or my money."

P was about to say something when One Eye hung up.

She got her bearings and noticed that the dank room had been emptied. *What happened?* She tried to remember—*drink of water—it must have been drugged. What day is it?* She shook her head alert and crawled towards the door. It was left ajar, a little light coming in from above. She reached to feel where her ear once was. Scabby Crustacea.

"It's okay, it's okay," she told herself. But she was frowning like a baby about to cry. The Beatles' song—"Cry Baby Cry"—went through her head.

Searching the house, she found it completely empty—ultra modernist and minimalistic—white on white—except in the middle of the living room—the only items were a vintage copy of the Beatles' *White Album* resting on top of a large brick, and a bright sunflower in a vase. Suddenly compelled, P looked down, and turning her foot, sure enough found an RMB 100 note sticking to it.

"That's very strange," she said aloud. Her voice echoed and sounded raspy. She took the note, stuffed it in her pocket, took the sunflower, put it in her hair, and picked up the brick. Standing it on end, she focused all her energy, and broke it with two fingers.

She left the Beatles album for the next visitor to enjoy.

Her phone beeped; she noticed Rook had called.

"P, it's Rook. If you get this, come on Rocinante and meet us up at Rishikesh. We know where they're taking Boudicca."

P stepped outside into the blinding sunlight, gasped at the humid air, and formed a plan. *First, back to the hotel. Clean up. Second, get the bike and head North. Third, get Boudicca back and protect client Rook. Fourth, return them both safely to Amsterdam. Fifth, get my ear back. Sixth, get the Van Gogh back. Seventh, get revenge on One Eye. In that order?*

And as she was walking back to civilization, bruised and barefoot, calling for a taxi, she bought a Thums-up! Cola, saw a picture of Rook in a tabloid, and decided that things were looking up. She noticed a copy of Gandhi's *The Story of My Experiments with Truth*, and couldn't pass up the bargain—only 50 rupees!

As she was drinking that lovely Thums-up!, she dropped the bottle cap, and being loathe to litter in a street that teemed with laughter, she bent down to follow the rolling cap. It led her to a strange item lying near a gutter— a severed ear! *Could it be mine? If so, how on earth did it fall there? My ear, that I have heard and felt so much with!* And she remembered that boy Cameron from high school and how he paid particular attention to that ear with his tongue, sucking on it, and what would he and his tongue think of her and her ear now? *I'll have to find him on Facebook,* she thought.

She quickly picked it up, her back aching as she knelt down, and brushed it off. She observed a broken mason jar next to it, and was careful not to step in the glass. She examined the curve of the lobe and the piercing and matched its shape to her missing puzzle. *It's mine. Okay, P, what next?*

A rickshaw rolled up. "Where to?" the gaunt and eager driver asked.

"Rajahranee Hotel," P said, cupping the ear ever so gently in her deadly hand. The driver stared.

"What you gots?" he asked as they began rumbling not too slowly over the potholed roads.

"I gots problems," said P. "Problems."

"Yes, this is true for many—*ah-cha*. What's your name?"

"What's in a name?"

"You do Shakespeare! I likes this! What, you like me?"

P smiled. "My name is Ming."

"And I am the Indian Slim Shady—I go by Phat Shady! Come see me perform tonight! I will be putting ons quite the shows!"

"I'll see what I can do. But I have to go to Rishikesh."

"Oh, the holy city. I likes, wishes I could go but I must sing—I'm very good, Ming!"

P looked down at her ear, withering away, and cleaned out some bugs that were just as lost in there as she was out here.

"Listen," said P, "this may sound unusual, but I need your help. Do you know somewhere to get some leeches?

Phat pulled over and stopped the engine.

"What is this 'leeches?'"

"You know, worm-like blood-suckers."

And she showed him her ear.

"Agggh! This is the fright! Leeches! Yes, you mean *jonk*?"

"Yes, Phat, *jonk*."

"I see you want it back. Don't have a heart attack. I will impact the scene with gasoline, so keep it real—word."

P smiled. They started up for who knows where, Phat evidently looking for leeches.

P remembered smiling more many moons ago. Ever since her kung fu training, she was taught to wear a mask of stern bronze. She remembered before that—putting cards and streamers on her bicycle with training wheels, and watching the wheel spin round and make that flapping sound. She rode the bike down the hill at the orphanage in Canton—watching the streamers flow colorfully in the wind, and she smiled at the freedom of the breeze in her hair.

Where had that freedom gone?

She touched where her ear had been, and hoped to be reunited with it soon. She felt disconnected, and wanted to get back to where she was going, for she was going somewhere with purpose and passion, she was going far beyond, and she wanted to help Boudicca go there too.

Phat stopped at some strange hut.

"Be back in a minute," he said, and he vanished beneath the flap of a shopkeeper's tent.

P opened up Gandhi's book and read about being detached from the things of this world, and holding firmly to truth. She held firmly to her detached ear. Then she noticed a child motioning to her with her hands out.

"Are you hungry?" asked P. The child nodded languidly, and extended her hands even further. P gave her some rupees, but the emaciated girl had developed a peculiar interest in the odd ear, and continued holding out her hand for it. Just then Phat reappeared from beneath the wetted-down canvas of the tent with a huge smile and an even huger jar of leeches.

"*Jonk!*" he proclaimed. "Look, Ming, your leeches!" He frowned at the child and batted her away but kept her at a distance—like some bothersome monkey with Herpes B virus. As they scooted off, the child pleaded with P with her distraught eyes, and P saw herself years ago. *I should bring her a bicycle,* P determined.

Soon, but not soon enough for P, they were at the Rajahranee Hotel.

"Thank you for all your help," P said to Phat.

"No problem. I hopes to see you at the show it would be very much welcome!"

"Yes," said P, and she paid him a rather handsome tip—handsomer than he was.

"Goodbye, Ming!"

P waved farewell, ear in hand, and headed past the Sikh doormen, who were all bows and smiles to her despite her ghastly appearance. She took the elevator, ascending up to their suite. Looking into the mirror, she took the sunflower out of her silky hair and spoke: "What am I doing here? What on earth am I doing here?" She cleaned the ear methodically, and her wound, and then somewhat squeamishly arranged the leeches on it, fitting it onto the scabby spot upon the side of her head. She leaned into the mirror and watched them begin sucking and winced. Putting on her motorcycle helmet, she headed down for Rocinante. *I'm going to find them. But am I falling for Rook?*

Engine roaring between her thighs, wind blowing freely, leeches sucking and working inside the helmet, P felt like a child again riding her bicycle; but this time she had purpose; this time she had intent. The monsoon began to fall.

***

Window open to the outside in Amsterdam, Hula studied a sunflower in a box that rested on her windowsill and observed how it leant towards the sun.

"I can't keep doing this," she said to herself, looking down from the Capri Club at the rain-slicked streets. "I'm at the end of the road."

She went into her own room at the top of the stairs and locked the door. She looked at herself in the mirror. She was not the spring chicken anymore that Rook had met in Iowa City all those years ago. Her body was still perky, but now it felt sore and she just wanted to take a shower and wash it all away. *Wash it all away. Down the drain. And where does it go? Out to the sea? And then?*

After her shower, she wrapped a scarlet terry cloth robe around her, made a pot of fresh coffee, and went outside on her balcony. She brushed the rainwater off the iron chairs, and sat down facing the overcast afternoon. She took a sip of java, lit up a Marlboro Light (she had switched to them from Reds years ago), and blew rings around the clouds.

"Oh Boudicca . . . ." and she swelled up with a love that surprised her. "I'm not a very good mother. I'm sorry."

And then an almost imperceptible red swirl and brilliant aura enveloped her, but she was unaware of it, as humble people are when such an authentic moment happens. And the halo circled her Hula hoop and something effortlessly and forever changed in her, and she felt this sudden sea change inside, but didn't know what to think or even how to describe it—it just washed over her, basking over the ridge of her gloom. The glow simultaneously* occurred from the inside-out to a young person who was watching TV in Basking Ridge, New Jersey, and, unbeknownst to the two of them, they had known each other in a past life and were best friends and would probably be drawn together again in this life but for what purpose it was unclear at this point. The girl in New Jersey sat absorbed in a documentary on Van Gogh, that spoke of one of his missing masterpieces of two lovers walking in a garden, and meanwhile Hula thought of strolling through the Van Gogh Museum later that day to blow off some

---

* Author's stickie note: What was I thinking? Synchronicity? Acausal? Fix!

steam and take in some emotion and then through cathar-
sis let her own art out into the beauty of the universes. And
all these things happened as Hula enjoyed a cup of coffee
and a cigarette with the sun now slowly sinking and
dancing over a wet cobblestone street in Amsterdam and
the light hit the wetness and certain spots just right making
everything feel clean and new again.*

***

S meanwhile toured his art gallery, admiring his own
work, his own forgeries, and his few original collectibles.
He rubbed an aging hand over the space where the Van
Gogh had hung. "I'll get you back, don't worry, old
friend," he promised the missing treasure. And he thought
of his mother, and how she had given him this work, and
then of the woman from long ago that he fell for, and
wanted to give the painting to; she had walked, or more
accurately—run out of his life before he had had a chance
to impress her with it. *Only she would understand it,* he
thought. "You were a good mother!"

As he walked, he stopped and took a long look out the
window, and thought of Hula. "I think I love her. If I am
even capable of love, that is how I feel," he said, perhaps
trying to convince himself, perhaps trying to articulate his
understanding to himself. "But why do I love her? But how
will I please her?" he asked aloud. He cupped his delicate
twig and berries and remembered Dr. Van Halen applying
the leeches just before he went to sleep. He shook his head
at the memory of them smooching his privates. "But

---

* Author's annotation: Bad Hemingway!

sometimes you need to lose a little blood to get things done," he said. "So far, so good," he whispered. "So far, so good."

He would never tell Hula about the leeches, as that would come between their lovemaking sessions, she being squeamish about all things slimy and insect-like.

***

Later that evening, Old One Eye arrived on the red eye into Schiphol Airport. Before going to the Genteel Hotel to pick up Vincent, he paid a visit to a prostitute by the name of Rachel he once had a crush on but now she was getting older.

"You've changed," she informed him.

"So have you," he said.

An hour later he got to the hotel and was greeted by its indefatigable manager. "Welcome, welcome," laughed the man. "Allow me to introduce myself. My name is Poop-jean."

"So you're named after a bowel movement, aren't you?" asked One, barely able to look at this lively charac-ter.

"Well, I can't remember, but someone once said: 'man is happy when his bowels work, and unhappy when they don't.' A more simple or profound truth you'd be hard-pressed to find."

"Yes, I can vouchsafe for that after my run-ins in India. Well, my art critic friend says that the painting is legit. So where is it?"

"Yes, it has been verified in its authenticity," said Poop, taking a long cardboard tube from out of a mink from out of the safe behind him and handing it to One.

"Show me to my room," said One, gravely.

Poopjean was silent for longer than he should have been. "Okay. You're right. You know, Mr. One, that most of S's collection, if you can call it that, are fakes. It's more of a hobby of his. But he does have some real masterpieces that he uses as collateral."

"So the Van Gogh is real?"

"As far as can be determined—from your friend's inspection, and my own research. It's called *The Lovers: The Poet's Garden IV*. It's been missing for years—ever since the Nazis confiscated it. Somehow it ended up in S's family. I'm not sure of the connection, but I do know that he values it for sentimental reasons; his mother gave it to him. I believe it was the art that inspired him to become an artist."

"A failed artist."

"Like Hitler."

"He wasn't as good in either respect," said One.

"I like the painting, for what it's worth" said Poop, honestly. "I like the lovers walking through the field, blending in with nature. It's touching. I think there's some melancholy there too, but the greenness all about gives them hope and sustains them."

"They have hope in love too," said One, surprising himself and quickly changing the subject. "I plan to get it checked out by my own sources. There will be issues if it doesn't match up."

"I sincerely hope not. This is too pleasant a place for issues."

"Then let us hope there are none." And One walked towards the elevator, past someone who looked like a rapper and past a man with a deep tan decked out in gold chains, looking at pictures of clothing designs.

***

As Hula was trying to get a catnap, she was awoken by S getting into bed and feeling her up.

"Honey, please, I can't," she pleaded.

"Come on, I need to let some steam off," said S. "If I can, that is," he laughed, trying to make light of his sensitive sac and its questionable functionality.

"Do what you have to do," said Hula, turning over and letting him do his business. To Hula, at some point S had become just another client in a long list of clients. She wondered if the life she had gotten accustomed to was really any different from that of most wives. Sure, she had gotten together with S in the first place because he had money, and he offered her an easy way to live well and support her daughter. But did she love him? *What is love?* she wondered. Were not many women in the same position, no pun intended? She thought about the first time S convinced her to dance at the club in London—and it was some dance. When she danced, she imagined she were with Rook at that wedding from long ago, dancing slow, dancing seductively, dancing with passion. From there, however, a slippery slope ensued, and no memories of weddings or romance entered into the sad picture. Nude cabaret—and although the first time it was embarrassing and her mind was on a million things and an abnormal fear that the father she had come to London to look for would suddenly be there in the crowd looking up at her, Hula got used to it after a while, like one gets used to almost anything. And she actually came to enjoy showing off her beautiful body and teasing the men and making good money doing so. When S moved everything to Amsterdam, Hula felt compelled to follow; she found it hard to give up the elegant lifestyle, and to be honest, for a while she enjoyed the strange allure of the mafia mystique that S brought along with him like a cloud of cigar smoke wherever he went.

When business at the Capri Club opened, S needed not only dancers, of course, but women who would offer their "services" to the clientele. At first she hemmed and hawed, but then reasoned that she had sometimes given party-favors at the club in London if the clients paid her enough on the side, and so it really wouldn't be much of a stretch if she now and then had sex with someone—*as long as I'm making more money and enjoying life, what the hell?* The first time she had sex with a John, she felt disgusted and almost threw up afterwards, but then she was able to find the proper frame of mind, and if a client really repelled her, S would usually give her permission to decline, unless of course it was big money or some business connection. Hula felt compelled to help S get his business up and off the ground in Amsterdam—but now, now that it was up and running, she couldn't see herself going on doing this any longer. It was finally over. Yes, she was still young—33, and S had really wanted her to do it for a few more years—

she looked 27 and was his biggest draw. Last year, when she let S know she wanted out, he took precautions to try and keep her in the business—sending Boudicca off to India, and she hated him for this, but she didn't know what she could do, honestly. She supposed if Rook had not so heroically appeared, she would have found a way to go herself, or hired someone like Pui to go for her. That was the problem—if she suddenly disappeared, she had a real fear that S would do something S-like, and kill Boudicca. And so she just took drugs, cocaine and pot and alcohol and extasy to numb the pain and get through the job. And she used lots of jelly and had herself checked monthly for STDs and HIV and so far had been lucky. But now, thanks to S losing his balls and Rook reappearing, S had softened and became jealous, or perhaps stopped taking Hula for granted and realized what a great woman she was?

"Oh, Hula, baby, oh!" shouted S, exploding with a hurrah. "I've still got it!" And S was beaming that his plumbing still seemed to be functioning. He made a mental note to give the surgeon an extra $1000 and a complimentary visit to the house.

"Honey, I'm glad you're feeling better," said Hula, cleaning off the goo. "Do you think we can have a baby when we get married?"

"Of course. I would love a son! I need a son!"

And S pictured raising a child he could give his empire to. But he would have to teach him the difference between right and wrong, or between necessary violence and unnecessary brutality.

Hula kept her back towards him and sat staring out the window past the Rodin statue and towards the fading rays of sunlight that cascaded across the row of houses that leaned forward ever so slightly. "I love you," she told S as she climbed back into bed, spooning with him. She pretended to go to sleep, wondering where Boudicca and Rook and Pui were right this second.

"I love you too," said S. And he wondered if he meant it and if Hula really meant it. And they both wondered what love was as all sorts of couplings went on down below in the club.

***

"Hey P, this is Rook!"

"Rook! It's so good to hear your voice!" P said as she stopped for a drink at a roadside stand and wondered about the possible pesticides in it.

"Listen, I got a lead on Boudicca and am on my way to Rishikesh to track her down. Where are you?"

"It's a long story. I was held—kidnapped—but I saw Boudicca."

"You saw her!"

"Yes, just after I got my ear chopped off."

"What the hell? Well, you know supposedly Boudicca's been sold off to some rich, famous actor; he's a crazy shit and thinks that, that a virgin will cure him of AIDS."

"I know. I met him."

"You met him?"

"Briefly."

There was a pause.

"I have the feeling his life will be even briefer," said Rook, in a manner that was so terrible that he made a mental note to utter it in Anatoli Anti's new Bollywood film if he made it through.

"Listen, I'm a day or so behind you," said Pui. "I'll catch up to you in Rishikesh."

"We're going to Arjun Alexander's estate."

"I'm hurrying," said Pui. "We'll get through this together. We'll help Boudicca."

"Let's hope she can help herself until we get there," said Rook, and he hung up, wondering about why butterflies flew the way they did as one landed on a nearby yellow flower in a meadow north of Nashik.

***

"Who was that?" asked Boudicca of Arjun, of a man naked and blue with a severe expression on his face, pointing a finger towards some indistinguishable point in space.

"Nobody," said Arjun. "Some crazy guru. Would you mind rolling the window down?" he asked Abhishek. "I'm feeling a little light-headed."

Abhishek looked over at him seriously. "Are you being funny?" he asked. "What is wrong?"

"I'm too sick," said Arjun. The window went down quickly, and Arjun actually threw up out the window, watching the vomit trail and a string of saliva blow in the wind from his once revered lips.

"Are you okay?" asked Abhishek, pulling over.

"I will be," he mumbled, looking at Boudicca tenderly and touching her knee. "I will be."

"Do you like my outfit?" asked Boudicca. "I can't wait to bring it back home! It'll be all the rage! It's from a new line called Rookster®!"

"That's nice, darling," faintly feeling déjà vu from one of his movies.

"Are you really a famous movie star? How come nobody's getting your autograph?"

"We're all movie stars honey, all starring in the movie of our lives. And that's the best acting—when you're not acting."

As Arjun was delivering this supercilious advice, the severe ascetic approached, in an entirely avant-garde movie of his own, with the most intense expression in his bold eyes that it jolted Arjun and Abhishek out of their drug-induced complacency and made them say simultaneously: *"Visar manisan! Visar attam!"*

"Does he want your autograph?" inquired Boudicca.

"Go go!" shouted Arjun. But the car had a hiccup and wouldn't start and suddenly this vortex of Vishnu was next to them and he raised a finger to the blue of the sky and thundered:

"Kimekam daivatham loke? Kim japan muchyate jantur janma samsaara bandhanaath?"

The ascetic's eyes mirrored the windswept wild azure of the yonder and they burnt through the two men. But when they set upon Boudicca, they smiled, and some strange darshan passed. He removed a gold and silver astrological bangle from his wrist, and gave it to her.

"Cool!" she said. "Thank you!" And she twirled it around her wrist.

The car suddenly coughed and started and they sped away, the ascetic nodding gently to Boudicca.

"What was that?" she asked.

"Oh, just some crazy mad man, down from the Himalayas, heading to the Kumbha Mela," said Arjun.

"He said something from the *Mahabharata*," said Abhishek. "I remember from when I was your age," he told Boudicca. "Something about who is the one Lord of All? Who commands everything? And what is that which by uttering any human can attain freedom from the cycle of births and deaths?"

"*Vishnu sahasranama,*" said Arjun, morbidly. "Chanting the thousand names of God will free you."

"Oh," said Boudicca, examining her new bracelet. "I like that. It's neat!"

"Yes, very neat," said Arjun. "Nice and neat. Everything so orderly." And a shadow fell across his already-ashen face. "Speed up, will you," he ordered Abishek.

***

Back in Amsterdam, the urologist with the uroboric tattoo, Dr. Van Halen, had sashayed out his office and went over the railing of the bridge and slid down below to a boat going by that was sailing steadily towards Centraal Station. He noticed a leech on the side of the vessel and thought of his recent successful surgery with the infamous S. *You are what you eat,* he thought. *You are what you eat. We're all leeches on the side of a boat.*

And he allowed his thoughts to drift strangely in the same obscure direction in which the river was flowing.

"Destination, Centraal!" called the captain. "Coming up!"

I feel like I've been here before, thought Van Halen. Somewhere, a baby was crying. Van Halen remembered the Beatles sailing down the canals in Amsterdam in the early 1960s, fans yelling and screaming. He wondered when the Little Bang would be touring next and hoped to see them again. *I wonder if I can get some good tickets?* he thought.

***

"Shit!" screamed Poopjean. "Shit!" He paced back and forth by the garbage bins in back of the hotel, disturbed by his inability to honor P's wishes regarding the Van Gogh and his fear of S and the man with the missing eye. He fired his gun straight up into the air and little did he know but the bullet came down upon a man a half-mile away who was working on the roof of his house and killed him almost instantly. The man was a distant relative of Van Gogh and he left behind a wife and three kids and a mortgage that was almost paid off and he died with the last thought that he had been faithful to his wife even though he knew she had cheated on him and he still loved her and his kids and flash there goes his whole life before his eyes as they closed he looked out over his beloved Amsterdam neighborhood one last time and hoped that his lawyer would properly handle his will in which he left his family a painting by his tragically-heroic relative that had been considered missing for many years: *Half Figure of an Angel (after Rembrandt).* And he looked at the buildings that were leaning half-forward, and he now too leaned half-forward and expired.

***

Back in 1888, Vincent Van Gogh walked down the wet cobblestones in Arles to show his favorite prostitute, Rachel, his latest work of art. Wrapped in a newspaper, she was taken aback when he presented to her his left ear. *It's not the reaction I expected,* he thought, beside himself with melancholy.

After he left, she examined it, noticed the odd advertisement in the paper for pipe tobacco (now bloodstained), and placed it carefully upon the uppermost shelf. *Odd fellow,* she thought, and never thought of him again until a month later when she came across the ear, almost threw up at its rotting stench, and tossed it out with some rotting potatoes that were sprouting.

I give everything and still no one's satisfied, thought Vincent, traipsing outside almost deliriously. *I need to go to hospital. I need to go. It's all going by so quickly! The pain!**

***

Holding Gandhi's book, Ming thought of Van Gogh, and felt where her ear once was, and wondered if this is how Vincent felt when he was falling apart. *The intensity of*

---

* At this point in the manuscript, there is a brief sketch, as if the author were imitating Vincent. Sadly, it is not a very convincing emulation. There were also many mostly blank pages, some with strange pictures and seemingly nonsensical ramblings (such as "Cinnamon, Synonym"), as if this chapter were going to be developed more fully, perhaps with additional threads connecting and expounding upon the theme of synchronicity.

life! But then she looked down at the Gandhi book again, and realized she had no business feeling sorry for herself.

She got up from the table she had been resting on, sucking on a lemonade, and inspected a road map, squinting at the paths that led to Rishikesh, and to Boudicca. She hopped back on Rocinante and roared to the rescue, to rescue a child who felt all alone in the world—just like she did when she was young.

As the Harley sped towards the Himalayas, far, far away, she felt the leeches working. She wondered if they would work the magic that she needed, the magic that Vincent never got—until after his death—that is. *What if Vincent had some leeches and some help? Maybe things would have turned out better? But what possible difference could leeches make to the most melancholy artist of them all? Now, there are other leeches after his work. Crazy mafia who have no business with art! What is this world coming to?*

P remembered the last time she had seen Cameron. It was on the last day of high school, and they made arrangements to meet at the graduation party. After a long talk about the future that led to nothing, they made love in a gazebo by a cherry tree that was blossoming and gave off a delightful fragrance. They sat holding each other, Cameron nibbling gently on her ear.

"One day, you'll remember this," he told her.

She said nothing at the time.

Now, however, all this time later, she said, "Wow." And she thought of their daughter that he never knew existed, and wondered how she was doing with her adoptive family. And P wished they could all take a walk together through a lovely garden and hold hands.

"I'm not a very good mother. I'm sorry," said P to the wind that blew gently. She stopped at a roadside stand, not knowing why. A delightful fragrance wafted through the air. The vendor was burning and selling cherry blossom incense.

"I want this," said P. "And this sunflower."

***

One summer day, many years ago, a young man named Vincent Van Gogh walked the streets of Amsterdam. The avenues bristled with early morning life and love and vivid colors glistened in rainbows in dewdrops that reflected off each other and he wondered how he could capture this moment for now and forever. He leaned against a railing, and noticed some leeches feeding off some dead bird to the side of the canal. *Is that a rook?* he thought. He turned and began walking, and almost bumped into a couple who had come bustling out of a house—then he saw that it was an old girlfriend of his who was caressing the stylish jacket of a handsome, roguish fellow, who was known to consort with questionable comrades. *I can't believe it! What is this world coming to? It's not right!* He hurried home, buying a sunflower in memory of the one he had given her, and painted his emotions out, hoping against hope that they could just take a lovely peaceful stroll together through that garden like they did in the old days, holding hands and speaking clearly and ecstatically without words.

Despite his best efforts, this painting never sold during his lifetime, and the old girlfriend who served as an inspiration had never noticed Vincent that morning, and never knew that he had painted such a masterpiece.

***

In his room at the Genteel Hotel in Amsterdam, a few miles from where the abovementioned happenstance happened, One Eye held a magnifying glass up to his one good eye and squinted at the Van Gogh painting, marveling at the thick, magical colors, and tried to guess the real story behind it, the real artist inside.

A sunflower suddenly fell out of a vase upon the table, its petals scattering upon the floor.

"Wow."

15

BUMPY ROAD TOWARDS RISHIKESH

Rook sunk into the leathery backseat as Pompeii pumped the elephantine Mercedes through the mad and mired potholed streets towards far-away Rishikesh. Rook longed to disappear down the rabbit hole, or more accurately—rat hole—down that sewer he noticed outside the tinted, bulletproof window. *But where does that go? Some disgusting tunnel and then out to the Arabian Sea? What's to become of me? What an interesting journey that would be!* He contented himself with enjoying the stale air-conditioning and the bright sunlight upon his buttery and slightly pungent face, covered with that ancient Indian cure-all— Neem Seed Oil. He took a starched white linen handkerchief which he had lifted from the hotel and wiped his famous face. He looked at the cloth, still forlornly hoping to see his image transferred there, but alas, nothing but a hot, sweaty towel; he thought of the last time he had sushi.

Rook rolled down the window to get some air, and immediately a tanned and weathered hand reached in— palm raised. It was an ascetic clothed in ocher, and Rook fished in his pockets and gave the holy man an American quarter. The sadhu looked at both sides with confusion and curiosity, perhaps perplexed by Washington's pock marks and periwig. They sped away, past the farms, full of paddies and cows and mosquitoes and children with undying hope. They got temporarily stuck in the mud near Nashik, and Rook looked at a Leer jet that was flying overhead and remembered the band taking their own on their last tour.

"This is when I need a jet," said Rook, confiding in Pompeii. "Where's my manager? This is when I need some damn teamwork, instead of fucking around in the fucking mud. I'm gonna kill that fucking bastard who has my daughter. Goddamnit!"

Pompeii paused, then tried to smile cheeringly. "Very well, sir. Very well. But if I may, let me says that now you are the father, and so be one. Fathers are very important. Just think of what's best. Here. Focus here." And he tapped Rook's heart and they got back in the car, some locals having very kindly freed it from the mire.

"Okay," said Rook. "Okay." He took a deep breath, then exhaled, yet he could not exhale his anger.

He tried to relax, picturing the blue fluorescence of diamonds; he stretched out his size 10s. He thought of Hula and how he wanted to be with her, but then he thought of Pui too . . . he dozed off in the lazy summer heat, reliving a long trip from childhood when he was jerked awake by the screeching of the brakes.

"Where am I?" asked Rook, gazing awkwardly around at the exotic scenery.

"Delhi," replied Pompeii from behind the wheel. "But that was the easy part of the journey. Now comes the rough part."

Rook put his hands to his head and licked his dry lips. "Do you have any water?"

Pompeii passed back some H2O then continued driving the black Mercedes SL 600 towards the roof of the world.

"Okay, Mr. Rock Star," said Pompeii, adjusting his dazzlingly clean shades. "if you need to use the potty, use it now. We'll be on some bumpy roads for a while."

"Sure," said Rook, "sure," looking at his reflection in Pompeii's glasses and thinking *I still look like shit.* Rook went over and sent a message to the mayor.

I just want to disappear, thought Rook. *Disappear into the air. But I can't. I'm rumbling and rambling and bumbling out here on this crooked road.*

Rook played with the lyrics and turned over the melody line in his head. "Could be a song," he said. "Maybe. " Rook turned and saluted Pompeii. "Ready when you are, Major!"

What the hell is this guy's problem? thought Pompeii and a spinning bicycle wheel nearby made him think of something but he couldn't recall it it was just on the tip of his tongue ti tum tum.

And so Pompeii bowed and very kindly opened the back door for Rook to enter and smiled and calculated and gracefully shut the door and rubbed his hands together like he was rubbing a magic genie bottle and then he slowly got in, careful not to upset his bad back, looked in his mirrors and adjusted them, and then proclaimed: "We'll have your little girl back in no time! So time *khoti mat kar!* Let's not waste time!"

Rook lit up a cigarette and touched the burns upon his face, massaging the neem oil around. He heard his skin crinkle. "I hope you're right, Pompeii. I hope you're right. But what if we run into trouble?" And Rook inspected the weapons in the back seat not-so-secret compartment: some semi-automatics, some grenades, even some Glocks.

"I'm well-prepared for such an event, Mr. Rook. We have the weapons we need. Have you fired a weapon before, Mr. Rook?"

"Yes," said Rook, trying not to remember his lessons.

"Now, of course we don't want to use them unless we must. Remember, Rishikesh is a pilgrimage town. A holy place—perhaps you will meet a holy man there who will give you all the answers. So let us not show our weapons—they don't even allow meat in the town!"

"The Beatles went there looking for the answers," said Rook, simultaneously thinking of the Alamo and the death of his family. "They came back with *The White Album.*"

"I'm well-aware of this facts as you states," said Pompeii. "Though I may have grown up in India, I am culturally literate. And I have good teeth."

"And high-fashion, I might add," said Rook. "Dig those glasses."

Rook tried to forget his name again and focused on the road ahead. He hoped he could sing his way out of this jam too, but realizing the improbability, he stared at the guns, picked one up, and imagined using it on that descendent of Alexander the Great—the not-so-great Arjun Alexander.

All we need are the windmills, thought Pompeii. *All we need are the windmills. And a Dulcinea.*

Four hours later, they made a restroom stop at a small little village stand. They relieved themselves and filled up on gas and water. Some young Indian boys were staring at Rook. As Rook was waiting for Pompeii to get gas, he decided to put on a show. He went to an old car-axle that was now weighed down with concrete barbells, and began jerking and lifting it as if he were in the Olympics. The kids began to laugh uproariously, and imitated Rook with motions in the air.

"American?" they questioned.

"Yes," said Rook. "American. From California."

"California!" they exclaimed. They evidently had not heard of Rook; they were just happy he was an American.

"One rupee! One rupee!" they asked.

Rook shook his head. "No money! Sorry!"

Pompeii came back and perused the scene with mild aggravation.

"*Shoo! Abe saale dhakkan, kyon time khoti kar rahela hai? Cut to cut baat karne ka, apun ko faltu bakbak karne ka aadat nahin hai. Jo kuch kehna hai, jaldi kar aur phoot le . . . .*" he said to them in a rhythmical voice, bobbing his head. The boys frowned and waved goodbye to Rook as he got back in the Mercedes, restraining their urge to follow.

"Wow, such great kids," said Rook. "I hope my kid is as nice as them. I hope she isn't spoiled. These kids here, they're so poor, yet so happy! Spiritually rich! I mean, look at them jumping up and down, just happy to be alive!"

said Rook, pointing out the back window at them bouncing as they disappeared into the climbing Himalayas.

"Kids," mumbled Pompeii. "I used to be one. Didn't like it much. Couldn't wait to get older so I could do what I wanted."

"And are you doing what you wanted?" asked Rook, watching the grimace on Pompeii's face as he blew a broken circle of smoke out the crack of the window.

"Don't talk philosophy, mate. We make of our lives what we can. If we're content, that's all we can hope for."

"Is it? Those kids back there seemed more content than you."

Pompeii slammed on the brakes, creating a dust storm of insignificance.

After a long pause, under muttered breath, he said, "Do you want to get out?"

"No," said Rook, holding back the anger he felt building from within his esophagus. "Let's just go and rescue a kid I've never met. Can you believe it? I've never met my own daughter! I never even knew about her until just the other day."

Pompeii slowly exhaled and pictured a cartoon with steam releasing from the main character's ears. He put the gas back on, and they resumed rolling along.

"Why do you think this guy believes this about AIDS and virgins?" asked Rook, as he downed a Thums-Up cola procured from the roadside stand.

Pompeii continued to navigate up the mountain and around the potholes. "Sometimes intelligent, desperate people, try crazy, desperate measures," he matter-of-factly stated as if citing from *Poor Richard's Almanac,* a book

Pompeii loved as a child and would still take down from the top shelf from time to time.

Rook stared out at a herd of cows off to the side of the road. *I don't want to eat you, my friend, and lucky for you, you're in the right place not to be eaten! I wonder if there's a place where someone wants to eat humans. I'm glad I'm not there—I couldn't chop them up and have them medium-rare!*

Rook took a now-warm vodka out of a beat-up canteen, and soon was dozing off, thinking of touring Japan and drinking saki. Then suddenly he was with his daughter and she hugged him, and together they had a lovely breakfast and talked about all the things they would do once they got Mom. They would go to amusement parks, and the beach, and the movies, and shopping, and all the things that normal families do. And they then met up with Hula and the three of them walked arm in arm out towards the sunset of the Santa Monica Pier where a man with a strange wheel blew magic bubbles that floated off into the dream of the sunset . . . and then Rook really awoke to the loud sound of music and chanting—kirtan—coming from just outside the car and at first he was discombobulated; and then he snapped to it and there was a group of devotees near the entrance to Rishikish, singing a song to Ganesh:

*"Jai Ganesh Jai Ganesh, Jai Ganesh deva
Mata jaki Parvati, Pita Mahadeva.
Ek dant dayavant, char bhuja dhari
Mathe sindur sohai, muse ki savari, Jai
Ganesh . . . ."*

"Do you mind if we stop and listen?" Rook asked Pompeii, rubbing the sleep from his eyes. "Perhaps you have sleep to rub from your eyes too?"

Pompeii smiled greatly, his amazing teeth sparkling in the strange sun, and turned off the car. "Welcome to Rishikesh and all the crazy holiness and people on holidays here! This is magic—pure magic!"

Smiling, laughing, Rook felt giddy for some inexplicable reason as he stepped out of the Mercedes like the asshole rock-star he was and nodded his head to the rhythms. It was a group of mostly Indian worshippers, but there was a Westerner who stood out from amongst the group—a blonde, German-looking gentleman who didn't pay the arriving royalty the slightest bit of attention. He just continued singing along with the rest of the happy haloers:

> *"Andhan ko ankh det, kodhin ko kaya*
> *Banjhan ko putra det, nirdhan ko maya, Jai*
> *Ganesh . . . .*
> *Pan chadhe, phul chadhe, aur chadhe meva*
> *Ladduan ka bhog lage, saht kare seva, ,Jai*
> *Ganesh . . . .*
> *Jai Ganesh, Jai Ganesh, Jai Ganesh deva,*
> *Mata jaki Parvati, Pita Mahadeva"*

They finished singing, the harmonium, sitar, and vocal melodies ending with a very soothing and melting *OMMMMMMMMMM.*

Everyone clapped; they were practically awash with bliss, like little children dancing in the sprinklers seeking relief from the scorching sky.

"That was beautiful," said Rook, smiling. "Would you mind translating what that meant?"

"Surely," said an affable and amiable young Indian college student, his eyes lit up like candelabra in the wind. "Salutations to you , O Ganesha, born from Parvati, daughter of the Mountain, Himalaya, and Lord Shiva. O Lord of compassion, you have a tusk, four arms, a bright mark on your forehead, and for transport the mouse. Glory, glory, to you O Ganesha. You give vision to the blind, cure the lepers, give sons to barren women and wealth to the poor. Glory, to you O Ganesha. People offer you gifts, while saints and seers attend you. Glory, to you O Ganesha." The young man bowed to a statue of Ganesha, and then to Rook.

"Why did you do that?" asked Rook. "Do you recognize me?

"No, brother. But I recognize the divine within you." And his shirt ruffled in the wind like an old ship's sail; his enthusiasm was a conflagration, and Rook suddenly felt a glimmer of hope. The young man cast a darshana; Rook felt a shiver as the saint floated away into the sea of pilgrims.

"I don't know how I got here," Rook said to Pompeii, shaking his head. Pompeii, who was at Rook's side, a confident confidant, listened intently. "But I do know my daughter is up there somewhere. So let's go and find her."

"She'll be the most happy to hear that, Sir Rook. And I have the weapons if you need them to be. Bang-bang slice-dice—whatever you needs, I have the recipe!"

"Yes," said Rook, chuckling. "It is good of you to bring those. You'll never know if we'll have to blast through some compound, huh?

"This is the thinking behind that," said Pompeii, adjusting his rear-view. "This is most definitely the thinking. I am a thinker and this is most definitively the way to take of this monkey in the business. I may do my laundries by the Gunga, but I wash my mind in the wringer of knowledge. Believe you me! Speaking of monkey, they belong at zoo. We have too many problems with too many wild and free! Nice but crazies! Here we go."

And without a flourish but with a flower (Pompeii had cherry blossoms pinned to his sweaty shirt), they entered the main town of Rishikesh, where a banner hung lively in orange, maroon, and yellow, flapping in the breeze, reading in Sanskrit and many languages: HOLY PIL-GRIMAGE TOWN, VEGETARIANS ONLY, NO MEAT ALLOWED!!! And as if to emphasize this point, a cow wandered freely and somewhat stubbornly down the middle of the road.

As they pulled up to the hotel they would be staying at, an eclectic affair named The Ganga—towards the hills by Muni-ki-Reti, a tiger suddenly and regally appeared in the headlights Pompeii had turned on only moments before to fight off the falling, inevitable darkness. Pompeii honked at it and the curtain of night furiously; it gave a condescending shake, and then ran away back towards the hills. The curtain, however, kept falling.

"I'm not sure whether to take that as a good omen or a bad one," said Rook, hesitant to get out of the car, hesitant to have to sign more autographs.

"I don't believe in omens," said Pompeii, getting out. "We create our own destiny." And he pulled out an old .38, spun the chamber, and smiled a crooked, yellow-toothed smile as he began to clean the gun. "Just in case."

"I really wish you wouldn't do that near me," said Rook, inching away and looking towards the dark mountains looming behind their bungalow. "I have a strange feeling about this," he said, getting out, slightly frowning that there were no fans to greet him.

"Well, India will do that," replied Pompeii, having some difficulty polishing the WW II relic, a British Webley MkIV. "Most definitely, it will make you feel the strangeness of the universe—look at Lord Shiva! Benefactor and destroyer! Householder and yogin! Why isn't this shining?" And he held the gun up to the light.

"I wish I could," said Rook. "I wish I could. Where are the manifestations? Why always the leap of faith? If I'm ever going to see Something, this is the place, isn't it?"

Pompeii shrugged. "I have lived in India all my life, dear sir, but I have never seen Anything. I am not advanced enough." And he looked downward sadly at the barrel of the gun as they walked towards the hotel.

"Have you met anyone who is?"

"Oh, there is definitely many of them. Perhaps you will meet some. Perhaps you already have. The kundalini is alive and well—but hidden."

"I don't know," said Rook. "I don't know anything anymore."

"Sounds like the beginning of wisdom to me," said Pompeii. "You best be the one to know, kind sir, but I will be in the readies with this just in case." And he cocked the trigger. "Samadhi or no samadhi, we need bes get your daughters!"

"Watch it!" said Rook as Pompeii almost dropped the gun—it bobbling in his clammy hands.

"Yes, indeed, watch it!" said the man at the front desk. "We like our guests, but we don't like any weapons! This is a pilgrimage town, after all!" said the middle-aged owner, calming down as Pompeii put the gun away. "Now, you must be the Rook? I recognize you anywheres! 'Los Angeles!'" And the man hummed the song. "Would you like a tour of the property?" he asked. "All this is mine," and he gestured with his lotioned hand at the wide expanse of the modernized hotel and its manicured grounds and gardens.

"Thank you, but just show us our rooms. We're very tired and we have a lot to do tomorrow," said Rook, staring at a mahogany table in the dark corner.

"This is the understatement, Mr. Rook, and also maybe an undertaker?" asked Pompeii, slapping the rocker on the back a little too enthusiastically.

"Oh, if you need an undergarment, I can most ably provide this!" said the owner. "I have many extras of the finest clothes and brushes! I have many extras of the luxury towels and pampered items! I have many extras of whatever you need! You need sari woman too, I can gets this, this is possible. All things are possible!"

"Good night," said Rook to both of them, withdrawing like a tortoise into his room. It was furnished in modest, yet appealing décor, as if the guest were about to embark upon a safari or a mountain trek. Rook picked up some of the literature left behind in the drawer where a Gideon's would normally be. It discussed some of the nearby retreats available. Another offered a tour of Maharishi Mahesh's old ashram, which was now abandoned. Evidently, the Maharishi had peacefully passed recently in the Netherlands; the old ashram, once a welcoming sanctuary for the Beatles, had now been taken over by wild tigers, monkeys, cows, the birds, the bees, and the forest itself.

Rook collapsed on the funky futon and stared at a gigantic insect on the ceiling that he could not identify. It pulsated in fluorescence as a ray of moonlight lit upon it. The aging rock star closed his eyes and thought about saving Boudicca tomorrow. *If I do, it'll be the first worthwhile, meaningful thing I've done in a while. Oh tomorrow, tomorrow, always tomorrow.*

Bug buzzing, walls perspiring, he drifted off down the Ganges of dreams, wondering when he would ever do all that fancy laundry that had piled up. "I'll just buy some new ones off the Rookster® line . . . ."

***

P got off Rocinante and stretched at the gas pump beneath the one working but twinkling fluorescent light. She started filling up her tank, shooing away strange bugs, as two men approached her in white shirts that contrasted brightly with their tanned complexions.

"What are you doing so far from home, pretty girl?" asked one with an eye that went askew, perhaps following the equator.

The other went to say something, but stopped. He had never seen an attractive woman before riding a motorcycle, let alone an attractive woman wearing a black leather jumpsuit. He imagined at any minute a song might break out, and he would dance with her away to the golden hills of marigolds and mountain snow. They would marry, have a family, and grow old together, drinking tea from earthenware pots.

"Are you lost, pretty lady? Do you need a guide to escort you?" asked Askew. "I am the best of the guides! I will show you the mountains as they are before time! Ancient India is the land of wonder, where anything is possible, even today!" And his eye drifted, as if anticipating the places they would go.

P turned to face them and slowly took off her helmet. She smiled and shook her long black hair loose.

"Come here," she whispered, motioning with one delicate yet deadly finger, drawing them nearer.

"Do you need help with the pump? Ha-ha, know what I mean?" asked Askew, gyrating into the air hopelessly.

"I need help, yes," said P. "Come closer."

They got so close they could smell the leather and perfume—Baccarat.

"Hmmm, shall we dance?" asked Askew, his good eye inspecting her, his ambling one gazing off towards yonder cloud in the shape of a camel.

"Sure," said P. And they sashayed a little; Askew even broke into song.

"Ali ali ali, are you the one for me? I stand here dancing, wee wee wee!"

Believe it or not, P responded, singing: "Kiss my ear, don't you please, but no kissing on the lips, it makes me too weak in the knees!"

Askew went to kiss P's turned ear. She pulled back her silken hair, and as Askew eagerly moistened his lips, his gag reflex acted up as he tasted the moving, happy leeches.

"Jonk!" he yelled to his mute brother who was now holding musical discourse and gyrations with the muggy air incorporeal. *"Jonk!"*

And Askew ran directly away, as fast as he could, towards a shanty on the hill. He spit and wiped his tongue but couldn't get the image of that kissed leech out of his mind.

His unfortunate brother unfortunately did not understand what all the fuss was about, and began to dance with P, never noticing the bloodsuckers working their magic on her severed and severe lobe. He too tried to work his magic with his strong silent ways. But P had all the tricks here, and she tongued him on his cheek, got on her motorcycle, and disappeared off into the sunset, towards the Himalayas, which were just coming into view as a mirage, as a multi-layered silhouette, in the not-too-distant distance.

***

Puroshottam popped into Schiphol Airport in Amsterdam in his own private leer jet, leering out at the orderly and colorful tulip fields below, and at the few remaining windmills of old that now provided entertainment for tourists who fought the giants of their minds as they rode past them.

Puro carried no baggage—only a briefcase. He always bought what he needed as he traveled, dimininishing by a moiety a portion of the cash he toted in his briefcase which no one ever dared to steal. He met One Eye after Customs.

"Eyeball, I need a coffee," he said as they brisked through the terminal.

"Let's stop in this shithole before we go."

"Okay, boss," said One, swallowing his pride and some phlegm.

"What does your good eye tell you?" asked Puro.

"Vanilla latte."

"Young man, I see you're missing your socket," said an elderly gentleman dressed in all white and a beard like Colonel Sanders.

"It's the eye, not the socket. Please let me know if you find it."

"See the emptiness. See the form. How does something come from nothing? How does an electric eel produce a jolt of electricity powerful enough to kill? Where does this force come from?"

"Never mind my father," said a professorial lady. "He's a little strange sometimes, as he refuses to censor himself."

"A man after my own heart," said Puro. "Life is too short to be afraid to look the fool."

"Dr. Kentucky," said the man in white, extending his hand. "This is my daughter, the novelist."

"Why, yes," said Puro, "I can't believe it! It's really you! I'm your biggest fan! I loved your first book and have been waiting years for the next! *Boudicca*, right?"

"That's right. I've been waiting for it too," said the professor, sipping her coffee very cautiously. "I've been waiting a long time."

"Have you ever read Kant?" asked Puro of the doctor.

"It's been years, but yes. Of course! I'm interested in what he says about intention."

One Eye stared as best he could at a Rembrandt replica in the corner of the coffeeshop and wondered if he would ever be able to capture the essence of life in such a way.

And the four of them stood there, a tableau vivant, striking their best poses unawares for posterity as the steam from the espresso machine rose and woke up sleepy little Amsterdam, while in the subterranean vaults below a mouse discovered some Super Aged Gouda and feasted with reckless abandon.

***

Boudicca bathed in the Ganges, her matted hair flowing in the water as she looked up at the Himalayan Mountains that cascaded endlessly. They had arrived yesterday in Rishikesh and were now relaxing at Arjun's ancestral estate. Arjun was preparing a nice supper for the two of them; Abhishek had gone off to see his guru at the ashram down the hot, muddy road. Boudicca splashed the water about, wondering if the famous Mr. Arjun would try and kiss her after a nice vegetarian meal. She wished she had brought some more clubby clothes.

***

The Bengal tiger paced restlessly about the ridge above Rishikesh, licking her lips majestically, looking for her next meal. By nature solitary, she was a very devoted mother, and would stay out all night until she found enough food to bring home to her cubs.

16

VEGETARIANS ONLY?

Rook knew he was dreaming, yet try as he might he couldn't wake himself up. He was falling, falling, falling, off a precipice that dangled in the remote regions of the Himalayas and there was no stopping the plummet. Tigers roaming, monkeys chattering, suddenly he was crossing a bridge and saw some people chucking pebbles at the furry fella sitting there. He decided to be nice when he passed the monkey and smiled at it and reached out as if to pet it and it snarled at him and made a hissing sound and Rook jumped back, afraid of all the rabies shots, and left it alone, wondering what was wrong with him. Later, as they found themselves on the precipice of the mountain, trapped there overnight because the sun had set and there wasn't enough light for them to get home, he stayed awake so he wouldn't roll off the ledge and he heard a pattering of something which wasn't rain. *Look! It was a monkey, perhaps the same one, a little bit above, as below, taunting them, throwing pebbles like they were answers to an insoluble riddle.*

Sounds off to the south indicated a big cat; Rook did not want to imagine what sort of *Panthera*, but he glimpsed a picture of the beast and it didn't please him—a white Bengal tiger with blue eyes, sauntering up to him, growling lowly, gutturally, as if arising from the depths to track, punish, and devour him.

The roars unfolded, as did the dream, and yet he couldn't awake from it. He tried to look at his hands, and yet couldn't summon the energy.

Kali suddenly appeared in the midst of an ethereal cloud with her arms busy writing and weaving and upholding the universe while the two remaining hands washed the dishes. Out of nowhere, Rook was riding on Ganesh, and the god said, "For once you used your talents to praise me. I actually enjoyed your voice—you should do it more often instead of singing about silly things—like Los Angeles."

"You're right," said Rook, "of course you're right." He chanced a glance about him. They were trodding along a continually expanding bridge of ice that appeared to lead nowhere. "Where are we going?"

"Is the universe expanding or contracting?" asked Ganesh, raising his trunk and tapping Rook on the shoulder to console him.

"Neither," said Rook. "It just is."

"Wise answer," said Ganesh, chuckling. "So what are you waiting for? There is no perfect moment. Every moment is perfect!"

"Yes," said Rook. "I'm in love." And he awoke staring at the dawn's light upon the strange ceiling. The scary bug was gone. Rook turned and noticed it on the pillow beside him. "Ah! But what on earth does the dream mean? I need a shrink." He looked at the bug, who also was dreaming.

"Hello, strange bug," said Rook, carrying it outside and setting it free. It slowly awoke and flew away, away from the sunlight. "This is going to be some day! I've never felt so alive!"

He proceeded to make himself look presentable for the daughter he had never known. Examining himself in the mirror—again—for a split second—he thought he saw someone—someone who looked like him—but then it was gone.

"I must still be dreaming!"

Someone knocked.

"Coming, coming," said Rook, spraying on a spritz of cologne and attempting to make the burns on his face not look so severe. "All ready," said Rook, opening the door.

"Let's have a cup of coffee first," said Pompeii. "Then we'll go and take care of the business. We best make lickety-splits. Let us find this actor and act like the *Gita* says! I am worried maybe we should have already done the acting last night. I know we were tired, but now I am worried. I am very most worried."

"Me too," said Rook, looking at the gorgeous sight of the Ganges as it rolled and sparkled in the morning sun all fresh and clean up this high. They sat down for their caffeine outside and brushed away the flies. "I'm worried about being a good father."

"Yes, this is tricky business, but we can do it!" exclaimed Pompeii, blowing on his coffee to cool it. "It is just like drinking this coffee. I keep one eye on it so I don't spills, the other eye on the world. I drink cautiously so as not to be burned, and I watch the steam disappear as we all will one day."

They both followed the trail of their steam towards the mountains as the early morning mist slowly lifted. Pompeii appeared as if he were about to cry. Rook nursed his java and observed the yoga practitioners, practicing pranayama down by the holy river. Rook wanted to reach out and touch Pompeii on the shoulder to console him, but he couldn't bring himself to do that. Instead, they both finished their coffee and got up in silence.

"So where is this place?" asked Rook as they got into the car.

"Oh, we will have to enquire," said Pompeii. "We will have to make some questions. Some very good questions, maybe you can write them down?" And Pompeii held up his gun and inspected it, frowning. "I really should test this befores. It's been many years since I fired it. It belonged to my uncle who was in the Indian army, and before that to a British officer in WW II. My uncle used it to fight drug smugglers. He killed many with this! But now he lives next door to an ex-smuggler and they are quite decent friends!"

Pompeii popped out of the car and went to the side of the road, picking up an abandoned Bailey's water bottle. He placed it on a fence post, then retreated some ten paces. Rook moved quickly so that he was not directly behind him, getting out of the car and crouching down on the other side.

The shot echoed loudly through the early morning air, missing the bottle by a good yard.

"I best need practice!" said Pompeii. He aimed and tried again. Again, he missed it, though this time only by a foot.

"Save your bullets," said Rook. "And if we have to shoot this famous actor, let's just put the gun to his head like they do in the movies."

"But I like the old westerns," said Pompeii, dismissively. "I like the honor."

"Will you be pleasing not to do that!" shouted the owner of the hotel, barreling at them in reckless abandon, hands pummeling the air. His hair stood straight up as if exemplifying his anger. "How you be waking everyone up with this shooting? All this shooting! How?"

They looked around; no one seemed to be paying them any mind, except for a solitary face in the hotel window. She was an American woman trying to figure out what to do with her life after earning an English degree from Yale. She recognized the famous rock star and smiled. Rook waved at her and she waved back, her heart leaping. She decided to get dressed and go down and meet him!

No, maybe it would be better to wear no clothes at all! she thought.

"We are on a mission," proclaimed Pompeii. "We are rescuing his daughter. Do you have the knowledge of the actor Arjun Alexander?"

"What? No!" said the owner. "Of what are you talking? Do you know this is a holy town? There is no shootings!"

"Thank you for your help," said Rook, handing the man a $100 bill.

"Oh, this is nice," said the man, smoothing it out. "Tell you what, I will make you a nice breakfast, then we can talk. This is nice!" And he smoothed out the bill.

"No time!" said Pompeii. "We are already much delayed. We have been traveling for days to find this nice man's daughter, whom he has never met, and now we are almost there. I will enjoy a nice mango lassi with you when we return."

The owner surveyed them with a mixture of trepidation and curiosity.

"Good luck, then," he said, extending his hands to them both. "I will have the lassis ready when you return. They will be so refreshing! But please be careful with that gun!" And then as if something dawned on him: "Are you going to shoot Arjun? Why?"

Suddenly the Yale graduate came running at them, half-naked and smiling.

"Rook!" she screamed. "I love you!"

The three of them gawked and inspected the woman. She was fairly attractive—though in a Midwestern sort of way. While she might be plain in ordinary circumstances, the method of her presentation made them stand up and take notice.

The woman put out her arms to hug Rook. Rook tried to turn his eyes aside, and allowed the woman to hug him, staring at the giraffe tattoo on her lower back.

"Imagine me waking up and seeing you out the window!" she said.

"Young lady," began the owner, "if you want to practice holy purifications in the naked, the river is right over there. Please be doing the bathings properly!"

"Listen," said Rook. "I appreciate your enthusiasm. But right now I am in the middle of something."

"Are you recording here like the Beatles?" she asked, taking his mangled hand and massaging it. "Oh, you should put some ice on that and get it looked at!" she said, inspecting the swelling of his precious guitar fingers.

"I know, I know. No time! We have to go!" said Rook.

Pompeii whispered to the owner: "He's famous!"

Rook pushed the girl's good hands away—gently.

"Listen," he said. "I have a daughter who's in trouble. I have to go find her, and find her now. Now if you want to help, that'd be great. But otherwise, we really have to go."

"Yes," said Pompeii. "And we be ready!" He showed her his gun that was tucked inside his too-tight Toughskin pants (he had gained a little weight over the years).

"I can help!" she said, turning serious, then embarrassed. "Let me just get some clothes. I'll be right back!" And she ran like crazy back to her room.

"What in the blazing hells is going on heres? This is the blazing hells!" said the owner. "I do not be liking this madness! I just want some peace and quiet! That is why I came to this holy town! Please, no celebrities! No trouble!"

"Let's go," said Rook, getting back in the car. "Peace and quiet will have to wait until later."

They started the car up, and were about to pull out, when the Yale student reappeared, this time in some sweat pants and a grey running shirt—collegiate wear from her alma mater.

Pompeii stopped.

"What are you doing?" asked Rook.

"She can help," said Pompeii.

Rook took a breath.

"You're probably right. Okay."

Yale girl opened the back door and hopped in, slightly frazzled, but now wide-awake.

"I almost didn't recognize you," said Rook.

She laughed politely.

"Allow me to introduce myself," she said, extending her trembling hand to the rock star. "I am Jane."

"And I'm Tarzan," said Rook, kissing her knuckles all suave and debonair.

Jane blushed as they rolled out—to where they did not know—just determined to find the long elusive Boudicca.

Why are they killing Arjun? thought the owner. *He is by far my favorite actor! His come-hither looks and tragic flair!* And he debated with himself and looked at the $100 and paced back and forth peripatetically then threw up his hands and finally went back inside his hotel, cursed, picked up the rotary phone, cleaned a smudge on the window, and called his old friend at the police station who answered with a don't- want-to-be-bothered "Ah-cha?"

***

"I didn't know you had a daughter," said Jane, brushing her blonde hair from her starling eyes.

"I didn't either," said Rook, startling himself with his sudden father pride. "Until very recently."

"I'll be back in a flash," said Pompeii, pulling up to a travel agency that beckoned with all sorts of acronyms: ATM, STD, EXC, etc.

"What are you flashing?" asked Rook.

But before the rocker could finish rolling out his line of misdirected sexual inquiry that would make many a paparazzi swoon, Pompeii was out the door and talking with the sleepy travel agent, who blew smoke rings and drank bitter coffee. They appeared to argue a little, then Pompeii came back, shaking his head.

"I tried to find out the places Arjun lives, but he wouldn't tell me."

"Let me try," said Rook, getting out.

They watched Rook approach the man. The sappy sapien seemed to wake up a little, and pushed aside his coffee, but still blew smoke rings, albeit forming his minigalaxies more slowly. He nodded his head as if contemplating Rook's question. He then started to shake his head, threw up his hands; Rook took the man's coffee and smashed it against the wall—against a poster advertising a getaway to Switzerland with a picture of a pretty blonde holding some lovely cocoa.

"He almost told me," said Rook, slouching into the car. "But not because I'm a rock star—he didn't know me—but because I'm American. Maybe if I pay him—"

"Let me try," said Jane, hopping out of the car.

They watched her saunter into the shop. The man stopped blowing his smoke rings, and his eyes lit up as Jane appeared to whisper something into his ear. He tried not to smile, but did anyway—like a kid in a candy store. He then said something, and tried to explain further, getting out a pencil and drawing something on a napkin that was wet with spilled coffee. Jane was about to leave when the man yelled something—Jane turned around and flashed him—mesmerizing him like a deer in the headlights.

"Now that's a flash," said Rook.

"I am not about to flash my precious body," said Pompeii, frowning. "I belong to my wife!"

"He told me," said Jane, returning with a winning smile. "Not because I was an American, but because I'm a sexy American." And she handed Pompeii the napkin. Upon it was a rough map—like a child would draw—with a road that branched off from the main, up a crooked hill, ending with a circled A.

"Ah-cha," said Pompeii. "I think we know where to go."

"He said we have to turn by the internet café next to the statue of Kali," said Jane.

"Yes, yes," said Pompeii. "I think we will be getting there soon. I think it is your time to be a father," he said to Rook.

"Yes," said Rook. "It's about time I took some responsibility." And he thought of himself as a child, playing Wiffle Ball in Iowa with his dad.

As they neared the actor's abode, an all-white palace with the name Kubla Khan above the gate, strange smoke blew from the chimney; bluish in color; Rook inquired.

"Oh, maybe it's for a ceremonial purpose," said Pompeii. "But maybe something strange in the air."

"So what are we going to do?" asked Rook, examining his mangled fingers, shaking them loose.

"We are going to ring the doorbell," said Pompeii. "And then we are going to ring the doorbell. Don't worry, I've got my friend here," and he patted his .38.

They walked up the reverse spiral staircase and hesitated slightly.

"Do you want to ring it?" asked Pompeii.

Rook took a deep breath and looked about.

"What are you waiting for?" asked Jane.

"I don't know," said Rook. And he tried to peer in the famous Bollywood actor's window, but all he could see was his own distorted and weathered reflection.

***

Inside, Abhishek had noticed them pulling up some minutes ago. He alerted Arjun, who had taken a shotgun off the wall and looked out from behind the curtain.

"Who are they?" asked Abhishek.

Arjun shrugged. Then as the three of them came closer, he squinted, then said: "I don't believe it!"

"What?" asked Abhishek.

"It's Rook! It's the Bang!"

And Arjun handed Abhishek the shotgun and went to fix his hair in the bathroom mirror. Unfortunately, he had been making them all blueberry pancakes and still had flour on his hands. He shook the white powder from his movie-star bouffant and washed up real good. *Why do I have to meet him in this state? I look terrible!*

***

Rook, placing his ear to the door, finally rang the bell. After a good thirty seconds, it creaked opened. A man in a white sari, some kind of servant, smiled and asked, "Yes?"

"We're here to visit with the actor Arjun," said Rook. "I'm from Hollywood and I have some work for him."

"Oh," said the man, cautiously eying Pompeii. "One moment, please."

And before he could even shut the door, the actor Arjun burst his face in and said with a smile: "Anybody home?"

Pompeii laughed; it was a catch-phrase from one of the actor's first movies.

"Rook! Come on in!" said Arjun. "I can't believe you are here! Do you really have work for me? Does someone from Hollywood want to hire this old has-been? Do not they know that I am long past my prime? Do not they know that I am a little crazy these days, if you believe the tabloids? Do not they know that I charge too high a price? Oh, my dear boy. What happened to your face? Oh, never mind, how rude of me!" And he soaked in the looks of the rock star he had fantasized about many a lonely night, thinking *oh my God he needs plastic surgery!* "By the way, could you please sing 'Los Angeles'? It's my favorite! I have been there once, you know!"

Rook shrugged and smiled: "'Los Angeles . . . city of the angels—'"

"Sweet!" said Arjun. "Love it! Love it love it love it whoop de doo! Please, come join us for pancakes. This is— Abhishek."

Abhishek bowed with professional courtesy, looking at his overgrown toenails and reminding himself to trim them. *People judge you by your well-groomed nails,* he thought. *You always must make a good appearance.*

"This is Pompeii and Jane," said Rook, thinking: *Why am I being nice to this bastard?* "And I'm sorry about my appearance—I fell asleep in the sun."

"It must have been quite a long nap!" said Arjun, adjusting his hair. "Ah-ha! Ah-ha-ha!"

Pompeii smiled, his heart warmed to the trademark laugh of the loveable actor; then he noticed the shotgun that Abhishek had inconspicuously set to the side and Pompeii's face grew heavy and molten. He breathed deeply and pretended to smile, feeling déjà vu, like he was in one of Arjun's movies that had never been released.

Jane looked at the fire and bent down next to it, warming her hands by the bluish flames. *This is the weirdest day of my life,* she thought, missing her parents.

Arjun led them into the kitchen, ushering them to sit down at the table. Suddenly, a young girl appeared from out of a back bedroom, half-dressed, rubbing her eyes and scratching her head.

"Arjun, honey," she said. "What's going on?"

Rook stared at her and saw Hula and himself and his mother and Hula's mother all wrapped up in one. His jaw dropped, and then his heart.

"Please sit down, I am making the breakfast!" said Arjun. "We have some lovely guests from America! So please, tell me about this movie offer! And I want your autograph! No, I *need* your autograph! You fantastic singer! You amazing performer! I wish I had your talents," and Arjun sighed and hoped to be reincarnated so as to achieve his musical desires.

Boudicca stared curiously at Rook, then went over and kissed Arjun on the lips and slapped his butt.

"Girl, please don't be exciting. Please don't be the exciter!" said Arjun, getting blueberries all over his hands. "You're making the stains in more place than one!"

"Make all the stains you want. I'll be your little slave and lick them off," said Boudicca to Arjun, snapping his Winnie-the-Pooh pajamas and licking blueberry from his finger. Arjun picked up the syrup, put some on Boudicca's wrist, sucked at it, looking hard at Boudicca, and then winked at Rook. He turned to grab something out of an official Little Bang coffee cup off the fine granite counter, while Rook simultaneously grabbed the first thing he could find—a Tiffany sterling silver pie cutter—and as Arjun started to turn around Rook thrust it with all his might into the back of the venerated actor's neck—deep into his medulla oblongata. Arjun gasped and looked up at his favorite rock star, handing him a Sharpie.

"Your autograph?" were Arjun's final words—and he collapsed to the floor, spilling the bowl of berries every which way, landing on his back—embedding his favorite pie cutter even further—his last thought being: *Why does the Rookster want to kill me? Me, whom everybody loves?*

Frenziedly, Rook got on top of Arjun and started pounding him further, uncontrollably punching him over and over again until his face and Rook's hands were a bloody pulp. Boudicca and Jane screamed over and over and hid under the table as Abhishek ran into the other room to get the shotgun and Pompeii reached for and cocked his revolver and pulled up his Toughskins as he followed him. Rook stared down at the actor as his blood pooled slowly and his eyes became vacant pools reflecting into Rook's.

"It's okay," said Rook, trying to calm the ladies, breathing heavily, heart pounding madly. "It's okay." He went over to try and console them beneath the table, but this only made them scream louder.

Just then a gunshot went off and Rook went to hide under the table too. The ladies started punching at him and then they were all silent as another gunshot went off in the other room, and then another. They could smell the burning powder and waited to see who would appear back in the room. After what seemed like an eternity, in came Toughskins. Rook got out from beneath the table, gasping.

"What the fuck is going on here?" screamed Jane.

"Who the hell are you?" Boudicca asked her.

"Shut the fuck up!" said Jane.

"Boudicca," said Rook, as calmly as he could. "Please get up here." It was silent. "Please."

Boudicca slowly emerged from beneath the custom-made mahogany table, her knees wobbling.

"Who are you?" asked Boudicca, her hair insane.

"I'm your father. Rook Heisenberg. I fell in love with your mother, Hula, in high school. I still love her very much. I just found out recently that you're my daughter—I didn't know I had one. Hula had me come to help find you."

"It's okay," said Pompeii. "Everything's okay." And he patted Rook on the back encouragingly. "He's a good father."

"What?" shouted Boudicca. "Everything's not okay!" What the hell are you all talking about? I was doing just fine! Why did you kill Arjun? He was the only person who's been nice to me since I got here!"

"He wasn't being nice to you," said Rook. "He was using you. I'm sorry, I was just trying to help, and something in me snapped."

Boudicca looked down at Arjun's crimson blood seeping towards her.

"What the hell's going on here?" came a female voice. They all turned and saw Pui standing in the kitchen entryway in a *Choy Li Fut* stance, ready to whip any adversaries with the tiger claw hand.

"It's a long story," said Rook.

"We need to get out of here," said Pompeii.

"I know you!" Boudicca said to Pui.

"And I know you," Pui replied. "But let's talk later. Rook, you get everyone out of here; head back towards Mumbai—I'll catch up with you after I clean up here."

***

The hotel owner and the local police chief made their way over to Arjun's estate in an aging squad car whose siren no longer worked (although they kept trying to get it functioning). Along the way, the chief stopped to buy a tabloid and get some sweets.

"Why are you stopping?" asked the hotel owner, tapping his foot spasmodically. "You don't believe me?"

"What's there to believe? That an American rock star would want to kill an Indian movie star? That they're fighting for fans, or a movie role, or for space in the gossip papers? This is not very credible at all!"

And they stared at a picture of Rook from *The Interloper*—he was indecent at his home in Beverly Hills with two beautiful ladies.

"Well, who knows? I cannot believe this, this is why I buy this! The lives these people lead!" said the police chief.

"It is crazy! It is beyond what I can imagine! I just want a pleasant life here in our village. There is no need for these guns and these activities of these wealthy things! Besides the matter, none of this junk in these papers is the truth! It's all made up!" said the hotel owner.

"Is it?" asked the police chief. "How do you know this information? Have you done all the investigations like me? Are you qualified?"

The hotel owner simply shrugged, and the two old friends took a moment to enjoy their sweets and outrageously far-fetched entertainment, chatting excitedly, dreaming of someday visiting the Hills of Beverly.

***

Pui quickly wrapped up Arjun's and Abhishek's bodies, having placed them side by side upon an expensive and exquisite Bengal rug the actor had been given after one of his first and more famous films (*The Magic Carpet*). With some effort, she took the leeches off her ear and placed them on the dead men's eyes. The annelids were very fat with blood now, but they quickly attached themselves to their new hosts and began sucking again. Pui made methodical and efficient work of it—dragging them out the back door, outside and up the hill—to let nature take care its course. She went back down to the house and did a speedy yet thorough cleaning of the blood and the fingerprints and the gunfight. While cleaning, she spied many strange items—swings, handcuffs, and pictures of all sorts of celebrities—even of Rook. Intermixed amongst these souvenirs were photos of the famous actor Arjun Alexander in better days, with many movie stars, smiling and appearing perfectly content. There was even a picture of him with some local sadhus, although one of the sadhus did not appear at all pleased to be seen with him, perhaps because the actor was smoking.

And Pui let the fire on the hearth keep burning, locking the door behind her, and hopped on Rocinante to go help Rook and his new-found daughter. *He will be feeling guilt now,* she thought. *And Boudicca will be feeling confused and lost, more lost than ever before* . . . .

***

The police chief and the hotel owner arrived at Arjun's estate some twenty minutes after Pui had left, still wiping the donut crumbs from their mouths. They moved in slow-motion, as she was already booking down the highway. They rang the bell, tried the door, found it locked, noticed the fire flaming steadily in the fireplace, and called out guiltily to the celebrities to no avail, almost feeling like stalkers or paparazzi. After plenty of snooping, they found an open side entrance and went inside.

"Hallo—hallo?" they called, searching, bumbling.

"There's nobody here," said the chief, eating a blueberry off the kitchen counter and licking his lips. "Hmmm, that is quite tasty! Leave it to the Arjun! I knew he could cook!"

They walked around some more, opening doors and cupboards. The hotel owner picked up a National Film Award. "Look! We could sell this on Ebay!"

"Put that back!" ordered the chief. "My God, man! What are you thinking?"

"I am thinking how our Arjun would never miss it— and I could really use the money." But he put it back.

The chief shook his head. "There's nobody here," he repeated, looking for more snacks to eat.

"No shitting," said the hotel owner. "No shitting! I just hopes Arjun is okay. He is by far my favorite. There are no new stars like him anymores!"

"I just hopes he makes another movie," said the chief, licking the batter from the pancake bowl. "Better than his last one. He can do so much better; he just needs to find the right part! Come on, let's go—I'm starving! I'll come back and check again later. He's probably off on one of those long walks of his. Let's put out the fire and go."

The two old friends secured Arjun's estate, and then walked hand in hand towards the police car, trying to figure out if and when they should declare the famous actor missing.

***

Rook told Pompeii to pull over—Boudicca was crying. They drove towards the Ganga that ran along the side of the road. It was not as powerful up here, for it started up above and developed force as it flowed; the kundalini-like nature of it increased slowly but surely then overwhelmingly.

Rook watched his daughter sit down on a rock and let the Ganga flow over her feet. Rook tried to wash the blood from his hands the best he could and after a long pause, hobbled over the rocks in a dream-like way like none of this could be happening but it was. And everything seemed so vivid and alive as his heart was racing and he sat down on a boulder next to his daughter and wanted to hug her and tell her everything would be all right but he couldn't. And so they both just sat for a while and tried to come to their senses.

"I think I'm going mad," Rook found himself saying.

"Don't," said Boudicca. "We don't have the luxury."

Rook scooped up the cold water with his hands and splashed his face awake. "We'll soon be back in Amsterdam with your mother."

Pompeii and Jane stood a ways away, watching in silence the river flow and witnessing this strange father and daughter reunion.

"What are we doing here?" asked Jane.

"What is anyone doing here?" asked Pompeii. And Pompeii couldn't get the man he killed out of his head—the way he mumbled emphatically—"My toenails will grow after I die," as he slumped to the floor and threw up blood.

***

Up in the foothills of the Himalayas, in the all-vegetarian pilgrimage town of Rishikesh, above the abandoned beehive meditation huts of the Maharishi's old retreat, above the crowded ashrams and busy market, and just above the famous Bollywood actor Arjun Alexander's family estate, a Royal Bengal Tiger wandered out of the forest, smelling her way towards two bodies wrapped in tiger skin. She dragged them slowly, awkwardly, but determinedly towards her den, snacking a little on the way, but committed to bringing food back for her cubs, doing the right thing that a mother should do—taking proper care of her young.

17

AVATARS & ELEPHANTS

"Here," said Rook, giving a handful of money to a girl in colorful clothing selling cow hairballs for good luck. She inspected them to make sure the bills were not torn. She, like many Indians, did not like torn currency, and gave several back to Rook to exchange for proper ones.

"Why did you do that?" asked Boudicca.

"We need all the luck we can get," said Rook, feeling the animal token.

"How long of a drive?" asked Boudicca.

"Oh, it depends on the big bumpity-bumps. It's slow going on these mountain roads. Perhaps eight hours or so until . . . until Delhi," said Pompeii.

Boudicca stared at her famous father for the first time really. Rook felt her staring and forced himself to look her in the eye, but this was one staring contest he could not win.

"What?" he asked, confounded that she had existed all these years without his knowledge.

"Nothing," she said, confounded likewise.

Rook looked at her unkempt fingernails and thought about reaching out. Instead, he just stared at them and wondered what on earth was under them and thought of if he had left fingerprints behind.

I just killed somebody. I can't believe I did that, thought Rook. *What have I done? What on earth? P will clean it up; P will take care of things. She has to help me . . . .*

Pompeii sneaked looks at Rook and shook his head. *We need to purify ourselves. How can he not feel more guilty? This is most urgent! Most urgent!* he thought, about to explode.

It started to rain, ever so slowly.

"Shit," said Pompeii.

"What?" asked Rook.

"It's going to take longer."

"Okay," said Rook. "Okay."

Jane rubbed Boudicca's hair. "It's okay," she said. "It's okay."

Suddenly P pulled up alongside them, catching up, giving them a thumbs-up signal.

"I am going to take a little detour," Pompeii yelled to her. "We need to stop somewhere for a little bit."

P signaled again and fell in behind him on Rocinante.

"What do you mean?" asked Rook.

"We need to purify ourselves," stated Pompeii, authoritatively. "I cannot go any further without doing so."

And nobody said anything. Pompeii shortly turned off the main road and headed towards a town called Dwarahat.

Rook turned to look at Boudicca once more. He opened his mouth to say something, but could not find any words to form. Boudicca turned to him. For the first time, he could really see her eyes; they were the color of Hula's—

hazel green. And they now seemed to have that other look Hula often displayed—of carnal knowledge.

"It's okay," said Boudicca. "We'll soon be back in Amsterdam."

Rook looked away and down at his hands; there was still blood on his mangled knuckles. He rubbed it on his khaki shorts, and it came off a little—and then it occurred to him that perhaps his blood had mixed with Arjun's. "Damn't!" Rook yelled, his face scrunching up and his fears growing. "Let's stop. You should wash up too," he said to Boudicca.

"We already did—in the Ganges."

"Wash more! Please." And then Rook spit it out: "He had AIDS."

"What?" Boudicca said, freezing. "What?"

"What do you mean?" asked Jane.

"That actor, that Arjun, in case you don't know, bought you. Don't you wonder why you suddenly were living so nicely? He *bought* you. I don't know how else to tell you. I may not be the best father in the world, but I am not going to lie to you."

"He had AIDS?"

Rook nodded.

"He thought, crazily, desperately, that by having sex with a virgin, he might be cured . . . and resume his Bollywood movie career."

Boudicca started breathing heavily, gasping, clutching at the back of the seat, pulling her hair, sticking her head out the window, and throwing up into the wind, the spit coming back at her.

"Pull over!" ordered Rook.

Pompeii pulled over. Boudicca got out and threw up a little more as the rain came down upon her.

"It'll be okay," said Rook to his daughter. "We'll get through this together."

"How can you say that? How can you possibly fucking say that?"

And Rook tried to rub his daughter's hair as the mud stuck to their shoes.

"There's a bathroom," he told Boudicca. "Jane, P, please help her."

And they guided her towards the dilapidated washroom; it offered few amenities—just a hole in the ground and some running water from an old rusty faucet.

Away from her father, Boudicca asked Jane and P: "Listen, what is this business about my dad being a rock star? I've never heard of him."

"They're an old band," said P. "The Little Bang."

"The Little Bang! So old school!"

Boudicca washed and cleaned herself as thoroughly as she could, not sure if any of it would help.

"Do you need a mirror?" asked Jane, taking out a compact.

Boudicca looked at herself and gasped, thinking: *Who are you? Who are you really? So you've been wondering who your father was your whole life, and now you find out, and now what? Now what? Now I have AIDS and I'm going to die? Now I might be pregnant? It doesn't make sense. Nothing makes any goddam sense.* She took a deep breath and inspected her tingling body.

"Listen," said P. "We don't know anything yet. As far as we know, you're perfectly healthy—you're just fine. So let's keep a positive attitude, okay? But we're going to help you wash up. Did he use protection?"

"A condom? No."

"How many times?" asked P, as delicately as she could.

"Two times," said Boudicca, remembering, trying to hold back her sobs. "I can't believe how stupid I am!"

"It's okay," said P and Jane. "It's okay."

They meticulously cleaned Boudicca, for whatever good that would do, for about fifteen minutes, with hotel soaps and shampoos and a lemon juice douche (telling her its efficacy was doubtful—it was a gamble) that they just happened to have in their purses. Then Boudicca exited the primitive bathroom like her namesake—as bravely as she could.

Maybe they won't catch me, thought Rook. *Who's looking? What are they looking for? Maybe they won't catch me. Even if they do, did I do anything wrong? I had to rescue my daughter! What choice did I have? So do I go to the cops? What do I do? Maybe I should turn myself in. But I have to help Boudicca!*

As he watched his daughter return, Rook asked Pui confidentially:

"What should we do? Go to the cops?"

"Are you trying to make your life more of a nightmare?" she asked. "I took care of things. This is my profession, and I do it well. So please, let me take care of things. Besides, they had it coming. Believe me, sometimes Nature takes care of things in Her own Way. Your job is not to worry about it. And your job is to be a good father. Boudicca needs you now more than ever."

"Yes, but now we need bes do spiritual purifications!" said Pompeii. "There is a cave just up ahead. We must walk just a little. But please let us go and make meditations! I cannot go any more without this!"

They followed Pompeii and walked a mile or so then stopped, at a rather isolated area—farms nearby, and little houses and huts, and lots of paths. They were greeted by several ladies carrying baskets of produce upon their heads—who nodded with their sparkling eyes. Rook bowed to them.

"I will be leading you to the cave. Make sure you have some water. You don't want to be the hydra," said Pompeii and he thought about killing that Abhishek—he thought of how the first two shots missed and how Abhishek was picking up the shotgun and something inside Pompeii erupted for the first time in his life and he aimed and then he was calm and he exploded.

Boudicca took a long drink from her bottle of Bailey's water, which she had learned to inspect the caps for to see if the protective ring was still intact or if it had been recycled and filled with shit. *If only I had taken the same precautions with Arjun!* she thought.

And they all took a step towards the top of the mountain. Rook noticed, as they traveled, that there were many paths that intersected this way and that, and they met more women with baskets atop their heads, and farmers plowing in the fields, and children working and playing, and animals toiling beneath the intensifying sun. The recent rain had turned the ground to mud and now it was baking. As they climbed, Rook thought of many things, and nothing at the same time. His mind and body felt numb.

Boudicca was amazed at the bulls pulling the old plows, and the dilapidated condition of some of the huts. *Did people actually live there? How? How is it possible to survive in these conditions?* she thought. And then a woman, or a girl Boudicca's age would happen by as they worked, and they would smile, and look happier than Boudicca had ever been in her life. And Boudicca wondered what her problem was. *Why am I so negative? What's wrong with me? Why can't I just carry my basket and be happy?*

"Oh excuse me," said Rook, almost bumping into a man who had suddenly come from working out 'neath a tree and practically bumped into them with a bunch of twigs and kindling. The man lifted his head slightly, and from beneath the brim of his Boss of the plains Stetson, his eyes and smile made contact with Rook. Rook felt some strange lightning, and fell to the ground.

Where am I? Who was that? Who am I? How many fingers am I holding up? What is going on? Here we are! All these thoughts circled Rook's noggin as he rocked and rolled in the dirt and his consciousness came back into focus and he saw a face in the single drifting cloud smiling down at him—it looked like his mother.

"Dad, are you okay?" asked Boudicca, gently touching her father's cheek.

"My kid is all right!" said Rook, hugging his daughter.

"My kind sir, why are you lying on the ground?" asked Pompeii, pouring water upon Rook's face.

Rook sat up. "I'm okay, I was just struck by, I just want to hear my mother pray again," said Rook, and he started crying, thinking of his mom praying at church in Iowa with the rosary beads.

"Let us go," said Pompeii. "We are almost there. You need be drinking some more waters. Drink the waters. Wake up."

Rook chugged and felt refreshed. He had not hurt himself when he fell—he just felt numb and nimble and tingly up and down the spine.

"I'm no good," Rook mumbled to himself. "I'm just no good."

And he looked at Boudicca and found it hard to believe that she had come from him and his first love Hula. And Rook thought clearly: *that is the only good thing I have done in my life. The only worthwhile thing in my entire life.*

Suddenly they stopped in a shady grove of trees.

"It is right here," said Pompeii, fumbling in his pocket. "Let me get it . . . ." And after fishing, he found a ring of rusty keys; he beckoned them to follow, and a minute later, after ducking several oak branches, they were at a cave with a gate. The cave's entrance was walled off and painted red and secured with a wrought-iron door. There was a ladder propped up against the side, along with a compass and some other tools; perhaps a worker would be back soon.

"This is where an avatar—incarnation of God— bestowed blessings upon humanity—with the keys to yoga. Feel the purifying vibrations and ask for any forgiveness that you need. Please pray for a blessing upon the world—upon every living creature, and even the rocks which surround us," said Pompeii.

They all looked at each other like he was a little crazy, but shrugged anyway and gathered closer. The gate creaked opened; they crept inside. It was damp, and it seemed like it went further back. There was the sound of water trickling somewhere.

"They had to wall this up to protect it from vandals and graffiti and such," said Pompeii. "There use to be a passage to the little stream, and the rest of the cave, but they had to block it off for the safety of the pilgrims. But there are still ways back there, if you like. But now, let us meditate."

And Pompeii folded his legs into the lotus posture. Rook sat Indian-style, and Boudicca actually imitated Pompeii. Pui and Jane just sat down quietly.

"Focus on your breathing," said Pompeii, "and the presence of the master about us. And on the white light, ever-increasing in intensity."

And Rook felt the gaze of the worker in the fields all over again, and felt a blast within, but this time didn't fall over and he took a deep breath of the ancient air. And he felt an energy charging up his spine and then he wondered if he were imagining all of it.

Just when they were starting to get comfortable, Pompeii said: "Okay, we must be going. We are purified, we are peaceful, but we really must be going. The cement truck of the world is still turning."

"So you come here often, Volcano?" asked P as they finished their return and neared the car.

"Not as often as I wish," said Pompeii. "How many lifetimes do we get?"

"I don't know," said P. And she thought of the Gandhi book she had started.

Rook checked his pockets to make sure he had his newly acquired, expedited, reissued passport—he did. "But honey," he said, looking at Boudicca, "don't you have a passport or anything?"

She shook her head. "I came to India with nothing but the clothes I was wearing. Unfortunately, spending all that time in that smelly cage ruined my fashion. The actor was kind enough to buy me this lovely new outfit! He was nice to me, you know."

Rook felt a rage building up inside him, but said nothing.

As they drove up and down and around on the winding roads of the Himalayan foothills towards Delhi, Rook wove in and out of sleep and at one point he jolted alert with a start and felt like he was going to vomit. He rolled down the window quickly and let the chunks fly towards the road that disappeared behind them that got lost in a mysterious fog.

"Are you okay, Daddy?" asked Boudicca.

Rook gasped for fresh air. "Yes, I think so," said Rook. "I just feel a little weezy." And he saw the dead actor's face staring up at him—as if it had come back to life—as if it were some strange movie where it was all fake and he really wasn't dead. *What am I supposed to do?* And then Rook pictured the tabloids and the headlines of the scandal. AMERICAN ROCK STAR KILLS INDIAN MOVIE STAR TO SAVE LOST DAUGHTER! He saw it play in his mind as a Bollywood movie—with dancing and mystery and all sorts of strange twists and turns.

Suddenly the car swerved to the side and almost teetered on the edge of the cliff. A bus had come around the bend of the one-lane road; normally, both cars honked when approaching dangerous bends. This time, no one did, and the result was a near-death experience. The valley of the gods lay stretched out—a nice flight for Mercury—quite a drop for a human.

"Idiot!" Pompeii yelled in Hindi.

"Jackass!" the bus driver yelled in Bengali.

And then the two of them shrugged. The bus driver and Pompeii both got out of their respective vehicles. They worked together to push the Benz off the grip of the cliff; little pebbles tumbled to the pit below. With Herculean strength, they were able to extricate the vehicle from its precarious position. They shook hands, everyone shrugged, clapped, and the parties were on their ways to their predetermined destinations.

We've got to do the same, thought Rook. *We've got to extricate our vehicles.*

He looked out over the ridges of the mountains silhouetted against the virgin purple sky and the clouds floating like faces of waiting-to-be-reincarnated souls with parched and tired lips.

Boudicca was shivering from the descending cold. The wind swept around them and night slowly fell, blanketing them.

"We maybe should stop for now," said Pompeii as a little village came into view. "It is getting late and dangerous to travel. And I have the sleepy times."

They stopped at the gates of an ashram. Pompeii rang the bell and a man in a white robe appeared. He had a long beard, and groomed it with the one hand he had left.

Pompeii had some words with the swami in Hindi. The swami nodded.

They were ushered inside and shown to some simple yet sufficient rooms.

"Rook, Dad," began Boudicca. "I don't know what to call you. But I want to call Mom."

"You're right. Let's let her know where okay and we'll be back soon. My cell has no reception, though."

"I'll try and see if they have a phone," said Boudicca, noticing there was not one in the room.

"Okay, okay, honey. Tell Hula, tell Hula I miss her."

"No problem, Dad." And Boudicca quietly exited the room, closing the blinds, turning off the lights, and gently shutting the door. She stood outside, waving goodnight to P and Jane, who were sharing a room on the other side of the ashram.

What is wrong with my dad? thought Boudicca. *He's been distant my whole life from me, and now he's just as far away.*

"May I be helping you?" came a seemingly disembodied voice. Boudicca turned around—it was Pompeii, leaning against his door, which was next to theirs, smoking a hand-rolled cigarette.

"Why, yes, I need to use a telephone."

"Let me see if we can be doing this. This is very much possible! Come."

And they went towards the office; inside, the swami was peering at his bookshelf, squinting, evidently looking for something.

"Swamiji," said Pompeii. "The young lady is needing a phone. Who will you be calling?"

"My mother," Boudicca stated, matter-of-factly.

"Oh, yes," said Swamiji, smiling. "We must all call upon Divine Mother now and again. Yes, where are you calling?"

"Amsterdam."

"Yes, let see if that is possible. One moment, please, and we will be seeing if that is possible here. But I don't know. Sometimes you can't get a message through, sometimes you can!"

Swamiji picked up the phone as if he were reluctant to use it; he hesitated, unsure of which number to press, then decided upon 00 with his one good hand.

In Hindi, he asked the operator some questions, then stated, brokenly—"Amsterdam." After a long delay, in which he looked up at the ceiling as if calculating the astronomical costs, he declared, "it will be done," and reached out to hand the phone to Boudicca.

"What number is it that you will be calling?" asked the operator in British English.

And Boudicca rattled off her mother's cell, which she had gotten so used to calling from school, from her friends' homes, from all over the Netherlands, but never from abroad.

"Hello?" came a voice from another time and place.

"Mom?"

And there was sobbing.

"It's okay, Mom, it's okay," said Boudicca, strangely comforting her mother. "I'm alright."

"Where are you?"

"With, with Dad. We're staying at an ashram in the Himalayas."

"What?"

"Well, it's a long story—" and Boudicca moved to a corner for privacy and whispered—"he, he, he killed someone to save me, and now we're kind of, kind of messed up. But don't worry, we'll get our shit together and be back home soon."

There was a long pause.

"I'm sorry, honey. I'm sorry you had to go through this. Everything will be okay. I'm sorry—I just can't believe this! It's like some nightmare! But really, we'll make everything okay. Everything's going to be okay. How is your father? Is he okay?"

"I don't know. I didn't even know him until this morning. He's sleeping now. He seems . . . disturbed."

"Well, he did just kill someone, huh?"

"I guess. He didn't have to. I just slept with the guy, that's all. We were having pancakes and dad went crazy."

"What?"

"Some famous actor bought me. Was obsessed with white virgins. He wasn't that bad—he got me out of that cage I was in in Bombay. But I guess he was sick."

"I'll say."

"No, really sick. AIDS."

There was a long, anxious silence.

"Well, I'm sure you're alright, but we'll get you tested real soon."

Suddenly, Boudicca became aware of the concerned eyes of the swami and Pompeii upon her. She looked at them, and could do nothing, so she shrugged. Their heads started gently swaying back and forth, as if they understood there was nothing at all that could be said.

"I love you, Mom."

"I love you too, honey."

And the swami and the driver nodded in agreement and approval at the exchange.

Boudicca handed the phone back to the swami and he took it gingerly, using his sleeve to grasp it.

"Is there a normal shower around here?" asked Boudicca. "I'd really like to clean up."

The swami smiled tiredly. "Yes, we have a shower in your room, but it is not Western. It is just a spicket and bucket, like many places. But you need to be careful."

Boudicca grimaced as if she were about to cry. *Is this how everyone is going to treat me now? Am I an outcast already? It's just not fair! I didn't do anything! I didn't do anything! Why is this happening?*

"There is only so much water," said Swamiji. "We must be saving water, there is only so much," he repeated. And he and Pompeii nodded together, then gently swayed their heads, as if communicating something untranslatable.

"But you will be making a good shower, still," said Pompeii, assuring her. "It is not many waters, but enough for cleaning. It is good for purifications."

"That's nice," said Boudicca. "You're both so nice. Thank you."

Pompeii got out some rolling papers and tobacco. Boudicca watched him begin to roll.

"Do you mind if I have one?" she asked.

Pompeii was obviously taken aback—his dark eyes said it all: *women here in India don't smoke.* But then, Boudicca was not Indian.

"I've had a long day," understated Boudicca.

Even Swamiji nodded.

"Roll one for all of us, babu," said Swamiji. "Sometimes the smoking is good. Sometimes it helps us relax and blow out troubles."

Pompeii nodded and expertly rolled the tobacco. As he lit it for her, Boudicca inhaled too strongly at first, and coughed violently. They couldn't help but laugh.

"It is making your first cigarette?" they asked.

Boudicca nodded, almost picking up their gentle head movements.

"It's been a day of a lot of firsts," she hoarsely said.

They suddenly became very quiet and stern and serious and looked at their tanned and sandaled feet, as if some answer lay there.

Boudicca's second puff was more measured, and she gently blew her troubles towards the open window and watched the smoke disappear with the gentle moonlight and subtle moonbow.

***

Hula stared for a long time at the cell phone she had just hung up. *My God, what has happened? What have I led my daughter towards? Does she blame me?*

And Hula thought for a long time about how she blamed her mother, and blamed her absentee father, and blamed Rook, and blamed Svidrigailov, and blamed God. And she thought how she now needed to patch up the patchwork quilt of her life once and for all, now, or else there was simply no going on from here. *First things first. Stop blaming others. Take responsibility—complete responsibility for your life,* she thought.

"Am I getting married?" she asked aloud, not able to believe it. She looked at S lying asleep on the sofa, curled up like a big baby, and woke him up.

"What?" he said, groggily.

"Do you have any idea of what has happened to Boudicca? Do you know that I just found out that she was sold?"

S got up quickly. "What are you talking about?"

And Hula told him what she knew.

"This is my fault," said S. "This is my entire fault. You have to believe me—I had her there only for safekeeping."

"She wasn't very safe," said Hula.

"Something's gone wrong," said S. "Something's gone terribly wrong. I will get to the bottom of this. I never meant for any of this to happen. You have to believe me." And he kissed Hula on the cheek and walked determinedly out the door.

Hula did not know what to believe any more.

***

Rook found himself reliving the murder in his dreams. He went over and over the killing and the look on the actor's face and then he saw P and wondered what she was doing in the room. They took the dead men outside and thought perhaps the tigers would clean them off. They pranamed and made an offering to Ganesh and hoped it would placate the gods; after all, Rook had only done this to save his daughter. But was there any other way around it? They left the body there and they wondered what was going to happen next. They sat and smoked as the sun went down and had a Kingfisher and then they felt a presence; it was a mother tiger and her cubs; they had caught the scent and followed their wet, black noses. Rook and P watched their nostrils sniff at the air; it was amazing how they were able to catch onto a hint and follow it impeccably to what they needed. They only ate what they had to to survive and they didn't like man encroaching upon their terrain. And there Rook and P sat like an old boring married couple watching this as if it were on their plasma screen TV.

The mother tiger gave a wary look in their direction, and her eyes glowed in the night. Sensing that they meant no harm to her or her family, she and her cubs went back to devouring the dead men. At one point the dead raised their hands as if to ask a question, like students at school, but then shied away and gave up, perhaps no longer interested in the answer. Rook watched while the tigers ate the actor's once famous eyes that had sparkled, and ripped out his tongue that had given so many clever quips; and his entrails trailed out like a movie trailer and then Rook suddenly became concerned—what if the tigers got HIV?

And Rook awoke with a start when he heard a door open, and he jumped up, thinking he was still at the crime scene.

"What? What do you want?" he yelled.

In the ashram doorway his daughter Boudicca, silhouetted, stood silent. Suddenly Rook realized where he was.

"I'm sorry, honey. I didn't mean to yell: I was having a bad dream."

"It's okay," said Boudicca, softly. "I'm just going to take a shower."

"You smell of smoke. Have you been smoking?"

"It's okay, go back to bed. Mom says hi."

"Oh." And Rook stared at the crumpled sheets and wondered if a doctor were available. He wondered about the dead bodies and the tigers. *But it was a dream!* he thought, pushing it out of his mind. *But what about Boudicca?*

As he heard Boudicca fumbling in the nearby bathroom with the bucket and the water, Rook's eyes slowly became accustomed to the light. He watched it cascade across the room and wondered if he were in a picture show. And then he remembered the commitment he had made to Anatoli to do a cameo in his Bollywood film. *I can't believe that. Is he gonna hold me to that?* And Rook realized that he was far from out of trouble—as a matter of fact, he pictured Svidrigailov back in Amsterdam. And then again he couldn't believe he had just killed someone. *I killed someone today. I really killed someone. That part wasn't a dream. I know that was real.* And Rook observed his breathing and observed his thoughts float down the Ganges and his right arm felt asleep from sleeping on it but he felt numb too—a deep numbness within that he didn't even know how to address. He observed it like some sort of deep chasm over which he would have to cross to get back to the world of the living.

***

Boudicca stared at her face in the mirror as the sun rose over the Himalayas: "Who are you? Who are you really?

Do you know who you are? You are the daughter of a rock star."

She had anticipated their wake-up call to see the silhouettes of the mountains in the distance, and just now the knock came upon the door of the room.

She heard her inept father fumble out of bed like some old man from a bad TV show, open the door, cough, and mumble that he would be ready in a minute.

"Divine Mother has whispered to me words of comfort and will lead you home," said Swamiji. And he lit up a smoke and watched the rings circle the sunbeams. Rook noticed the brand he smoked was called Hello! and it had the colors of the American flag.

"Can I bum a smoke, Father?" asked Rook, putting on his shades in the habit that paparazzi would be waiting outside.

"Sure," said Swamiji, "but we both know we should both quit."

As Rook lit up, he noticed Swamiji staring at him in a way that made Rook feel uncomfortable.

"What's your deal, old feller?" said Rook, half-jokingly.

Swami laughed outright.

"I am being sorry," he said. "I am not meaning for the staring. I just have always wanted to try on a pair of designer sunglasses, such as you have, and I hate to be the asker, but I would not want it to force me to reincarnate for that desire."

Rook handed him his mirrored Armani shades and watched, taking a mental picture of the swami as he put them on and looked about.

"How do I look?" asked Swami.

But Rook could not help but just stare at his own reflection. "I am not as good looking as I used to be," said Rook, aloud.

"What?"

"You look great, Swamiji! Like a real rock star!"

Swamiji smiled and blew smoke rings towards the rising sun, then gestured with his hands in a type of mudra that blessed the awakening day.

"Mr. Rook, I bless you and your daughter, and wish for only God's wishes upon you and your family." Swamiji bowed to the god within Rook and anointed him with a mixture of ashes and oil.

"Why do you do that?" asked Rook.

"Oh, I am a man of all religions. And once you experience that bliss, you are forever in a state of wonder and ecstasy—isn't it amazing?!!!"

"Yes," said Rook, smiling, then wondering if his teeth were becoming as rotten and yellow as the swami's. *I need to go have a check-up in Beverly Hills,* he thought. "Hey, can you get us a doctor? We need some help."

"Sure, no problem." The swami went to make a phone call, and then returned. "He will be here quickly. Listen, will you be good enough to join me in a glass of Glenlivet Scotch before you go?" asked Swamiji. "I usually am not of the drinking, but I have always wanted to party with a rock star."

"If it will help you from reincarnating to fulfill that strange wish, fine," said Rook. "But it is awfully early for such activities."

"You sound like you are CIA!" laughed Swamiji, and he disappeared with Rook's glasses and into a room. He quickly reappeared and poured them both a drink and Rook stopped twirling and began swirling his liquor, toasting with the swami the ineffable beauty of another day in the Himalayas.

"I think I believe that it all started here," said Rook.

"Yes, I think we are all believing, when we see; it's all flowing down from the beginning, up in the blinding snows," said Swamiji.

Suddenly, Boudicca, Pompeii, Pui, and Jane appeared. Rook noticed his daughter's frown at the fact that he was drinking this early, and quickly handed the glass to Swamiji. Swamiji stood there, guffawed, and momentarily not knowing what to do with the double-fisted drinking image, he began juggling the empty shots. Everyone laughed.

An Ambassador car burst up the drive and pulled in very quickly. A man in a white smock with a Red Cross symbol got out just as speedily. He ran, carrying a little black bag.

"I think you know who I am. I am the doctor. Doctor Vajpayee. Who is needing the help?"

"Doctor!" said Rook. "Thank goodness!"

And Rook took him aside and explained the situation in hushed tones, careful not to implicate himself or anyone else.

"Have you been drinking?" asked the doctor. "I can't believe you! People look up to you and this is how you act? Listen, you and your daughter should begin post-exposure prophylaxis. I actually have some here. It is a course of antiretroviral drugs; you will need to continue this treatment once you reach Mumbai, for a month total. And you need to be very strict. No laziness! Follow the regimen! I will give you the name of a colleague in Mumbai—he can help you from there. Let me warn you though, the regimen can have side effects, and there is no guarantee."

"It's better than nothing, isn't it?" asked Rook.

"I suppose so," said the good doctor, organizing the medicine, writing some info on a business card, and placing it in a brown paper bag. Vajpayee then cleaned and bandaged Rook's mangled hand, wrapping it with gauze.

Rook, wincing, got out a large sum of rupees and handed it to Vajpayee.

"That is far too much," said the doctor, shaking his head. "Please."

"Consider it a donation," said Rook, insisting. "Please buy more medicine and give it to whoever needs it."

"Very well," said the doctor. "Thank you."

"Thank *you*. You're a lifesaver!"

"Maybe. Maybe sometimes."

Rook took the bag of drugs from the doctor and headed back to the Mercedes, where the others were waiting. Swamiji poked his graying, white head in. "May you have the blessings of God," said Swamiji. "May you find what you are looking for, and always remember—there is no beginning, there is only the Eternal Now."

Rook looked at himself once again unflatteringly reflected in the swami's shades; this time it was an extreme close-up, and stretched like Goo, relative to the strangeness of the lenses and the early hour, and also in the glasses Rook saw the majesty of the purple mountains surrounding him like royal angels crowned with a snowy diadem. Not knowing what else to do, Rook blessed the swami with the sign of the cross, and as they pulled away from the ashram, Rook watched the doctor and the swami waving at them, as they examined the expensive sunglasses Rook had left behind.

"Daddy," said Boudicca, "are you a drunk?"

"No, honey. Maybe at one time. But no, not now. Swami, well, never mind . . . ."

"Are you wanting the drinking?" asked Pompeii, looking in the rear-view.

"No! I am not wanting it!" Rook said, a little too angrily.

"Yes, I believe you! You are the drinking too much already," said Pompeii, shutting his mouth and thinking of how to change the subject. "We are maybe by an elephant park today? Are you the ready for it?"

Rook was about to give a very loud no when Boudicca spoke up:

"I'd love that! Elephants! What fun! Come on, dad, we could use some fun!"

"It will be good to get rid of your karma," said Pompeii. "Of course, your karma will not be as bad, for you had no choice in this killing matter. It was to save your baby. And the man was dying already. But he is a quite beloved actor. How will you make up for the country's loss?'

"Perhaps I can play a character in a Bollywood film and offer that. I am supposed to anyway when I get back to Mumbai."

"Oh this is most welcome! Most welcome! I remember! Who will you be?"

"I don't know. Probably a character they love to hate. Some asshole foreigner that people will love yelling at in the theatre. And when the real hero comes to save the day, the audience will cheer tremendously, relishing my downfall."

"Yes, this is a great news! I will buy my ticket prematurely! Will I be able to play your driver? I hope I still have a part! I am quite the good driver, as you know." And as if to demonstrate this, Pompeii swerved the wheel, and the car went to the side of the narrow road and almost down a dry gulch and then he pulled the wheel the other way and the car regained its footing and continued belching along.

"I don't know. I would like you in the movie, but that's not up to me."

"Sure it is," said Pompeii. "You are the famous rocker. You can ask and they will put me in—if just for a cameo. Will you be singing and the dancing too?"

"Perhaps," said Rook. "Perhaps I will be kissing the beautiful lady too."

"Oh no, that is forbidden," said Pompeii. "There are many crazy things in our excellent films, but none that crazy yet. It would cause an uproar!"

"Why, what is wrong with kissing?" asked Boudicca, staring out at the passing scenery as if it were a film.

"Oh, you tell her," said Pompeii to Rook.

"Oh, well," and Rook was truly stumped and could only now relate to his father not being able to have the sex talk with his kids all those years ago. And he thought of the strange letter he had read from his daughter to that boy, and how poorly written it was, but how she obviously had a secret life, like we all do, and what was he supposed to say now?

"Kissing should be only done in private; why show such intense personal emotionals in public?" *I'm a living, walking contradiction and hypocrite,* thought Rook, thinking of all the times he would play around in public on tours. "And of course it should only be done when you truly love the person." And Rook thought of all the tired and tried clichés and empty platitudes and Platonic advice that really meant everything and nothing at the same time.

"What's in the bag?" asked Boudicca.

"Oh, we need to start taking these right away. Where's some water? Now look at these directions, we have to follow this strictly. It might help!" And Rook squeezed his daughter's hand.

"Oh," said Boudicca. "Thanks."

And they both cautiously popped their pills.

"You didn't kiss that actor?" asked Rook.

"Well, yes, he was nice," said Boudicca. "Remember, before you came, he was the only person here that was nice to me. I was locked in a cage, goddamit. Wouldn't you have feelings for someone who rescued from that?"

Rook said nothing.

"Look at the changing sky," said Pompeii.

"Look at the wonderful birds!" said Jane.

"Besides, I didn't know he had AIDS. I thought he was just getting old. And plus he was a famous, good-looking actor. Who wouldn't want to kiss him and feel famous too?"

Now this Rook could regrettably understand, from his own experience of dealing with women who didn't really want to sleep with him—they just wanted to sleep with the image—and they would love it if they were seen in public making out. He remembered at a certain Hollywood movie premiere, making out against a brick wall on the red carpet with a certain hot groupie who wanted to be a star, and cameras were flashing and he didn't care, he just wanted to feel the passion. The tabloids had a field day with it.

"It's okay, honey," said Rook, sighing. "We'll get everything straightened out. It'll be okay."

"Everyone keeps saying that! Just stop! You mean I'll be tested for HIV. Fine, that's fine. But Jesus, I'm too young for this. I shouldn't have to worry about it. And what if I'm pregnant?"

"The whole world has to worry about AIDS," said Rook, feeling like he was filming a commercial. "We're not doing enough to find a cure. We're not doing enough to help the people, and to overcome this, this stigma. And if you're pregnant, well . . . ."

"Have you been tested, Daddy?"

After a long silence, Rook said, truthfully, "A long time ago. I should go again, you're right. We'll all get tested together. Mommy too."

"Mommy's already been tested—many times. But I'm sure she won't care about being tested again."

And Rook pictured all of them in the doctor's office in Beverly Hills, going through the psychological torture of waiting for the results.

"I heard the mafia runs everything," said Jane suddenly, brushing her hair, still trying to find balance after the last day of insanity.

"What is this?" asked Pompeii. "Yes, they run many things in India, but not me!"

"I mean in Bollywood."

"Yes, they do do a lot of that. That is unfortunately the business."

"Well, let's not think about that today. Today is a very special day for my daughter, Boudicca. Today she is free, and today if she wants to go and see the wild elephants, by gosh she will!" proclaimed Rook, smiling at his child. After a moment, Rook's little girl smiled back. *She's got my smile!* he thought, smiling.

***

"Well, I am hoping you enjoyed and refreshed from the cave," said Pompeii as they were now nearing the Rajaji National Park. "It gives energy!"

"Actually, I was tired and lazy at first," said Boudicca, "and I didn't really want to do it. But now I'm glad I did. I do feel more energetic."

"Yes, this is real believe you me. Mr. Rook, how are you being?'

"I am being, just fine, my friend. I am being just fine. But I feel like a drink of Scotch. It's not everyday you kill a man. It's not my line of business."

"Indeed," said Jane, repressing a light smile. "You're a lady killer instead."

"Please," said Rook. "Not in front of the children."

"Well, maybes you can get some of your precious liquor from the elephants," said Pompeii, chuckling to himself. "They are heavy drinkers!"

They pulled into the entrance of the park. Three men looked at them, half-warily, half-expectantly. Pompeii got out and carried on a short bargaining session, and then told Rook and Boudicca: "Three hundred rupees each. They wanted 1000, because the park is officially closed during the rainy season; I told them that was not right."

"Thank you for watching out for us, Pomp and Circumstance," said Boudicca, brushing the hair out of her eyes. With that simple gesture, Rook, once again, noticed the similarity between her and her mother.

I've got to get us out of here, thought Rook. *I've got to get our family together. I've got to snap out of this dream and act!*

They paid their Gandhis and got out of the taxi. The men, clad in dirty white, introduced them to the elephants. There were two—chained up by a withered and weathered and wuthered rope to a little stake in the ground that could have easily been pulled out. As they prepared to board the beasts, the baby elephant, separated by a cement wall from her mother, reached her growing trunk around—searching. The mother reached out hers and comforted her daughter, intertwining trunks and grunts until the driver hit the mother with an iron rod and yelled something to get it going.

Boudicca and Jane hopped on the baby, Rook and P on the mommy. Rook noticed his daughter crying, her face turned in front of him, wiping her tears with the back of her sunburnt hand. Rook thought of saying something but instead put a hat on and thought of the cave and wondered what the truth was. He turned back and waved at smoking Pompeii, who had decided to wait behind.

The drivers urged the animals onward, striking them steadily with the heavy metal instruments. Rook looked at the aged, wrinkled skin of the mommy pachyderm and wondered about its pain and the pain all mothers go through.

They continued riding in silence, looking at the birds and hyenas and water buffalo; Rook was amazed when the elephants navigated a narrow path with their mammoth feet, precariously balancing their weight as they went downhill in the sloppy mud. *Everything in this country is precariously balanced,* thought Rook. *And yet it somehow works.*

The driver kept hitting the mommy with his iron staff. Rook noticed Boudicca reaching out and petting the baby beast on its grisly hide. It followed its mother earnestly.

"Be careful, Boudicca," said Rook. "Hold on."

"I'm okay, Dad. I'm okay. Stop being so father-like all of a sudden."

"Just being safe. Your mother would kill me if you were trampled by an elephant."

Boudicca half-heartedly laughed, and at this point the driver turned around and smiled a yellow, crooked and missing teeth smile and laughed too, and nodded gently, his head swaying from side to side. Boudicca made a googly face and did a farting sound with her armpit and everyone felt that the ice was broken.

Shortly, the sky took on a surreal orange-brown color, like an ocher-robed swami, and suddenly the birds became quiet. The driver held up his hand and his amiable face became serious and silent.

"What is it?" asked Boudicca.

"Sshhhh," said Rook, looking about.

And momentarily, a tiger, a white Bengal tiger with blue eyes—came out from behind a near-bare oak tree and looked up at them. The mommy elephant ignored it and reached its long trunk up to gobble some of the few remaining leaves.

The tiger slowly pranced away and toward a shady, watery area. They watched it until it disappeared out of sight.

"Wow," said Rook. "This is one of the few times I wished I had a camera or a paparazzi!"

"Why's that, Papa?" asked Boudicca. "Why don't you want any photos of me when I was a baby? Why don't you want some of you and mommy getting married?"

"Of course I want that," said Rook, surprising himself. "Of course I do. And if your mom will have me when we return, I'll say 'I do!'" And he thought of Hula in her wedding dress and Boudicca as a baby and the possible moment of conception was unclear. And then he thought of Arjun giving his last and possibly best performance, bleeding, dying, with his eyes staring at him for his last Cecil B. DeMille, backwards and fading to black. And he thought of Hula with those bastards at the Capri Club taking advantage of her, and he thought of how he wanted to kill Svidrigailov and send him down the river in a body bag.

P and Jane both thought of saying something, of how they wanted to be with Rook (they had shared secrets as they shared a room), but how? They kept silent as the elephants made their way.

Boudicca sniffled and wiped her rugged face again, this time sweat, not tears, and Rook thought of the joy he now felt in having rescued her, and helping Hula, and the future the three of them might have—a normal, beautiful

family—for Rook had always believed that marriage and
family life was not serious—people dying in Sudan was
serious—no, marriage was sacred, but not serious. It was
not the stuff of soap operas, but more like *The Osbourne
Family*. Rook thought of his neighbor down the street, and
laughed at how now MTV might want to do a reality show
on Rook's newfound family life. And Rook looked at P and
Jane's bodies in front of him, and remembered all the times
Ted Southhampton slapped him, and of all the times with
his wild and crazy bandmates, and his ever-receding dead
family in Iowa, and of the strange man with the old hat
and the magnetic eyes by the cave they had just visited.
How does it all connect? thought Rook. *Or does it?*

And suddenly the mommy elephant gave a start and a
turn of the head and one wild eye looked up at the invisible moon and the driver shouted commands in Marathi
and tried to calm the savage down. In the distance stood a
group of wild elephants, memories calling out to their
cousin, all trunks in the air, sniffing, and one, the male in
the distance, let out a painful grunt and chortled something
so inhuman yet so profound that it echoed over the darkening park.

"Maybe that's her mate?" asked Boudicca.

"Maybe," said Rook. And the wind blew through their
hair and a strong gust of the creatures' overwhelming odor
enveloped them. The driver hit the mommy hard to make
it turn around, but it was reluctant to do so, snorting and
heaving and crying. He then withdrew a pistol and fired it

into the air: the other elephants turned and scrambled away—something in their experience telling them to hide.

"Let's go back," said P. "Let's go back home." P wished to achieve harmony with nature, and wished she could click her heels three times and be back with her parents before the disaster. Then she thought of all those faces she had been hired to kill. And she wondered how she could ever stay in business and still practice *ahimsa* and *satyagraha* as Gandhi advocated.

We're all just as chained and trapped as these elephants. Living in the open, we're still prisoners, thought P. *What was that quote from Rousseau?*

Suddenly, the sky turned quite dark and rain started to fall; the drivers tried to hurry the elephants, but they would only go so fast, and Rook became concerned that they were in danger of tipping over at such a reckless speed and he would lose his daughter as soon as he had found her and would never hear the end of it from Hula. But somehow they made it back to the station, just as it started to pour buckets.

"We will be waiting here under here for now," said the still-simmering Pompeii, nodding to the roof that protected the beasts and them. "This is a good place to wait. But we must not wait too long. It is not good to wait too long in life."

The rain pelted down and washed everything clean, yet made everything less passable and muddier than before. After about forty-five minutes, it stopped, and Pompeii proclaimed that they would have to make speed now to get to Delhi.

"You can be sleeping in the car, if you be liking," said Pompeii. "I have done my sleeping and smoking here, and am ready to go for you. But you think of the Mercedes as a hotel, and we will be doing just lovely!"

The three men received a tip from Rook, much to the protest of Pompeii, and Rook asked him to translate about why they had to hit the elephants so hard.

"It is the only way," explained Pompeii, going back and forth with gestures and talk, and taking pains not to offend the workers. "Their skin is so thick, it is the only way to communicate."

Just like me, thought Rook. And Rook stared once again at the flimsy ropes that kept the elephants in place and wondered why they did not burst free.

"You are thinking," rambled Pompeii, "perhaps why they are staying here away from their family out there?" And there was more talk in Hindi between the men— serious, reflective talk. "Well, it is a long story. These elephants, there are maybe 500 here in the park, are having problems. Some are sick, some are running out of rooms, and also the peoples are running out of rooms. And so we must learn how to all live together. We need some of these elephants to take away from the problem of the neighboring villages, and also to give these men work and tourists something to see." Pompeii continued translating. "Did you not see the white tiger? Did you not hear the songbirds? Did you not see the family of elephants? The only way this all can exist at all is for everyone to work together, do you follow? Yes, it is painful to be separated from loved ones, yet take a looks around this; the world is pain and suffering, yes? And so we all do what we can to get by, you see? And these elephants use to be kept locked down with heavy chain and steel, but now they are so accustomed to it, they are unaware that it is a mere string that ties them down, that they could really break at any second if they only realized it! But sometimes it is better to live in ignorance."

"And sometimes it is not," replied Rook. "Sometimes we have to realize!"

"We have to break free," said Boudicca. "We can be free."

They all nodded cheerfully goodbye, and got into the Benz. Pompeii started it and the wheels just spun, spitting and coughing up chunks of clay and spraying dirty water upon the already dirty white clothing of the men as they approached to help push the car out of the rut; they trudged slowly, their sandaled feet becoming unrecognizable—like hooves of some strange new creature, and they lifted their heels heavily, and then lifted the car lightly, and waved farewell as the four of them were on their way back to Delhi, with P puttering behind on Rocinante, soaked yet determined. Just as they were nearing the main highway, and as Rook was about to doze off to sleep, they drove through a sleepy little village that bordered the park. The first thing that Rook noticed was a small crowd gathered around, looking at something: it was a man standing on his head, no, buried on his head in the ground, hands clasped in prayer.

"What the heck?" said Rook, pointing it out to Boudicca. "How strange!"

"It is holy man," explained Pompeii. "Sometimes they do this form of yogic, tantric penance for days. Sometimes no breathing, sometimes breathing through a straw airhole. It is very cathartic."

"It looks crazy," said Jane. And she thought of the dorm parties at Yale.

"No, now that's danger!" shouted Pompeii, suddenly swerving the car and pointing. A pack of pachyderms were coming their way; one elephant crashed through one of the village huts like it was made out of paper mache, and let out a triumphant, trumpeting clarion call, and six other elephants soon appeared and followed it, trampling down the hut even further, which people had luckily scrambled out of, and now the beasts were drinking from a large vat.

Pompeii discreetly rolled down his window and gently yelled something to one of the people who had left the upside-down yogi to observe the thirsty guests. They exchanged words and nods and laughed heartily, and then tried to be quiet. Everyone watched the elephants drink.

"They are coming across from the park. They used to have this village as part of the park, but it is too many people and too many elephants. They are only going where they used to go, and we are only going where we have to go for lack of room. But what is not as before is the drink. Maybe water was the lovely for them, and other foods that were done nicely. Everything was done so nicely. But now they are hungry and thirsty and take what they can get. And they have become most accustomed to the rice wine these villagers make; it is a mad scene."

"I'll say," said Rook. "Rice wine. How bizarre."

"Daddy?" asked Boudicca. "Do you drink a lot?"

"No. Why do you keep asking?" And then he thought how he never wanted to lie to his daughter. "I used to, but no, I won't be drinking much anymore. Just socially." And he thought of how his life had changed in an instant, and he really needed to clean himself up.

"You'll need drinks after today!" joked Pompeii. "You'll need many drinks, for no one will believe you what you have been up to! How will you explain it, but only drunk will it make sense!"

They watched the elephants drink with eager, wild abandon. Then suddenly, the leader, had evidently had his full, and let out a stupendous horatio hornblower. The rest of his little gang echoed his call, and the drunken elephants spun around with Dionysian glee, and someone near the upside down yogi asked him to pray to Ganesh, and the elephants pounded past the cowering crowd, one of their trunks touching the yogi's dusty feet, which twitched and twinkled baby-like, and the herd was off down the street, kicking up cleated clods of clay and pissing and shitting as they ran, rumbled, and roared.

The villagers were left shaking their heads, and one of them gently placed her aged hand on the foot of the buried yogi to comfort him, but evidently it tickled him, because a muffled laughing and giggling could be heard, which encouraged the woman to funny him more, and soon children and everyone joined in on the tickling and laughing, until the holy man couldn't stand it any longer and scraped and dug at the earth around his head, breaking himself free—doing an acrobatic backflip and emerging out of the earth like some strange living perennial philosophy—his head all asunder and caked with old mud and crazy eyes spilling out that were still on the other side and he bestowed a blessing upon them all, smiling and laughing.

"He's been gone a while," said Rook, remembering the Alamo.

"I'll say," answered Pompeii. "It is a blessing. *A darshan*—the gaze of a saint does wonders." Pompeii seemed to possess the pre-requisite knowledge that all Indians had about spirituality.

And everyone started dancing happily in the streets, mosquitoes buzzing nearby in a game of malaria roulette, and Pompeii said it would be a sin not to get out for the saint's blessing, and so they hopped out of their mobile hotel and jumped about with the maddening crowd— sometimes on one leg, sometimes two, sometimes none— as there was one handicapped child with no legs who did his best to hop about on his hands. The child had a hard time keeping up—until the yogi noticed him and scooped him up upon his shoulders—and never had Rook seen such a look of happiness in all the years he had entertained thousands, millions, as he had seen upon that unfortunate boy who was beaming more brightly than those silly artificial lights that cascade out of the Vegas hotels and casinos and theatres and towards the night sky. And everyone went to touch the feet of the guru, but he shook his head, and instead insisted that they all touch where the feet of the boy would be, because this boy was the same as he, just not realized yet. And so everyone touched the phantom limbs of the boy and a strange tranquility came over all. Slowly, people dispersed, and a few minutes later, Rook, Boudicca, Jane, and Pompeii found themselves back in the Benz, not knowing what to say. P yelled at them from her motorcycle—"I don't know what that was all about, but let's get moving!"

"That is India," stated Pompeii, as he started up the car and they began to drive away into the orange glowing sunset. "That little experience in that village back there is India all rolled into One."

And Rook thought of the microcosm and the macrocosm and the microscope he had used in Biology class in high school in Iowa City, sharing it with Hula—his lab partner. And he placed his arm around Boudicca, and she leaned against him, and for the first time in his life Rook felt like a father and they both soon fell asleep on the bumpy ride back to Delhi, which Pompeii managed to expertly navigate, considering the lack of streetlights, the potholes, and the abandoned cars and people sleeping on the sides of some roads. They stopped once to get some gas, and to use the non-existent bathroom. Rook went into the brush and wondered, half-sleepily, what he would do if a tiger burst out of there. And then they were back in the Mercedes, chugging along to the growing city of Delhi, and as they entered the gates of the metropolis, there was no celebration, no royalty, no pampered treatment, for who knew they were coming or could even see who they were in this darkness? In their REM states, they didn't know who they were either, and they didn't care—they just floated about in the ether, on the edge of a fantastic dream and horrible nightmare and reality (which was more substantial was hard to say) and presto it was 3AM and they were near the Delhi Airport, waiting for the sun.

"We will be stopping here," said Pompeii. "We will be stopping and with the light we will be making eating and getting a flight to Mumbai. I will drive and meet you there. It is faster and easier this way. It is better for Boudicca."

"Oh," said Boudicca. And she nudged her father.

"What is it?" asked Rook, scratching his growing stubble. "Oh, well, here . . . ." and Rook pulled out a wad of rupees and handed it to Pompeii. "Your help has been invaluable at extricating us from a sticky situation."

Pompeii reluctantly took the money and slightly shook his head.

"What?" stumped Rook.

"I think he wants something, Dad," said Boudicca.

"You mean the movie?" asked Rook.

At first he didn't say anything, then Pompeii ventured: "Yes, that would be much liking to mine. I will just telephone up the wife and let her be aware of my plans to star in this Anti movie. I cannot be waiting until I see my handsome face on that big screen—and all my neighbors and friends from when I went to school will see me and shout—there's Pompeii! There's Pompeii! He made it! He made it big! He made something of himself!"

And Pompeii was so happy that they were all happy. And they and the city stretched and slowly awoke from their dreams into a dream of another sort.

"Bollywood, here we come . . . ." said Rook in a gravelly voice.

"Bollywood—oh boy!" shouted Pompeii, hand in the air, triumphant over what he did not know.

"Bollywood—oh Lord!" prayed Boudicca, wondering if there might be a spot in the film for her too—perhaps she could sing and dance or just play Rook's daughter! *That would be really cool,* she thought. And she looked at the multitude of beggars swarming the streets in dirty clothing that was colorful underneath and the people living out of cardboard boxes with litter blowing to and fro.

"I will be meets you there!" said Pompeii. I'll meet you at your hotel!"

"Sure," said Rook. "Sounds good."

A homeless beggar child wandering by put out his hand. Jane gave him her camera and asked him to take a photo. The boy gawked at the strange shiny device and did his best to capture the odd, haggard, ramshackle group. He handed her back her magic box and she gave him a rupee in return. Jane would later study that photo and remember how this whole little adventure with the rock star Rook was a life-changer; it served as a catalyst for her to switch her focus to med school to become a cardiologist for she wanted to help people—she wanted to fix hearts and prolong the joy of life.*

They all lingered a moment longer. Jane gave a long, passionate kiss and her number to P.

"Wo—what's goin' on here?" asked Rook, surprised.

"Nothing," said Jane, smiling. "Nothing at all." And she and P kissed one more time.

Jane then quickly gave her number to Rook as well. P proceeded to present Rocinante to Jane, and told her to let it take her wherever she wanted to go. In reality, it took her around Delhi for about a week until she went to the old zoo one day and decided she had had enough—she

---

* There was a phone number here, Jane's (verified), along with some notations. Evidently, the author had followed up and interviewed Jane, who speculated on her future plans. Jane's photo of the group outside the Delhi Airport is currently on her Facebook page.

wanted to set herself free. And so she donated Rocinante to an orphanage, went back to the States, and to Yale.

Pompeii kept squinting; perhaps it was because he was thinking of all those bright Bollywood lights. And then he started crying just a little.

Rook hugged him. "It's okay, guy," he said. "Look, here." And Rook gave Pompeii his other pair of expensive shades. "You'll need these when you're a movie star."

"We are all movie stars," said Pompeii, thinking of the cosmic drama. "I am just taking it to the next level! I will be seeing yous soon! Definitely! Most definitely!"

And Pompeii exploded off in the bumpity Benz, and Jane roared off on the supercharged horse, both waving to the strange trio they had grown so close to in such a short time. At the same time, they all wanted to forget all the murder and mayhem forever, forever erasing it from the shores of their memories.

As the motley crew of Rook, Boudicca, and P made their way to the ticket counter, Rook was recognized by the pretty agent behind the desk.

"I've got all your music!" she said. "Will you autography this for me?" And Rook signed the back of last year's Diwali calendar—which was all the woman had handy. "I can't believe it! Rook, my favorite rock star! Do you know how popular you are here?"

"Is that a good thing, or a bad thing?" Rook asked.

The woman laughed. "My name is Maya. Where would you like to go?"

"That's a loaded question," said Rook.

And Boudicca looked at her father and this Maya and then up at Pui.

Pui smiled and tousled Boudicca's hair, and Boudicca tried to smile but wondered if she were going to die soon as she popped another series of pills and reminded her dad to take his too.

As they headed towards security, Rook noticed his mangled and bandaged hand trembling as the guards with rifles in green army uniforms waited for something unknown to happen. And try as he might, Rook couldn't stop his hand from shaking and imagined his guilt would give them all away. And then he looked down at his daughter and felt a strength and knew somehow everything would be okay.

"Excuse me sir," said a guard to Rook. "But what is the nature of your stay here in India?"

"To kill a famous movie star and then take his place," said Rook.

The guard burst out laughing. "What?"

"I'm in a movie."

"Okay, go ahead," said the man, distracted by P's winking at him.

The three of them sauntered to the gate, with P whispering to Rook: "you've really got to watch it. What the hell do you think you're doing? You've got to be careful and professional about this."

"I'm sorry that I'm not a professional killer like you. I'm sorry if it's taking me a little bit of time to get over it."

"Here's a newsflash: you never get over it. Those memories and faces stay with you for the rest of your life. So get use to it and keep on moving. That's all you can do—keep on moving."

Boudicca, who had been holding both of their hands, let go of them and tried not to think about all the madness by focusing on her Manolo Blahnik's that Arjun had bought her as they sashayed elegantly yet uncomfortably across the piss-poor tiles of the Delhi Airport.

As the trio kept on moving, a man in mufti named Shanti Degvan, Detective Constable with the Indian Special Branch in Delhi, scrutinized a faxed version of an autographed glossy photo of Rook with accompanying text—**Watch with discretion!—American rock star Rook Heisenberg possibly complicit in Arjun Alexander's death or disappearnce?**—that had been sent over the wire from the Rishikesh Police. Constable Degvan carried his masala chai carefully and followed the celebrity and his companions ever so surreptitiously.

"What's this world coming to? I can't escape the tabloids!" Degvan said to himself. He stopped momentarily, making sure to pick up a copy of the latest *Interloper*, which his wife read avidly every week.

18

A BOLLYWOOD HOMECOMING

As they landed in Mumbai in the early morn and exited the airport, Rook once again had a feeling of déjà vu. He noticed a military man approaching—it was the same one who had wanted his mosquito spray before. They recognized each other and laughed, but this time his face took on a more serious demeanor. His rough hand stretched out, tentatively, palm-up.

"Excuse me," he stuttered, "but I have been hearing some strange things over the system, Mr. Rook."

Rook cleared his throat and hoped he wouldn't have to sing.

"What strange things? That I found the daughter I never knew I had?"

The officer looked at Boudicca, shook his head, and said, "Never mind. Please just be comfortable in your stay here with your new family."

"Yes, my new family," said Rook. "Thanks." And he slipped the guard 100Rs.

"Let's get out of here, father," said Boudicca. "I'm feeling nervous and dehydrated."

"Those might be side effects of the medications," said Rook, feeling a very dry throat himself. "But you know, P's here; she'll protect us! That's her job!" Rook winked at her.

P winked back. "I'll do my best. Now let's head back to the Rajahranee."

"Don't forget our movie appearance!" said Boudicca, tugging on her father's hand.

"My whole life sometimes feels like a movie appearance," said Rook, tiredly, wiping the sweat from his peeling nose with his bandaged hand.

They flagged a cab to the hotel; Rook and P kept looking back to see if they were being followed, but only noticed a mad crowd of cars and horns.

Rook rolled down the window to get some air and allowed the hands of the beggars to reach inside. He closed his eyes and felt life grasping at him, clutching at him, tugging at his shoulder, pulling him up and pulling him down. He looked over at Boudicca as she gazed out at the colorful saris blowing in the wind.

"Life is a series of performances," said Rook. "One show after another. You have to do your best and play the game to win!"

Boudicca almost laughed; suddenly, she could not look at her father, this man who had shown up fifteen years too late.

"Easier said than done," she whispered, wondering if the needle would hurt that would take her blood and test her for HIV. She didn't like needles, and had to look away as the blood flowed out of her, speaking of anything to get her mind off the loss.

"We'll turn it around together," said Rook. "I'll do everything I can to help you, honey."

"Can we just skip to the last page? Can it just be a happy ending?" A tear began to well up in Boudicca's eye.

"Sure, darling, sure." Rook reached over and held her hand and kissed his daughter on her cheek as Pui smiled at them.

I'm so selfish for thinking of Rook in that way, thought P. *I shouldn't think of him like that!* And she went back to her Gandhi book.

Off to the side of the road, a crowd had gathered, for some reason pummeling a man for having accidentally hit into a roadside stand selling tobacco and Thums-Up cola.

Their new driver eased the process, greased the wheels, and knew exactly where to go to get the best ride to the Rajahranee Hotel. As they journeyed through the streets, it occurred to Rook just how much had changed recently. *Last time I was taking this trip, I had no idea who my daughter really was. It's suddenly like fifteen years of fatherhood has caught up to me in a week. And these people on the streets. They don't shock me now. It's all such a carnival—a bazaar—a bizarre painting.*

For Boudicca too, the city seemed much changed. She remembered the first trip though these streets was very different—tossed about in a box—bumping her head and feeling every pothole in her knees with an "ouch." And the colors and smells which had seemed so violent to her before, so hostile, now reached out to her and consoled her—*these Indian people—they're the friendliest, on earth,* she thought. *But I miss Mommy. I really miss my Mommy!*

An hour later they were back in the royal suite at the Rajahranee. Rook stretched out on the big bed, feeling like the Big B as one of his movies played in the background, and dozed off. Boudicca, meanwhile, had the adjoining suite. She listened to her newfound father snore, and wondered how she could possibly be the only daughter of this mega-star. She flipped through the TV, then went to the window and stared luxuriously out onto the sprawling city she had not too long ago been surviving in in squalor and captivity. And then she thought of all the other young girls, and boys, who scraped by out there. And how they still were out there and had no rock star father to swoop down and rescue them. But what could she do? *Of course I care about them. How can you not care? But what can I do?*

She sat down at the desk and rifled through the mahogany drawers. When opened, a whiff of a grandmotherly, inlay of pearl scent rose up. Instead of the Gideon's Bible, she found a copy of the *Bhagavad Gita.*

She put it aside and breathed heavily. She tried to remember what her mother looked like. For a second, she panicked: she couldn't picture her face in her mind. But then suddenly it swam into focus, and she wanted to hug her tight.

Boudicca got up and paced around the room, absent-mindedly observing her feet making twirls in the thick, plush red carpeting. It felt good upon her feet. She stared at her face in the full-length beveled mirror.

Do I have HIV? Do I have it already? She popped more of the regimen, noting the time.

She looked away, down at a fancy broach that someone had left behind. She picked it up and put it on. *I know I have to get tested; I'm just afraid to know. One way or the other. I'm afraid.*

Boudicca suddenly went back to the TV and a Bollywood film that was playing. The hero kissed the world goodbye as he was dying, hurtling from a plane with a bomb he had removed, saving everyone on board.

"What a strange, sad ending," Boudicca said to herself. And she determined right then and there that she would make sure there would be no sad ending for her.

Rook awoke and jotted down a quick note about a song idea he had in a dream. Then he wrapped a rubber-band around the pile of little ideas he had stacking up on his nightstand; in a moment he was transported back to his childhood and thoughts of collecting and sorting sports cards by the Iowa River.

Before he could fully enjoy his reverie, a knock came upon the door.

"Who is it?"

"Anatoli," said the voice. "Let's get going! We're shooting bright and early!"

Rook opened the door and hugged his old friend.

"I heard you had quite an adventure," said the director, framing a scene in his mind. "Found your daughter, hey?"

"Why, yes." Rook coughed and looked for his pills.

"Killed Arjun?" asked Anatoli, looking at Rook's hand.

"Well, sadly yes, I killed him," said Rook, the words hard to form. "And Pompeii killed the other."

"Uh-ohh . . . police won't like that. But it's part of the job. What can one do? You had to save your daughter!"

"Yes, he did," said Boudicca, now standing beside her father. *He really did go overboard though*, thought Boudicca.

"Ohh! And you must be the lovely—" And Anatoli pictured a future star.

"Boudicca. I'm looking forward to being in your film."

"And you will be! I have discovered you for the ages!"

And Anatoli wandered about the room, looking at things as if he were about to film there, tapping at furniture with his cane, rubbing his black goatee, and picking up sundry items, examining them, then placing them down in ideal, orderly, but seemingly random positions.

"Do we have everyone?" asked Anatoli.

Suddenly, P and Pompeii both appeared, as if psychically aware of their chance to play a key part in a great, or possibly not-so-great, movie, entitled: *Mujhey Doctor Kee Zaroorat Hai! (I Need A Doctor!)*.

The limo drive to Film City was smoother than any taxi's ride. The white leviathan cascaded through salient streets, salient mobs reaching out to the dark tinted windows, as if the white whale offered some hope of salvation. Rook, for a second, was back at the Hollywood Bowl, leaving that last concert. *It feels like a million years ago,* he thought. He looked over at Boudicca and grabbed her hand, patting it. She looked at him and yawned.

Pompeii was all astonishment. He had never been in the world of the sleek and sexy. He ran his hand against the cold leather interior, the seats adjusted to the right temperature, looked out at the crowd and waved, and he almost started salivating. He looked up at the pregnant sky through the sun roof, rolled it open, and stuck out his tongue to catch the drizzle of rain that hinted at the monsoonal rains of the later afternoon. Closing the window, he put headphones on and started listening to the radio stations. He also turned on the TV in the back of the seat, and began absent-mindedly flipping through the channels. His head swayed from side to side. *I am not a servant any more! I am a celebrity!* he thought. *I love it love it oh yeah!*

Entering the gates of Film City, the limo was waved right through by the guards, evidently accustomed to the driver. The car weaved in and out of little islands of make-believe, until it finally came to a monstrous set that looked like it covered the space of ten football fields.

"Here we are being, my friends," said Anatoli Anti. "This is not Burbank, but you are in for a treat, nonetheless. We will show you the magic behind the making. Mr. Rook, I apologize if this is not a surprise to you, but you are old school."

"Yes, and I am old and getting older. We really can't stay for long."

Anatoli slapped Rook on the back and pretended to laugh. As they entered the stage, Boudicca and Pompeii's eyes gaped, not just at the vastness of the set, but at the ensemble of dancers in electric blue saris who giggled and pointed at the foreigners. P sat to the side, intent and content on reading more of Gandhi.

One young lady, about Boudicca's age, ran up to them, brimming with excitement and something else. She spat the betel juice to the side, wiped the red crap from her mouth, and began animatedly talking in Hindi.

"I'm sorry, I don't understand," said Boudicca.

"It's okay," said the girl. "My name is Rashmi. I am famous from Tiraputi to the jungles of Kashmir. Do you not know my famous face? I wanted to ask you if you knew me in America." And she lit up a smoke. "Want one?'

Rook stepped in. "My daughter doesn't smoke!"

"How do you know?" said Boudicca.

"Oh gracious, it is the famous Rook! Goodness gracious! How bizarre! Let's make something fun! Let's dance!" And Rashmi grabbed Boudicca's little growing hand that might one day wear a wedding ring and they jumped up onto a wooden platform.

"These are the moves—they are sick!" said Rashmi, demonstrating them to Boudicca.

"Rook, you're needed on Stage 34!" called Anatoli over the loudspeaker.

Rook meandered over, squinting at the early morning sun and gently touching his slowly healing face. He listened to Anatoli go on and on animatedly, and then repeated back what he thought was important.

"Let me get this straight, you want me to run across this fake jungle, jump at the couple, look at them both, and then start singing?" asked Rook.

"That is correct, sir," said Anatoli. "Then, the next scene, you will kill the male star; or at least it will look that way. And the audience will hate you. He looks a lot like Arjun Alexander, by the way."

"Lovely. Simply lovely. Why are you making me do this?"

"You owe it to India! This is your penance! And make sure to look guilty and sorry!" said Anatoli.

"I won't even have to act," said Rook.

"And you won't even need makeup!" said Anatoli. "You look like you've already been through hell!"

Rook did not say anything, but moved to the side and waited for his cue.

Pompeii, meanwhile, waited for his cue as a face in the crowd. And he was happier than all of them put together, thinking of how all his friends and family's respect of him would rise like a new offering on the India Exchange.

As P sat reading, off in the corner, looking up from time to time to make sure all was fine, she noticed an older Indian man dressed up like a fakir, apparently waiting to be called for his part.

"Hello, sir," said P, smiling.

"Namaste," said the man, nodding.

"Who are you supposed to be?"

"Well, it just so happens that my real profession and my movie profession are one today! I really am a psychic!"

"Well, since we're waiting around, could you do some readings for us? I had some questions . . . ."

"Sure," said the man, smiling mysteriously. "What would you like?"

And as if on cue, a break on all the stages was called. Rook and Boudicca and Pompeii found their way over.

"Rook," said P. "This nice man is going to help us. He's going to give us a reading!"

"Great!" said Rook. "An actor reading my future!"

"Are we not all actors?" asked the fakir, smiling.

"Come on Dad, it will be fun," said Boudicca. They all gathered around the psychic, who pulled out some items from an orange cotton bag. When Pompeii saw the tarot cards, however, he walked away and busied himself with calling his wife on the phone.

"Show him what's in your locket," said P.

Rook opened the pendant, and pulled out the Jupiter Magic Square.

"Hmmm, yes, yes, I've seen this before," said the fakir. "It's a good luck charm, it helps protect you so you can get your work done. In *I Ching*, it also has to do with balancing your chi power, your yin and yang. The numbers 3 and 4, however, also have special meaning. Multiplied, they equal 12, the number of The Hanged Man."

"What's that?" said Rook, shifting his weight.

"In Tarot, it has to do with the Fool who finds himself through an epiphany. Let us do your cards!"

The fakir allowed Rook to cut the cards. The first one to appear was indeed The Hanged Man.

Rook gasped. "This is silly," he said.

"You must make a sacrifice. You must give up your youth to find your youth," said the psychic, seriously. The prognosticator was about to continue, when Rook grabbed his wrist.

"What are you doing?" Rook asked. "What the hell are you doing?"

"Rook, please," said P.

"Daddy—"

"Don't you realize we've just been through an awful lot?" asked Rook.

The fakir paused. "I do. But there is more to come. Excuse me, I'm needed for my part now," and the man wriggled away and headed towards Anatoli, who was waving for him urgently.

Rook collapsed upon the stage platform, almost upside-down with his foot in the shape of a "4." He tried to take some deep breaths.

"It's okay," said P, holding his hand. "It's okay."

Boudicca was about to say something, when Anatoli arrived.

"Rook," Anatoli said in an unusual tone, "I'd like you to meet someone. An old friend . . . ."

Rook looked at the man approaching from his odd angle.

"This is Dr. Cartwright, Rook," said Anatoli. "He's a very old friend of mine and just happened to be in town. He heard you were about and wanted to meet you."

"A doctor?" said Rook. "A real doctor? Good, I can use some help. I'm all messed up still. And we'll need some refills."

"I'll say," said Boudicca. They only had a day's supply left of their regimen.

"I'm a psychiatrist, Mr. Heisenberg," said Dr. Cartwright, struggling with the intense humidity, padding his face delicately with a monogrammed handkerchief.

"Oh," said Rook. And he sat upright. He had never been to a psychiatrist before, mostly because he felt they would eventually take whatever he had confided to them and turn it into a best-selling book.

"Well, would you like to talk?" asked Dr. Cartwright. "Anatoli here tells me you've all been through a lot lately."

Rook looked over at Boudicca, and reached out for her hand, but she didn't take his.

After a pause, Rook said, "Yes, we've been through a lot lately."

"I'd be happy to talk with you all, if you'd like," said Dr. Cartwright, itching his face. "No charge!"

Rook was about to say no, but then looked over at Boudicca. She shrugged her shoulders.

"Okay," said Rook. "For her sake."*

***

Later that night, Rook washed the makeup off his face, very carefully, lest he peel some new skin away, sprayed his best Versace cologne, and turned around to open the door for P, who had been wanting to talk with him.

"Expecting someone else?" asked Ted Southhampton, smiling ear to ear with arms wide open.

"What took you so long?" asked Rook, laughing.

---

* Editor's note: Some of the chapters of this book were partially assembled from the sessions and notes here between Rook, Boudicca, P, Pompeii, (and later Ted Southhampton), and Dr. Cartwright (aka Aitchkiss Killawathy?). These transcripts are highly anachronistic. However, certain annotations (although incomplete) assisted in a somewhat helpful reordering and clarification of the narrative. Certain editorial inferences were also drawn, where it was deemed to provide possible insight. It is also worth mentioning, that whoever the author was, it is probable that he/she was not an authentic psychiatrist, as the notes do not at all follow standard DSM-IV or ICD codes.

"God, you look like shit! Man, I'm gonna have to hire somebody to really fix you up! Okay, let's get to it." And Ted was making all sorts of phone calls to find the best dermatologist and plastic surgeon in the city.

"Tomorrow, Ted, please. I'm about to have dinner."

"Okay, okay," said Ted. "Who's coming?"

"Now I remember why I left LA," said Rook.

"Now I remember why I get paid the big bucks! You'd be falling apart without me! You'd be nothing without me! I'm glad you're here, by the way. We can do some clothing business too!"

"They've already started plastering me up on billboards," said Rook. "I saw the first one, of me wearing those sexy clothes, as I was lying naked and torn in the dirt."

"Stop exaggerating!" said Ted. "Let's make some money!"

"That I do need," said Rook, thinking of Boudicca and Hula. "That I do need."

***

And so, for the next week, they filmed their scenes (Rook had a stunt double for the most dangerous segment; after time in the make-up chair, his replacement really did look very much like the rock star, which scared Rook to death), they had their psychiatric sessions, and they did their clothing and other business.

Rook and Boudicca met with Dr. Vajpayee's colleague, and refilled their regimen. Despite the fatigue and constant thirst (which in the Anatoli film gave them an odd, raspy quality—for Rook as the villain it was perfect—for Boudicca, it gave her instant acclaim as a new face to the method-acting world), their side effects weren't too bad. The doctor told them they should have an HIV test at three months, and another at six months. Rook and Boudicca breathed long sighs as they conveyed this information to Hula, who would talk with them on the phone every night, asking what was taking so long.

"When are you coming?" asked Hula, from her flat on the outskirts of Amsterdam, far away from the Capri Club.

"Any day now, Hula," said Rook. "We're just wrapping things up down here. Don't worry, everything's fine. I just really owe a favor to Anatoli to finish making this film. We wouldn't have Boudicca back without his help."

"It's okay, Mom. We're having fun! I'm getting to act!" said Boudicca. "Maybe this will be my career!"

"Well, darling, hurry. Mommy misses you! I love you," said Hula to Boudicca, trying not to cry.

"I love you too, Mom," said Boudicca, trying not to cry.

Rook did not know what to say, so he said nothing.

"Well?" asked Professor April Kentucky, crying. "Is he on his way?"

"He'll be here soon," said Hula, looking out the window, waiting.

"Just what I thought! He's like all men. They all leave when you need them!"

"I'm not like that!" said Grandfather Louis Kentucky, waking up from the recliner and looking at a bird soaring by, bringing a worm back to her young.

"I have to go out now," said Hula, getting dressed.

"You must have a big date!" said Grandfather.

"Darling," said April, "you must learn that if you try too hard to impress a man, you'll just ruin things. Less is more."

"Oh Mom, when will you realize that your writing techniques don't always apply to real life?"

"What's real life?" pondered Grandfather, getting out his pipe and an old book that smelled like a wine cellar.

And Hula walked out the door to go meet S. They were going ring shopping, taking a quick flight to Belgium, and then setting up a trust fund for Boudicca.

"You should have done all this in the first place," Hula told S as they slowly patched things up.

"You're right," he said, honestly. "But I am a criminal. I am not familiar with such sensible approaches."

***

Meanwhile, in Mumbai, Detective Constable Shanti Degvan walked in the door of the Rajahranee Hotel, nodding politely to the doormen who seemed to recognize him. He sat down in the lobby and waited and observed, something he was very good at doing. He ordered a masala chai and the most recent *Interloper,* something he was very good at doing.

***

Late at night, after he had tucked Boudicca in, Rook would quietly watch all of Arjun Alexander's best movies; he would study at least one a night, sometimes two, and sometimes P would join him, cuddling beneath the silken blankets until they fell asleep. Rook marveled at the acting skills of the legend he had killed, and chuckled to himself as he witnessed onscreen the actor's trademark laugh, and the classic line: "Anybody home?" *These are some of the best performances I have ever seen!* thought Rook. But to Rook, Arjun's quintessential performance came in real life—in his death scene, which no audience would ever see—with his line: "Your autograph?" uttered with such sincerity and confused hopefulness. And Rook began to cry, and then he started sobbing.

"What have I done?" Rook asked the TV screen. "What on earth have I done? I've killed a national treasure!"

19

THE GREATER GOOD

"**M**y dear Mr. Heisenberg," said Shanti Degvan at the old Victoria Station on the last day of filming. "Allow me to introduce myself. I am Detective Constable Degvan, of the Indian Special Branch, Delhi Office."

"Are you in the movie too?" asked Rook.

"No. But I do need to speak with you."

"Perhaps I can help. I am Mr. Heisenberg's physician, Dr. Cartwright."

"And I am his manager, Mr. Southhampton."

"And I am his security, Ming Dynasty."

"And I am—" and the detective interrupted Boudicca, patting her affectionately on the head.

"It's okay. It's okay," said Shanti. "I know. You are Boudicca Kentucky Heisenberg."

They all looked at him suspiciously, except for Dr. Cartwright, who seemed impressed.

"I'm sorry," said Anatoli, approaching. "Is there something I can help you with? Hey, would you mind working crowd control with your colleagues?"

"I am not a traffic officer," said Shanti. "I am Detective Constable Degvan, and I am piecing the puzzle."

A bell rang and Anatoli nodded for a servant to approach. He tiptoed hesitantly and brought forth a calling card printed on a sheen white business card with bold, glossy, raised black lettering: CALYPSO—ART AND ANTIQUITIES.

"Show him in by all means," said the Anatoli.

A gentleman dressed in blue and smoking an accompanying blue-smoked charras sashayed in and spoke.

"My dear Anatoli, so good to see you again. I have something you may be interested in acquiring. Black Box."

The man pranamed to all present, however, when he saw Constable Degvan, his face started twitching.

"Excuse me," said the man in blue. "I must be going." And he turned and left, moving quickly this way and that.

Anatoli shrugged. "Now, what is it Constable?"

"That happens a lot," said Degvan, evidently referring to the man of antiquities who had just left. "People get so afraid when they're guilty."

"We're all guilty," said P.

"That is true," said Dr. Cartwright, scratching a pimple that was poking out and wiping his forehead.

"I know what you're doing here, Mr. Heisenberg," said the inspector. "Just an American rock star on holiday, huh?"

"Listen, how much will it take for you to go away?" asked Anatoli, getting out a wad of bills and preparing to count.

"Another sure sign of guilt," said Degvan. "Mr. Heisenberg, it is quite apparent that you have left quite a wake behind you. A trail of disaster stretching from country to country. So my dear Rook, you will have to explain what happened to Arjun Alexander?"

"Well," said Rook. "It's a long story . . . ."

"I'm sorry," said Southhampton. "What's this about?"

"A famous actor is missing," said the inspector.

"He must not be that famous, then, huh?" said South-hampton. "Just follow the paparazzi."

"Well, he is not in the hey-day," said the detective.

"I am Mr. Heisenberg's manager, and if you want to talk with him, you need to make an appointment, just like anyone else. I am quite sure he doesn't know anything about this Arjun Alexander."

"But I did not say his name," said the detective.

"Oh, it's all in the tabloids," said Southhampton, brush-ing him off and turning away.

"I could make up a story," said Rook, confessing.

"Rook—?" said Southhampton, urgently.

"But why should I?" continued Rook. "I did nothing wrong. I was just trying to save my daughter. I did what I had to do. I am not proud of killing, but I saw no other option. *Uska kaam kiya,*" Rook said, throwing in the Hindi phrase he had learned from the movie they were making as off-handedly as he could.

"Ha! Rook, he's quite the actor!" said Southhampton, attempting to pull his client towards safer waters.

"I am a reasonable man," said the detective. "But you need to be reasonable too. Where is he?"

Rook looked to P. "Um . . . ."

"I understand the situation. I am not stupid. Ha? I know what happened. I know Arjun had AIDS; that's pretty common knowledge. I know he was desparate, and was trying to cure himself by that old myth. I know you were only trying to help Boudicca. But I have to fill out a report, and that report will be in the media. We can't have one of our major stars stay missing! It looks very bad!"

"The tigers got him," said P, and she went on to explain how she carried the bodies up the mountain, knowing the nearby cats would lick the bones clean.

As she related the story, Ted Southhampton paced back and forth, mumbling how he was going to fire her, and how everything was now "curtains."

"Come now," said the detective as he made notes on his yellow legal pad. "It's not as bad as all that. Listen, there is no need to turn this into a circus. Do you think we want to ruin Arjun's reputation and cause great dishonor by telling the whole sordid story? My report would look like *The Interloper!*"

With this comment, Dr. Cartwright fell into a laughing fit for some time, covering his face in his hands.

"No," said the detective, still writing. "Mr. Arjun Alexander and his servant Abhishek were killed and eaten by tigers as they were meditating peacefully at their estate in Rishikesh. There will be a national day of mourning in their honor."

"Excellent!" said Southhampton. "This is a very good idea. I couldn't have thought of a better solution myself!"

"Not so fast," said the detective, walking about, thinking, or pretending to think. In reality, he had planned the entire episode.

"I want Puroshottam Petro and One Eye."

"What can I do?" asked Rook. "You all want a song?"

"No," said Degvan, curtly. "You have an in. You get me them, and we'll forget all this," said the detective.

"They're up at the Kali Club. Go ahead and knock," said Anatoli, laughing. "I don't have time for this!"

"Do you have all the permits for filming here?" the detective asked Anatoli, taking a sudden interest. "Where's your passport?"

"I think I can help," said P, moving closer. Everyone suddenly looked at her. "I think I know where they are."

"Where?"

"Back to where we want to go. Amsterdam."

"And how do you know this?"

"Because I was held captive. Heard it. I had to give them a Van Gogh for my release, and to help Boudicca. They're going there to get the painting, and to take over S's operations."

"Bloody mafia wars," said the detective. "In the old days, it was all local. Now days, it's all internationals. Listen, I need to take them down. You help me, you help the greater good."

"What can I do?" asked Rook.

"Lead me to them. I'll do the rest," said the detective. "Now finish your movie. We have a plane to catch!"

"Okay," Anatoli yelled. "Everybody back to work! Rook, I appreciate all the hell this movie is for you, but it'll all be worth it in the end! You will be the American rock star they love to hate! But in a good way!"

They all took their places.

"Action!" yelled Anatoli.

Rook, assuming his role, sang his new, beautiful and tender song, "Look What's Become of Me," and near the end of it, everyone broke into dance. Rook kissed the lead actress (which later gave the censors quite a headache). The dance scene ended with Rook panicking, dropping to the floor as a fake bullet exploded fake blood upon his chest, Rook screaming: "I need a doctor!"

"And cut!" directed Anatoli with a great smile. "Rook, that was great; we didn't even need to use your extra!" he championed, running up and hugging the rock star. "You know, you did a much better job with your part in this film than in that other."

"I know."

"What happened?"

"I guess you could say that I was inspired with a creative frenzy. And guilt."

"Well, whatever happened, keep it up! See you at the screening!" shouted Anatoli, disappearing to talk with his accountants and marketing people.

Rook then noticed his daughter off by herself, looking at the floor. Rook wanted to go over there, but didn't know what to say. *I don't know how to be a father,* he thought.

Instead, P, who also noticed, went to hug Boudicca.

Later that evening, back at the Rajahranee, Rook took Boudicca to one of the jewelry shops in the back of the hotel. He busied himself in looking for something to get for her and Hula. He found a lovely Lapis necklace for Boudicca, and for Hula, on a whim, a rather large diamond engagement ring. And he bought them without hesitation or regret.

"You think she'll like this?" Rook asked Boudicca.

Boudicca said nothing.

"What? What?"

"I don't think you know what you're doing."

"Sure I do," said Rook. "I'm making a commitment. To you and to her."

And Boudicca walked away and reached for a copy of the nearest paper and pretended to read it. It just happened to be *The Interloper*. And there happened to be an article about her father: **Where Is The Rookster?**

Rook glanced over her shoulder.

"I've been wondering that myself," he said, smiling.

And Boudicca walked out of the store and started talking to a young Indian boy who had been staring at them for some time.

"I am Boudicca," she told the boy, smiling.

"Well, it is very good to meet you. My name is Scott."

"Scott?"

"I'm actually from California. I can't believe you know Rook! I've been standing here, wanting to go up for an autograph, but . . . ."

"Really?" She paused, looking down at his beautiful feet. "I'll introduce you." And she tugged Scott by the sleeve. "Where are you from?"

"Santa Monica."

"What's it like?"

"Why don't you come visit and find out? Want a smoke?"

"Sure," said Boudicca, reaching out for the Kool that Scott was offering.

"Have you smoked before?"

"A little. Little by little."

As Scott reached out, cupping his hand to shield the slight wind, and gentlemanly tried to light Boudicca's cigarette, Rook exploded on the scene, grabbing the coffin nail out of his daughter's mouth and smashing the lighter to the ground.

"What the hell do you think you're doing?" yelled Rook.

"Be cool," said Scott, "be cool," not seeing right away who it was. When he noticed it was Rook, he said nothing, then, "Your autograph?"

"Rook," said Dr. Cartwright, who had wandered upon the scene. "Deep breaths. Deep breaths."

"I'm really having a hard time right now," stammered Rook, clenching his fist. "Who the hell are you and what do you want with my daughter?" asked Rook.

"What?" said Scott.

"Please," said Boudicca.

"I'm Scott. We just met."

Dr. Cartwright pulled Rook aside.

"Rook, just relax—he doesn't know about Arjun. You know that. Now, it might be a good idea for Boudicca to socialize with people her own age. Let her live a little. The boy's from California too," said Cartwright.

"Really?" said Rook, still breathing heavily.

The good doctor pulled Rook away, allowing Boudicca and Scott to get acquainted. Still, Rook watched them from behind a display of watches and cologne, slowly unclenching his fist.

"Doc, I'm trying, I'm really trying," said Rook.

"I know you are," said Dr. Cartwright, making some notes on his patient. "And so am I."

20

THE BIG BANG

Pompeii waited outside the Rajahranee in the wee hours of the morning, waiting to take them all to the airport. As he sat in the limo, he looked at an unusually large group of people out at this hour—evidently preparing for the total solar eclipse. Some were buying extra umbrellas, others stampeding towards temples, and one ambulance attempting to take an expectant mother to the hospital. She and her family were insisting on not going and postponing the birth until afterwards; they thought it bad luck to be born during such an astrological event. Still others were preparing to journey to the Ganges; it was considered auspicious by some to bathe in the holy waters during this day of unusual alignment.

I don't know why the Rook has chosen this day to fly. Why this day? thought Pompeii. He recalled his strange dream, about a plane crash, and when they found the black box that contained the secrets and the Mystery of Mysteries, how that exploded too, leaving even an even greater Mystery. And then he remembered how the gun exploded when he shot and killed Abhishek and how that opened up secrets of tremendous guilt. And he thought about the beginning of the universe and how it exploded with a big bang and everything somehow came out of the blackness of nothing. And he wondered when he too would explode. And thinking all this, and thinking again about his dream, he wondered if the universe too were a dream and how many cycles would it take until he broke free from the wheel? He clutched his heart, feeling a slight palpitation. He opened his mouth and said, "But it's not Kali Yuga, it's Dwapara!" but then realized no one was there to listen.

Suddenly, Dr. Cartwright knocked upon the tinted window. As Pompeii was helping him with his bags, except for a briefcase that he refused to part with, Pompeii asked, "Dear Doctor? I know you listen to people for a living. I would like to be listened to. I would very much like to be listened to."

"Okay."

"But I can't pay you. I am very poor."

"Okay."

"I have a dream, a story to tell you . . . ."

"Okay. That's okay. We all have a story to tell."

"But I want you to tell me what it means."

"That, I can try and help you with. But I don't know if I can. A story can mean so many things, as well as nothing at all."

Pompeii's cheeks sucked in, and his eyes bulged out.

"But I'm listening," comforted the good doctor. "I'm very much all ears."

***

"I know I haven't been much of a dad: I'm sorry. But the fact of the matter is, I didn't know you existed. I was ignorant. I'm still ignorant—of a lot of things. Anyway."

Rook sat talking to his daughter on the plane as they headed back to Amsterdam. He did not look into Boudicca's eyes because he could not reconcile his lame excuses with the fact that she had no dad for years, just like her mom, Hula. And so he just whistled nervously.

Rook instead looked out the window, until finally he had the courage to bring his eyes up. Boudicca was staring at the aging red carpeting; she wiped her eye with the back of her hand, but did not reach out to hug her father.

"I'm nervous," said Boudicca.

"Why?"

"About what's going to happen next."

"It's okay. It's okay."

"Ladies and gentlemen," came the pilot's voice over the intercom. "You're lucky enough to witness the longest total solar eclipse of the century from 41,000 feet! Today, the earth is at its farthest distance from the sun for the whole year! If you'd look out your windows . . . ."

And Rook, Boudicca, P, Ted, Dr. Cartwright, and Constable Degvan all peered out like infants as the moon began to block the sun, casting a shadow over the world.

***

They were silent as they made their way through the gentle air towards Hula in Amsterdam. Rook stared out into the surreal sky and wondered what else the dark would bring. He tried to fall asleep, but couldn't. He got out *Either/Or* and flipped through some pages:

"In addition to my numerous circle of friends, I have one more intimate confidant—my Melancholy. In my joy, in my work, she waves to me, calls me to her side ... she is the most faithful mistress I have known; is it any wonder that I love her in return?"

"What is that you're reading?" asked Dr. Cartwright, walking by and snooping over Rook's shoulder.

"Oh, some old stuff," said Rook, showing it to the doctor. "I find strange parallels to my life."

"Indeed," said Cartwright. "Fascinating." And he got out a yellow legal pad.

Rook put the tome aside and looked around. He noticed that P was still reading Gandhi's autobiography—*The Story of My Experiments With Truth.* Ted was flipping through some paperwork and fashion shoots for Rook's new clothing line. Dr. Cartwright had sat back down, and was now studying a black and white engraving; he began writing feverishly on his psychiatrist's pad, holding it at a strange angle—perhaps so any passenger nearby could not spy what he was scribbling. At some point, Rook watched Boudicca sleep—her gentle breathing was somehow reassuring that life went on. Then, before he knew it, Rook was dreaming. Dreaming of what Hula's reaction would be when they showed up on her doorstep. He felt her turning them away. They rang the bell again, and this time some stranger appeared, frowned, and pointed in some askew direction. Rook turned to look where he had pointed, and noticed a lake shimmering. He went to its edge and looked in, holding Boudicca's sweaty hand. As he gazed into the water, he couldn't bring himself away from his own beautiful reflection. Boudicca kept pulling at him, Hula kept calling, and still he studied with wonder the glorious details of his Rubenesque face.

"It's nice to have a face," he said. "It's nice to have a lovely face and a handsome one, together we're going to walk in the sun . . . ." and a song was born.

Suddenly he was swimming the backstroke and floating somewhere long off when a tug came at his heart. He turned and awoke and saw outside the neatly delineated polder landscape—a fresh beauty of orange and greens and yellows and shades of amber to greet them after the darkness of the eclipse.

When Hula and her mom and grandpa met them at the airport they ran up and scooped up Boudicca. Everyone hugged, and Rook watched this with a tender tear. Then Hula looked at Rook in a way he had never seen before, but couldn't quite place his finger on. He felt the box with the engagement ring in his pocket, but couldn't bring himself to propose just yet.

Mrs. Kentucky stood standoffish; Rook approached her in the same way he did as a teenager.

"Hi! Professor Kentucky, you haven't aged a day!"

"No, I've aged about fifteen years," she replied, not smiling. "You look like hell," she said, honestly.

Rook tried to hug her, but she did not reciprocate.

"Hello, Rookie," said Grandfather, with a warm smile. "How are you, son? It's been a while."

"Yeah, well . . . ." said Rook. And they hugged.

"Grandpa," said Rook, "I have a puzzle you'd like," Rook said, taking off the pendants and showing them to him. "I've been trying to figure this out . . . ."

"Rook!" said Dr. Cartwright. "Don't you think you should do that later?"

"You're right," said Rook, putting them back around his neck.

"It's just some old thing, remember Agrippa?"

"Sure."

"It's just a magic square."

Grandpa nodded. "Old as the hills," he said, smiling. "Is it Jupiter?"

"I think so, right P?"

P nodded.

"The classic square for artists! Have you been whipped into a frenzy?" asked Grandpa, slapping Rook upon the back. "Gematria. Very interesting subject. From the Gnostics to Tolstoy! Let me see, if you don't mind."

Grandpa opened the locket and took out the vellum.

"Ah, yes, but this is Dürer's. It's a slight variation of the Jupiter square. In his famous engraving, *Melencolia*, the square acts also as a window to the house, but it's all obfuscation—you can't enter. So you must climb Jacob's ladder. Also, the total sum is 136, so . . . ."

"Enough!" shouted Professor Kentucky, as if her word would put an end to all the speculation.

"Don't forget, I have a PhD too!" said Grandpa to his famous daughter.

"You haven't taught in years!" scoffed April.

"And neither have you!"

This cut was deep, and Grandpa knew it; he apologized right away. "I'm sorry, honey. It's just why do you always scoff at art history? Don't you know scholars have been pondering Dürer for years?"

"I'm not scoffing, father. I'm just tired of hearing this nonsense over and over!"

"There she goes again!"

Hula shot Rook an *I'm sorry* as they scurried along, then admired the shuffle of her blue translucent slippers blending in with the blue lights that reflected from the walls. As the two professors argued, Rook chuckled and made a cuckoo sign alongside his head.

"You two haven't changed a bit!" said Rook, holding Hula and Boudicca's hands gleefully, feeling like he had almost come full-circle back to high school.

"And neither have you, you young hooligan!" said Grandpa, repeating to himself: "136 or 137? 136 or 137?"

But Rook felt very much changed, drastically, and now he was changing yet again—going backwards, yet advancing at the same time.

As if to echo this, the escalator they were on jerkily stopped, went backwards for a moment, and then forwards again, climbing little by little.

"Let's go," said Hula, trying to get everyone to hurry up. They all glided along, got off, and went up a glass elevator. "I have a surprise for everybody!"

"Very well," said Rook. " So where to?"

"Grand Centraal Station."

Rook thought Hula was speaking metaphorically, but thirty minutes later he discovered she was not. Their caravanserai headed to the main train station in Amsterdam, and went to a special entrance.

"What's all this?" asked Boudicca.

"S and I are getting married! We wanted it to be a surprise for everyone! We thought it's about time! We've been living in 'sin' for far too long," she joked.

Rook moved towards the door, opening it as the car was still slowing down. He got out and gasped for air. He started walking away, towards the river.

"Rook," said Hula, running after him. "Will you just grow up for once? What did you think? That you and I would get back together and we'd raise Boudicca and all that fairy nonsense? Get real!"

"But this S? This horrible lifestyle! I will not have my daughter raised in these conditions! He sold Boudicca!"

"No, he didn't. That was a mistake—something his business people did without his knowledge, and believe me, he's going to make them pay for it. He just wanted to keep me—to hold on to me. He didn't know any other way! Come on, as if your lifestyle is much better! Come on! You're a killer too!"

Rook was silent for a long time.

"We can change," said Rook. "We can all change."

"Yes, and so can S and I!" said Hula. "Don't you know that we've been together longer than you and I? And he's giving up his club, and we're both taking on new careers, opening up an art museum!"

"Great!" said Rook, "I'm really happy for you! But you should ask what Boudicca wants! I can't believe you really feel something for this guy!"

"You don't understand," said Hula. "You only see his bad side. But he pulled me from out of the gutter in London and helped give Boudicca and I a chance."

"This is crazy!" yelled Rook.

And they both looked over at Boudicca; she was watching them yell.

"Boudicca, honey?" asked Hula.

"I want you both to stop yelling. Please. No more drama. I've had enough for a lifetime." And Boudicca walked away, listening to her father's music on her iPod, unbeknownst to him.

"Dear," said April Kentucky, coming close to Hula. "Why did you not tell me about your marriage?"

"We wanted it to be a surprise!"

This was partially true, but the whole truth was that Hula and S did not want her mom, or Rook, or anybody throwing a monkey wrench into the whole schedule, especially when they found out how much older he was. And they did not want Professor Kentucky to ask what S did for a living.

They entered the station and proceeded to a rather formal room, gilded in gold leaf. Everyone was searched from head to toe by the twin bouncers. As Rook and P entered (P had quickly disguised herself with a black veil), the rocker nodded at them, but the brothers did not return the sentiments. Hula, meanwhile, slipped into an antechamber to change into more appropriate attire. A magistrate appeared, smiling, and welcomed the unusual party. Already in the room were some of S's friends and cohorts, which unbelievably included One Eye and Puroshottam (who had just had a long, intense meeting with S). Upon seeing the back of their heads, Constable Degvan tried to hide his face behind a tabloid at the back near the exit, sitting between Dr. Cartwright and Ted Southhampton.

The magistrate called everyone to attention, announcing that the bride and groom would be out shortly.

"Welcome all!" he said, with too much enthusiasm. "In a few moments, we will witness the wedding of S and Hula. I have known S for years, and am very happy to be here today to perform this ceremony. S would like you all to know, that in due time, there will be a more formal wedding, in the Russian Orthodox tradition, but that the couple has been waiting a long time for this day, and wanted to make it official as soon as possible. I'm sure you all understand."

There was a low murmur, and people began to talk amongst themselves as gentle music piped through the room.

Suddenly, a wall slid open, and S appeared in profile in a Savile tuxedo, then turned his back, awaiting his bride's entrance.

Momentarily, the wedding march played, and all rose to see the beautiful Hula walk down the red carpet, her long trail held aloft by her young daughter, Boudicca, who was doing a very good job with no notice and no rehearsal.

The music stopped, and the magistrate welcomed all again.

As he continued with the short service, he got to: "And if there are any objections, let that person speak now, or forever hold their peace—" when blaringly Professor April Kentucky, who had been coughing much and straining her neck forward as if to get the frog out of her throat or to get a better look at her lovely daughter's special day, suddenly shouted:

"No! I object! This wedding cannot take place!"

Hula looked at her mother with daggers, and even Rook, who smiled inwardly, could not believe the audacity. Somewhat oddly, Dr. Cartwright began writing in his journal more frantically than ever before, his thoughts and the present action outpacing his cursive abilities.

"Mother!" said Hula. Grandpa tried to make April sit down, but she would not.

"This wedding cannot take place!" The professor paused, dramatically. "Because that man is Hula's father!"

And Professor Kentucky marched forward with all the energy of a mad professor.

"April?" said S, jaw dropping, literally.

"Sven?" said April.

"Sven?" said Hula. "This is not Sven."

"This *is* Sven," said S. "That is my old name, before my life went haywire . . . ."

Hula almost fainted, and she would have, if she were not so angry, and if Boudicca wasn't standing right there next to her. *I have to be strong for her,* thought Hula.

S turned away from Hula and turned towards April. As April neared him, he reached out for her. April slapped him.

"I suppose I deserve that," he said. "But you left me! You left *me,* April! You left me haywire!"

"I know I did." The professor tugged at S's tux sleeve.

"Mom, I thought—" said Hula.

"No, it was me. It was me all along. I just couldn't."

"But now things are different," said S.

"Yes," said April. "Things are very much different."

"I brought you a painting," said S. "I've been saving it for you for years. I was going to give it to Hula today, but it's really for you. One Eye?"

One Eye suddenly rose, and so did P and Degvan. One brought up an old canvas that had been rolled up, and dramatically unrolled it to show everyone.

"It's Van Gogh's *Lovers*," said S. "They remind me of us. So beaten down, but still hopeful."

"That painting has been missing for years!" shouted Grandpa. "I can't believe it!"

To top off the presentation, One Eye popped open a bottle of Cristal. "Courtesy of Puroshottam," said One, handing S the bottle and taking the Van Gogh back. Puroshottam and One then began heading toward the exit.

"Well, I don't know what to say," said S, smiling. "Thank you, Puroshottam. But we still have business!"

"Later—congratulations!" said Puroshottam, exiting.

"Excuse me, best to you and the missus," said One Eye, exiting out the wall door that S had entered in through.

"Where's everyone going?" said S. "I know this is a bit strange, but—Hula, honey—" But Hula had turned away. "A toast," said S, "to—"

As he was raising his glass, and pouring one for April, April said: "Sven, there's something in the bottle!"

Before anyone could take a closer look, April pushed Hula and Boudicca out of the way, and tried to cover the Cristal as best she could—it promptly exploded, blowing April and S up in the air like a pair of rag dolls.

As the dust settled, and people shook the blindness and deafness of the big bang from out of their eyes and ears and quickly took stock of their body parts, and whether they still existed, it was apparent that S and April were the ones who suffered the cruelest fate.

S reached out his trembling hand towards April, brushed off glass and plaster from his $5000 tux, and attempted to hold his guts in. "I'm not doing so well," he said. He gazed over at April, who was struggling to roll over, and at Hula and Boudicca, who were crouching, holding each other, and S mumbled, "I'm really the worst ever . . . the worst ever. I'm not feeling so good. I'm sor—" And he collapsed, as he stretched and kissed April on her melting lips, his innards spilling outwards upon the delicate berber champagne carpeting.

April was not faring much better. She had turned over as S kissed her, for a moment thinking she was okay (like a character in her unfinished novel), but then realized that her bowels were now mixing with the earth as well.

"It's okay, it's okay," said April, reaching out for Hula and Boudicca. She pulled them close, and staring into S's now untenanted eyes, she recited, softly, yet determinedly:

"Mad and maddening all that heard her in her fierce volubility
By half the tribes of Britain, near the colony
Doubt not ye the Gods have answer'd
These have told us all their anger in miraculous utterances
Thunder, a flying fire in heaven, a murmur heard aerially
Phantom sound of blows descending, moan of an enemy massacred
So they chanted in the darkness, and there cometh a victory now
So the Queen Boadicea, standing loftily charioted

> Brandishing in her hand a dart and rolling glances lioness-like
> Yell'd and shriek'd between her daughters in her fierce volubility
> Yell'd as when the winds of winter tear an oak on a promontory
> Thought on all her evil tyrannies, all her pitiless avarice
> Till she felt the heart within her fall and flutter tremulously
> Then her pulses at the clamoring of her enemy fainted away . . . ."

And April trailed off.* Then, taking one last breath and reaching out for her family, turned to her daughter and granddaughter, and said: "You are my conclusion. Do something great!"

Rook, not knowing what else to do, put his arms around Hula and Boudicca, and began to quietly (and it could be argued, somewhat inappropriately) sing "Free Fall." Grandfather Kentucky placed his hand on Rook's shoulder, and shed a tear, inconsolable that his last talk with his daughter had been unpleasant.

"Somebody get somebody!" cried Grandfather, shouting to the windows with the bright sunlight streaming in.

Meanwhile, P had kept on One Eye like a tiger. She followed him out the secret passage, and nearing him, said: "Stop!"

---

* Professor Kentucky recited here part of the Tennyson poem ("Boudicca"), which rumor has it serves as an epigram to her as yet unpublished novel of the same name. It is cropped and disjointed, which practice is anathema to Kentucky, but this is hardly surprising given her condition. Supposedly, this almost-finished novel is currently being readied for a posthumous publication. The preface, so the trades say, will be written by her granddaughter Boudicca.

But he didn't stop. He kept going, speeding up. P—with a burst of energy—shortly overtook him—and performed the "Typhoon" move in a burst of anger.

She lay on top of him, pinning him down.

"I give up! Please!" he begged.

But P forgot her Gandhi, and overcome with adrenaline, dug her nails into his one good eye.

"An eye for an ear," she said. "You are now officially 'No Eyes.'"

And he began screaming and crying like a baby.

P escorted Now No Eyes outside, and turned him over to Constable Degvan, who was arresting Puroshottam. They would be extradited back to India to stand trial for an extensive list of felony crimes.

A few days later, after sorting everything out and sprinkling S's ashes out of a plane over the North Sea, Rook, Hula, Boudicca, Grandpa, and P returned to Iowa, along with the body of the heroic April Kentucky.

With events and wounds still fresh, wills in probate, and criminal and civil cases still in motion, it is too early to speculate, at least with any hope of accuracy. Still, as soon as this odd family arrived back in California, all the tabloids and entertainment shows, as well as the news media, ran wild and rambling stories about the rock star's holiday so far-fetched that no one with any sense really took it seriously, despite a somewhat real-looking photo of Rook buried in the sand in India with a fool's expression on his sunburnt face (and other photos and "proof" turning up on blogs, and Facebook and elsewhere). Nevertheless, the "news" is selling like hotcakes, and the press and public want more. There have been sensational pics of a possible "love triangle"—involving Rook, Hula, and P—published in the respected *Interloper*. Other magazines have run the gamut on all sorts of rumors—including a possible custody battle over Boudicca (whose existence has not yet been confirmed publicly). The entire matter has become such a circus, that even the media covering the event has become a story unto itself. Just today, on the international wire, the news cycle kept repeating every two hours a clip of the paparazzi driving by Rook's house in Beverly Hills, but the gates were closed and a sign read in large letters: RESPECT OUR PRIVACY. For now, in this gossip-frenzied world of up-to-the-minute-stories, it seems that the press will not be content for long with that message of non-disclosure; indeed! Just now out! A video of Rook's neighbor's dog Princess who had gotten loose, and who evidently had her vocal cords cut to keep her from disturbing the community. The clip ends with a shot of the canine attempting to bark, but no sound comes out.

It is with suspense and anticipation that this undercover writer looks forward to providing a whole new lens into the rock star Rook's recent holiday. This angle, unlike any other, is truly breakthrough journalism, providing a fly-on-the-wall perspective. Dots still need to be connected, and obscure and arcane ideas need further exploration, but in order to get this out while still fresh, and to satisfy the insatiable demand of the public for more on this celebrity and his incredulous story, the publisher hopes to*

---

* It is at this point that the manuscript, and perhaps the anonymous author's life, ends. So much for "breakthroughs." Please see the following postscript.

21

POSTSCRIPT

Well, gentle reader, if you have made it thus far, you will realize there remain many aspects of this tale that are opaque, disjointed, and onerous to verify and connect. It is this editor's hope that my humble efforts to piece together and corroborate this far-fetched story serve as an accurate mirror for the portrayal of the characters within this rather fanciful series of events. If there exist any other eyewitnesses with knowledge of the situations related who could come forward to help ascertain the facts herein, it would be much appreciated. Additionally, scholars are welcome to peruse the primary documents; qualitative research and triangulation would be much appreciated and help to complement this rather holistic picture. I am sure that the rare book room at the Library of Congress would be more than happy to assist, as long as you make an appointment in advance.

As already stated, it is nigh impossible for this editor to tie this romance up with a pretty bow. There are too many loose ends and missing elements—too much under water.

But there are a few more facts and suppositions I can add for clarity.

As to the unfortunate death of the possible author, Aitchkiss Killawathy, most of you have already read the news reports of that event. If you haven't, there are abundant conspiracy theories online. The gist is that as Killawathy/Cartwright was flying back home to Los Angeles from Amsterdam (where he had spent approximately two weeks after Rook left, working on an "undisclosed" project), he was tossed out the emergency door of the plane. Eyewitness accounts vary, and the FAA investigation is ongoing, but most say that Killawathy was minding his own business, working in his seat, when another man confronted him. Visibly shaken, Killawathy got up to use the bathroom, and when he returned, this same man had a gun and was sitting in Killawathy's seat, bizarrely demanding to be left off the plane immediately—even though it was almost ready to land. Everyone got strapped in and held on for dear life as the door was forced opened at gunpoint by a scary man with windswept hair and shattered periwinkle goggles, who grabbed Killawathy's briefcase, threw Killawathy out (who, careening backwards, yelled—"Read it! I can't—"), laughed and then leaped, an old parachute on his back, and Killawathy's precious portmanteau handcuffed to his wrist.

It is this editor's speculation, and leaked preliminary federal reports sustain this, that Ted Southhampton discovered while in Amsterdam (where he too was also working, setting up Rook's new clothing line and lining up European distribution for Anatoli's *I Need A Doctor!*) that Dr. Cartwright was not a psychiatrist, but a reporter—

Aitchkiss Killawathy from *The Interloper*. This supposed revelation came as Southhampton was confiding in the good doctor; whatever Southhampton had disclosed was so horrifying that it caused Cartwright to sweat profusely, causing his make-up to melt enough to reveal the spy beneath. Evidently, Killawathy, knowing the jig was up, snuck out of the hotel and booked the next plane home. Southhampton, in an effort to kill the story that would be most damaging to his client and to himself, decided to kill Killawathy and destroy the work-in-progress. *The Interloper*, as well as Mr. Heisenberg, have remained suspiciously silent, as international investigations continue. At this point the speculation is just a theory, along with a lot of other theories—some outré, some not.

An additional hypotheses has the unfortunate Mr. Killawathy hitting the water of the Pacific about a mile out from shore. His body washed in later that same day with high tide, getting tied up near the Santa Monica pier. He was not alone, however. Ted Southhampton, or whoever the suspect may have been, or should I say his skeletal arm (most of the flesh was gone), and the handcuffed briefcase, was holding onto Killawathy. Evidently, his parachute did not open completely (some witnesses claim to have seen a hole in it), and his parobolic plunge went off course, thus leaving the manager to grab the only support he could find. Why sharks chose to sup on Southhampton (?) and not on the bleeding Killawathy (?) is a matter for marine biologists. Perhaps it was a semiochemical occurrence—something in Killawathy's boils or possible chronic osteomyeletis?

There was nothing in the briefcase, after all, save some recordings, which, due to water damage, were irretrievable. Apparently, the author was perhaps acquiring some of his information surreptitiously through advance surveillance techniques and black box type equipment.

It would be remiss of me not to mention that there are some rumors that these "tapes" actually did survive the crash. A supposed FBI raid on Killawathy's Beverly Hills office also discovered another mysterious "black box." Avid followers of the rock star have actually surrounded the building in which it is now kept under guard. I suppose some light will eventually be shed on this secret, as the truth will eventually come out as the investigation is unsealed and international public support is sought in piecing together the tapestry. In the meantime, we must do our best to assemble this continually unraveling quagmire with the threads we do have.

One such thread is rock star girl, or Monique. I was fortunate enough to track the aspiring actress down. She spun quite a tale herself, and to be honest, I do not know if she was putting on a performance, or relaying accurate information.

In any case, during her interview, she claimed that once Rook and his family got back to LA, she made an effort to meet with him to apologize for not acting truthfully. She said she tried to make it up by putting some "protective" talismans in his "pendants" that she had acquired from a renowned psychic.

Monique "ran into" Rook as he and Hula, Boudicca, and P were visiting a lovely garden near the ocean off Sunset. Evidently, Rook and Boudicca were trying to find some kind of peace as they finished their HAART regimen, recovering from some unknown adverse effects, and mentally preparing for their HIV tests. The three-month test supposedly had already been scheduled, and now they just had to wait to go in, but Boudicca especially was nervous. The new family (including P) had all agreed to go in and be tested together, supporting each other.

"What if I do have HIV?" asked Boudicca.

"I'm sure you don't, dear," said Hula.

"But what if I do?"

"Then we'll deal with that as a family."

"Will you still love me?"

"Of course we'll love you," said Hula, Rook, and P in a chorus. "We love you no matter what."

As they continued walking about the garden grounds, around the lake, they stopped at a place that held a portion of Gandhi's ashes. P sat down to meditate (evidently she knew about the retreat and brought them all there), and told Monique that she had made a vow to practice ahimsa (non-violence). This sounds somewhat strange, as P supposedly is Rook's new bodyguard.

As they stood around the Gandhi Memorial, Rook mumbled something like, "Why can't I do something worthwhile like him?"

At this point, Boudicca took his hand, and said, "You have, Daddy."

And Hula said, "And you can."

And Rook said, "Yes, I can . . . ."

According to Monique, a bird, a rook, at this point flew down to nibble on some crumbs of a Hostess blueberry pie that someone had left behind next to a red bandana. As it

nibbled, Rook inspected it, and a glare of light that reflected off the water caused the bird to take skyward. As it
did, their eyes all followed it, and then noticed something
else in the smogless sky.

"Are those angels?" asked Boudicca. "A meteorite?"

Two figures were falling spectacularly from out of the
clear blue over the ocean.

"I don't think so, honey," said Rook and Hula, holding
hands, swinging them innocently like children.

"What makes you so sure?" asked P. "'There are more
things in heaven and earth . . . .'"

(Supposedly, these two figures falling from heaven to
earth were Killawathy and Southhampton.)

"I never realized that what I was looking for was right
in front of me," said Rook, smiling at his newfound family
in the garden as a man in a strange hat climbed a ladder to
trim an apple tree.

Monique concluded her interview with me by plugging
a TV commercial she had coming up, and relating that she
had asked Rook for his address, wanting to stay in touch.*

As for the other characters, Grandpa Kentucky's heart
nearly broke as he buried his daughter in Iowa. They all
attended the funeral, and so did many famous writers and
celebrities, while the press was kept at bay. Professor
Kentucky's will ordered for her unfinished novel to be
buried with her, but Boudicca refused to agree with this,

---

* Normally, I would not mention this. But Rook's address contains the number
137. This is the fine structure constant in physics, which has given many a
scientist a headache. Of course, it may just be an odd coincidence, or perhaps
synchronistic. My taped and annotated interview with Ms. Monique_____
is not yet available (as her waiver has yet to be signed); please check my
website for updates.

and others concurred with her; as mentioned earlier, she wants to write the preface for it someday, and have it published posthumously in honor of her grandmother.

Grandpa Kentucky is supposedly at work on a book on the enigmatic Dürer. According to his publicist, it is intended to offer an entertaining and fresh approach to the almost 500 years of scholarship and mystery.

Speaking of artists, the Van Gogh painting *The Lovers: The Poet's Garden IV,* was indeed authenticated and is now at the Van Gogh Museum in Amsterdam, a testament to the endurance of true love in the face of overwhelming obstacles.

One Eye, or Now No Eyes, and Puroshottam are currently in jail awaiting trial in Mumbai. Detective Constable Degvan promises they will get a very lengthy sentence. Degvan, surprisingly, is considering leaving the force, and becoming a tabloid journalist, starting a magazine along with his wife. "The business of gossip is really booming!" he told me, as I attempted to interview him long distance. (He asked me more questions than I him!)

If you are a reader of such entertainment magazines, you've probably been exposed to the non-stop rumors regarding how Rook now has to choose between Hula and P. As of this writing, the family of four are living together in the same house in Beverly Hills. P, despite her practice of non-violence, is supposedly serving as some sort of bodyguard/sensei. This may not last for long though, as P is still wanted for additional questioning by INTERPOL; there is some confusion, from a legal standpoint, as to "proof" of her guilt in several political assassinations. Apparently, as of the moment, no government is willing to bring up charges, perhaps in fear of self-incrimination. Without any charges, she is currently free to walk. Evidently, she has chosen to walk in a very nice neighborhood indeed.

S, shortly before his death, had changed his will and left almost everything to Hula (except for establishing a trust fund for Boudicca). Hula is currently consulting with US and Dutch consulates as to how best to reconcile her father's estate, selling S's holdings, hoping to make reparations to all injured parties.

Boudicca is continuing to adjust to life in California. She rendezvoused with the boy she met in India—Scott—and he introduced her to some Hollywood friends her own age. Supposedly, for Boudicca, Tinseltown is Bollywood on steroids. Boudicca, by the way, has officially been confirmed to exist, having been issued a United States Passport under the name Boudicca Kentucky Heisenberg.* Boudicca was also introduced to another new friend—Dawn Jam (Rook was so happy to see his daughter and Jim's meet!). Boudicca now also has an agent, and apparently a movie role, in Hollywood, to build off her early Bollywood success: the tentative title is *My Friend Kali.*

The reader should be aware that as there are continuing developments in this story, that future additions of this work will incorporate any new and vital information or speculation. In fact, just today, *The Interloper* printed a conversation (with scandalous photos, of course) supposedly "overheard" by the poolboy as Rook and Hula swam at their home in Beverly Hills:

---

* On file with the U.S. Department of State.

"What do you want from life?" asked Hula, splashing playfully.

Rook smiled and there was a long silence between them. He then swam under water and surfaced next to her.

"I feel butterflies," said Hula, kissing him.

"So do I," said Rook, gasping, out of breath. "You know, this whole experience has been my worst nightmare and my best dream coming true."

"That's how life is," said Hula, matter-of-factly. "You wouldn't know one without the other."

"Hmm," said Rook, both of them now treading water and holding hands in the deep end . . . .

As far as the traditional newspapers go, it has just been reported that Rook has hired Billy Todd to help manage not only the success of his new clothing line (at least the Western Office), but to also line up an American release of Anatoli's Bollywood film (which Anatoli dedicated to Arjun Alexander), and perhaps take on the management of The Little Bang. As of this moment, Rook is supposedly also working on a new version of "Los Angeles," with a slight change in some of the lyrics: "Los Angeles. City of the Angels. What to make of this? This city of the angels?"

Having finished compiling this manuscript, I took a long look back at the imbroglio of yellow legal pads I started with, and am somewhat amazed that I was able to make any sense of this nonsense whatsoever. In retrospect, I don't know how I managed to untie this Gordian knot. In truth, parts of it are still tied. Honestly, I do not know if it was worth the effort. I now wonder, after months of editing and pre-publication work, if I should have just left that bulky folder on the plane; perhaps the world would be better off without one more celebrity exposé. But then, maybe it is these far-fetched stories that push the envelope and the world forward, as people stand around the water cooler, evolving.

Before rushing this book off to the printers, I decided I would make one last effort to go to the source; I drove past the rock star's house today, attempting to bypass the normal gatekeepers and see if I could get get the story straight from the man himself. As I stopped at 137 _____, I made my way past the press. I looked at the security cameras in front of and behind the giant wrought-iron fence, waved, and buzzed the door repeatedly, holding up the original manuscript. No one answered. There was a ladder nearby—at the corner of the estate. I thought of using it, but a gardener wearing an old Stetson was employing it, pruning some cherry trees, and ignoring the press that kept snapping photos, filming, broadcasting, and tweeting. One tweet was speculating on some recent books that Rook had just bought at Book Soup (apparently discovered by going through receipts in the trash)—one was Dostoevsky's *Crime and Punishment*, another on fatherhood, and a third on opening the chakras. Such information may be valuable to critical theorists in the future (although it could just as well be garbage), but to resort to such lengths as the subject lives and breathes borders on the intrusive.

As this book goes to press, it is unclear if Rook is working on a new album, reuniting with The Little Bang, or performing again anytime soon. There exists a veritable "radio silence." In any case, should he happen to be reading this, Rook should know that his true fans and friends wish him and his family the very best of health and hope he returns soon.

Finally, despite the cliché, one remaining question begs to be asked: Did the rock star find the rainbow he was chasing for so long, or perhaps something even better along the way? That is something only he can answer, and perhaps someday he will choose to when he emerges from his retreat—with a new work of art.

Let me end this hodgepodge with one final disclaimer: I cannot speak to the truth of any of the matters contained herein, and any fan that seeks some sort of affidavit would do better to wait for potential court proceedings. On the other hand, if the reader feels that I have gotten the general arc of this anonymous and far-fetched story across, however imperfectly, and is obliquely inspired to chase his or her own rainbow, however improbable, no matter what anyone says, then it was worth the gamble. Now if you'll excuse me, I have a flight to catch to Vegas.*

---

* If there is any fault or confusion in the telling, this editor takes the blame. It is entirely possible that the unknown author never meant this work to see the light of day. However, it does seem probable that he very much wished it to be published. The overwhelming demand of the public has decided the issue. Please note that I have tried to be faithful to the writer's style, altering the text as little as possible so as to allow the prose to speak, or not to speak, for itself. Some necessary editorial decisions had to be made, however; the fragmentary nature of the manuscript necessitated assembly and imposition, so some coherence could be achieved. Finally, it should also be noted that as the frantic journey of the narrator and his tale hurtled to their conclusions, there was not much I could do with the last-minute scribblings, as they were penned under the gun, and obviously not treated with as much care as the author's earlier revisions, which while by no means perfect, were scrawled in a slightly calmer and more legible hand.

Kevin Glavin's ancestors hail from the Emerald Isle; he hails from the Windy City. After receiving his BA in English and MAT in English Education from the University of Iowa, he sashayed like his forefathers—westward. Mr. Glavin has taught for some thirteen years, mostly at Claremont High School, in Claremont, California. Last year, Kevin got married; he and his beloved wife Brenda have settled just a little farther west—in Orange County—with their dog Ciao, a chow chow, golden retriever mix adopted after a trip to Italy. In December 2009, Mr. Glavin formed his own publishing company to learn the entire art of bringing a work to market, in print and digitally, and to maintain creative freedom.

Far-fetched stories that don't go far enough.

KEVIN GLAVIN PUBLISHING
IRVINE, CALIFORNIA